In The Company of Whispers

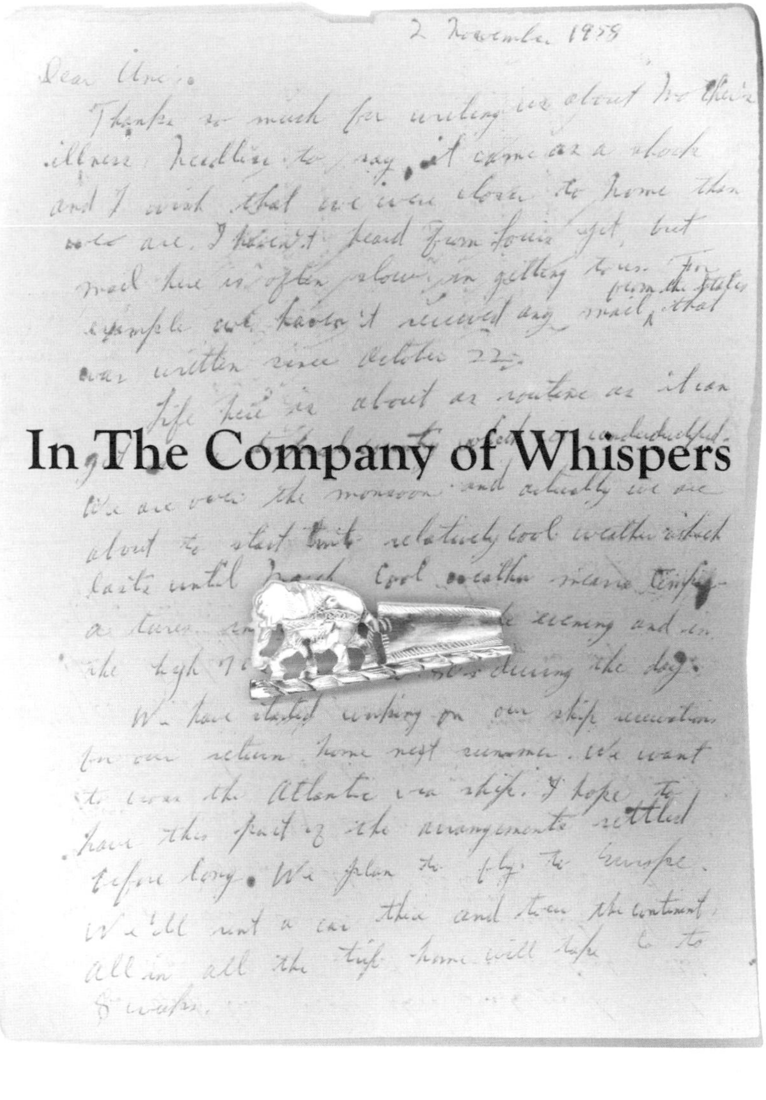
2 November 1958

Dear Urie:

Thanks so much for writing us about Mother's illness. Needless to say, it came as a shock and I wish that we were closer to home than we are. I haven't heard from Louis yet, but mail here is often slow in getting here. For example we haven't received any mail from the States that was written since October 22.

Life here is about as routine as it can

We are over the monsoon and actually we are about to start the relatively cool weather which lasts until March. Cool weather means temperatures the evening and in the high 70 during the day.

We have started working on our ship reservations for our return home next summer. We want to cross the Atlantic on ship. I hope to have this part of the arrangements settled before long. We plan to fly to Europe. We'll rent a car there and tour the continent. All in all the trip home will take 6 to 8 weeks.

First Edition published by Lion Stone Books
10 9 8 7 6 5 4 3 2 1

Cataloging-in-Publication Information.
Lowenstein, Sallie
In the Company of Whispers / Sallie Lowenstein
p.cm
Summary: In 2047, Granna, who lived in Burma as a child in the 1950's, bequeaths her memories to her orphaned granddaughter and the mysterious, intricately-tattooed Jonah.

ISBN 0-9658486-7-1
ISBN 978-0-9658486-7-1
Library of Congress Control Number: 2007907226
1. Burma—Fiction 2. Science Fiction—Fiction
3. Burma—Photography 4. Burma—Memoir

Includes bibliography and glossary

Lion Stone Books
4921 Aurora Drive
Kensington, MD 20895
Tel. 301-949-3204 Fax: 301-949-3860
lionstone@juno.com
www.lionstonebooks.com

Book Design by Sallie Lowenstein
Cover Design by Rachel Kenney

Printed in China
by Anderson International Printing, LLC
Glenn@Andersoninternationalprinting.com

In The Company of Whispers

A Novel by

Sallie Lowenstein

Lion Stone Books
Kensington, Maryland

For my father,
who taught me to delight in story;
And for my mother,
who taught me the dream of being a writer.
I will be eternally grateful for their voices
and influences upon my life.

Many thanks to my friends and family who supported
this book through its many incarnations over a period
of years.

"Humanity has been led astray by three evils: greed, hatred and ignorance. Whether we are Buddhists, Hindus, Muslims, Christians, Animists or Atheists, we cannot escape...old age, disease, death...nor can anybody deny that property is transitory: no one can carry away his property after death."

U Nu, Prime Minster of Burma
Mandalay, 1953

Rangoon

February 23, 1958

Dear Mama,

We arrived at Mingaladon Airport before lunch and were met by the entire "company family", which included Jack's new boss, his wife and their six-year-old son Sammy who was dressed in American cowboy chaps, fringed vest, Stetson hat and dime-store six-shooters, glistening in the tropical sun. The air was so heat-drenched it made the metal on our plane shimmer as if we had vanished into a parallel universe. Maybe we have...

Love,

Blanche

The Greater East Coast Metropolis, 2047:
[This is to inform our residents that the cost of Net
time will increase by 15% at the end of the month.]

Flying. A great white bird, I spread my tail feathers, stretch my shady pink neck into warm updrafts that carry me away, away from the towers below. Swooping down, I snatch at a water bug, dark and ugly...

A huge water bug, the oily tortoiseshell brown kind, was crawling on my blanket near my toes—exactly the kind of roachy insect the bird had been about to grab in my dream. Yuck. I kicked, hard. The blankets rearranged themselves but there he came, crawling from between the folds. No respect at all. I switched on the light, didn't matter to the bug. He kept on coming, but then I glanced at my clock and figured it was just as well. Almost time to get up, to go to my last day of classes before summer break. I didn't want school to end. There they exterminated vermin the likes of which roamed free in our apartment. I'd learned the hard way not to just swing my feet out of bed. First morning we moved here, I'd done it once, and only once. Crunch. I'd taken out six black carapaces in one step. Bug juice, thick and white, had coated my heels. *Eggs*, Dad had told me. I'd squished the females. Gag. I had gagged into the bathroom sink. Did that stop the things from crawling out of the drain? Nope. No way. I'd thought the bugs would convince my parents to move us back to the old place, but nope, no way for that either. *United we stand*, my mother had said. United they stood, against all my pleading and begging and outbursts.

"But Mum, Dad, you can't afford the place. All you do is work, work, work, and for this!" I'd screamed, yelled, waved my hands at walls where previous tenants had hung pictures, leaving nail-studded ghost-squares of faded paint. Could I count the number of tenants since the apartment had been painted last by the differences in the colors of those squares?

"You're going to be late," Dad called to me.

"Coming." I put my feet directly into my shoes and stamped on the floor, watching skittering bugs race for cracks under the baseboards. I'd been known to sleep through school sometimes, so Mum and Dad had taken to being sure I was up before they left. And they left earlier and earlier, which meant I had to groan and crawl out of bed, earlier and earlier—yet another annoying effect of living here.

Dad was already at the door. "See you late tonight. I have that extra job, remember?"

Mum didn't speak, but when she turned, I could see she'd been crying.

"What's the matter?"

"Nothing."

Another fight. I knew it, even if she didn't say so. "What was it over this time?"

"Dad thinks we made a mistake moving here."

"Yes!" I said triumphantly. "Yes!"

"Zeyya, we're not giving up this apartment. It's safer from Quarantine here. You know that." She turned her face from me, but I could still hear sobs.

I hated it when she cried, making me too guilty to pursue a victory. When would I stop caving to this? Not today. The quicker I made nice, the faster she could leave for work. "I'm sorry, Mum, it's just I never get to see you guys, and the roaches, and..."

Now she was crying full force.

"I'm sorry, I'm sorry, but Mum—what do you expect me to do here all summer by myself?"

She wrapped her arms around me. "It'll work out."

Oh, good job, Mum, I thought, but for once didn't say it. No point in engaging her over this. The only solutions she had these days were paltry offerings of comfort like, *It'll work out.* I'd found my own source of comfort, anyway. Alejandro. If Mum and Dad knew I'd been hanging with Alejandro all year, they'd chain me to the walls or something, but they were never home, so they didn't know. I repeatedly toyed with telling Alejandro our place was available, but never did, making up all kinds of excuses to myself, like what if Mum or Dad came home early? Dad would roar at me about the possible dangers I'd exposed us to by bringing a stranger into our living space, much less getting hung with him. More likely I'd get sick from the vermin in the apartment than by bringing Alejandro home.

Mum turned away from me and swept into the bathroom, closed the door and I heard the water running. When she came out, she managed a smile and a reminder that she, too, would be late getting home.

That left the apartment to me and the roaming roaches. I boiled some water, made some tea and concentrated on getting out to school. I took a quick peek at the Net News, just to be sure of what the weather held. Our budget didn't allow for many minutes, so it was on and it was off. Mum and Dad had promised me more time during the summer, but I knew it unlikely. No money. It all went to rent for the bug-house, which was way overpriced.

Our old place had been sunny and the landlord had painted the walls regularly, and even fumigated when needed. He lived on the first floor. Or he had. Maybe by now he'd joined the other tenants who'd gotten Quarantined. That was the one truth about this rat hole we lived in. So far, no yellow tape across doors. Nobody missing or dragged off in the night. Didn't make sense that the disease had taken the better building first, but as the news was fond of saying, disease knew no boundaries of age or wealth.

I grabbed a slicker in case of rain and headed out the door. It was going to be a pretty lame last day because Principal Jaster had canceled all final activities until we turned in the pranksters who had busted into the Senior Dance in gorilla suits. I wished I'd seen it. The Seniors described it as having been sensational, a worthy testimonial to Junior nerve. Of course, nobody owned up to knowing who was in the suits, but I noticed Alejandro beamed with pride at each praiseworthy adjective uttered.

"Hey, Zeyya," Tracey called to me, "what're your plans for the summer?"

"Not much, how about you?"

"I'm getting shipped off to shovel manure and bale hay for the whole ten weeks. My folks claim its good preparation for my future if I don't bring up my grades."

Tracey sauntered off down the hall. Truth was, she'd been asking for it since the beginning of the year. Her grades were lousy, she was cutting from orchestra, her one true talent, and if I didn't miss my bet, was peddling Snap-up for spending money and maybe using a little on the side.

First period orchestra was the only full period of the whole day. We had locker cleanout and inspection after that, then registration for next year, then a few half-periods of classes.

Mr. Pompandow, the music teacher, handed back our final compositions, moving along, routinely dropping them onto desks until he got to mine. He stood over me with my notations dangling from between his fingers and said one word before he let them drop. "Interesting." After the papers fluttered onto my desk, he added, "With some work, we may be able to perform it next year. See me after class, Zeyya."

Perform it? My piece!

I waited until everyone was gone before I walked nervously to his desk. He looked up pretty quickly for once. "Well now, for such a mediocre performance musician, you prove to have hidden talents."

I stuttered a thank you and waited.

"Do you like composing, Zeyya?"

"Sure, uh, yes, I do, but I, uh, I wasn't so sure I was any good at it."

"No? Well, surprise, surprise! So do you have time to work on it this summer?"

"Yeah, yes, sure. I have time."

He nodded, drummed his fingers on his desk before speaking again. "You need to listen for the music in things around you. You know, rhythms, and notes, melodies you haven't noticed before."

His fingers were still moving. Was he demonstrating his point, or was it an ironic accident? I stood there waiting.

"That's it. Let's see what you can do. Have a good summer."

I got to the door and looked back, hoping for a little more, but he was rummaging through his desk and never looked up.

Listen? That wasn't much help. I liked music a lot, but we didn't have the money to go to concerts or to buy time to listen on the Net. I was really on my own, and that was all Mr. Pompandow had to offer? Great! Some teacher.

I stomped through the rest of the day, trying to find something musical in the cafeteria, in the hallways, but the sounds in my life were all cacophony and coarse. And worse yet, I had built my concerto on the sound of a single instrument. How did I blend cymbals or drums or horns into a composition based on violin?

At the end of the day, Alejandro waited for me on the sidewalk. "I'm going to miss you, Zeyya. Wish you had more Net Mail time."

"Sorry. No money."

"None? Come on, just steal a little extra time for me."

"A little time is all we have, Alejandro. Nothing extra. Besides, you're going to be at your cousin's for most of the summer."

"You could come with me," he said.

Tempting, but I wasn't ready to be his hung girl. Maybe if we made it through another year together, then, yeah, I'd think about going the rest of the way and getting hung with him. But not this summer. Not with Mum and Dad so unhappy already.

"Not this time," I said. He opened his palm and dropped my hand, just as I was ready to squeeze his fingers in reassurance. "I'll write when I can."

He frowned. "Sure, okay." He walked off without kissing me.

By the time I got home and dumped my papers onto the kitchen table, hunger was what demanded my attention, and I pushed Alejandro to the back of my mind. I sliced some cheese, grabbed up some crackers, content to nibble until I noticed the edge of my composition sticking out of my pack, pulled it out and flipped up the title sheet. The pages were covered in red scribbles and comments, notes and instructions. They must have taken hours for Mr. Pompandow to write out. He'd given me a B, but noted the potential was amazing—*surprisingly imaginative and original*. On the last page—*good luck*.

I fell asleep on my bed with papers spread across my stomach and chest until around eleven, when I heard the door creak open twice on its un-oiled hinges as Mum, then Dad dragged in from work. Moving the papers aside, I rolled over and stared out the small window that lay at the top of the wall, barely wide enough for me to see a star. Mainly it leaked air—good in the summer, bad in the winter—but I liked it because once in a while a stray ray of sun would meander down my wall from it.

I fell back asleep, only to wake to the sounds of the toilet and water in the sink. Mum was standing in the bathroom with her face close to the cracked mirror, pulling at the corners of her eyes.

"Mum?"

"Oh, oh...Zeyya, uh, I was just noticing..." She dropped her hands to her sides. "Wrinkles."

"No, Mum, you're just tired."

She brushed my cheek with the back of her fingers as she grabbed her hat and coat, waved quickly, departed, closing the door behind her. Dad must have left earlier, his bag no longer set where it always sat. I was alone, an empty day ahead of me without a single plan.

Maybe work on the concerto? I settled into the big chair near the window that looked out onto the walls of other buildings. Not much to see from this apartment.

Got up, washed my hair in the drip of the shower and combed it out into long straggling locks that would all too soon knot up into curls and hang only to my shoulders. Mum said I got my hair from Granna, although when we went to see her now, it was hard tell because she was old and refused to have her hair restored, or her teeth, or her eyes. Despite living in her own little house, perhaps she wasn't rich enough to afford the procedures, but I couldn't be sure because Mum wouldn't talk about it, and Dad mostly swore under his breath about Granna. I shook out my hair and piled it into a towel. What was I going to do, all alone, today, tomorrow, the next day, until fall? How was I going to find the sounds and melodies that Mr. Pompandow had assigned me? Plopped down onto my bed, felt a crunch that sent me lurching to my feet, where I stepped on something. I didn't have to look down to know what it was. That was it, I was getting out of the apartment for at least the day. Pulled on my pants, scrapped the bug off my foot with an old piece of tissue and stomped out the door. I hated our apartment and I hated the idea of spending my summer days in the company of a bunch of dark-bodied, crispy bugs.

"There is a strange beauty in the remote flowering of Burmese music.
…a circle of drums, a circle of gongs, the big putt ma drum, cymbals,
clappers and wind instruments, such as the hnè…and the palwé…
accompanies our…many festal occasions…"

<u>Burmese Music</u>
by U Khin Zaw
Perspective of Burma
An **Atlantic** Supplement, 1958

Rangoon

1958

Dear Mother,

There really isn't much news from here. We seem to be going to one party after another, some large, some small. I'm getting a little fed up with it, but of course, this is the principal form of recreation here. There are no concerts, no legitimate theatre, no TV, very little radio in English and what English language movies they have are hot and stuffy—not air-conditioned.

They do show American movies outdoors under a shelter at the Kokine Swim Club. The kids sit at the front and the parents in the back. We went the other night and in the middle of the film, all the kids started screaming. The bigger boys stood up and began stamping on the ground. Two pairs of scorpions had been crawling under their chairs.

Life is certainly different here.

Love,
Jack

The Greater East Coast Metropolis, 2047:
[Coastal displacement continues to impact the Metropolis:
Quarantines increasing with influx of new residents.]

The fifth morning alone, while eating toast with jelly and drinking tea until I couldn't hold it anymore, I tried penning romantic poetry composed of saccharine imagery in bad verse. For the fifth day my concerto languished in my pack. I had not one inspiration. I piled my dishes into the sink and soaped them up. Mum had spent ten minutes lecturing me on my lack of cleanliness and how it encouraged the bugs. Actually, it had the main effect of keeping them all in one place, which had a certain appeal to me, but I did the dishes anyway.

By the time I was ready to go out, the little boy who lived next door was waiting in the hall for his mother.

"Hi."

He had jug ears that went up when he smiled at me and came down when he stopped, as if they were waving.

"I'm Zeyya. What's your name?"

"Ethan," he lisped out. He was maybe four.

His mother slipped out her door to stand next to him. "Hi, I'm Mary. And you're?"

"Zeyya. You and Ethan are new?"

"Just this week." She locked the door. I never bothered. Nothing worth stealing in our place. The computer, for what it was worth, came with the apartment and if someone came and took some of the roaches, well, so long buddies, it was nice knowing you.

"How do you like it?"

She wrinkled up her nose as Ethan announced, "We got a cat."

"You aren't supposed to have animals," I whispered to Mary.

"I know, but we aren't supposed to have bugs either. Cats keep them down."

"I won't tell," I promised as we walked towards the front door.

They were going to a park, a little patch of concrete with a seesaw and a slide, and I tagged along. When we got there it was crowded with toddlers, screeching joyfully. The sounds were fresh and crisp. What instrument would make them?

I was mulling it over in my mind when Mary asked me, "Are you working this summer?"

"Can't yet. I'm not seventeen until the fall."

"Next year then?"

I nodded without answering, listening to a mother on the next bench, who was probably my age, humming to her child.

"I was wondering, would you like to earn a little money, I mean not much, but for taking care of Ethan so I can work?"

"Huh?" It wasn't legal. I wasn't allowed to take a job, but then again, I could use the money—new clothes, Net time to talk to Alejandro, Marilyn, Tracey. And who would know? "Yeah, sure. For how long?"

"So far, only in the mornings. After your parents leave. I'll get you cash, not pay in credit. And he's a good boy, really."

"I don't have anything better to do. Tomorrow, then?"

We walked back together and Mary took me into their apartment to show me around. They had more windows than we did, but only one bedroom. She showed me what worked in the kitchen and what didn't, which included the freezer. She showed me where Ethan's clothes and toys were, and he showed me a beautiful longhaired grey cat that lay curled under a chair. Their things were nicer than ours. They had a working computer, fairly new model and they had thick towels in the bathroom, though it was no bigger than ours, and in either you were likely to bang your knees on the sink when you used the toilet.

"Why'd you move here?" I asked curiously.

She answered in a voice so pained, it was little more than a murmur. "Quarantine. My husband while he visited his sister."

All I could think to say was, "Sorry. Was his sister sick?"

She shook her head. "Not that we could tell. She'd just arrived, but she wouldn't have let him come over if she was ill."

What my English teacher would have called a pregnant pause followed, before Mary filled the void with, "Well, we should be getting on with our day, Zeyya. See you in the morning."

I slipped into our apartment, gathered the trash and had descended to the basement to dump it in the garbage bins when the rain began again, so I stood in the doorway and watched the water rush down the sidewalks. I listened to the rain, pounding then retreating, drumming on concrete, on wood, on tin, coming to a crescendo and decrescendoing into little more than a whisper. Music.

Soon all that was left of the storm were puddles. In a surprise urge, I tore off my shoes and bunny-hopped into the nearest patch of water, splattering my pants, laughing as I imagined how I looked to anyone watching. I stepped my wet feet back into my shoes, trudged upstairs to dry off and by the time I finished, it was pouring again, the storm surging violently, slamming its fury at the windows and walls of the building, trapping me in the apartment with my little friends. I sat down at the kitchen table to work on my concerto. I started with rain patter. Drums. And when it hit the tin downspouts? I was chewing on the end of the pencil when I noticed I could hear Ethan and his mother through the wall. They were singing together, sweet and clear, their voices rising above the growling thunder. I scribbled notes across pages until my hand ached.

Mum came through the door before Dad, but he was close behind.

"Want to go to a vid-show?" he asked us as soon as he was through the door. "We haven't done anything for a long time, and here we are, all of us at home at the same time."

I answered by grabbing my bag and heading for the door.

"Whoa, hang on. Dinner first."

Mum started things rolling, I set the table and then guarded the food from the famished hard-shelled hoards until we were all sitting down to dinner, together. It was nice.

"So how's it been going, Zeyya?" Dad asked me.

"Little boring, but not too bad. I've gotten some musical ideas."

He put a piece of re-cooked chicken in his mouth and chewed for a long time. "Have you thought about the future? Past next year?"

"Music."

"Music? As a job? It doesn't pay well," Mum noted as calmly as she could.

"What's the dif? Nothing pays well anymore. If you're rich you're rich, if you're poor, poor you'll stay, right?"

"It's years of training. For that amount of training you could become a doctor. You have the grades."

"But Dad, I'd flunk out when I had to disect a human cadaver. I vomit when I step on a bug! Come on, please, I'm good at music."

Their only responses were side-eyed glances at each other.

"And it's my life," I pointed out.

Dad cleared his throat. "Not totally. Not if you need to live with us while you train."

Hated to admit it, but I understood their hesitation. No singing voice, mediocre violinist. "Look," I cried, jumping up and pulling my concerto, in all it's red-marked glory, out of my bag. "Look, Mr. Pompandow says if I can finish it, they'll perform it this fall! I want to be a composer."

Dad dutifully read through the comments on the sheets of paper and put the sheaf down precisely, as if it was something either fragile or something unsavory, couldn't tell which.

"Okay, Zeyya, we'll see."

I rewarded him with a smile.

We cleaned up, grabbed our stuff and dashed out the door to the vid. Got there, argued over what to watch, finally decided on a musical, which pleased everyone, and splurged on more expensive tickets to a three-viewer room so we didn't have to share the show with anyone. It was filled with the stale smell of popcorn and the sickly smell of old soda, but the seats were soft, and the screen was a decent size. Halfway through, we heard a ruckus in another room loud enough to come through the walls. I shrank up against Dad.

"Our neighbors must have chosen an action vid," Dad reassured me. I moved away from him, embarrassed at my reaction, and tried to concentrate on our show.

"Can we turn up the sound, please, Dad?"

He hit the volume button on the controls, but the next time I jumped, Dad jumped, too, as the wail of Quarantine sirens drowned out the piercingly high notes being sung by our soprano lead.

"Let's get out of here," Dad said, pointing at the emergency exit, pushing the door open enough to see that no one was waiting outside to stop our escape. Would they quarantine the whole building? Were they after specific people? If they had wanted everyone, were we carrying an infection? No, no, we weren't sick, we had nothing to fear. That didn't stop us. We ran, stopping to catch our breath, running again until we got home where we fell exhausted onto our ratty sofa. Dad looked okay, but Mum was pale, panting heavily.

"Bed," Dad announced.

I don't know if my parents lay in bed going over the night's events again and again, but I did, tossing, turning, wondering if I might be sick, promising myself I would sleep, then going over it all again, again, again until daybreak when I dozed off. Mum and Dad were up and off to work by the time I shuffled from my room. I was about to eat breakfast when I remembered—babysitting! Ethan!

Rushing, throwing water on my face, running the toothbrush over my teeth but forgoing flossing, a comb through my hair, my pants on, out the door to my first day of a job. Was I late?

Mary parted the door and let me in. Ethan was playing with the cat, swinging a ball of yarn for the beast to lunge at.

"I've left a clinic's number, because there's no way to reach me. If something should go wrong, try to wait for me. If you can't, then use your judgment." I wanted more explicit instructions, but she dashed out before I could demand them, and there I was with a four year old and an illegal cat, illegally earning money. My anxiety from the night before pasted my first-day-jitters to my fear that my toe-the-line father would find out, but at least I wasn't bored, just sitting in my kitchen writing bad poetry.

Ethan pulled out his bricks and little blocks and began setting them up, then knocking them down. We made bridges and ran antique toy trucks over them with *vrrooom's* and *zzzzzz's* and assorted beeps and honks. I didn't notice the time until his mother walked in the door. Noon already. She handed me some bills and said, "Tomorrow?"

"Sure."

It had been easy and I could see why little kids gave comfort to their parents. They didn't notice the Quarantines or the yellow tape, or the exhaustion that coated people they passed on the street. They didn't notice that there were roaches running the baseboards or that the windows didn't keep out mosquitoes. It had been a good day, and the sounds of play were starting to repeat in my head as music.

Once, people could get anything they
wanted from the Padaythabin Tree. But
people became greedy and spoiled the
Tree of Fulfillment, so that it shriveled and
disappeared. Some became poor, while others
flourished, which is why crime began.

A Burmese Myth

March 24, 1958

Rangoon.

Dear Helen,

Josephine, the nanny, says the night yowls we hear are two wildcats they've seen on the hill behind our house! I think I told Connie the insurgents blew up the pipes leading into Rangoon the day before we arrived, and the city was without water for five days. Drinking water and water for one john flush a day was brought from artesian wells to our hotel room at the Kambawza Palace. It has happened before and everyone else was very blasé about it, but it seemed quite dreamlike to me.

I'll add more to this after I say goodnight to Susie and Sis.

The Greater East Coast Metropolis: 2047
[The great immigration debate rages, but we notice that behind
the scenes, everyday people are trying to survive and barely notice
where their neighbors come from. People move eagerly from one
building to the next, searching out the safest sanctuary from
Quarantine they can find.]
Subterranean Net Site

It's a dream because Ethan is in my grade, playing a full sized cello in a performance of my concerto. He plucks strings to thump out raindrops on pavement. It's a perfect performance save that the cello keeps tilting backwards because he's four. He ties it upright to a post that appears out of nowhere, picking up the tempo immediately. I'm feeling good as I swing my baton to direct the orchestra.

It was dark when I woke. Hadn't meant to take another nap, to sleep away another afternoon. Had planned on working on my concerto, but taking care of Ethan was tiring. Also paid well. I had a small stash in my pack. I was hoping, if I didn't squander it, to save enough to be able to subscribe to better Net Service so I could surprise Alejandro in the fall.

Rubbing my eyes, I headed for the bathroom, flicking on lights as I went. By the time I got to the sink, I wasn't squinting anymore. Drank some juice from a bottle in the kitchen and looked at the clock. Still hours before Mum and Dad came home. This was their latest night. Pulled out the notes I was making on sound. Now that I had started listening, I heard music everywhere, but I liked it best when there wasn't too much surrounding it. I found myself keeping my style and notes sparse and precise, not flowery and expansive like I'd thought I would.

Still tired, I put my cheek on the kitchen table just for a minute, and without meaning to, dozed off again only to jerk awake with a start at a heavy pounding out in the hall. Quarantine?

I held my breath, straining to hear what door they were at. Mine? My heart sounded like it was going to explode. I wanted to hide, but where? In a closet? Would I fit? How many bugs would be in there? I heard Ethan crying, screaming; I heard Mary yelling, "No, no, we aren't sick! No symptoms."

"You were exposed," a rough voice called. "Come quietly now."

"No! Run Ethan!" Was that a window opening? I pressed my ear against our common wall.

I heard something, what was it? Somebody groaned.

"She stabbed me! Get the witch."

Screams, shouts, yelling. Who said they had the kid? Which voice? Why wasn't he screaming anymore?

"Hey, stop her!"

Then nothing for a few minutes. Nothing until, "Too bad."

"Yeah, well, what could we do? Guess she didn't want to go to Quarantine. Just pick her up. Let's get her to the morgue, and the kid to processing."

A few grunts. "Come on kid! Stop it! Ow! He bit me! Damn, now I hafta get shots."

"Hold him. I'll gag him. There. Come on, let's get out of here!"

Then nothing more. I sank to the floor, tears dripping off the bridge of my nose and onto our rug. Ethan. Mary. I wanted to peek out into the hall, but was too afraid. Something scratching at the window made me twist around. Bellisima the cat wanted in and I opened our window to her. She leaped off the sill and slid beneath the couch. When I peeked under, trying to coax her out, her eyes glowed neon, and her claws were extended. I let her be and sank into my bed. I heard the door to our apartment open, I heard my parents' humming whispers, I caught the words tape and Quarantine, but I didn't come out. I prayed Bellisima would stay hidden under the sofa. I prayed for it, and as I did, I made a plan. Bellisima and I were going to Granna's first thing in the morning. She would stay, I would come home. I hoped Granna liked cats, because I didn't have anywhere else to take Ethan's pet.

I tried to sleep, but kept half-waking, half-listening, dozing, half-waking until I heard the alarm go off in Mum's and Dad's room, and darted quickly into the living room. I had at most ten minutes to coax Bellisima into my bedroom and under my bed before they were out of their room.

"Come, come, Bellisima," I clucked, swinging a little ball of rubber bands her way. She pounced, I pulled it, she pounced, I pulled it until she was in my domain. I threw the ball under my bed and she skidded after it as I pulled the door closed. Phase one accomplished. Now, to wait until Mum and Dad left.

"Zeyya," Mum said softly through the door. "Are you awake?"

"Sort of," I said, slipping under the covers as the door cracked.

Mum didn't come in. "Honey, next door—tape!"

"I heard them last night."

"Okay, then. Be careful."

How was I going to be careful? There were no secret doors or escape hatches in our apartment, and I wasn't able to balance on a ledge like a cat. I coached Bellisima into my lap and scratched the crown of her head behind her ears. Her diaphragm vibrated under my fingers like my violin when I played my best.

Mum and Dad called their goodbyes and I followed theirs with my own. I waited five minutes and jumped out of bed, hanging onto the cat and plunking her into my extra pack. I put my violin into my other pack, then dashed into the bathroom for a quick get ready, back to the kitchen for a slab of bread and gulp of water and we were out the door. The cat was a weighty lump on my shoulder, but she was quiet. Now, if only Granna would take her.

It started to drizzle while we rode the walkways, but it never got too bad and by the time I stepped off, sunlight was tweaking the edges of the clouds suspended in the heavy summer air. Visiting Granna's was always like stepping into a past of lazier days. No matter how Dad complained about her and her obsession with the past, my visits with Granna comforted me. I turned down what could barely be called a lane and there was her house, squatting between the back-alley entrances to towering high rises.

Buildings to the right of her, buildings to the left, stuck in the middle with you—it was a corruption of some song I had once heard that had lodged itself in my brain.

And there, painted in stripes of rain-fresh sun and shade, Granna rocked in an old oak chair she'd pulled onto her front porch.

"Hi, Granna."

She greeted me with a grin and a small wave. "Come to visit?"

"Yes."

"Did you bring your violin?"

"Of course." She always wanted me to play for her, seemingly unaware of what a mediocre musician I was. "Can we go inside first?"

Her rocking ceased and her eyes narrowed. "That isn't the custom, is it? Pay the price of admission if you want to come in—my performance, please, Zeyya."

"Okay." I carefully laid my packs on the porch floorboards. I pulled out my violin, tucked it under my chin, slid the bow across the strings and watched Granna's eyes close as her fingers tapped on the arm of the chair. Her eyes snapped open, bird-bright behind her thick glasses.

"What's in the extra pack? It's moving you know."

"A surprise." I smiled hopefully.

"A surprise that moves? Bring it on in and let's see what you've brought with you."

"Alright, but Granna, keep an open mind, okay? It's a refugee."

"Oh!" she exclaimed when I lifted the cat from the pack. Bellisima's long fur hung softly between my fingers as she mewed her protest.

"I think she needs some water."

Granna found an old bowl, filled it and I let the feline down on the floor.

"Where'd you find that?"

I sighed. "The lone survivor of a Quarantine raid next door to us."

The cat was rubbing against Granna's leg, its motor rumbling in its chest. "Bellisima likes you, Granna."

"Uh huh." She looked at me over the rims of her glasses. "You want me to keep her?"

"She belonged to a friend of mine. He was four."

"Ooooh, Granddaughter, you know how to pull at my heartstrings. Okay, okay, I'll keep her." She stroked the fur some more. "Did they tape it?"

"Of course, but I think, well..." I began to cry. "Granna, I think Ethan's mom got killed."

She let the cat jump out of her lap and opened her arms to me. "You heard it through the walls?"

I couldn't speak, so I let her wrap me in her thin arms, accepted the hug as if I was a four-year-old, until finally I managed to utter, "Mum thought we'd be safe."

"No, she hoped you'd be safe, my darling. Hope is all she has now."

"Granna, they weren't really sick, I know they weren't. I'd been playing with Ethan in the mornings. He was fine."

"Probably was. His mom, too."

"Then why'd they take them away? Why'd they kill Mary?"

She stroked my hair now, catching her fingers in the knots and curls. "Oh, baby! I'm sorry."

"But why, Granna?"

She lifted my face, stared right at me and put her fingers to her lips as she whispered, "They have to find cheap labor somewhere, don't they?"

"You can't believe that!"

"No? You don't like that one? Then—they need test subjects for medical experiments?"

"Granna! That's against the law."

"Well—was Ethan a suspicious political dissident?"

"What? He was four. He and his mom were harmless."

"If you're sure of that, then I suppose they took them for no reason at all."

She got up, got us each a glass of water, sat back down and began to hum a song softly under her breath, tapping her fingers on the tabletop to the rhythm of it.

Abruptly breaking off, she asked, "Would you like to eat lunch here? I can make a pot roast and vegetables. How would that be? And the cat can join us."

My mouth watered at the thought of pot roast. Mum and Dad couldn't afford much meat anymore.

"Granna, do you ever worry about Quarantine?"

"No."

"Why not?"

"If they want me for labor, I'm too old. If they want me for experiments, I'm too old. If they're after political dissidents, I'm too old."

"What if you get sick."

"I'm old enough. I'll die quickly."

"So you're lucky to be old?"

She laughed before sobering up. Putting her face close to me, meeting my gaze eye-to-eye, she said, "Better than the alternative."

"Being young?"

"No, Zeyya, being dead."

I felt myself flush. "I wish we lived somewhere safe, that's all."

"Let me know when you find such a place."

She turned to the oven and shoed me from the kitchen. I sat in a living room chair in a patch of sun and Bellisima jumped into my lap. The clatter of the dishes and the click of the knife as it sliced vegetables filtered into the living room. Water gurgled in the kitchen sink and the breeze stirred old brass chimes that hung on the porch, and I felt calm and safe. Time passed slowly as the smell of the roast filled the house, causing Bellisima to stretch and strut towards the source of the aroma.

"Lunch," Granna called.

There was a place set for Bellisima on the floor. A dish of milk and a wedge of tuna lay neatly on a plate. Granna watched her sniff, then nibble, before confessing, "I've never had a cat before. Wildcats lived on a hill behind our house once, but that's it. Anything I need to know?"

"You're asking me? I've never had a cat, either."

"In that case, you'll have to come over more often to help take care of her."

"Thanks, Granna."

"Well, I suppose it's the least I can do, seeing as how your father would never consider keeping her—seeing as how it's against the rules."

I helped her clean up, kissed her goodbye and promised to return in the morning.

I was halfway down the block when I turned around to look behind me. The tops of the city towers blocked the afternoon sun and draped Granna's little home in shadow so that it faded away as if vanishing from existence. Then a light filled a window with pale yellow and the house was back, a little anchor in a sea of tilting skyscrapers. I felt my stomach settle and hurried towards the walkways.

"Our recent history is such…that in the minds of the people of Burma, alliance with a big power immediately means domination by that power."

U Nu, Prime Minister of Burma, 1955
National Press Club, Washington, DC

September 21, 1958
Rangoon, Burma
Dear Mother,

It seems strange to think that the nights at home are turning crisp and fall is in the air. It's still hot and humid here. The monsoon will be with us for another three weeks and it will be about mid-October before we get a break in this weather. So far, we've had 60 inches of rain since January first. Normal rainfall for the year is about 99 inches and there is no rain after October 15.

We didn't take Labor Day as a holiday. We're forced to take so many Burmese holidays that we just ignore a good many American ones. Sis is growing so fast that if we return home in the winter, she won't have anything to wear, as nothing we brought will fit her and you can't buy winter clothes here.

I'm sorry I can't be with you for your birthday. Have a happy one!

Love,

Jack

The Greater East Coast Metropolis: 2047
[Official Weather Report: No rain warnings. Total rainfall this month: 22 inches. Total ground absorption due to violence of storms: 5%. Today: Sunny-haze. Please wear sunscreen for your protection. High temperatures will be in the upper 90's. Sidewalk and walkway coolers will be turned on Thank you and have a good day.]

I'd forgotten the yellow tape until I stepped off the shaky elevator that seviced our building. We lived on the fifteenth floor, so I almost always took the lift, even though every time I stepped into the rickety box, I was sure its cable was going to snap and send me and it to be smashed at the bottom of the shaft. I was whistling when the color caught me in its glow. I was going to hate yellow for the rest of my life.

My hands were shaking as I turned the key in the lock and let myself inside, closing the door tightly against the neon glare of the Quarantine tape. Roaches scattered when I turned on the light and a mouse slipped under the door to the bathroom. I dumped my bags on the sofa, gulped some water and went to the Net. I hadn't used it in a long time, so I had a little time saved up, not enough for Mail, but enough for a quick search. Straight to search mode. Looking up *Quarantine*, adding *tape*, I waited. The connection was slow, but finally coughed out a few lines. I wanted to know how long I was going to have to pass by the neon yellow next door, how long before I could try and forget without a daily reminder. I clicked off. Nothing specifically about what I wanted, but it did say: *Any quarters taped off remained permanently uninhabitable.* Why? What was in Ethan's apartment that was so dangerous? By the time Mum and Dad came home, I had a long list of questions about Quarantine, but had whittled it down to: *Could we try to find Ethan?*

Dad shook his head. "No, Zeyya, we can't."

"Why not? Has anyone ever tried to find someone they took? What if he's cured? Where'll he go?"

Mum hugged me. "You're a kind person, Zeyya, but he won't come back. We can't do anything."

I kicked a chair and slammed the door to my room. He was four. He had to be scared. I opened the door and yelled through, "Why do they leave the tape up?" When they didn't bother to answer, I slammed the door again. It was good I'd eaten a lot at lunch, because I wasn't eating with them tonight. They could try to find Ethan, they just didn't want to.

Minutes passed. My frustration dwindled. I wasn't being fair. I crept into the kitchen. Mom silently put a plate at my place, cleared her throat and asked what I'd done with my day.

"Went to Granna's. She fed me."

Dad turned his head to me. "And?"

"Nothing. It was nice. The food was good. Why can't we live with Granna, Dad?"

"We live here," he said, pushing his chair away from the table. "She only has two bedrooms."

"I could sleep on the sofa."

"This is our home, Zeyya."

"That's lame, Dad."

"Zeyya!"

It was his warning voice. Dad was a stickler for rules and one of his rules was—*Don't talk back to your father*. Tough. I was too old for that rule.

"I bet it's because it'd be embarrassing for you to have sex there."

Their heads snapped up. I could tell I had definitely stepped over a boundary when it took Dad a few minutes before he came back with, "Is that the kind of thing Granna discusses with you?"

"No, of course not! Just tell me why can't we live there."

His lips snapped together, parted and he spit out at me, "It's not possible," before he stalked into his room.

"Mum?"

She shook her head.

"Mum, you're not being reasonable. Look at this place! We could live at Granna's for nothing! You wouldn't have to work so hard."

She stood. "The law is specific. Granna doesn't have the square footage to take in three people."

"That law is to stop the diseases. Come on, Mum, we're less likely to get sick at Granna's than in this rat hole!"

"That's enough!"

"Mum," I called, following her. She didn't answer.

Neither of them came out that night, so I washed up, put things away, read in bed for a while. When I closed my eyes, I slept like a rock. When I opened them, Mum and Dad had left already, leaving a note taped to the front door. "Bye. Love you. Talk to you tonight. Have a good day."

I took it easy for a while, postponed going to Granna's until after I worked on my concerto, but couldn't get any notes down, so it wasn't long before I headed out. I had to walk by the tape again. No way around that. I put my hand out, just one finger touching it and I didn't drop dead. I wanted to yank it down, I really did. Looked around to see if anyone was coming, but at the last minute, I chickened out. I was a coward. I hadn't even tried to help Mary and Ethan. I bit my lip when I relived the memory of that night, but what could I have done? At least I'd saved Bellisima who came purring up to me the minute I stepped over Granna's threshold.

"So there you are! I was wondering if you'd forgotten your obligations to this cat."

"Nope. I was trying to compose, but no luck."

I slumped into the sofa cushions and scratched the cat's back. "Granna, you didn't really have wildcats in your backyard, did you?"

"Not in my backyard. In the jungle-covered hillside that butted up to the edge of our compound. Of course, they couldn't get over the fence, but we could hear them, and Josephine, she told us about them."

She reached over and scratched the cat's ears. "We were living in Burma at the time."

I'd never heard about Burma before. Last year, she had spent two-hundred-and-twelve days—I'd counted—talking to me about books I'd never heard of, and then finding me old copies of them from used bookstores. Most of the spines were splintered, the pages barely held together, and one day while I was out, Dad had thrown them away. I hadn't thought I'd care, but once gone, I'd gotten a tight feeling in my chest.

"Burma? Where's that?"

"Oh my, it's called something else now, but it's still Burma to me. It was so beautiful there—cerulean skies with Flame of the Forest trees flowering in our yard and neatly trimmed hedges framing the perimeter of our front lawn. In the back, an old banana palm stood next to our house, the kind with little red bananas cradled in its broad leaves. So unimaginable here."

"Sounds nice," I said, trying to remember how often I'd seen truly blue skies instead of blue haze.

"In unexpected places, the jungle grew right up to the edge of Rangoon's roads, while in other places, rice paddies were planted in the middle of the city."

"I read growing rice takes a lot of water."

"Oh, you got plenty of water there in the rainy season and afterwards bursts of blossoms and greenery." Her eyes closed as she spoke and her voice mellowed into something smooth and velvety as if the years had dropped away, but it scared me a little, she sounded so young.

"Granna? Are you okay?"

"Of course, I am. My goodness! Do you want a snack?"

Bellisima must have recognized the word because she dropped out of my lap and followed Granna to the kitchen, mewing all the way.

"Let's just bake a few cookies. I made dough already." She handed me a spoon and we dropped dough through the idyllic afternoon, carefree, laughing, ignoring the rest of the world.

"Sometimes I wish I hadn't grown up, Granna."

"You? Grown up? Well, not quite yet. Don't rush it. You've got a lot of years to be older."

"Okay." I flashed her a smile.

"So how is your concerto coming?"

"Not bad. I know how it's going to end—on a wailing sound. I'm calling it *Ethan*."

She looked up at me. "You know, it must be real hard to be young right now with all this Quarantine mess."

We dropped the remaining cookies in silence after that, baked them in silence, too. By the time we finished chomping on some and relaying the trays in and out of the oven, it was past time for me to go home.

"I'll see you tomorrow," I said.

"Take these to your mother and father," she instructed, handing me a bag of cookies, "and no eating them up on the way home!"

By this my gift, whatever boon I seek,

It is the best of boons to profit all;

By this abundant merit I desire

Here or hereafter no angelic pomp

Of Brahmas, Suras, Maras; nor the state

And splendors of a monarch; nay, not even

To be the pupil of a conqueror.

But I would build a causeway sheer athwart

The river of Samasara, and all folk

Would speed across thereby until they reach

The Blessed City. I myself would cross and drag

The drowning over. Aye, myself tamed,

I would tame the willful; comforted,

Comfort the timid; wakened, wake the asleep;

Cool, cool the burning; freed, set free the bound.

Pali Verse, by King Alaungsithu (1112-1167)
Shwegu Temple, Pagan, Burma
An **Atlantic** Supplement, 1958

AIR LETTER

AEROGRAMME

July 22, 1958

Rangoon, Burma

Dear Louis,

Susie really had a birthday that was out of this world. I thought the kid was going to explode before it was over. She got a doll of a Burmese prince of the olden days, an American doll that we brought with us, a pink sari that Josephine, the nanny, made for her, a longyi and angyi from Ab and Sil, umpteen presents from her party guests—what a party! The servants decorated the house in a most professional manner with crêpe paper and balloons. Sebastian baked her three marble cakes, as well as cookies. The kids had a fabulous time.

Life here in Rangoon is settling down, but I can't say it's humdrum. For one thing, there are never the right parts available for our equipment. Two of the headlights for our car burned out and there are no replacements available. The pictures of your children made me a little homesick. Everybody is changing so fast.

Love,

Jack

The Greater East Coast Metropolis: 2047:
[This is an official announcement: WARNING
We have had a number of incidents of runners. Remember,
Quarantine is for the greater good. Do not associate with
the homeless, or anyone you think might be in hiding.
Contamination by association will mandate your Quarantine.
Please go willingly if approached by a Quarantine Squad.]

It'd been great, nestled between the walls of Granna's house all afternoon. Swinging the bag of cookies from my hand, I barely noticed how late it was, how dark it had already gotten before I got home. Smelling those cookies, my mouth watering, I barely noticed the dingy halls of our building. Relaxed, at ease, I skipped off the elevator thinking about the boy who said he'd never grow up in an old book on Granna's shelf, tipped my head back, said hello to the bugs on the ceiling, and stopped in front of our door.

Yellow tape? Yellow tape across our door?

I'd made a mistake, stopped at Ethan's door, not ours. I walked past it, stopped, looked back. Two doors with yellow tape.

Ethan's: one.

Ours: two?

I walked back, every step impossibly drawn out, stretching physics, keeping me from really getting to our door. Then the pause ended. Motion, time began again.

Was that me who screamed? I wasn't sure. "No! Open the door!" Now I was howling. I tore at the tape, pounded on the door. "Open up, let me in! Open the door!"

I pulled at the knob, tried to force the key into the lock, but the door was sealed, the lock was filled. I was on this side where I didn't belong. I belonged inside. I belonged with my parents, wherever they were.

"Let me in! Let me in!" I screamed until my voice wouldn't make a sound, then slid to the floor, a wretched wet-faced bundle, shaking and shaking until my hand brushed a slip of paper. I shook a bug off it. A message in Dad's handwriting: *Go to Granna's.*

The yellow tape, hanging where I had torn it off one side of the door, brushed my neck.

Go to Granna's.

But everything was inside. Everything. I had no clothes. I had nothing except my pack. I stared at it, unable to remember what I'd put in it when I'd gone to Granna's in the morning. My violin. My concerto and all my notes. What else? A jacket? The little that was left of my stash of money from Mary that I hadn't spent on clothes or a few Net Mails to Alejandro, still unanswered, never to be answered now that the apartment was sealed. Blood money, I thought. It's blood money. I fumbled in the pack and pulled it out, crumpled it into a wad in my fists, dropped it on the floor and kicked it away from me, rubbing my hands on my shirt to wipe away the stain. My mind floated off. Did I sleep slumped there? Did I? I couldn't remember. What time was it? What should I do?

What was that? Somebody beating on a door? *Quarantine.*

I jumped up, heart hammering, blood rushing through my ears. Quiet, girl. Quiet. Tiptoe. Take the stairs. No one uses them and it's fifteen floors down, not up. You can do it. You can. Quiet as a mouse, as a roach. Crawl under the cracks. To Granna's. *Go to Granna's.*

Going down, I counted ten floors with tape across the stairwell doors. Ten. They had cleaned out ten floors. But not the basement, not the lowest level with exits to the garbage dumps. I pushed the stairwell door open as softly as I could, froze when it squealed and then hurried through. Halfway down the hall, something popped like a gunshot. I froze again. It was Old Stella, cracking the door to her apartment. I could only see one of her eyes and a tiny bit of her mouth.

"Do you know what happened?"

"It was Mr. Porter what brought them."

I didn't know who that was, or why or how he'd brought them. Had he been sick? Had he exposed the whole building?

"Was he sick?"

"Sick?" she asked with a cackle.

"You should leave," I told her. "Get out. They're going through the whole building." She cackled again and sealed the crack to her apartment with a bang.

I ran. They'd be in the lowest levels soon. Ten floors already. I looked back once, but no one was behind me. There was the door. I pushed with my shoulder, spun out into fresh night air, ran again. Running, running, my feet pounding, the pack slamming against my shoulder and back.

Run!

I didn't watch which way I was going, just away, away from the yellow tape, the booming voices: *Quarantine*.

Run.

I didn't look back or slow down until I felt the shock of my heels on the pavement pulse up my legs and cramp my muscles. I slowed and wiped at my streaming face and nose, only to realize people were staring at me where I stood. I whirled around and ducked behind some trash bins, gulping back my sobs and wiping at my face with the edge of my shirt until I had enough control to find a break in the crowd and step back into the swarming mass of bodies. People going home. Walking.

Walk.

I put one foot in front of the other, tried to look inconspicuous, sure that everyone knew I belonged in Quarantine, sure that someone would turn me in. Barely keeping the tears back, I stepped onto a walkway. I didn't know or care where it was going, and was afraid to ask, just got off at the first street I recognized.

In a daze, I trekked sixteen blocks into Granna's neighborhood. I started to shake and it took me a few minutes to realize I was angry. Why had they taken everyone? What right did they have? Where were Mum and Dad? Where? Where was Ethan? Everyone was disappearing! I wiped at the tears that were running down my cheeks, rubbed my finger under my nose and tried to compose myself. What was I going to tell Granna?

I sat on her steps the rest of the night, shivering even though it wasn't cold. I didn't sleep, but I didn't think, either, until I heard her through the open windows, putzing around inside. I picked up my stuff and raced to the other side of the street. I didn't want her to find me like that. I'd hide until it was a reasonable time for me to appear and then I'd wait to tell her what had happened, wait for a moment when it wouldn't give her a heart attack, when I wouldn't burst into tears. Found a place where I could watch the house from the behind some empty cartons and trash bags, and sat on the ground. Very few people traversed this alleyway, so I was pretty safe.

She came out on her porch. Had I ever noticed how frail she was? She sat in her rocker in the warm morning air, sunlight pooling in her lap as she started to move the chair with her heels, up and down, pumping it into a rhythm. I watched her, trying to get up my courage to go across the street. The morning got warmer, but still I didn't move. Finally her head drooped and I could see she had fallen asleep in the sun. I stood, straightened my shoulders, brushed at my hair and took a deep breath.

I got up the third step before she opened one eye.

"Hi, Granna," I said, plopping a kiss on her soft cheek, hoping my nose wasn't red or damp, that my eyes were clear.

Her fingers were wrapped in yarn and intertwined in crochet hooks which rested in her lap. She was dressed all wrong, in white, not black. White was the color of brides, not the color of mourning.

"You aren't getting married, are you, Granna?"

"What?" She patted my hand in greeting.

"White is a bride's color, isn't it?"

"Not in Burma. There it's yellow."

I jerked away from her hand as if burned. Yellow. Quarantine. Breathe I told myself, stay calm.

"You look tired," Granna said, keeping her eyes on my face. "What's wrong."

"I had a fight with Mum. Can I stay a few nights with you?"

Her fingers began moving quickly as she wove the yarn. "Did you tell your mother you'd be here?"

"She knows."

And it wasn't a lie. They had told me to come here, left me the note I had carefully folded into my pocket.

"I can just slip into Mum's old room, okay?"

She kept her eyes focused on me even as she gave her consent. Could she tell something was wrong? Should I tell her? I couldn't. I just couldn't. I gulped and kissed her, then gratefully slipped away and into the house. I put my bag down and pulled out my violin, an almost empty portfolio of compositions I'd been carrying around and the pages to my concerto, laying everything neatly on the chest of drawers. They were all I had left of my music. I had some pens, my jacket, an extra pair of socks I couldn't remember putting in there, and a couple of books. It was everything I owned in the world. Bellisima followed me into my Mum's old room and made herself at home on the bed. My bed now. I had wanted to live here, but not like this.

I fell face down on the clean bedspread and Bellisima walked onto my back. "Off," I hissed through my teeth at her. "Not now." I closed my eyes against the tiredness that was overwhelming me, demanding that I sleep, and let myself fade away to wake to Bellisima walking on me again. One paw then another, one paw then another up my back until she jumped down onto the floor and with her tail in the air, strutted from the room, leaving me to smell something delicious wafting through the whole house. When I sat up, I realized I had an odor, too. A bad one. I needed a shower which would clean my body, but not my clothes. I looked in the small closet in the hopes of finding a change of clothing. There were three items in it. A sheath of rosy silk fabric hung over a hanger, an old flannel shirt hung on a hook, and a pair of worn out shoes that lay on the floor. I pulled out the shirt and sniffed it. Clean. It'd do.

Washed, hair combed, huge shirt swamping me, I found Granna in the kitchen. "Can I do laundry?"

"Sure. Pop it in and then come back for some lunch."

Lunch? Only lunchtime? I wished I'd slept the whole day away, not merely half of it. Then I would have been a day further from everything. Absolutely everything.

"I see you found your grandfather's shirt?"

"Uh, is it okay? I forgot to bring clothes."

"That must have been a humdinger of a fight you had with your parents, you leaving with nothing but what was on your back."

"Uh huh." I hurried to Granna's ancient washer and stuffed my clothes in, drizzled laundry detergent over the load and stood there listening to the swish of the water as it filled the machine.

I turned around to face Granna standing in the door, staring at me intently. Her mouth opened, but before she could ask me what had happened, I asked her, "What's that pink stuff hanging in the closet?"

I knew I wasn't off the hook, that I'd only distracted her, but it bought me a teeny bit more time.

"A sari. Josephine made it and gave it to me on my ninth birthday. It came with the choli and a slip and a pair of golden-threaded Burmese slippers."

I could have asked what a choli was or what a sari was, but I only asked, "Who's Josephine?"

"Oh, she was our nanny and her husband Sebastian was our cook."

I'd barely processed that Granna had once had servants, when she spoke again. "I had some party that year, though I'd set my heart on ice cream and only got the cake. Actually, Sebastian baked three cakes and the whole house was decorated in balloons and streamers." She made a sort of smacking sound with her lips. "Lunch is ready, Zeyya."

I followed her back into the kitchen. "It must have been nice, Granna—your birthday party, I mean."

"Mostly, except my mother got amoebic dysentery that birthday and it kept her from getting my ice cream from the commisary. Still, it was a good birhday. Let's eat."

I sat down quietly until Granna cleared her throat. I had to stop her from asking about Mum and Dad. "Granna, what's a commissary and dysentery, and what's a choli?"

"For goodness sakes, you are just full of questions! A commissary was a place where American goods were available to foreign nationals. Stuff from home, like powdered milk and sometimes freezer ice cream mixes or chocolate syrup or chocolate chips. A choli was the blouse Indian women wore under their saris and as for dysentery, that I'll leave for a time other than lunch to explain. Now..."

"Wait, Granna, what's a sari?"

She stood up suddenly. "Zeyya, can't I get a question in edgewise?"

I hung my head. Here it came.

"What were you fighting over? You aren't pregnant, are you?"

My eyes popped open. It took a second before a giggle bubbled from between my lips, then another moment before the giggle turned into eye-watering, unstoppable peals of laughter that took my breath away. When I finally got control, Granna was staring at me suspiciously.

"Have you run away from home? Because, this isn't a good place to hide, Zeyya. It'll be the first place they'll check, and I won't lie for you."

"I told you, Mum and Dad sent me..." My voice trailed off. I was going to have to tell her. I couldn't keep this up. "Yellow tape." It was all I could get out.

She cocked her head, obviously mystified for a moment before realization passed across her face. She sat back into a chair, hard.

"Quarantine?"

We sat there, the two of us, each in a chair, separated by silence, by disbelief and then Granna rose, picked up my plate with the food pushed around on it but barely touched, went to the trash, threw it in, turned on the water and surprised me with, "Liar, liar, pants on fire."

"Granna, please, I'm sorry! I should have been there. I should have saved them."

She stood with her back to me. Silent. Not crying, at least. In a whisper I heard her say, "There are some things you can't stop."

It was late afternoon before Granna muttered another sound. "Darn these skyscrapers, hanging over my house, casting me in shadow and running up my energy bills." She moved around, flicking switches, until the whole house was lit up. "Got to hold back the darkness."

Before I could speak, she headed out onto the shade-laden front porch. Beyond the house, between the skyscrapers, sunlight still shone.

"Granna?"

She put her fingers in her ears, shook her head at me and plunked into her rocker. Her porch wrapped around the front of the house and down the sides. A bicycle with flat tires and rusted spokes leaned in a corner like some lame animal. The wind chimes moved in a hot breeze and sang with a clean sweetness. Granna's eyes closed and her face relaxed into soft folds and wrinkles. I tried to imagine her as a young woman and then as a teen and finally as the child who had lived in Burma. I couldn't. She had been old my whole life.

"Granna, why don't you have your face restored?"

Her eyes remained closed, but she answered immediately. "So I could look young again? Who would I be fooling? Besides, I don't mind people knowing I've lived a long time." One eye opened behind her glasses. "No denying it, I'll be one hundred in two more years."

Most adults didn't want anyone to know how old they were. Aging was equated with ugliness, followed by death and wasn't to be spoken of, but my Granna sat there and announced her age with pride. "A century! When we lived in Burma, the average life span was twenty-eight-years-old. That would have given you about eleven more years to live, Zeyya."

"Will you at least let me get your glasses repaired, then?"

She reached up and touched the frames. "No, but I guess I should get a new pair."

"You could get just your eyes restored," I suggested gingerly.

She glared at me.

"Okay, okay, forget it."

The sun slanted onto the porch for a brief moment just before real dusk fell across the sky. Sounds from the city floated around us, but remained distant, removed from where my Granna rocked. I kept sneaking glances her way, still attempting to imagine a young Granna. What color had her hair been? Her eyes were walnut brown, her skin was pale and sun robbed, but still slightly olive. When had she started wearing glasses? When had her hair turned white? What had she looked like when she lived in Burma?

"Granna, was it safe in Burma?"

She laughed. "Safe? Ten poisonous snakes in the compound and in the house, eleven scorpions and two thieves. And yet, yes, I felt safe."

Scorpions? "Okay, uh, how about plain old roaches, Granna?"

Her laugh was a little tinny when she answered. "Roaches? Roaches are everywhere. When humanity is extinct, roaches will still be here. My mother even found them baked into bread our cook bought at the market."

"You ate that?"

"Don't be silly. Sis and I shrieked and jumped around about it, but Daddy proclaimed calmly, 'A little protein never hurt anyone.' Mommy threw it away anyway, after which the cook baked our bread."

"A little protein?"

She laughed at me. "There are plenty of people who eat bugs."

"No way! You're making that up."

She shook her head slowly, eyeing me seriously. "No, I'm not. Some Burmese tribes, like the Padaungs, fry cicadas. And the Karens consider the queen of the white ants to be a delicacy."

I had no idea what a white ant was and I didn't want to know, so I just squinched up my face in disgust.

"Looked bad to me, too."

"You saw people eating bugs?"

"Well, I saw our servants roasting the queen of the white ants on a stick over a fire on our front lawn. Kind of an ignominious end for a queen, don't you think? But then, she was just a big white grub."

Grub? I gagged and tasted bile in my throat.

"My goodness, you have a weak stomach, don't you? I'm the one who saw them dividing her into portions, not you."

I ran for the bathroom and by the time I felt less queasy, it was truly pitch black out.

'Fire, Fire, come with me,

To burn the Forest,

To clear the Land,

To grow the Grass,

To feed the Buffalo,

To wallow the Mud,

To mend the Pot,

To fetch the Water,

To wash the Beak,

To eat the little Wren.'

'I will come,' replied the Fire. The Crow in great joy flew
back towards the Forest with the Fire in his beak, but before
he could reach it, his Beak had become so badly burned that he had to
drop the Fire. Giving up all hope of eating the little
Wren, the Crow flew home in disgust.

The Crow and the Wren
from *Burmese Folk-Tales*
by Maung Htin Aung, Barrister-At-Law
Oxford University Press
21st Impression, 1958

Tuesday, April 29, 1958

Rangoon

Dear Mama,

U Tun Khin was a guest at our house the other nite. He's a much traveled young super salesman, selling rice to importing countries. He just spent ten days in a Buddhist monastery and maintains Buddhism to be philosophy rather than religion.

Thursday and Friday are holidays for Peasant's Day and the Full Moon of Kason, which celebrates the anniversary of Buddha's birthday, his attainment of Buddhahood, and the day on which he entered Nirvana. I am being called to dinner, so I'll continue this before bed and send it in the morning.

B.

Greater East Coast Metropolis: 2047
[Hospitals are unable to accept new flu patients.
If you become ill, please log into
Networksmedicalemergencies.consol
and help will be dispatched as soon as possible.]

I open my eyelids, or do I? Are those cat-eyes, neon green in the dark, glowering at me, changing to yellow? Something yellow slithers in the blackness. There! And there! Wind catches it up, whips it, snaps it. It flaps in the wind. Tape. Neon yellow blinds me.

Granna slept late, but neon yellow woke me before light touched the porch or the windows. I was up in time to hear a storm drive the rain onto the slate roof of the house and batter at the windows. *Let me in,* it screamed. It drummed on the trash bins by the back entrances and ran out their drain holes. I stepped onto the porch, and the wind drove the storm under the roof, against my body until my clothes were soaked. Puddles collected where the alley pavement had collapsed into potholes. When the water-drenched morning dawned, I went back inside.

The house was still dark, but shadows were starting to form on the walls, washed in by a pale sunrise. I flipped through a stack of books on an end table. Granna had more books than anyone I knew, and less tech. I stopped, picked up *Burmese Folk-Tales*. I felt the old pages, blew the dust from them, fingered the simple line drawings.

Bellisima padded into the room, her eyes glowing and right behind her came Granna, a fluff of white robe and flow of white hair.

"What are you doing up, Zeyya?"

"Couldn't sleep. Bad dream."

She sat down next to me. "What have you got there? Oh my, I remember the morning Mommy bought this at the English speaking book-shop down on Sule Pagoda Road. Maung Htin Aung." She pronounced the author's name with a tonal twang as she took hold of the little book.

"Granna, can we talk about Mum and Dad?"

"I'd rather not," she said, taking my hand in hers and patting it. "Later, when I'm more awake." She flicked on a lamp. "There, that's better, I don't like dim light. I remember this book. Moona couldn't read, but if we told her a title of a story, she'd tell us a tale from the book."

"Who was Moona?"

"Our nanny."

"Wait, I thought Josephine was your nanny."

"She was our first nanny. Moona was the second and all of about this high." She raised her hand to her shoulder height. "She was sixteen and Sis was already as tall as she was. Burmese are small, trim, and they have great posture." She straightened her shoulders.

"I was babysitting Ethan. For money," I admitted for no real reason.

"It's good to get paid for your work."

I had expected an admonition. "It was illegal, I'm not seventeen yet."

"It's all relative, isn't it? Moona was sixteen and she was an old maid. You're sixteen and still a child in the eyes of our society."

"Wait," I said as she stood, "wait a minute. Was she ugly?"

"Ugly? No, Moona was pretty. Now, let's get some breakfast and get this day on the road. Don't you need some new clothes?"

Huh? Yes, I did. I had nothing except the oversized shirt I'd slept in and the clothes I'd been wearing. I tugged at the shirt. "Was Grandpa a big man?"

She looked wistful for a fleeting second. "Yes, tall, six feet and thin, with beautiful blue eyes. Over the years, lost a little height, filled in a little, but his skin was creamy, and his hair always had that squeaky clean smell of baby shampoo." Her eyes looked misty.

"You miss him?"

"I miss him." She shook her hair as if to shake something from her. It fell like snow drifts down her back. "I miss many things. I miss the blight of crows frothing over trees at the edges of Burmese roads. I miss the blue-black backs of water buffalo in the fields of waving grass, right in the heart of Rangoon—like cool spots of shade in the burning sun. And your grandfather, yes, I miss him."

I scooped the little book up and followed her into the kitchen. "So which story do you like the best, Granna?"

"Oh my, it's been years...read me some of the titles."

"Rabbit Has a Cold, How the Galon-Bird Became a Salt Maker, Rain Cloud and the Crocodile, The Opium Eater and the Four Ogres, and The Crow and the Wren."

She threw her hands up. "You can't expect me to remember! It's been almost ninety years since I read those stories."

She dropped a bowl of cereal and a cup of milk on the table in front of me. "Get us spoons, dear."

"Come on, Granna, tell me why Moona was an old maid."

"How do I know? I was nine. But they didn't live very long over there, so you had to have your family young. They didn't have many doctors, but they sure had lots of diseases. Yellow fever, typhoid, typhus, diphtheria. I should know. Sis and I got twenty-one vaccinations before we left the United States. Nowadays, what is it, one shot when you're born?"

She sat down and dribbled milk onto the table as she gobbled up her cereal.

"Now, go get dressed and we'll go to the store. I'll wait on the porch."

"Granna, you're in a robe!"

"Ta da!" She whipped the robe off and there she was, fully clothed. "Good trick, huh? I'll take my morning rock in my chair while you get ready."

Who could help but laugh at my crafty old Granna? The shower felt good and some of the tension of the day before washed down the bathtub drain, but came back when I looked around Mum's old room. There in the corner was a picture of her with Granna when Mum was maybe twelve. There was a picture with Grandpa. On the dresser was a silver backed child's brush with Mum's name engraved on it: Debra. I picked that brush up and held it, clutched it as if it would bring Mum back. I forced myself to tie my shoes and sniffled up the threatening tears. What good would they do?

"Granna," I called out morosely as I walked towards the porch. "Granna?" She was standing at the railing talking to someone I couldn't quite see. "Granna? Who's that?"

"I'm not sure. Who does he look like?" she asked.

No one I knew. No shirt, no shoes, no socks—he had on nothing but a black suit hanging loosely off his frame, a coating of dust on his feet, and a broad-brimmed, high-crowned black hat shadowing his face.

"Hey," I greeted him. He took a few flat-footed steps forward so that he was standing just at the bottom of Granna's steps. "Can we do something for you?" I asked more directly.

Up came his head, exposing his face which was stained disconcertingly blue by detailed portraits etched on his skin in tattoos. His mouth opened, spewing a rapid-fire series of words at us so quickly they were unintelligible until he stopped and added, "Eldest?"

"Me?" Granna jabbed her thumb into her chest. "I'm old, but not the oldest. Not hardly. How about you? Are you an undertaker sent to prepare this poor body for the other side?"

He didn't seem to understand. "Undertaker?"

"You know, the person who prepares the dead for burial? You're dressed like one, sort of, well—in a way," I tried explaining.

"That is not something I do." Or at least that was what I thought he replied.

"Slow down. Don't talk so fast, I can barely understand you." And while I said it, I tried to figure out how old he was, but he didn't lift his face again, so it was pretty hard to make a guess.

"Then why're you all dressed in black, young fellow?" Granna inquired, her eyes twinkling now.

"I am not an undertaker," he insisted.

"No? Then are you the Grim Reaper?" She was on a roll, her mouth tweaking up, then straightening out. "Is that why you're dressed..." She waved a wrinkled hand at him.

I watched his face, watched delayed comprehension dawn on it.

"No. Uh..." He paused again as if searching for words.

"What's the matter?" Granna asked. "Don't you speak English?"

"Granna, everybody speaks English."

She twisted around to me, put her hands on her hips and stated firmly, "I've seen this before. He's translating from English to some language and back. Take my word for it."

It took him several minutes to speak again. "Please! Please, I do not represent death in any way. That is not why I'm dressed this way. Someone gave me this suit. It is black only by happenstance."

"Didn't they have some shoes and socks to give you while they were at it?" I asked skeptically.

"I don't know. They said something about Quarantine?"

I took a step back. "What do you mean? What about Quarantine?"

Granna was gesturing to me to calm down, but I felt my stomach fluttering and my heart beating. How could I stay calm?

"The man who owned the suit was sent away," he said very simply. Now my heart was really going. "Perhaps he took his shoes with him."

"You, go away!" I demanded.

"Now, now, let's be reasonable here," Granna said. "Why don't you just take that suit off and thrust it quickly into one of those trash bins."

He picked at it with his fingertips. "It's a perfectly good suit," he said slowly, "isn't it? I found a card here, in this pocket. Perhaps you know how to contact this man to see if the suit is good or not?"

He offered Granna a business card and before I could stop her she had plucked it from his fingers. "Phillip Masoneri, Taxidermist."

"That is not funny! Granna you should go in and wash your hands with a disinfectant, and you, Mr. Masoneri, you get out of here, leave us alone!"

Granna handed him back his card and he turned it in a puzzled fashion between his fingers.

"I am not Phillip Masoneri. This is his card, not mine."

"Yeah? Well, whoever you are, go away. Go find yourself a tailor and a pair of shoes, okay? Just leave!"

Granna hadn't budged from where she stood. "You look tired," she said to the guy. "Why don't you rest here on the front porch for a bit. Zeyya and I are going out to do shopping. Stay as long as you like."

"Uh, Granna, maybe that isn't such a good idea," I whispered, following her back inside as she made her way to the sink and washed her hands. "He might be sick. He could die on your stoop."

"Oh, Zeyya, he's not dying. He's just tired. Can't you tell the difference? We'll just lock the house, if I can find the darn keys. Have you seen them? Oh, there they are. Now let's get a move on it or the stores will be busting with people. We're already off schedule."

She pushed me out the door, turned the key in the lock, and gave me a grin. The taxidermist was sitting on a step, looking truly droopy.

"Up in the chair, boy," Granna said.

He rose unsteadily as we pushed by him, and when I craned my head around, he was sitting in the rocker slumped forward, the hat completely hiding his face.

"Granna, do you really think we should just leave him there?"

"Come on, come on, let's go."

She hurried along much faster than I had thought her capable of.

"Aren't we going to hop a walkway?" I called after her as we passed a stop.

"Don't believe in them. We're walking. Now move it."

It took us twice as long as riding the walkways would have, but luckily, once we got there, we got an order station quickly and I punched in Mum's account number. A buzzer went off: *Account Canceled.*

"What?"

Granna squeezed my hand, while deftly punching in her account number. "The minute you get sick they confiscate your money to pay for your care. Guess you're on my payroll now. Just remember, I'm on a limited budget, so only the basics, Zeyya. I'll be back in a bit."

I called up the menu and chose the cheapest things I could find, but when Granna returned, she deleted about half of what I'd picked.

"You don't need all that, Zeyya. We have to eat, you know. Come along, I want to get out of here as quickly as possible. I hate these hi-tech markets. One little mistake and it takes forever to straighten it out."

I scurried after her, noticing that she had a long menu printout.

"Is that all food? Can I get some pudding?"

"Zeyya, you should have asked before. I'm not adding anything else. It'll take too long. Now come along."

We fed the list into a chute, walked to the checkout, picked everything up, all prepackaged into sealed brown bags except for one white button-down shirt which she had added at the very end of her list, and so was spit out separately in clear cellophane.

"Who's that shirt for, Granna?"

"It's for emergencies. You never know when you'll need one."

It looked like a man's shirt from the picture pasted on the packaging. "Are you sure this is the one you want?"

"Humph. Won't know till I get it home, will I?"

She grumbled all the way home, still forcing us to walk. "Darn these hi-tech markets! Can't be sure that you got what you wanted until you unwrap it at home. Stupidest idea ever. Didn't used to be like this." She turned her face to me. "When I was small, a bald man with a pencil-thin mustache weighed all our produce, put it in a bag and marked the brown bag with a black crayon. So many pounds for such and such a price."

"Was that in Burma?"

"Heavens no! In Burma, either we went to the commisary or to a fresh air market where everyone tired to sell you anything they could."

"That must have been nice," I commented unthinkingly.

"Nice? Hmmm...Do you like mosquitoes and flies? If so, I guess it was nice. But maybe lively was a better description." I made a face at the thought of more bugs and she grinned at me. "I went with Mommy once when we were between cooks. We strolled between piles of food, squash, fruit, rice, spices spread out on bamboo mats, glancing at this and that as casually as possible before we made an offer."

"An offer?"

"Yep, they expected you to haggle."

"So, what'd you buy there, Granna, the time you went?"

She shrugged. "Don't remember. What I remember is all the hawkers and peddlers carrying fish and cold drinks for sale in buckets of ice, hanging off the ends of long poles, and if you understood Burmese, you might get a free story thrown into the purchase price. The hawkers were cackling and calling, 'Come buy, come buy'; and the chickens and roosters were cackling as they wandered between your legs; and the ducks were squawking and waddling wherever the chickens weren't! Day I went, there was a snake in a basket and a monkey in a sack. Oh, how I wanted that monkey!"

The sun went behind a building as we walked and Granna looked up, shielding her eyes with her hand. "Think it's going to rain today, Zeyya?"

I looked between the buildings, and saw hazy blue. "Probably not."

"In Burma, we knew precisely in which month, by which day the monsoon would come, and by exactly what day it would end."

"What's a monsoon?" I asked.

"Rainy season. But dry or rainy season, Burmese ladies carried big round black umbrellas overhead. When it was dry, they kept the sun off their skin, and when it was wet, well, they stayed dry."

It was nice walking and talking with Granna, listening to her past come into my present. It kept my mind from circling Mum and Dad.

We were almost home, which was good because the packages were getting heavy. I shifted their weight. Another block and we were on the alley that led to Granna's. I shifted our bundles again and stopped. There on the porch sat the taxidermist.

Granna was already at the door, turning the key in the lock by the time I got there.

"Can I help you?" he asked me.

"Yeah, by leaving. What are you still doing here?"

"Your Granna just offered me a drink. I'm pretty thirsty."

"Dirty, too. What's all that blue stuff on your hands and feet?" Granna asked over her shoulder.

"Granna, he's tattooed." How could she have missed it? She really did need to have her glasses fixed.

"Everywhere? He's tattooed on his toes, and his fingers and his teeth?" she asked.

Teeth? I turned to look and he smiled and yes, his teeth were scrimshawed in blue drawings. "Yeesh!"

"These are portraits of my ancestors."

Granna took off her glasses and wiped them on the bottom of her shirt, put them back over her eyes and said, "You have a lot of ancestors, Mr. Masoneri."

I caught a glimpse of tattoos on his chest beneath the suit jacket, on his hip where the pants were slipping, on his ankle beneath cuffs that were too short.

"Thank you," he said, as if she'd paid him a compliment.

She winked at me as she spoke again. "The Burmese believed a bug could be one of your ancestors. You have any bug ancestors on your body anywhere, young man?"

"Granna," I hissed, "don't encourage him."

"That's not possible, Eldest. Bugs cannot be an ancestor."

"Why not? Because you say so? Because Zeyya says so? Keep your mind open, Mr. Masoneri. You might not believe it, but the Burmese absolutely did."

The taxidermist looked confused, and I could almost sympathize.

"Granna, maybe this isn't the time to be reminiscing." I really wanted her to end the conversation, to give this person some water and send him on his way.

Instead she said very quietly, "But there's a lot back there."

That's when the taxidermist announced he'd check on what the Burmese believed.

I expected him to press one of the computer interface buttons some people got embedded in their wrists so that they were in direct contact with the central database. But no—he sat plop-down on the porch floor, crossed his legs Indian style, put his hands palms-up on his knees, rolled his eyes back in his head and had a seizure.

I shrieked frantically, "He's having a fit! Do something, Granna!" She should have been rushing into the house to call someone, but instead she was watching with calm curiosity. "Granna, what should we do?"

"Leave him be until he comes out of it," she said and started into the house.

I grabbed her arm. "Wait! What if he's contagious?"

"Then don't tell anyone. Quiet as a mouse unless you want Quarantine for all of us. Besides, I don't think he's having a seizure." She pointed at him. "No foaming, no twitching—not a seizure. A trance maybe. Maybe a vision. He reminds me of something."

She chewed on a fingernail while I tried to hold back my panic. Here we stood, in plain view of anybody headed to make a delivery to the buildings rising all around us, visible to some of the apartment windows, while this taxidermist-weirdo had a fit on Granna's front porch. What was she thinking? We didn't have to be the ones to call him in. If anyone saw him, they'd do it for us.

"Buddha!" she exclaimed, surprising me out of my fears. "Yes, he looks like a sitting Buddha." She walked all the way around him. "Except he's covered in blue not polychromed or gold leafed, and I can't tell if he has a lump of knowledge because he's wearing that silly hat."

She was about to pluck it off his head, when I saw his eyes start to roll forward.

"Quick, Granna, inside and lock the door!"

"Don't be silly, Zeyya, I want to see what happens."

His lids fluttered open, his eyes covered in a milky film, but before I could point out that it was a sign of illness, he blinked and it vanished.

"You were right, Eldest."

"Uh huh. So what did you find out?"

He rubbed his eyes, shaking himself to and fro like a dog with an itch before he spoke again. "Theravada Buddhists, like the Burmese, believed that if they did something bad in one life, they would return as a lower life form when they were reborn."

"You know, you didn't have to go into a trance to find out. I could have told you about reincarnation."

"Or you could have gone to a database," I suggested.

"I do not carry databases around with me. Eldest, did you know the Burmese followed the teachings of Sidhartha Guatama?"

Granna scratched at her ear. "You mean the Buddha, Mr. Masoneri."

Wait—how had he known that? How many people knew about Buddha and Burma? I hadn't. Yet according to Granna, the taxidermist had been sitting like a Buddha, and now he knew about Buddha. I was getting more and more nervous.

"Look, I don't know what you're up to, or who you are, but you need to leave now," I insisted.

"Where should I go?"

"I don't have the vaguest idea. Pick a place. I don't care where. Let's go in, Granna."

"My name is Jonah, Eldest. Tell me where to go."

I whirled on him from just inside the door, wishing Granna would follow me right then, immediately, but she stood with her feet planted firmly where she was.

"Let's let him explain, Zeyya. Now then, how did you come up with that information?"

He lowered his voice and his eyelids closed again, which made me even more nervous. "Granna, please!" I begged.

"I went to my ancestors for it."

"Pardon?" she asked, her eyes narrowing.

"I had to roll past my usual informants to a most ancient and rarely accessed ancestor."

"And where are your ancestors?" Granna asked, taking her first step backwards.

He laughed, a very small, musical sound, a perfect note that caught my ear. "With me always, of course."

Granna looked around. "I don't see them anywhere."

"No, Eldest, I carry their memories in my mind with me."

"Me, too, but I can't talk to them. They're pretty silent since they're deceased."

"I am sorry, Eldest. It must be very lonely for you."

"Sometimes."

That did it. "Stop," I demanded. "What do you want? What do you think you're pulling?"

He ignored me completely. "I'm tired and hungry now. Is there a place I can rest?"

"Oh no you don't! Out of here, you. Now. Go. Enough is enough! Begone. Right now."

He didn't budge. "I have nowhere to go."

"Go ask your ancestors what to do, then. We're not helping you. Leave us alone!"

"Aw, what the heck. He's the most interesting person I've met in decades. He can stay if he takes a shower and gets all that dust off him. I'll turn on the water."

"Thank you, Granna," he said.

"What? No, Granna, it's not safe! You can't let him in!"

"You've got a great imagination, Jonah," she said, ignoring me. "Come on, to the shower with you."

"What's a shower?" he asked as he followed her into the house.

"What do you think it is? You clean in it, you numbskull," I answered in despair.

"I clean in rivers, but if Granna wishes this, so be it."

"…my mother also told us of how beautiful he looked when he was playing chinlon, which is a light cane ball to be kept in the air by tossing with legs, shoulders or any part of one's body that agility can devise, his short strong body, bare except for the longyi tucked about his loins, with tattoo marks in a blue-ringed pattern from waist to knee, and his long thick hair in a knot on the crown of his head…"

Burmese Family
by Mi Mi Khaing

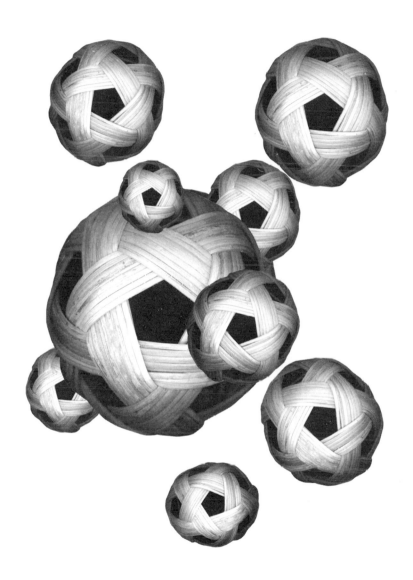

April 3, 1958

Rangoon

Dear Mama,

Today I went shopping. A friend took me to the "Brass House" to buy ashtrays and a vase or two. It's really not limited to brass, but sells things made of any metal at all—old and new items varying from old junk to real antiques. Then we tried to find lamp shades, but they must be made and although the labor is available, the materials are not. Rowe's is the local department store, but is being squeezed by a lack of import licenses, so it's quite empty. I think the government is trying to put a quietus on British-run businesses and also those owned by Indians, who seem to be the omnipresent businessmen here. I suppose this is hard for you to imagine.

Love,

Blanche

Greater East Coast Metropolis: 2047
[The new administration of the Metropolis is considering
limiting the number of organ restorations allowed within
any one family in order to deal with overpopulation.]
Subterranean Net Site

"Granna, you can't do this!"

"Now boy," she said, ignoring me, "when you're ready to step into
the shower, just take off your clothes and hop on in."

"Why?" Jonah asked.

"To get clean. You can't be in my house all dusty and dirty."

"I bathe in rivers," he repeated.

"Well then, it's been a long time since you bathed because there
are no rivers around here. Now, into the shower. Go!"

"As you wish," he said, but he was frowning and as he frowned, I
could have sworn every tattoo on his cheeks and forehead furrowed their
brows as well.

He stripped then and there, keeping only the hat sitting tightly on
his head, but his body was incised with so many faces, they seemed to clothe
him. Despite the many high school kids I knew who had gotten tattooed, I'd
never seen tattoos inscribed with such precision and expression. I should
have looked away, I wanted to, but I couldn't. The eyes of the portraits
reached out for me and held me in their stares until Granna spoke and
broke the spell.

"Don't just stand there buck naked dressed in your ancestors, boy.
Get in and pull the curtain!"

Jonah clamped his eyes and mouth shut and stepped in, hat and
all. The sound of water broke on his body and we heard him giggle. "The
water tickles me. Make it stop!" he called, jumping out of the shower, water
rivulets dripping down the blue lines, like small rivers running across the
landscape of a map.

"I guess that's good enough." Granna grinned at me conspiratori-
ally. "Come on, give the boy some privacy while he gets dressed."

We had only gone a few steps down the hall when she stopped. "Let's go back and peek at that incredible picture-covered body."

"Granna, no!"

"Oh, you sound just like Mommy when she caught me and Sis watching the servants showering."

"You were doing what?" I was shocked.

"You don't need to be indignant. I was nine and we didn't see anything juicy."

Yeah, right!

"We were in an upstairs window watching the servants bathe under the water tank spigots. Even if we'd been closer, we wouldn't have seen anything. All they did was unknot their longyis, hike them up under their arm pits, hold them open and let the water run through."

I didn't stop to ask what a longyi was, just exclaimed, "But you were spying!"

"For goodness sakes, loosen up." She giggled and it sounded like the laugh of a little girl, not of a centenarian. "Come on, come on, hurry now, or we'll miss our chance to see all those beautiful blue tattoos again."

"Granna, no! Why're you doing this?"

"Because I want to, silly. Come on, hurry!"

Already halfway down the hall ahead of me, I watched her go.

"Fraidy cat," she called back to me, leaving me where I was, all too aware that my mouth was hanging open. Who would ever think of Granna spying on naked people? She was old. She was wrinkled. Too old for sex, right? Yet there she was, trotting off to voyeur at a naked man less than a quarter of her age. Had Mum and Dad's Quarantine knocked a screw loose in Granna's brain? I needed to think.

I looked for my shoes, but couldn't find where I had kicked them off, so I stepped barefooted onto the porch, plunking into Granna's chair, rocking slowly at first, then pumping into a maddening frenzy—heel-to-toe, heel-to-toe—until exhausted, I stopped, letting the rocker slow to a halt. I walked gingerly back into the house, trying to keep from stepping on the soles of my feet which had taken a beating. Where were they? Murmuring from the kitchen? About to go in, instead I stood shamelessly outside the door and eavesdropped.

"So, where did you get your tattoos, Jonah?"

"A long way from here." Nice evasion.

"I'd love to get a few. Can you give me an address?" Granna was tricky.

"It's too far. Further than Burma."

"I see. Well, that's too bad. I have a little money saved, maybe I could bring the tattooist to me."

"I'm sorry Granna, but he who did most of mine has passed on."

"So he's one of your ancestors?" Go for it, Granna, I thought, thinking how canny she was, forgetting my earlier fears.

"It was my grandfather."

There was a brief pause, and I heard a plate being set on the table. "Too bad."

"Granna, do you believe me? About my ancestors?"

I waited, holding my breath. "Well now, Jonah, I can't honestly say I know what to make of you."

"Well, I do." I stepped into the kitchen. "You're a fake. I don't know where you got those tattoos, but I do know you're a fake. And I don't know what you're trying to do, but I do know Granna should kick you out because you aren't what you claim. Taxidermist! Hah!"

"I never claimed to be a taxidermist."

"Yeah," I said, surprised at the snarl in my voice, "you just had his card."

"Zeyya! Watch your manners. Jonah is a guest!"

"Guest? Granna, why are you letting him stay?" I stabbed at the air in front of Jonah. "He shows up here without a shirt, or shoes, or socks or even underwear on."

"He has a shirt now," she said, interrupting me and handing him the white button-down shirt we had bought that morning.

"Granna, don't give him gifts! Don't encourage him to stay—he's going to get us Quarantined. Maybe you don't care, but I do."

She clucked her tongue. "Zeyya, Zeyya, be patient. Hear him out."

"About what? That he can talk to his ancestors? Granna, he's playing up to you. Please, kick him out."

He stepped up close to me. "So who do you think I am, Zeyya?"

"I don't know. I don't care. I suppose you'd like me to think that you—I don't know—you're Burmese?"

"Burmese? No."

"Okay, you're from—oh, I've got it! You're from another planet! That's it, right?"

I waited for his denial, but he just stared at me. Oh, no! He couldn't expect me to believe—to accept that. No. "Granna, send him away now! He's crazy."

She smiled her crooked smile. "Maybe, but I like him."

"Granna, I don't understand why you're being so unreasonable."

It was her turn to stare at me. "Zeyya, when I mentioned ancestor bugs, Jonah didn't believe me. He probably still doesn't believe, but that doesn't mean he's right, or that you're right about him, either."

The thing I believed about bugs was that there were a lot more of them than us. If all the bugs in the world were the reincarnated souls of people, then more people had done bad than good. But was that really so hard to believe? I shook my head, trying to clear it so I could make a good argument.

"Granna, he can't carry around the precise, exact memories that belonged to his ancestors. That's impossible."

"It would seem that way, but there are so many things we don't understand, much less know. When I was little and went off to Burma, I never dreamed our world could turn out like this." She waved her fingers in an outward spiral. "Sometimes I don't feel real." She felt herself where she stood near the kitchen sink as if to be sure she was actually there.

"Are you okay, Granna?" She looked odd. Distant. "Granna?"

"Oh, yes, I was just thinking. Look here, Zeyya, who would have thought that two little girls being raised in the middle of the 20th century by parents who had been Tennessee children of the Great Depression..." She stopped to poke herself once, twice, before she spoke again. "I mean, there I was, eight, sledding with my Daddy on an American Flier down snow-covered golf courses and playing with baby dolls named Angel..." Her voice grew wistful, the pauses grew longer and longer as if her thoughts were physically disconnecting from the moment. She sighed audibly.

"Granna?" I put my hand on her arm. "Why don't you sit down."

She squatted creakily onto her heels and as if she had never paused, began again. "Who on this earth would have thought we would move to the other side of the planet and live in Rangoon, Burma?" She looked up at me. "So who's to say Jonah can't talk to his ancestors?"

Oh, she was tricky, but I wasn't buying it. "Granna, people cannot hear their ancestors' voices speaking to them in their heads. They can't."

"I just accessed a memory, didn't I?"

"That was your memory, not anybody else's."

"True, but now you have that memory in your memory, and now you can pass it on to your children."

I wasn't going to answer her. I was merely adding fuel to the fire. "I'm not talking about this anymore, Granna. I'm done with it."

"Then it's settled. It could happen."

I couldn't leave it at that without tacitly agreeing, so I answered with the simplest thing I could. "No."

"No, Zeyya? Then what's your explanation of Jonah's belief?"

I threw my hands up. "He's crazy? Or, if you don't like that, he's a medium and can talk to ghosts, or—no, he's just crazy, that's all."

"There is no such thing as a ghost," Jonah said with a sanctimonious smile.

"No ghosts? But you can converse with your dead ancestors, right? Not their ghosts. Them, right?"

"Admittedly, when the phenomena began, everyone thought they were being haunted. They tried to exorcise the ghosts, but you can't exorcise memories. So finally, we gave up and listened to the voices, to their advice, to their wisdom." The smile had become a condescending smirk.

"You think you're so clever, but your inherited memories are a crock." I spat the words right into this face. He opened his mouth to say something and I got a close up view of his teeth and their tiny, blue lined portraits. I backed away.

"Young lady, I do not allow rudeness in this house. My mother was from the Southern part of the United States of America, and she taught me to be polite."

"Well, Granna, your mother's world passed away long ago, just like this charlatan's ancestors, so tough!"

"But my Southern upbringing didn't and you either abide by my rules or you'll end up in your room with no supper."

I was about to ask her how she was going to make me stay in there, that I was bigger than she was, when the doorbell cut off the dispute. Granna straightened her dress, pulling it so the wrinkles fell more properly, and I slumped into a chair, fuming mad and close to tears again, while she went to the door.

Voices. Jonah cocked his head, as if listening to something more than just the conversation in the other room, stood, opened the broom closet and stepped into it. "Hide and seek," he whispered to me, his finger to his lips as he pulled the door closed. So he didn't want to be seen. Great.

I went to see who had arrived. Granna was conversing with a portentous looking uniformed woman in a tightly coifed hairdo who was in the middle of a sentence. "...their return is not imminent."

"Whose? My parents? Are they okay? Are they coming back?"

The woman turned to me coldly. "There is no way to tell you that at this time."

"Are they dying?" I whispered, feeling a lump in my throat move up and down.

"You must be Zeyya. I'm your social worker." She put her hand out for me to shake, but when I failed to respond, she lowered it with a distasteful expression. "We are leaving you in your grandmother's care for the time being."

"If they don't come back, I can stay here, can't I?"

"Don't count on that. It depends on many variables. In the meantime, I'll be dropping by to check on the living situation here. Oh, and we'll be sending you a new school assignment soon."

"What? No! Please, don't take me out of my school."

She shook her head disapprovingly. "If you want to stay here, as soon as you get the notice you'll have to switch." She turned on her heel to leave, almost tripping over Bellisima who had curled herself up on the porch steps.

"Wish she'd broken her neck," Granna hissed.

The woman turned her head back for a moment and hurried on. Had she heard Granna? If she had, what would happen? I was shaking, my legs like rubber. We sank mutely into chairs, Granna and I, separated by an aphonic void. Her face looked pinched, more wrinkled than ever. I had to clear my throat several times before I managed to ask, "How did they know I was here?"

"Your parents told them." Granna shivered. "The State is not taking you away from me. We're family. You stay with me until your father and mother return."

My voice trembled. "If they return."

"Nyuant Maung came back. They will, too," she stated with absolute confidence.

"Nyuant Maung? Granna, you know someone who came back from Quarantine?"

She clamped her lips into a thin, determined line, but it only lasted a moment before her mouth went slack and her eyes watered on the verge of tears.

"No, no, but he was really sick, and he came back."

"Where'd he come back from?"

"A clinic."

"So what was wrong with him?" Jonah asked from behind us.

Sarcastically, I commented, "You came out of hiding, I see."

"Yes. What was wrong with this Nyuant Maung?" he asked again.

"Leprosy," Granna said. "Sis and I used to play chinlon in the yard with Than Swe and Nyuant Maung. Well sort of. We didn't play with the cane balls the servants used. We used balloons, jumping all over the yard chasing them, trying to keep them in the air without using our hands, laughing and giggling. Then Nyuant Maung got sick and my parents sent him away for treatment, and we stopped playing, but he came back. Your parents will come back," she repeated, her head shaking ever so slightly. She got up and wobbled unsteadily towards her bedroom.

"They had Quarantines in Burma?" I muttered questioningly to myself.

But Jonah was still there. "Do you want me to check for you?"

"You mean ask your ancestors? And why would they know about it? They're aliens, right?"

"I never said that."

"Doesn't matter. Keep your ancestors out of my ancestor's home, got it?"

"Known as Ohkala, way back in the mists of
history, and later Dagon…being renamed Rankon,
meaning, "End of Strife". After the conquest of Lower
Burma by King Alaungpaya in 1755, the city came
to be Rangoon."

Rangoon (Sights and Institutions), circa 1955

Wednesday nite, June 19, 1958

Rangoon

Gertrude Dear,

Our staff is unbelievably good. Sebastian's food is varied, the fancy and the simple pleasantly intermingled. He is much more protocol-conscious than we and will be sure to feast us tonight when our friends come over. I need especially to check the menu, or dinner will be an eating marathon with umpteen courses and six vegetables or so.

Have I told you about our house? It's a two story "Western style" pukkah house, though by no means a colonial, which has a rather typical stucco exterior for pukkah houses. (Burmese style houses would be black teak on stilts for the well-to-do or woven basha, one room huts for the poor). Our house has such atypical features, even for a Western style house here, as bathtubs, hot running water (although no water runs upstairs if someone is using it elsewhere) and real baseboards instead of painted ones. Our formal lawn with its hedges and Canna was once jungle and today the gardener killed a snake on the sleeping durwan's (watchman's) head.

Love,

Blanche

Greater East Coast Metropolis: 2047
[Dogs, cats, rats, raccoons are invading the city
from the countryside. Traps have been set, but
the animals are allusive. Caution is advised.]

I tiptoed into Granna's room. She lay on her bed, with her arm slung loosely over her face so I couldn't tell if she was awake or asleep. I pulled the afghan at the end of the bed up over her.

"Wish I could sleep," she said, opening her eyes, "but I can't."

"Can I get you anything, Granna?"

"I wish you could get me a little betel nut to chew."

"Uh, do we have any?"

"No." She giggled. "It's a stimulant—maybe it'd give me some energy. The Burmese kept it in lacquered betel boxes."

I sat down on the edge of her bed. "Granna, I'm scared."

"Me, too." We sat like that a few minutes before she pushed herself into a sitting position and swung her legs over the edge of the bed. "No point in sitting here moping. Let's see if I can find that betel box of mine." I must have looked surprised because she added, "No betel in it, just pins and buttons, but it's pretty."

She was bent over, pulling out cardboard cartons from the bottom of her closet when a horrible howling arose.

"What's that, Zeyya? What's going on?"

Without waiting for my answer, she set off in her bare feet down the hall, stopped near the kitchen, shook her head and kept going, following the noise to the front porch. There they were, big dogs, little dogs, hairy ones, hairless ones.

Granna waded right in, yelling, "Shoo, shoo, get out of here. Go on!" She grabbed a long, black straight-handled umbrella from the corner near the door and began swinging it overhead in wobbly circles.

"Darn blasted mutts! What're you doing here? Scat. Scat! Take your mange-ridden behinds off my porch."

"Granna, the Jo-Boys came to visit me," Jonah said from where he sat in her rocker. "Why are you chasing them off?"

"Dogs and me, we don't get on, especially not me and packs of dogs." She went into the house, slamming the door behind her.

"I didn't know Granna didn't like Jo-Boys or I wouldn't have called them here."

"Yeah?" I stopped myself from telling him not to do it again. Why warn him? Maybe the dogs would encourage Granna to kick him out.

"At home, we run together on the river beaches. There they are free and gentle and rarely give wild voice like these Jo-Boys did."

"Most be another breed of animal, huh, Jonah?"

"Like you and me?"

This guy was just full of it. I went inside to find Granna, but this time she had really fallen asleep. I sat down in the living room and picked through a stack of books on the lamp table. I was about to open a small volume when I felt something behind me. I turned to look and it was a dog, it's head resting on the top of the sofa, it's tongue dripping saliva onto my shoulder, it's eyes big and dark, too close to mine for comfort.

"Er, Jonah!" I called softly. No response. More loudly. "Jonah." I didn't want the dog to overreact. As loudly as I dared, "Jonah."

"Did..." He broke off in mid-sentence. "That Jo-Boy seems to like you."

"Get it away from me."

He whistled and for the second time I heard him hit a musical note. The dog withdrew, the door opened, and then it was Jonah who was standing over me.

"Don't stand there like that, okay?"

He came around and sat on the opposite end of the sofa. "It's strange to sit on this." He bounced up and down on the cushions. "It's soft."

"And you don't have soft cushions where you come from?"

He shook his head.

Leaning against the back of the sofa, I looked up and for the first time in months, there were no bugs crawling across the ceiling. "Do you have a lot of insects where you live—I mean inside your home?"

He craned his head back. "Do you see insects up there?"

"Uh, no." No more bugs to step on, and no more banging my knees on a sink, and no more mother or father and... "No."

"We don't have houses like you do."

"Most people don't have houses anymore. Everybody lives in those towers out there. Have you ever been in a house before?"

"No."

So he lived in high rises like most people. He'd actually let a clue slip out.

"So you live in an apartment."

"No."

"Okay, where do you live? Come on, tell me. Give it up."

"You want to know about where I'm from?"

Sure, why not, yeah, because despite myself, I wanted to see how he'd imagined it and along the way, maybe he'd tell me something I could use as leverage to get Granna to make him leave.

"We dwell in communal buildings, but they spread out, not up."

I had to consciously keep my mouth closed if I wanted him to go on, and I did. "One floor?" I asked.

"Some are two."

"And? I mean where are these places built?"

"On the tops of cliffs where we can look out over the land. We see the sun rise as it reaches the lip of the earth and see it spray burnt-out colors at its setting. In the summer, we open the walls to let the high breezes blow through the buildings."

"You don't have air conditioning?"

He shrugged his shoulders in a small gesture of apology. "No."

"How much land do you have to be able to spread out like that?"

"There is much land. Vast spaces rest between dwellings and it's easy to walk a long way without meeting anyone."

"You walk everywhere? No walkways? What about vehicles?"

"We have few vehicles," he said, thrusting his arms into a long stretch, "and those we have use the sun for fuel."

He was obviously delusional, but it seemed a gentle fantasy, a true Never-Never Land, like the one in Granna's book. Would I mind believing in that instead of this?

"So how do I get to where you live? It sounds nicer than here."

"You are tricky, Zeyya."

"No, I mean it, I'd like to be able to go there."

"There are no maps or instructions that you can follow to get there. It isn't easy to reach."

More and more like Never-Never Land. "First star to the right? Hey, wait, where are you going?"

He was by the door. "I'm going to sleep on the porch."

"Okay." Surprisingly glad he wasn't leaving, I threw him a quilt off a chair which he hugged to his chest. "See you tomorrow, Jonah."

I heard the patter of feet and the whine of dog voices outside. Didn't think I needed to lock the door with them sleeping on the porch, and Jonah might need the bathroom in the middle of the night. So I did the unthinkable—I left the door unbarred and went to bed, except I couldn't sleep. I kept thinking about a place where you could see the whole sky without end. I could almost feel the wind tossing my hair, caressing my skin. Jonah's delusion was an easy one to adopt if you needed one. Me, what I needed was—no—what I wanted was to find my parents. Or for them to come back and find me. If they were cured, how long would it be before they'd be released? I closed my eyes, I saw their faces, but they didn't see mine. They stared blankly at me, as if they were holo projections. Sightless, translucent, they faded into the darkness and I was left with nothing until morning when I smelled Granna frying something in the kitchen and drawn by hunger, got up.

"Here," she said as soon as I sat down. "We forgot dinner last night."

"But Granna, I mean, burgers for breakfast?"

"I won't waste food. Now where is Jonah?"

"On the porch," I replied, poking the burger with a fork. "Granna, Jonah claims that buildings where he's from are built side-by-side, one story high. Is there any place left like that?"

"Nope, not enough land left for that. Used it up years ago."

I stamped on the floor and asked, "What about your house?"

"It's the last of a breed."

"How about in Burma, what kind of houses did they have?"

"Where is Jonah?" she asked again. "Go get him, will you?"

He was still on the porch, dogs all around him, but as soon as I opened the door, he gave them a look, a nod, no sound, no command, only a nod and they rose leisurely, casually stepped off the porch and pranced down the street as if they owned it. Except for one. It stayed, tightly up against Jonah's leg.

"How'd you do that?" I asked.

"Can this one stay, do you think, Zeyya?"

"Uh, I don't know. You'd better ask Granna."

I called her to the door, noticing Bellisima standing with her back arched by the sofa. A dog and a cat together? In one small house? I wasn't too sure about that. Granna was already frowning as she saw the dog. "Now where'd you find that?"

"He's lost."

"Purebreds like that one don't get lost. They get stolen. We should report him."

Jonah put his hand out and gently stopped her. "Granna, he is my Jo-Boy. He has taken me for his." I wished someone other than me had seen

Granna's expression. It vindicated all my reluctance to accept Jonah. Surely this would make her ask him to leave.

"Okay, if he gets along with Bellisima, you can keep him—but just this one. The rest, never in the house. Got that?"

He didn't answer. He put one finger on the dog's head and it stayed at the door. Then he walked towards Bellisima who skittered under the sofa. He sat on it and picked up a book.

"This is going to take a while. Come on, Zeyya, come eat your burger." Granna vanished into the kitchen.

Not me. I didn't really want a burger for breakfast, and I did want to see what happened with the cat. I stood just outside the room to watch. Jonah did nothing. After about five minutes, I was thinking it wasn't worth it except to avoid the burger, but, of course, that was the moment the cat's front paws extended from under the sofa and out she came, a big ball of fluff. She jumped into Jonah's lap, draped herself over one of his thighs, and a second later, the dog pattered over and laid its head on the other leg.

"I'm hungry," Jonah announced and stood, sending both animals sliding off his lap. And the three of us, cat, dog and girl followed boy into the kitchen, where he dug into a burger, and I fed mine to the dog but ate the roll and drank my juice.

Jonah was finishing his last bite when Granna asked him about his home. "So you have a lot of land where you come from?"

"Yes, we have a lot of land."

"How about people? Lots of them, too"

"I don't know the population count, it wouldn't be easy to come by." He took a gulp of juice. "It's lovely there."

Granna sipped some tea and the conversation came to a dead end. The sun streaked the kitchen and Bellisima curled into a spot of it, but the dog made the mistake of trying to nuzzle its head into Granna's lap.

She stood up abruptly, pushing him out of the way. "I'm not a dog person, Jonah. Make sure that animal knows that."

I gathered dishes, feeling something akin to pleasure at the morning, which turned almost instantly to guilt. My parents were neither safe nor receiving comfort. They were in a hospital bed somewhere, or else in the morgue. It wasn't right for me to be happy. As punishment, I volunteered to clean the bathrooms and the kitchen.

"I'll help," Jonah said.

"No, it's my penance." I didn't want help.

"For what?" Granna inquired. "What have you done?"

I hung my head. I didn't want to tell her, but I couldn't think up a lie fast enough, and all my guilt and regrets spilled out in a rush and then she wrapped her arms around me and said, "Jonah, you do the clean up. Zeyya and I are going for a little break out on the porch."

I sat on the steps, she in the chair, but she didn't say anything for a long while and when she did, it had nothing to do with my parents.

"Zeyya, I've been thinking about Jonah. Tell me what he said about where he lives."

"Do we have to talk about him, Granna?"

"No." A long pause, in which we talked about nothing again, until she asked me what I did want to talk about. My parents? I hung my head and couldn't look at her. What would we say? That they were dead, that they were coming back, that they weren't? No, there was nothing to say about my parents. Another morose moment of silence slipped between us, but Granna wouldn't give up. "Then let's talk about Burma, Zeyya, and don't say no, because this exhausts my suggestions." When still I didn't say anything, neither did she for a while.

"Okay, what would you like me to tell you about Burma?"

"You pick, Granna."

"Then you'll get what you get, you know?"

The door creaked open and the dog streaked down the steps, followed by Jonah who stopped next to me. "The Jo-Boy needed some space."

"And he told you that?" I asked, squinting up at him.

He smiled down at me, revealing his blue teeth.

"Close your mouth over those teeth, please. They freak me out."

"What are you and Granna talking about?" he asked, sitting down uninvited next to me.

"Nothing, yet," Granna answered, shaking her head gently. "Zeyya doesn't want to talk about anything. She's sad, I think, but she won't tell me that, either. So how about you? What would you like to know?"

"I have many questions, Granna. Where shall I start?"

Their words faded into background buzz as thoughts of my parents washed over me and I paid no attention to their conversation until I heard Jonah ask, "So why is your house still here if all other short dwellings were torn down?"

Why was it? Why hadn't I ever thought to ask that? I waited for her answer, trying to pretend I wasn't really listening.

"I've often wondered that. Maybe the lot is too narrow to put in a big building. Anyway, I hold the deed and I won't sell even for a trillion dollars, so it doesn't matter."

Unless they dragged her away to Quarantine and then they could take it with no one to stand in their way, which was a scenario that suited Granna's paranoid views. But as if in contradiction of her own theories, she was still here, virtually unnoticed, undisturbed.

"We don't have these problems where I live," Jonah said.

"So where is this paradise?" I asked, breaking my silence and getting a smile from Granna along with a remark that she was relieved that I could, after all, speak, hadn't been struck dumb—which I ignored by asking Jonah, again, "So?"

"I never said it was paradise."

Granna laughed the slightly cracked laugh of the very old. "Paradise. Now there's a relative term. What would you consider paradise, Zeyya?"

"There is no such thing. I don't even think about it."

"How about you, Jonah?" Granna wagged a finger at him when he shrugged as an answer. "You don't know either?"

He swiftly turned the tables by asking her, "And you?"

"Now, I've thought about this a good bit. I doubt true paradise exists, yet I did have a very magical couple of years in Burma, except for the scorpions, the snakes, a little bit of leprosy and a fair amount of thievery." A smile licked at her mouth. "But all in all, I hold it in my happiest of memories."

"What kind of house did you live in there?" Jonah asked. I had the feeling he was directing the conversation as far away from his home as he could, and the way Granna liked to talk about Burma, it'd be pretty easy.

Before she could answer, I interrupted with a question of my own. "Granna, why do you keep looking back to Burma?"

She tipped her head so she could stare at me over the top of her glasses. "I told you before, there's a lot back there and I want to pass it on to my progeny. That's you, Zeyya. You're all I have now."

"What if I don't want it?"

"Oh, Zeyya, you aren't going to deny an old lady her dream, are you? You aren't that cruel." She had properly put me in my place, left me staring at my feet and unable to look her in the eye.

"Now, to Jonah's question. Many Burmese lived in basha huts made of woven bamboo mats tied to poles covered with thatched roofs. We lived in a Pukkah house left from when the British occupied Burma, but you could hardly call it modern. The servants had to stoke the furnace to get hot water. Red ants lived on our play porch and bit me when I played there. No closets, only wardrobes we called almirahs that rose almost to the top of the fourteen foot ceilings. Heat rises, you see, so the worst of it hung at the top of the room far above us."

"Why didn't they take the walls out to make the rooms cooler?" Jonah asked.

Take out the walls? What next? "You can't take out plaster walls, Jonah. I'm going inside. I've got things to do," I announced irritably.

"Like what?" Jonah asked, following closely on my heels.

"Like," I said, whirling around in the hall, "practicing my violin and working on my composition, so leave me alone. Get lost, okay?"

"You make music," he replied, unmoved by my suggestion, "and my mother makes music."

He was incorrigible, impossible to discourage, a total pest, but the longing in his voice when he spoke of his mother was undeniably genuine.

"What instrument does she play?"

"None now, except when I visit her memory. She died."

I managed to say I was sorry, just in case she was really dead.

"Would you like to see the instrument she played when she sang?"

"Uh, sure?" What could I say, although I couldn't imagine how he was going to show it to me since he had arrived with no luggage, wearing only a suit with empty pockets and the oversized hat that had not yet left his head.

"Look," he said, lifting that hat at that exact moment. Hair tumbled out. Long bronzed tresses fell over his shoulders, strung with beads, rings, pieces of bone, even a cluster of tiny silver bells that hung like a bunch of shiny grapes near his cheek. It all wobbled and clanked as he tilted his head.

"Good Lord, what is all that?"

"These bells were my mother's instrument." He stroked them with a fingertip and a pure note rang out, but I was too distracted by the rest of the clutter in his hair to pay much attention. "You don't like them, Zeyya?"

"Huh, uh, no it's just—what's the rest of that junk in your hair?"

His face fell at the word *junk*. He moved his head only slightly, but everything in his hair clashed together. "These are the tangible belongings of my family that I carry, along with their memories."

"Uh, okay, uh—Granna, come see this!" I yelled out.

"What?" she asked from the doorway. "What's going on?"

I just pointed.

"Oh my, Jonah! Who did your hair for you?"

He raised his head higher. "This is traditional."

"Yeah, like having movable walls," I remarked.

Granny's tongue snuck between her lips and she got a goofy smile on her face. "Actually, the Japanese used sliding walls to let the outside in when the weather allowed. It was a philosophical approach to the connection of man to nature—and it cooled their homes."

Oh, Granna, please don't give him a way out, I thought. Make him own up to either his fantasy or else to reality, please. But she said, "This is very nice." She gingerly flicked at the bells that let loose with a series of lovely notes. "I'm going to fix lunch."

"Now?"

"I'm making a big meal and it'll take a while."

I turned back to Jonah. "So, did you bring anything else with you from your home?"

"No. This is all. Should we help her with the meal?"

"Yeah, I guess so."

It would be a relief to help fix lunch. It was an everyday act in a world gone crazy.

"Hey, Granna, what can we do to help?"

She scowled for a moment. "You set the table and Jonah, chop some vegetables on that counter over there."

He was whack-a-whacking in a beat I coveted for my concerto, when out of nowhere, Granna absently instructed me to, "Set that table in formal British style today."

"What? I don't know how to do that."

"Yes, well, it's about time you learned, girl. Butter knives over the plates, three forks, one for salad, one for the main course, one for desert. Two spoons outside the knife, and then fold the napkins like peacocks, put them inside the soup bowls, which go on top of the salad plate which sits on top of the dinner plate."

Jonah had stopped chopping as the river of instructions overflowed its banks. Granna told me to close my mouth and get on with it.

"Granna, can you repeat the directions?" I asked.

She ignored me, except to scowl again, so I started, although folding the napkins like peacocks was definitely not going to happen. I finished and Granna shooed us out. "Out of my kitchen. Can't possibly get this meal finished on time with you two underfoot."

Disconcerted, I fled to my room. I'd never seen Granna like that before. She was usually patient with me, so patient, but she'd practically snapped my head off and the look in her eye—I didn't recognize it. Bellisima crawled out from under my bed and jumped lightly onto it. It didn't seem possible that it had been such a short time since she and I had become refugees in Granna's house. I scratched her ears, which perked up when Jonah's bells dinged as he tapped on my door.

"Yeah? Come in."

"Is Granna all right? She seems—distracted?"

"Or something. Maybe we should go back and check."

We stood at the kitchen door again, the four of us: boy, girl, cat, dog—the last two salivating from the smell of dinner, the first two nervously waiting for her to notice us.

"You two? Don't you know when to leave a cook alone? If I'd gone bothering Sebastian like this, he'd probably have eaten me alive."

"Who's Sebastian?" Jonah whispered to me.

"The cook in Burma."

"You betcha and I'm telling you, you wouldn't have dared come into his kitchen like this. Everyone was afraid of him. Absolutely everyone. Than Swe, the houseboy-bearer-sweeper stayed out of his way. Nyuant Maung, U Kyin—they were watchmen, they shouldn't have been afraid of him. They weren't afraid of snakes or of scorpions, but Sebastian... And Hla Maung, the driver, jeeze Louise, he tried to become a shadow if Sebastian was lurking about." My eyes were wide and I saw Jonah shifting from foot to foot uneasily.

"Oh, go on with the both of you!" She waved her hand at us, but just as we turned to leave she demanded, "Zeyya, where are the peacocks?"

I turned back slowly. "Granna, I have no idea how to fold napkins into peacocks."

She scratched her head a moment. "Oh, it was your mother I taught." I heard a funny little wheeze and was about to go to her, when she looked up and scolded, "Out, or else go squat under the table while I finish."

"What?"

"There," she pointed, "that's where Dak always sat to stay out of Sebastian's way. He was a smart one."

"We're leaving," Jonah said, and pushed my shoulder gently toward the door. "I don't think she's okay." He looked the Joy-Bo straight in the eye and the dog turned, as if he'd been spoken to, and padded back into the kitchen. "He's under the table like Dak," he told me. "He'll get me if she needs us."

I should have made some skeptical remark, but I didn't, because I hadn't figured out how he pulled off the trick with the dog, which left me with the uncomfortable possiblity that he really did speak to them in some silent way. I went back to my room, scolding myself with a *no, no, no* playing in my head, grateful that Jonah hadn't followed me. I needed some time alone.

It couldn't have been but a few minutes when Granna yelled out, "Soup's on." A bell rang.

Jonah and I arrived at the kitchen at the same moment. I took a deep breath and stepped in, with Jonah right behind me.

"Sit, sit."

There in my soup bowl was a peacock-folded napkin.

"No soup tonight," she said, lifting the peacocks delicately from the useless bowls and setting them aside. She served some salad, then sat with us, flipping out the folded bird and putting it across her lap.

She seemed calmer as we ate, until Jonah asked, "What happened to them?"

"Who?" she asked.

"Sebastian, Dak, Than Swe and..."

"Oh, they must be dead. Gone. All of them. Josephine. Mary. Moona. Sylva. Ba Kyi—the durwan who replaced Nyuant Maung. All of them, long gone."

Had all those people worked for her family? That was a lot of servants, but something told me not to ask anything else right then.

"I'm sorry," Jonah said.

She looked up at him with a sweet smile. "Thank you, Jonah."

We ate in silence, using only two of the forks and none of the spoons and there wasn't any butter on the table, so at the end of the meal, I put most of the silverware back in the drawer. I had just finished when Granna put her hand on my back.

"I love you," she said quietly and kissed my cheek.

I hugged her. "Me, too."

"Today a whole new nation is being built in Burma—
politically, socially and economically...Under the Pyidawtha
("Happy Land") program, grants are made to communities,
which are matched by voluntary contributions of labor or money,
to build wells, irrigation systems, water storage tanks, disposal systems,
roads, bridges, schools, libraries and other social welfare buildings..."

Building a Nation
by The Honorable U Thant
Perspective of Burma
An **Atlantic** Supplement, 1958

April 29, 1958, Rangoon

Dearest All,

I'm mailing you under separate cover a postcard of the Padaungs, a famous tribe of Burma whose women wear brass rings around their necks beginning at age 5. Eventually, they so stretch their necks that they are referred to as 'the long-necked women of Burma'. If you get the postcard, save it for me. Last night we met a young couple. He's an artist whose works are bringing in several hundred dollars a piece. He was brought here to help design books to be used in the villages, which are almost entirely illiterate. The books have to be largely in pictures.

We do have some disturbing news. We've had to fire Sebastian and Josephine. They came so well recommended that my suspicions that they might be stealing were slow in coming, but now I learn from really old-time residents that they were fired before. We must have lost several hundred dollars plus food, pots and pans, clothing and even bobby pins. It was so hard to believe. They were so dignified, they appeared so fond of us and the children, and were brighter than most and apparently, also hardened criminals, but of course people here have so little, we must seem truly wealthy.

I think I have a cook and a nanny coming next week to replace them, but until then, every drop of drinking and cooking water must be boiled twenty minutes and dishwashing water, too. Thank heavens I'm not an average Burmese housewife for the rest of my life!

Love and xxxx's,

Blanche

Greater East Coast Metropolis: 2047
[Weight of rainwater on the roof of the 35 story Central
Library Towers has caused the collapse of the roof, destroying
the collections stored on the top two levels of the building.
The library will be closed indefinitely for repairs.]

I set an alarm to wake me at first light because I needed some time alone, without Granna, Jo-Boy or Jonah interrupting. Even if I didn't go back to my school, I had to finish my concerto. For Ethan and Mary, for myself. I tiptoed into the bathroom to throw some water on my face, unexpectedly scanning the walls for shiny carapaces I hadn't seen in weeks. I didn't want to go back to the apartment, not ever, not for any reason, but I did want to go back to my school.

I sat on the toilet lid in a trance or something, because I was still there when I reconnected and looked at my watch. Thirty minutes had passed. Darn. Didn't want to lose these early morning quiet hours.

Hurried back to my room, forewent getting dressed until later, except for pulling on socks. I sat cross-legged, sheets of music spread on the bed. It was complicated. I had so many melodies and rhythms and changes I wanted to make. Here in a pile went the percussions, here in that pile the sounds of rain-beaten tin and silver bells. Lost in notes and notations, I didn't notice the time passing until the door opened to Jo-Boy's nosy push, and right behind him came a flash of grey fur that leaped onto my bed, right onto my carefully placed piles.

"No!" I screamed, which made the cat twist around, sending more papers flying and sliding along the bed. "No," I moaned.

"What, what?" Granna asked as she came hurrying to the door in her nightgown, tiny in its long folds, her wrinkles more awry than usual, pressed into place by sleep. "What happened?"

"The cat! I had it all organized," I groused as I started picking the papers up into one big stack. "I'll never get this straightened out again."

"Of course you will."

I felt the tears, but didn't expect the temper tantrum that overtook me. I threw the papers at the wall, not that they hit it, they simply floated in every direction, which the dumb cat took as an invitation to play, jumping and pouncing as they landed here and there.

"Get out," I roared at it and sat down on the bed sobbing.

Granna waited by the door for several minutes before stepping into the room, picking a path through the papers to get to me. "I'm sorry, sweetheart. I know how hard this is."

"How? How would you know? You don't know anything!" I screamed at her in jagged sentences broken by tears.

She kept her eyes fastened on me until I calmed down. "My parents were never dragged away in the night, Zeyya, but I've lost people I loved."

"Who? Who did you ever lose?"

She startled me when she said in a small voice, "Your mother."

I sniffled loudly, she handed me a tissue.

"Your grandfather."

I blew and wiped at my eyes.

Free-running, unobstructed tears dripped down my cheeks, down my neck. "At least you and Sis had your parents until you were adults."

"Yes, we did." Did I hear her mumble, *But they're gone now?* She patted my arm. "You still have me and Bellisima and Jonah."

"The cat that just ruined my work? Jonah the nut job? Thanks a whole lot."

"Sometimes we make do with who's available. Sis and I had Sylva the peculiar. She was Sebastian and Josephine's daughter, and I can tell you, I'd take the mysterious Jonah any day over the sly Sylva."

"She couldn't have been that bad!" The tears were stopping, caking in the corners of my eyes.

"I suppose she looked more normal than Jonah does, except that she was too much like Sebastian. Thin-faced, deep-eyed, pointy-chinned, a budding reflection of his darkness. They claimed she was thirteen, which conveniently made her Sis' age. She could have been older, or younger, no way for us to know, but her eyes glowed, that I can tell you for a fact.

"She'd play hopscotch with Sis and me in our front hall which was made of black and white squares of marble, so we didn't have to draw the board. After she'd fix us in the gaze of her dark eyes, she'd hitch up her skirt and tuck it into her underwear with an unnerving grin, and we'd know she was ready to play. It was always the same: she won every time because we were afraid to win, afraid she'd curse us—or worse, tell her father."

"So she was creepy. So what?"

"Ah—then the nuns called."

"What did they have to do with it?"

"You see, Josephine and Sebastian were Catholic—at least she was. He was from one of the Indian sects that walked on hot coals."

"Now that's scary!"

"Uh huh, but it really had nothing to do with anything. My mother and father believed in education, and couldn't bear for Sylva to remain illiterate, so they arranged to send her to a Catholic school."

"And," I prompted her.

"And she'd barely been there two weeks when the nuns called demanding that my parents remove her from the school immediately because she was a nasty, dirty girl. Sis told me sex made a girl dirty, but Mommy said we shouldn't judge Sylva. And I didn't know what to think. Besides, at eight, I wasn't sure what sex was about."

"Big deal, lots of girls at my school get hung with their boyfriends by the time they're thirteen."

She grimaced. "Hung? That's an ugly word for it."

I raised my eyebrows. "I guess."

"Well, Mommy and Daddy suspected she was getting 'hung', but the nuns refused to be specific, and in those days, it was scandalous for thirteen-year-olds from our world to have sex."

"But she wasn't from your world, so maybe your parents shouldn't have been so judgmental."

"No? And Jonah, he isn't from yours, is he? Get dressed and come have breakfast. Maybe I can help you reorganize this mess after."

I pulled on some pants and a shirt, picked the papers up into a pile and weighted them on the dresser top under a heavy glass jar full of shells. In the kitchen, I slurped up some cereal and washed it down with juice.

"Granna, did you make friends in Burma?"

"Of course. Judy, Lainey, Kyle, Marion. I made lots of friends. You'll make new friends, too, even if you have to go to a different school."

If I wasn't Quarantined or sent to a work camp first—then, maybe.

She looked over at me. "Life is just full of surprises, Zeyya."

So far, all bad surprises. Concentrated on my cereal so I didn't have to say anything else for a while, but of course, it didn't work. There came the terrible threesome. Bellisima, who just had to get into more trouble by jumping on the table and getting her backside swatted by Granna; the Jo-Boy, who immediately crawled under Granna's chair and got swatted by Granna and banished to the porch; and Jonah, who sat down and just had to annoy me—only Granna didn't send him running.

She plunked a bowl of cereal and a glass of juice in front of him unceremoniously and announced, "Zeyya doesn't think you're her friend."

He turned his head very slowly, hat back on, shading his eyes again. "Perhaps she's right, Granna. We haven't done anything very friendly yet."

"True. We'll have to remedy that. I'll send you two to the Amusement Arcade on a play date."

"What? No, Granna!"

"Yes, right after breakfast. Off you'll go. I'll contribute the admission fee. You'll have fun."

"Granna, no! I'm not going on a play date with Jonah."

Jonah was grinning ear to ear, his teeth shining blue. I wished he'd keep his mouth closed.

"Granna, I can't go anywhere with him! Look at him!"

"Oh, looks aren't everything, you know. Things aren't always what they appear."

I scratched my brain trying to think what Jonah appeared to be, but I couldn't come up with a single idea. Like nothing on this planet... I stopped myself. I wasn't going there.

"No," I repeated, determined Granna wasn't going to win this one.

"Zeyya, Josephine was a beautiful woman with a sweet smile. She gave Sis and me hugs and kisses. She made me that Sari, hanging in the closet. On Mommy's and Daddy's anniversary, she gave them a beautiful teak box. But the whole time she showered us with smiles and gifts, she and Sebastian were stealing our stuff. Money of course, that might have been expected, but you know what my mother missed first? Bobby pins."

"What are bobby pins?" Jonah asked. I couldn't answer because I didn't know either.

"Oh, they were little black, wire clips that held your hair in place. My mother was very proper and tidy. Hair spray is still around, but bobby pins were abandoned long ago."

I had no idea what hair spray and tidiness had to do with anything, There was nothing for it but to demand, "What's your point, Granna?"

"Obviously, the point is, Jonah may look one way and be another."

I couldn't help it. It was too perfect. "You mean, he might look harm-less and really be planning to steal your life's savings? Is that what you mean?"

He denied it fiercely. "That isn't true! I would never do that!"

Immediately, I wished I hadn't vocalized the idea because it made me wonder if maybe he wasn't crazy, just canny. Granna obviously had some money. She owned the house. Could be he was biding his time, waiting to find everything worth stealing. A complex scam, but far more conceivable than an itinerate alien.

"Zeyya, I am not a thief!"

"So you claim, but how do we know? My great-grand-parents entrusted their children to Josephine and Sebastian and they were thieves."

"Go to the Amusement Arcade by yourself," he said, thrusting the money into my hand and whistling to the Jo-Boy who leaped from the porch and followed on his heels as Jonah stormed from the yard.

Granna shot me a dirty look, throwing her hands in the air and shaking them. "Zeyya, Zeyya!"

I'd finally done it, finally driven him from us. It was what I'd wanted, right? Yeah, it was exactly what I'd wanted, so why did I feel empty? I looked at the money in my hand. I'd go to the Arcade. I'd have fun, maybe go by the old neighborhood and see if Tracey was back from roughing it. Maybe she'd go with me to the Arcade. Maybe.

I trotted off and it wasn't until I was halfway to Tracey's that I noticed a dog was following me. I looked behind me, but it was a regular old dog, poking in a pile of garbage at the edge of a street. I sat down on a bench at a walkway stop. What had I done? What if Jonah never returned? I leaned my head into my hands.

"Hey, what's the matter with you?"

Looked up. It was a cop.

"You aren't sick, are you?"

"No, no, I'm not sick. Just tired. Stayed up too late with my boyfriend last night."

"Yeah? Okay, then. Maybe you should go home and get some sleep."

Sure, I would, right away. And when I got there, I'd stay there. I was about to turn down the street when I realized the cop was right behind me.

I swung around. "Hey, what do you want?"

"Wanted to make sure you got home okay. You live around here?"

What to say? Something made me not want to show him where I lived, but he was moving closer.

"So—do you?"

"Not far," I replied as evasively as possible. My palms were sweating.

117

He was stepping way too close and he had a sensor out.

"What do you need with that? I'm not sick."

"Just checking." I swore I heard him mutter, "You, and I'll only need one more for my quota."

Quota? How did you have a quota on sick people? They were either sick or they weren't. He moved closer, one step, another as I moved back, trying to think where I could run to, not coming up with any ideas.

He: a step up.

Me: a step back.

He was a little overweight. I might be able to outrun him, especially if I didn't have on my shoes. That was when I was at my fastest, but even with them on, I was fast, placed regularly, if not first, at least third on the track team. I was about to cut and run when a pack of dogs came howling out of nowhere and crashed into us. Unexpectedly, the cop was too busy to keep his eyes on me. Panicking, I ran from two snarling dogs who chased me, herding me away from home and safety. Turned to look back, and the cop was still surrounded. I ran backwards, the foaming jowls closing in, when my feet went out from under me. Putting out my hands, I waited to hit the ground, waited to be torn apart by snapping jaws and gnashing teeth. Where was the ground? Why was it taking so long?

Blue-etched hands caught me.

"Come on." Jonah set me on my feet, yanked me into a run. "This way. I found it yesterday." He pulled me in, out, between buildings, this way, that way—my head was spinning, my side was aching before we stopped.

"What?" I gasped. "Where?"

"Granna's backyard," he announced, not winded at all.

I bent over until I caught my breath. "Thanks, I mean for the Jo-Boys, if you sent them, I mean, thanks for rescuing me." Breathing deeply, my panic waned, then blossomed into anger and I turned it on Jonah. "Wait, you followed me, didn't you?"

"Jo-Boy followed you."

"On your orders? You expect me to believe that?" Did he think I would believe that he had enough of a connection with the wild dogs that slept on corners and tore through the trash and prowled the streets like they owned them to send them on a complex rescue mission? I was never going to believe that. I still had other choices: he'd escaped from a circus where he trained dogs to do his bidding; he was a rich kid slumming, and these were his highly trained purebreds. No, that was ridiculous. Just look at the mutts that followed him.

I sighed and sat down on the back stoop. "Why'd you have to show up at Granna's?"

"To keep you safe, perhaps," he suggested calmly, "and Granna, maybe."

I was exhausted, scared, too tired to protest—and unprepared for Granna's appearance at the back door.

"What are you two doing out here?"

"Nothing much," he said.

"Then why does Zeyya look so pale?"

Neither of us got to answer because someone hammered so loudly on the front door that we jumped, even though we were in the backyard. Granna gave us a skeptical look, put her finger to her lips and told us, "Stay out here. I'll take care of it."

I began to shake. Nobody but Quarantine squads hammered on a door like that. What had I done? What if they took Granna, instead of me? I waited. Jonah waited. He put his fingers around mine and I didn't stop him because, at that moment, I was too scared to shake them off. Minutes passed that took forever to slide by. More minutes. The back door opened and Granna beckoned us inside, gesturing for us to hurry.

"What happened?" I whispered.

"Police all around, looking for wild dogs."

"Did they find them?" Jonah asked.

"No, no, apparently they scattered too quickly. Your Jo-Boys?"

He nodded and sat down on the floor.

"Well, you darn near got us all arrested," Granna scolded him.

I shook off his fingers which were still wrapped around mine. "He was protecting me."

She sat on a footstool and sighed. "I should have known. In Burma, my parents hired durwans. Here we have Jonah." She stopped to wag her finger at me. "And it's a good thing, isn't it? What happened, by the way?"

"Nothing, not really, I mean, I was sitting on a bench and this cop came up and maybe he was just concerned, but he was getting so close and asking so many questions and then he pulled out a scanner."

Be calm, I told myself, calm. It's over, you're safe. I closed my eyes. Granna's voice sounded young with my eyes closed. It was a delicious illusion. "Zeyya, you have to keep your guard up all the time. You can never assume you're safe. Never!" She had such authority to her when it was only her voice.

"I told him I was fine, that I was just thinking, but he kept asking me if I was sick and where I lived." I kept my eyes closed, waiting for Granna to say something else.

"In his favor, you can't always tell if someone is sick, you know. And people will lie about it, especially today."

Jonah agreed with her and there was another silent pause and then I heard her turn on the water and put the tea kettle on, and still I didn't open my eyes because it felt safer like that. Granna asked Jonah if I was asleep and I suppose he must have said yes, or nodded, because they got very quiet. I decided to let them assume I was. I was too tired to talk anyway.

Granna's muted voice: "Even when I was a child, disease scared people."

Jonah: "We don't have disease."

Listening like this, his voice was soft and deep, tinged with something different. A cadence? A slight emphasis on sounds or syllables that wasn't usual, but seemed natural, integrated, not rehearsed to play a role or a part. Genuine. He'd had to have practiced for a very long time to perfect it like that. My mind refocused on the conversation.

Granna: "Burma had more disease, scary ones. Malaria. Typhoid. Hla Maung and his wife had worms. And Nyuant Maung, he had leprosy and they didn't tell us."

Still, only the sounds of their voices.

Jonah: "Who didn't tell, Granna?"

Granna: "The servants. They all knew. Do you know what leprosy is? No? Oh my, I think I'm too tired to tell you right now. Another time."

Only Jonah remained when I opened my eyes.

"She looks very small," he said.

"She is small. She's old."

"Why are there so few other elders, Zeyya?"

"You're pulling my leg, right?"

"Pulling your leg?"

"Yeah, what's the punch line, Jonah?" I waited. After all, we had the highest population of aged in the history of mankind, we all knew that, but because of restoration we couldn't tell who was who. A perk to modern living, according to all the ads. A few restorations on public money, and most people died. Unwrinkled. Youthful. But in the end, still dead. What was the average age of death these days? Did it include all the people who died in Quarantine? The figures used to include people who died in childbirth, why not Quarantine? My mind was getting murky. I didn't want to think anymore. "I'm going to nap right here for a few moments." I put my head down on the tabletop and closed my eyes. "I don't want to play these games with you, okay? So when I wake up, just tell me the truth, Jonah." Already half asleep, I faded into a vivid vision with everything tinted in irridescent blues and outlined in metallic golds.

Perched at the top of a cliff, I am a bird of wide wingspan. Jonah perches next to me, he too a bird, blue of beak and feather. We watch a storm roll in beneath us. Rain pelts the ground far below, but floating above it, we are dry, separated from

the drenched earth. A shadow casts itself over us, the sky turns coal black and we
vanish into it.

I woke with a start. I had so wanted to fly off that cliff with the other bird. It was terribly quiet in the house. I was pretty sure Granna was napping and Bellisima was curled up next to Jo-Boy, but where was Jonah? The house was dusky. Time to turn on lights. I'd find him after I went to the bathroom.

Done, I went to the porch. No Jonah. No Jonah in the kitchen. That left Granna's room or mine. Mine first, so I didn't wake Granna.

There he was, sitting nude in the middle of my bed, legs crossed, eyes just opening.

"You didn't—not here, not on my bed!"

His voice was slightly muffled as he spoke. "But you didn't wish to have people see me on the porch the last time."

Had me there, but what I really wished was he wouldn't go into any trances. "Thanks a lot, I mean, for how considerate you're being."

"You don't mean that," he said, rubbing at his eyes. "But it's okay, I understand. I frighten you."

"So, you spoke to your ancestors again?"

"Accessed them. About leprosy. Do you know what it does to you?"

Bothering to answer would have been pointless because he was going to tell me, I was sure. So I waited expectantly while he casually stretched his arms over his head, casually slipped into his pants, buttoned his shirt and stretched again, more like a cat than a person.

"It's a terrible disease where the nerve endings atrophy and cause the limbs to fall off, first fingers and toes, then arms and legs until you are only a stump of a body."

"That's disgusting...I feel sick." I ran for the bathroom.

"You really do have a weak stomach," he said, standing at the door watching me.

I slammed the bathroom door in his face and finished throwing up in private. I was in the shower when I heard the door open, then heard him audacioualy ask, "Are you naked?"

"Get out of here."

"But..."

"Out! Out!" I shrieked, sticking my head around the edge of the shower curtain. *Out. Out, Out. Out.* The bathroom echo doubled the effects of my voice.

"Jonah?" It was Granna. "It's inappropriate for a young man to be questioning the state of a young lady's attire."

"Especially in the shower, where he knows what state I'm in."

"He's gone, Zeyya. Perhaps lock the door next time?"

"Thanks, Granna. Don't worry, I will."

By the time I got out, dried, brushed at my hair, Granna was back in the kitchen, clattering pots and pans, rearranging her shelves.

Still pulling at my hair, I asked her, "Granna, if Nyuant Maung had leprosy, how come your parents didn't help him?"

"At first, they thought he just needed vitamins, Zeyya."

"So, did he become a stump?"

"What? A stump?"

"Lose all his limbs?"

Granna patted a seat for me. "To answer your question—no, he didn't."

"Why not?"

She stirred something in a pot and checked something else in the oven. The smell of the food and the sound of the bubbling pot was soothing.

"My parents talked him into going to a clinic for treatment, which they paid for." She smacked her lips as she licked a spoon. "Yum! A few more minutes and it'll be ready. Now where was I? Oh, yes, Nyuant Maung. See he was a Karen from a little jungle village. At first he planned to return to his village to die. He thought he was being punished for something he'd done in a previous life. Therefore, he had to accept it. Burmese Buddhism is rather fatalistic in that respect."

"But he didn't go back to the jungle?"

"Nope. He got treated and never became a 'stump'. He was one of the lucky ones." She began serving food, paused, went to the door of the kitchen and hollered for Jonah before she sat down, glancing my way. "But there were plenty of people who weren't so lucky. I remember—no, I'll tell you another time, not during dinner. Now eat."

None of us said anything much. I didn't know about Jonah and Granna, but I was really tired. All I wanted was sleep. I cleared my place, washed my bowl, my plate and while the water ran, I heard Granna ask, "Jonah, can you get the Jo-Boys to guard the house tonight?"

Did he say yes? Would they? I had to admit, I hoped so. I doubted any nighttime visitors seeking to fill quotas would risk venturing into a Jo-Boy-protected home.

"Goodnight, Jonah. Goodnight, Granna."

"Set in a tropical woodland, Rangoon…is a garden city. The Rangoon River gives it…a peninsular look. Modern buildings jostle with wooden ones on stilts. The…Inya and Kokine Lakes…afford fishing and boating. At the foot of the Shwedagon you see the Royal Lakes where the local boat races are generally held."

Rangoon (Sites and Institutions), Circa 1955

AIR LETTER

AEROGRAMME

Rangoon, 1958

Dear Liz,

I can't learn the streets here for watching the crowds! People carry bricks, and anything else heavy, on their heads. Oxen pull wagons of straw, trishaws weave through the crowds. English racing bikes with Indian and Burmese riders zip in-and-out between cars. Everywhere is filled with staccato motion. Nothing is what I visualized before we got here. Our help in the house is either Indian or Karen (a Burmese tribe) and our nanny Josephine wears a sari. She stretched all six yards of it out to dry today. Six yards! Nothing is what I expected and it is so distracting.

Will I ever get used to it?

XXX's,

Blanche

Greater East Coast Metropolis: 2047
[Fields Park has been closed. The site will be converted
to temporary housing. In order to alleviate the effect
of the rising summer temperatures, new trees will be
planted in any spare patch of ground around the city.]

Thrashing, turning and tossing resulted in twisting myself into a knot of arms, legs and sheets that woke me in the middle of the night, leaving me with the uncomfortable feeling, that inch by inch, reality was being stripped from my life. My parents gone. Jonah and Jo-Boys guarding a house filled with century old memories of a place whose name no longer existed. It felt as if some ravenous monster had gobbled up my present.

I got up in the dark. It was funny how after I slept, I could see in the dark, while when I first turned out the lights, I was light-blinded. I went onto the porch in my night gown, not expecting to find Jonah sitting on the steps with a Jo-Boy draped in his lap, but there he was.

"What are you doing out here, Jonah?"

"Thinking. Wondering."

"About what?" I asked as I reached over to rub the Jo-Boy's head.

"About Burma. About you and why you don't trust me."

"You know why."

He shook his head.

"I'm not discussing it with you. You already know," I insisted.

"Then will you talk about Burma?" he asked, seemingly unperturbed by my rejection of his first choice of topic.

"What about it? Shouldn't you be talking to Granna about it?"

"She makes it so vivid."

"Yeah, you'd think after all these years, it'd be fading a little."

He scratched the dog's ears and our hands brushed. I saw a shadow out in the alley, then another. More dogs? On sentry duty? It was a little chilly out, the first hint of fall when summer nights cooled. Vaguely remembered, the image of a particular tree, aflame with fall oranges and reds, flashed behind my eyes.

Jonah kept his voice low, as if not to break the silence of the night. "It worries me a little. She's bringing it closer and closer all the time. And in the meantime, things are going on that she ignores."

I nodded. It was true. Maybe it was why I was awake. "Jonah, you don't think she could just step off and stay there one day?"

"It's too far away," he replied.

That wasn't what I'd meant. "I meant that figuratively. I meant, just stay there in her mind, with her mother and father and Sis and the servants where it's safe."

He pulled at the brim of his hat and shifted position. He had his shirt off and the tattoos caught a gleam from the streetlamps that lined the alleyway. He shook his head. "I don't think she'd leave you like that. I really don't."

Clenching my hands, hoping he was right, I still had to ask myself, how would he know? He wasn't exactly grounded in reality himself. He'd probably done just that—stepped off into a fantasy to escape something in his own past. Probably. Just stepped into a private Never-Never Land.

"It wasn't my intention to stay here so long, you know, Zeyya." He smiled in a way that made all the tattoos on his face smile, too. "I should go home soon."

Did it make me nervous—the idea of his leaving?

"Right." Standing to avoid opening the discussion up to his return to his imaginary homeland, I announced, "I'm going back to bed."

"Zeyya," he called after me in a low tone, "why can't you trust me?"

"Because," I whispered back, "because you claim to be heir to a bunch of ancestral memories from another world. Who would believe that? And how can I trust someone who lies?"

I swore every face on his chest and stomach came alive, little frowns passing over their countenances. His lips were clamped tightly together. He cocked his head, pain passing over what I could see of his face and then, did his eyes began to twinkle in the dark?

"No, no! Don't you say one word! Not one! I'm too tired for a debate," I instructed him.

He blinked wide-eyed at me with a look that was all too similar to one Granna and my Mum got when I was being obstinate. I sat in the rocker, too tired to stand and unwilling to sit where he could sit next to me. He was still staring at me.

"Oh, okay, go ahead, speak if you must, but not one word about your ancestors!" Was that triumph on his face?

"A violin can make beautiful music, Zeyya."

"Can?"

"Well, I've heard you practice and..."

"I'm not that good, I admit it. No argument."

"My uncle played well. You would have liked him."

"He'd be an ancestor, now, right? Dead?"

He shrugged. "You've forbidden me to speak of the topic. I'll stick to music."

"What's your point then?"

"Uncle Lew made the violin sing, made the notes cry and moan. He made music that carried you away. It's how I know what a violin should sound like."

He was insulting my playing, but I couldn't deny that my playing was mediocre, and it had probably suffered from a lack of regular practice since school had been out.

"I can help you, Zeyya."

"No! And goodnight—to you, too, Jo-Boy. Oh, and tell your Uncle Lew goodnight and no thanks."

"You do know that Granna reveres her ancestors?" I didn't turn around. I waited. I knew there was more. "She has a whole collection of letters from her mother, bracketed together in rubber bands."

"Her mother has been dead for more than fifty years. She wouldn't save letters from somebody dead."

"Perhaps she takes comfort from them since she can't access her ancestors directly."

"That does it. You broke your promise!" I barely kept from slamming the door. Was he laughing, or was I projecting?

Tried to sleep, but tossed again, angry, frustrated, scared that I was disinherited, without heirlooms, with nothing tangible of my mother or father to hold in my hands or to hang onto. It was all sealed behind Quarantined doors. Nothing. Not one item except a hastily scribbled note and a few pictures that Granna displayed from Mum's childhood. Oh Mum, Dad, I cried silently. It isn't fair! You weren't sick. You were probably just a number, a Quarantine quota. A statistical piece of data.

After another hour of sleeplessness, I got up and stamped back outside He was still there in the dark, his head lolling forward, his hat lying on the stoop. I scooped it up and slapped him with it.

"You—don't you ever go snooping in Granna's stuff again! If you do, I'll call the cops myself to take you away, even if it gets us all arrested. You got that?" I was furious, the red anger of that fury gathering at the corners of my eyes.

"Please, don't, Zeyya, it wouldn't be a good idea!"

"And neither is having you here. Why don't you go back to where you came from?"

"I will," he said, "as soon as I can."

"Good. Soon?"

"I don't have a date yet."

"Why are you here, Jonah? The truth for once!"

"I made some errors, some miscalculations. I didn't intend to be here more than a few hours. Really. I'm sorry."

"A few hours here, with Granna and me?"

He made a bigger gesture. "In this city. And now I can't go home, not yet, anyway."

"And home is where?"

He smiled in such an infuriatingly condescending way that it made my fury burn brighter and without my wanting it to, it spilled over and I could hear myself screeching something about what a weirdo he was, what a first rate con-artist, and not in polite language, either. Afterwards, when words failed me, sobbing, I raced to my room and threw myself onto my bed, hitting the pillows with my fists until I ran out of steam and lay there, drained, exhausted, disconnected from everything.

I heard the porch door open. In another minute, Jonah's blue shadow slipped into my room.

"Did I say you could come in here?" My voice was empty, without affect. Weary.

He ran his hand down my violin where it sat upright against the back of a chair, his fingers sensually caressing the polished wood.

"Don't touch that!"

"I just want to make you feel better." He lifted his fingers from the instrument and began unbuttoning his shirt.

"Don't do that either!"

He laughed and pulled his shirt off anyway. "I want you to meet my mother," he said, pointing to a blue-lined portrait near his naval just as I was trying to get up the energy to scream. A face smiled at me, the eyes sparkling and laughing. It made me shiver as I watched the expressions on that face change until I realized that Jonah was tightening and loosening his stomach muscles to create the phenomena.

I didn't mean to laugh as he wiggled and swayed like a belly dancer, but I did. Here I had thought he was trying to rape me, or get romantic, or something—not perform a gyrating jig.

When he stopped, while he buttoned his shirt, it occurred to me that I wished I had a picture of my mother as she had been the last time I'd seen her. "I wish I had a portrait of my mother." I sounded far away, as if my own words were barely in my range of hearing.

"No, you don't."

"I do!" My words were close this time, loud, said with such certainty, I surprised myself. "I want to carry her around with me, always."

"You do not, Zeyya. Scribing only takes place after someone dies." He spoke ever so gently, with such longing it was painful, but I almost laughed anyway.

"I don't want a tattoo. God, the only people who have tattoos at my school are the losers who think they're all so tough, or the girls who do it for their boyfriends and then break up and are stuck for life. Have you ever seen some old, overweight broad with tattoos wrapped into the folds of her fat? I don't want a tattoo, just a holograph to carry in my pocket."

"Ohhh," he said, drawing out the sound. "What's a holograph?"

His face remained perfectly blank. Too tired to argue that he had to know, I just gave him a simple explanation. "It's a three-dimensional image of someone or something recorded on a photo plate, then illuminated by laser light."

"And you can have such a portrait made while people still live?"

"It's the only time you can have it done, but it's too late for my mother and father."

"Granna says they'll come back, like Nyuant Maung. She says they'll be cured, then you can get a holograph of them."

"Nobody comes back." There, I'd admitted it. No one was ever cured, no one returned. There was nothing more to say. I climbed under the covers, lay there, wide-eyed for the rest of the night. In the early morning, there was a light knock at my door. It was Jonah.

"What?" I asked him.

"Can we get a holograph made of you and me and Granna?"

"Do you think we're going to die soon, or something?"

"I want to have a record of you before I leave."

"Uh, yeah, why not?" If he was going to leave, what did I care, as long as he left?

"Then I will have a picture from which to have you scribed upon me when I return home."

"What? Oh, cripes no! You're not scribing me anywhere on your body. Anyway, I have to die before you can do it, right?"

"I don't know the custom in this case," he answered sheepishly.

"Doesn't matter because I'm going to outlive you, so there!"

"Perhaps, but then you will have a hologram to guide you in having me scribed."

He was really irritating me. "Listen here, Jonah, I'm not having you *scribed* on my body."

"So you have no use for a hologram of me?"

"Jeez, I don't mind the hologram, I'm just not making a tattoo from it. Got it?"

"But you don't object to the hologram? Good."

"Okay, okay, I'll talk to Granna, but no scribing, absolutely none— not on you, not on me!"

He grinned, but didn't promise. Instead he caught me off guard when he said, "Zeyya, I'm sorry about your mother."

"Uh, yeah, thanks. I'm sorry about yours, too."

He smiled. Were the lips on the portrait of his mother beneath his shirt smiling?

"Thank you. I miss her, but not in the same way you must miss yours."

"Does time make it less painful?"

"Perhaps. Perhaps time will make the bad parts fade away for you."

"Has it for you?"

He shook his head. "Remember, I can access her memory. I can hear her, I can see her. I know what she thought when I was born.

"That must be nice," I said. I couldn't bring myself to attack this particular branch of his delusion.

"It is, but I can feel her pain when my father died, too, and I can hear her decision to pass away."

"She killed herself?"

He smiled. "She did not. She simply let go of life, peacefully."

I wanted to say something, but I couldn't think what. Maybe Jonah was some rich kid who had run away from home because his mother had committed suicide. How long ago? How old was he? It was hard to tell under the tattoos. Had he gotten them before or after her death?

"Do you want breakfast?" he asked.

"I'll be there in a few minutes. I want to lie here a bit."

I was sleepy, I didn't have any plans. I'd just doze, get breakfast later. Why not? I let myself go into a dream, in which long hazy moon-cast shadows slid across mountains and sprinkled patches of light on the walls of a cave where Jonah stood clothed only in his tattoos, his belly dancing while I played the violin like a virtuoso.

"It is in the monuments devoted to the glorification
of Buddhism…that one can look for Burmese artistic
expression…[but the] magnificent wood-carving for which
the palaces of Burmese Kings were justly famous is, alas,
a thing of the past."

Rangoon (Sites and Institutions), Circa 1955

Rangoon

September 21,

Dear Helen,

If only I had artistic talent, there is so much to be inspired by, but, I remain talentless. Instead, we are collecting artifacts and art works while we're here. Our friend Carl, who knows much about local art, took us to a copper burnishing shop where we purchased two copper trays, and then to places in a strictly Burmese section of Rangoon, composed of alleyways so narrow and dark that anywhere else we would have hesitated to enter them, but here it is where items for pagodas are made—rows and rows of Buddhas with marble shining smooth, or, painted over with gilt. Rows and rows of gilt pagoda spires, sized for family pagodas in private yards or monasteries; and marble nats (Burmese spirits) with faces and postures similar to the standing Buddha. Standing, sitting and reclining Buddhas have different hand positions called mudras that mean different things. We bought a solid marble nat about 2 feet tall, with a rough spike at the bottom that we will mount in a teak or padouk base. He has a head shaped like a Buddha's with the bump of knowledge, but also with an Apollo-like look, as Buddhas were influenced by ancient Greek and Roman sculpture which was popular in India long ago. So our nat looks slightly Greek with Oriental diversifications. Wait till you see him!

Love,

Blanche

Greater East Coast Metropolis: 2047
[Outdoor dining has been banned due to weather
hazards. Lists of facilities offering indoor dining
will be posted on Gooddining.xnet.]

By the time I woke up it was mid-afternoon. I hated sleeping too long during the day. It left my internal clock set wrong for days. Tried a cold shower, shivering my way through it, but it didn't help. Wrung dry—that was the feeling that gripped me.

I was rummaging in the kitchen for something to eat when Granna appeared. "Hurry, hurry."

"Why?"

"We're going to get the holograph taken. I made an appointment. Go change into something nice."

"I just woke up. Give me a few minutes."

"Too late for that. Go change!"

Clean shirt and into my one skirt, that was all I could do with my limited wardrobe, but it satisfied Granna. "Better," she said, standing on the porch watching it rain. "I guess we'll have to take the umbrella."

"Where's Jonah?" I asked.

"I'm making him put on a clean shirt," she said. She meant a shirt, any shirt, as he rarely wore one, and since he only had the one she'd bought him, really she meant that particular shirt. "Ah, there he is. Doesn't he look nice?"

"Uh, Granna, don't you think..." I pointed at his feet.

"What?"

"Shoes? Don't you think?"

"How?"

"I don't care how. We can't go out with his feet exposed!"

"Because?"

"Everyone will notice—the tattoos."

"You're only worried about my feet?" Jonah queried.

"Pretty much." With a shirt on, with the hat shading his face, if he walked with his hands stuck into his pockets, the tattoos would be virtually concealed, except on his feet.

"So he has strange taste in body decoration. I've seen that come and seen it go and come again over the years," Granna commented.

Jonah beamed at me.

"Now come along, Zeyya, we've an appointment in half-an-hour." Granna snapped open the umbrella and urged me and Jonah off the porch. "Come on. Hurry it up."

"Granna, I'm not sure about this." She ignored me, scurrying along, supported by Jonah's arm.

"Come on, come on or you'll be drenched. Here, here, grab onto Jonah's arm and snuggle in close, or even this monster of an umbrella isn't going to keep you dry."

Jonah's arm was wire hard under the black suit sleeve. He wrapped it around my shoulders and despite the wet chill and his lack of shoes, he felt pleasantly warm through the jacket.

"Pick it up a little, you two," Granna groused. "We're going to be late."

Heavy early rains were usually the harbinger of a cold, wet winter. "I wish I lived somewhere warmer and drier," I complained as my shoes got soggier and soggier.

"If you like warmth, you'd have liked Burma, but it wasn't dry. The mighty drum roared, the dark face poured its tears, the dead lived, the hid came to life."

"That doesn't make sense, Granna!" I protested.

"It's a famous Burmese riddle translated by U Wun. Solve it."

"Uh, since I've never been to Burma, uh, maybe I don't have the references to solve it."

"Oh, alright, I'll explain this one. The mighty drum is the thunder; the dark face is the sky weeping rain, quenching the thirst of the land, bringing back to life all the hidden plants waiting for the rains."

"Okay, I get it now."

"The rains started by the same day every year, and when they were over, everything was lush and green against robin-egg-blue skies with coconut palms wafting next to the spires of pagodas." The picture she painted pasted itself over the slick grey rain.

"See if you can do better with this one, Zeyya. Look up and up and up, past the stupa's spire into the night until a cup of cow's milk floods the countryside."

"You have to be kidding! I don't have the slightest clue."

"Jonah?"

Right. He was going to be able to solve it.

"The moon flooding the land with light," he responded quickly.

"Right you are, Jonah!" Granna cried out delightedly.

"How'd you know that?" I demanded of him, truly amazed. "She told you the answer beforehand, didn't she?"

"It's not your fault, Zeyya. You've never seen the moon look like that. I have." He gave me a kindly smile, which just made me madder. They had to be tricking me.

I took a brief breath to calm down before I asked, "Granna, can we wait to get home for more riddles, please?"

"We'll have to. Here's the shop."

She hammered on a mouse-hole-sized door at the back of a towering building. There were probably lots of shops tucked into the backs of buildings, but they weren't allowed signs, so if you didn't know they were there, you couldn't find them. All around us, metal skyscrapers soared, reflecting the raw, grey sheets of rain. Granna banged again and at last a stooped man came to the door. His clothes were smoky colored, his hair, his eyes, even his skin were cast in grey, his back hunched. He lifted his head to take us in.

"Don't move! Don't move a fraction of an inch!" he immediately exhorted us. "Stay until I get my holocam, please. I haven't seen anything as interesting in twenty years." He vanished back through the door, leaving us wet and shivering, waiting under the waterfall of rain that rolled down the umbrella and dripped off its points.

"Are we an artistic vision, an inspiration, do you think?" Granna asked, smiling broadly, swinging out her hip and posing.

"Come on Jonah, take a pose," I said, hamming it up by showing some leg on the stoop like an enchantress in an old vid, trying to get a ride from a passing vehicle.

Jonah swooped off his hat and bowed to me, his cluttered hair falling forward in an undignified clatter that brought an outburst of laughter from us all. The door creaked and we quickly righted ourselves, Jonah only just replacing the hat before the holographer stood in the doorway snapping shot after shot.

"I like your umbrella, Susannah." I'd never heard anyone call her by her given name before. Mum, Dad, me, even Jonah once he got over the *Eldest* bit, all called her Granna, but this old grey man called her Susannah. "Did you get it around here?"

"No," she answered promptly.

"Too bad. Would you consider selling it?"

"No!" we all said in chorus.

"I never sell anything my family got in Burma," Granna told him.

"When will the holos be ready?" I asked, as much to change the subject as anything.

"I'll send you notification via one of your interfaces or Net Mail. Leave me a net address."

"We'll just come back," I said, not wanting to admit that none of us had either an interface or a Net Mail address. I was too poor, Granna too old, and Jonah apparently only interfaced with his ancestors.

Granna turned without warning, leaving me and Jonah standing out in the rain as she blithely went on her way, dry as a bone under the big black circle. "Come on, you two. You're getting drenched out there," she called to us, but didn't pause for us to catch up.

I shivered in the cold rain and for no real reason, I was afraid. The sky opened and the rain increased. I could no longer see Granna, only the black umbrella as it wobbled off in the downpour. Jonah grabbed my hand and we ran through the tears that fell from the dark sky.

"Any man, within himself, possesses the power
to make himself good, wise and happy. All the teachings
of the Buddha can be summed up in one word:
Dhamma [Dharma]. It means truth, that which really is."

From <u>The Meaning of Buddhism</u>
by Bhikkhu U Thittila
Perspective of Burma
An **Atlantic** Supplement, 1958

July 30, 1958, Rangoon

Dear Louis,

    I'm writing to ask a favor of you. There are so many things you can't get here. Nobody has a vacuum cleaner. If you want your floors cleaned and polished, the servants use dried halves of cocoanuts. You can imagine that we can't get parts for any of the American appliances we brought with us. So, can you order some parts for our air-conditioners and have them shipped over? What I need is two front fans. We need these parts desperately as otherwise our belongings will all mildew. The humidity around this town must be 100%, with rain and more rain.

    One amusing incident. The Burmese wear very comfortable sandals as footwear for all occassions. They have no heel-strap, only two straps, each of which comes from the side of the sole of the shoe and meets the other between the big toe. The other day, I was at a ceremony of graduation for the State Agricultural Marketing Board Training Center. I was seated with officials, including a Cabinet member. Since most of the speeches were in Burmese, I found it difficult to keep my attention focused on the speaker. I looked down at the floor and all the big shots, including the Cabinet member, had slipped out of their sandals. My eye-brows raised a little as I noticed they were all sitting with their bare feet tucked under them. Here they were in cotton jackets, formal shirts with gold collar buttons but no collars, longyis (tubular skirts) and no shoes! Wouldn't that be a strange sight back home?

                               Jack

Greater East Coast Metropolis: 2047
[Anyone wishing to participate in the new mural project
on the buildings on Metropol Avenue should send a message
via Net Mail to Arts Rehabilitation Ministry. You will be
credited with community service.]

When we got home, Granna made Jonah and me drip on the porch while she went for towels. I was drying my feet, hair falling across my line of vision as I bent down, when I caught sight of Jonah's clothes, discarded on the porch floorboards. I straightened up. He was happily toweling himself off, newborn nude on the front porch.

"No, Jonah." I shoved him inside, picked up his clothes, and followed right behind. "What did you think you were doing?"

"Drying."

"You can't do that out on the porch. You can't just stand there naked as a jay bird."

"Why not?"

"Because."

He looked puzzled, honestly confused. Had to be an act, didn't it? He couldn't think it was okay. "Does it have to do with nudity customs?"

"Wha...? Listen, I'm not giving you the birds and the bees talk. If you want to know, ask somebody else."

He dropped his towel, sat on the floor, still unclothed, crossed his legs and rolled his eyes back and while water dripped off him in slow plinks, his eyes moved behind their lids and the faces on his body glistened from the water.

I hadn't meant for him to ask his ancestors.

"He's being Buddha again," Granna made note as she bent creakily to pick up his sodden towel, then stood with it dripping onto her old, black galoshes. Her eyes focused somewhere else.

"I saw my first Buddhas in Japan when we stopped on the way to Rangoon, the next in Hong Kong, then on to Bangkok to stand under one molded of white stone, its face brooding many stories above us." She tipped her head back as if she could actually see something standing over her.

"Granna?"

She brought her head down and looked squarely at Jonah. "He wouldn't be a Japanese or a Chinese Buddha. No, Jonah resembles the Indian or Burmese Buddha. Fine bones. Thin nose. Delicate features. He even glistens a bit." Noticing the water on her boots, she gave each one a little kick that sent drops flying.

"Better go dry these," she said, shaking the towels just slightly, leaving me alone in the living room with Jonah. His features were chiseled, but it was hard to tell what he really looked like behind the tattoos. His eyes matched his skin and teeth. Blue. The tattoos extended over his lips, setting off the only piece of him that wasn't blue—his tongue. He didn't give any sign of moving so I went searching for Granna. I didn't see her in her room, but the door was open.

"Granna?" I called in.

Her head popped up from behind the bed. "Help me up, Zeyya. I'm not as spry as I once was."

"What're you doing down there?"

"Look what I found! Go on, open it." She handed me a green booklet. "That's me right there!" She put an arthritic finger on a black and white, two-dimensional photo of a child.

"You, really?" I'd never seen an antique photograph like that before. It was flat shades of grey. Staring at it, I couldn't overlay the young face on the old one before me. Years had taken too much of a toll.

"That's my passport from Burma. Thought you might like to see it."

"Oh." It could have been any girl-child in that photo as far as I could distinguish. "What was a passport for?"

"It proved your citizenship, so you could legally go from country to country. Look at those stamps of entry. Japan. Hong Kong. Thailand. Burma. India. Turkey. All the way through Europe, too. Seventeen countries all told."

I'd never even been to another metropolis, much less another continent. I recognized some of the countries, others I'd never heard of. Stamps of entry overlapped each other, some clearly lettered, some smudged, and there among them was the word *Burma*, clear and still bright as if just stamped in fresh purple ink.

"And you had to have proof of shots so you didn't take or bring diseases with you from place to place. See there. Those are some of the shots we got. Typhoid. Asia Flu, Typhus, Diphtheria, Tetanus, Salk 4, TRB. Sis and I got so sick of shots that we hid from Nurse Jelli every time we went to the doctor's office for one. The worst was Yellow Fever. You should have seen the length of that needle!"

Now we got one dose of vaccine when we were born. It supposedly protected us from everything. I sat on the bed holding the papers. "Did the vaccines work?"

"I guess they must have. We didn't get any of the diseases we got shots for."

"So this new disease they're Quarantining people for, do you think they'll find a vaccine for it?"

"We had this discussion once before, didn't we, Zeyya?"

"Huh? Not about vaccines."

"About the Quarantines, remember?"

I dropped my head. "I want Mum and Dad."

"I know. Me, too." There we stood, in silence, neither knowing what to say until Granna cleared her throat. "Let me show you something else. Maybe it'll make you feel better. Look here. This is a letter from my mother to her mother. Go on, read it."

I shook my head, but she thrust the thin white sheets of paper into my hands anyway.

"Why's this paper so thin?" I fingered it gingerly, afraid it would tear.

"The less it weighed, the less postage it took, the less it cost. No E-mail; no Net Phone or Zippy Messages; no Visual-Voice Computers. No computers at all in those days. There wasn't even overseas telephone service. Mail and telegrams were our only contacts with home while we were in Burma. That's why I still have this letter. It's permanent and unlike communications today, you don't need anything but two eyes and a brain to read it. No machine. Now, read, Zeyya, go on, please." She pushed the paper under my nose.

I had rarely seen longhand and it was hard to read as I struggled not to cry.

July 5

We arrived in Burma and trotted off with our 21 suitcases to the hotel—the Kambawza Palace, rather than the downtown Strand. It's central tower resembles a Chinese style pagoda with two big wings off it. The tower is decorated with pink and blue porcelain tiles. The seven downstairs halls form a lobby, dining room, plus six bedroom suites, one of which is ours. It even has a painted dome and ceiling. Decorative columns look like marble because they're inlaid with mother of pearl.

Our suite has 20 foot ceilings and more of the big columns and a single, dangling light bulb covered by a tiny pink boudoir shade. Transoms without glass run across the windows so there is no privacy and if one of the girls screams, everyone hears it. Jack dubbed the place the 'birdcage' and he was prescient in that because we woke with birds literally in our room, singing sweetly as the morning dawned.

Granna watched me expectantly until I dried my eyes on my sleeve. "Well, Zeyya?"

"Is that all true? Do you remember it?"

"Yes, I remember it. And our suite wasn't the only place that had birds in it." She patted my hands with her thin fingers. "When we went to breakfast the first morning, the whole dome over the dining room was filled with birds. All the ladies were wearing hats except my mother and Sis and me, and they all tssked at us, telling us how we should wear hats because of the sun. By the time breakfast was over, my mother thought we should wear hats for other reasons." She stopped and stroked the paper. "I'd know this handwriting anywhere. Seeing it is almost like hearing her voice."

Gulping back more tears, how I longed to hear Mum's voice. "Can I read another?" Anything was better than thinking about Mum and Dad.

"Here, here, try this one." She pushed a thin blue form at me this time. "It's an airmail letter form. They were even cheaper than the thin paper, but you couldn't add any sheets so, see how small my mother wrote."

Have I told you about the Post Office here? This morning Lillie and I went to the commissary and then the Post Office to see what had happened to the package you mailed me, Mama. We had the usual experience with the P.O., a place one should go ten-thousand miles to avoid. It's a large hull of a building with many desks in one room, all stacked with sheets of paper. There are no file cabinets. As packages arrive, they are listed on those sheets of paper in no set order, not alphabetically by recipient's name, nor by street nor by date—simply not organized in any way at all. If a package notice of arrival doesn't come, and you are expecting something that is a month or two overdue, you go to the Post Office and ask if it's there. Of course, they have no idea, so they give you all their stacks of paper to sort through, page by page by page to see if you can find your name. Lillie and I divided the stacks up and began, wondered if we shouldn't have brought a crew of searchers with us, began to feel as if we worked at the Post Office. Miraculously found my name, but never hers. Now the Post Office will send us a notice of arrival, then we fill out a customs exemption form, and then we firmly go and refuse to leave until they find the package in the heap it has been dumped in. It's amazing we get any mail at all.

And with that, I will mail this and hope you get it.

Love and XXXXX's

"What was in the package, Granna?"

Her voice became wistful and her tongue circled her lips. "Melt-in-your-mouth Belgian chocolates. Two months sitting in tropical heat, in an unairconditioned post office—yet not one had melted. See, miracles do happen, Zeyya."

"You really think Mum and Dad'll come back, Granna?"

"Miracles are always unexpected. Mommy served that candy at a party, and there was another miracle—nobody ate even one because chocolate was so precious there. But it didn't stop Sis and me." She ran her tongue across her lips again. "Now, where's Jonah?"

"Probably still visiting his ancestors," I said with as much sarcasm as I could summon.

"No, I've returned," he announced, standing in the door frame of the room. "I apologize to you, Zeyya, Granna. I had no idea you had such strong prohibitions against nudity." As if to prove it, he held a towel up in front of him so all we could see was his face, fingers and feet.

Couldn't help it—I laughed even as I thought, Mum, don't be angry at me for finding something funny right now.

Granna clucked her tongue. "I'm too old for it to offend me, but Zeyya..." She took a sideways glance at me as if to say, it's all your fault he's embarrassed.

"Still, I apologize," he said seriously, catching my eye. "Truly, Zeyya, I didn't mean to make you uncomfortable." He was so sincere, it was hard to keep a straight face.

"You know," Granna said, moving smoothly on, "in Japan they have very fine tattooists and they also have public baths where everybody swims in the nude. You'd fit right in there, Jonah."

"Yes?"

"No question, but I've never seen tattoos as expressive as yours. Turn around." I wished I hadn't gotten her glasses fixed the other day. He skillfully flipped the towel sideways and wrapped himself in it, but his shoulders and chest were still exposed and most of his legs. Granna pointed to a particular tattoo. "Now that's a handsome man!" Jonah strained around to look at the back of his right shoulder.

"Oh, that's Grandfather Nathan. His nose seems a bit hawkish to be handsome."

Granna solicited my opinion. "What do you think, Zeyya?"

I thought Jonah was thin and muscular, and if Granna had been younger, I would have thought Grandfather Nathan was an excuse for her to stare.

"Nice," I replied obligingly, trying hard not to focus on Jonah's body. "Get some dry clothes on, Jonah."

"I don't have any spares," he said. "That's what I came to ask. Do you have something other than the towel I could wear?"

"Oh, oh, except for that shirt Zeyya's been wearing, I don't have men's clothing anymore."

"He can't run around like that, Granna! You must have something?"

"Well—oh, wait. I know!" She began digging around in her closet. "Aha, a longyi." She held out a yellow and black plaid tube of cloth with a wide black band of fabric at the top. "Just step in, pull it up and I'll show you how to tie it at the waist." She tossed it to Jonah who struggled to step into it while keeping the towel in place, but finally managed the timing so that almost nothing was exposed in the exchange.

"Now, then, a man knots it like this, but a woman just tucks it in at the waist, like that," she said, demonstrating both techniques. "The nice thing about the man's way of holding it up is the little pocket that it forms in the knot. You can put your change into it if you don't have a Shan bag. Now Zeyya, you lend him that shirt you've been wearing around and he'll be decent."

By the time I returned with the shirt, Jonah was toweling off his hair, polishing at each artifact woven into it, the jingle of it all muffled in the towel.

"Oh ho, look what I found," Granna announced, bending down again and straightening with a pair of warn, maroon suede flip-flops in her hands. "My father's old Burmese sandals. How about trying these on for size, Jonah?"

"Why?"

"Just try them on for me," Granna coaxed him. "Please."

"What if I need to run?" he asked. "It seems to be a good thing to be able to do here." He was right. If you wanted to stay out of Quarantine, you might need to run—and fast.

"Sis and I got pretty good at running in them. Here, let me try."

She dropped them on the floor and slid into them. They were huge on her, but she squinched up her toes and took a step, then a quicker one, and quicker. The backs of the shoes slapped the floor as her speed increased until, as we watched, she took a few running steps, right before she fell. I thought, this was it, she was going to break a hip or an ankle, but Jonah caught her before she hit the floor. He gently set her on the bed, then, equally gently, removed the maroon Burmese sandals and put them back in her closet. "I think you should stick to regular shoes, and I to none," he remarked sagely.

Granna pursed her lips and frowned, but couldn't hold the expression. Her face broke into a smile and a laugh exploded out of her. "My, my, aren't we just the ones. Look at the three of us."

"Hey, I'm normal!" I protested.

She laughed again and shook her head. "Maybe, but then why are you keeping company with the two of us?" She wrapped her arm around Jonah where he had sat next to her on the edge of the bed. "Are you with us or agin us, Zeyya?"

I sighed. "Okay, yes, with you." I sat on the other side of Jonah who wrapped his arm around me, and he was warm, as if he'd been lying in the sun for hours, although outside a cold rain still fell.

"Okay, let's break this up," Granna said abruptly. I jerked, pulling away from Jonah's warmth. "Now then, let's attend to business. Zeyya, school is starting soon. Do you need school supplies? New clothes? A haircut?"

Yes, I needed all those things, but could Granna afford them? If not, which was most important? I hadn't gotten my school lists yet—Wait! How was I going to be notified of anything? Granna didn't have access to the Net. Did the school, the social worker, did anybody realize that?

I was about to say something when Granna started circling me, flipping my hair up here and there with her finger. "Nope, no way. I was going to offer you a new hairstyle, but your hair is too curly."

"What kind of hair style?" I asked warily.

She didn't quite succeed in suppressing a small laugh.

"What kind of haircut?" I repeated.

"Burmese top knot?" she said almost sheepishly. "Shave the sides of the head, keep it long on the top, bowl cut it all the way around the skull and knot the top piece into a long tail—but you're hair is too curly and knotty. You're safe." She poked me playfully.

Now it was Jonah's turn. He put his finger in my hair and lifted. "That is a lot of hair."

"You're a great one to talk!" I flipped my fingers at his locks.

"Now, now, no bickering, children," Granna instructed, adding, "time for bed."

We scattered to our rooms and I slipped into my night gown, then knocked softly on Granna's door. She was already under the covers.

"Granna? How do you get notification of official things?"

"A delivery boy knocks on my door and hands me the papers."

"Really?"

I could hardly see her, swaddled under the quilt she kept on her bed.

"Actually, I don't remember when someone last served me with anything official. I think they've more or less forgotten me. Why? Have I missed something?"

"School." One word hanging in the air washed all the good feelings of the evening away.

"Oh, yes, there is that. Hmmm."

"We can't take it lightly, Granna. It starts soon and I haven't heard anything."

"That might be good, Zeyya. That old biddy of a social worker said you'd have to change schools when they notified you, so if they don't, then I guess you can go back to your old school. That's what you want, right?"

That would be ironic justice—like we'd learned about in English. No way to contact us, so they couldn't force me to leave. But what if they notified my school, just not me, then what? I opened my mouth to say something, but in that brief moment of thought, Granna had fallen to sleep. It would all have to wait until morning. I closed the door softly.

The rain sliding off the roof sang to me, and the chill it brought to the air reminded me, fall was very close.

"They will now be climbing mountain paths, going down the valleys deep,
treading lonely trails to villages far and distant, crossing fields
and streams, bearing the torch of knowledge [so] that those who never
before had been given the opportunity in life may now freely enjoy
what had been the monopoly of a few. On this Mission of Love
and Light, go forth our Mass Education Organizers."

Prime Minister of Burma U Nu
On the occasion of a graduation ceremony

AIR LETTER

AEROGRAMME

November 23, 1958

Rangoon

Dear Mama,

    I sent our Nanny to the doctor in our car and told our driver to wait, so I am stuck at home until they return. We switched Susie from the Calvert System Kirkham's to the International School, a small school with problems in hanging onto teachers in this ever-changing community, but whose 4th grade teacher, also the principal, is an American married to a Burman. Susie missed the stimulation of the class situation which Kirkham's didn't provide and to my distress, I realized without group work in a class, she had not learned her number facts. She simply refigured all multiplication answers by addition, etc. Working alone, she could do that. Only her answers were checked which were correct regardless of the inefficiency of her methods. So we switched her and I spent the 2 weeks of school holiday that she had teaching her 3 months of arithmetic. Such a whirlwind life we live here. By the way, Buddhist customs determine holidays here, as Christian ones do at home—an interesting switch for the American Christians here, who sometimes have odd reactions to finding themselves in a minority.

                          Love,

                          Blanche

The weather never reverted to summer. The last days before school grew damply chilly and one morning, Granna promised me a trip to the store site for more clothes, but while I went to get ready, she dozed off in the rocking chair which we had brought into the living room. Jonah and I tiptoed into the kitchen and put on the teakettle.

"You should come when we go shopping. You'll need some warmer clothes for winter, too."

"Why?"

"Why? Because it's going to get cold, of course. Doesn't it get cold where you live?"

"Yes."

"Snow?" I asked.

His eyes seemed to move away from me, to focus on some distant place. "We can watch the storms roll in across the valleys. The sky grows thick and heavy, and if we're lucky the storm clouds hang below our homes for a while so that we can look onto the fluffy mountains and continents they form, suspended like mystical new territories begging exploration. Then the new lands rise and shower us in snow, until deep drifts form yet more new countries and icy mounts."

He had painted what he was describing so beautifully, so clearly that I found myself hoping it was real.

"So you do need heavy clothes." He shook his head. "Oh, come on, Jonah, either you made up the storms or you're lying!"

"No. My body stays warm without clothes."

I rolled my eyes. He only wore his tattoos? I opened my mouth to say something sarcastic when there was a knock at the back door and the social worker popped through, saying loudly, "Surprise!"

"I'd say so," I said as calmly as I could, but my fingers and stomach had the jitters. Why hadn't I thrown the lock when I had let the Jo-Boy out earlier? What had possessed me to leave the door unlocked?

"Where's your grandmother, Zeyya?" She was eyeing Jonah suspiciouly as she spoke.

"Napping in the living room. Can you keep your voice down?"

She continued staring at Jonah. What did she think of him, with his blue-dyed skin and his artifact infested hair?

"Who's this?" Her finger pointed accusatorily.

"Oh, Jonah. He's the son of a family friend." I was surprised at how easily I lied to her.

"Really? Where do you live, Jonah?"

"He's visiting us right now," I answered for him.

She ignored me, addressing him directly. "Where are you from, Jonah?"

Oh no, his eyes were sparkling. That wasn't a good sign. Speaking clearly and more slowly that usual, he answered, "It used to be called Burma. Have you heard of it?"

"No. Would you like to try again, this time with the truth, Jonah?"

"What do you mean?"

"Oh, give it up! You're Zeyya's boyfriend, aren't you?" Now she swiveled her head towards me for a minute, back to Jonah, back to me. "Not a very savory choice, Zeyya. A liar and a gang member at that."

"Huh? Gang member?"

"The tattoos. Gangs. Surely you can't be in high school and not know about them."

I stuffed my fingers into my pockets so she couldn't see them shaking. "Not my boyfriend. He's visiting us is all." My palms were clammy. If she thought I was hanging with a gang-guy, she'd have a reason to take me away from Granna. I crossed my fingers as I uttered the only defense I could think up. "And have you ever see tattoos like these on a gang-member."

She smirked, ignoring me completely, except to say, "Zeyya, neither of you lie well." Impassively she began making notes, when in walked Granna.

"I thought I heard an unwelcome voice. What do you want?"

"Who's this with your granddaughter?" The social worker pursed her lips which smeared the over-applied gloss she had slicked on them.

"Jonah. He's visiting. A friend of the family," Granna replied glibly, accidentally confirming our story. "He's been lent to me by his parents to help with some repairs."

"From Burma?"

"We already told you that," I said quickly, gulping as I realized I was complicit in a big lie about both Jonah and Burma.

Granna's voice was poison as she asked, "You already knew? Are you accusing my granddaughter of being a liar?"

I remembered Mum had always advised me not to make Granna really mad, but the social worker didn't know that, and without noticing the edge on Granna's voice, asked, "Who has custody of him?"

"He's of age. Now out. You can't just sneak in the back door of my house and start snooping. I'm going to report you!"

The woman looked startled. "You can't do that," she whined.

"Oh, yes I can! I know my rights. I read up on this after your first visit. You have to announce yourself. You have to present me with a permit to visit. You didn't. Now get!"

Crimson crept up the woman's face. It looked like she was going to burst. I stepped back as Granna stepped up and raised her head as high as she could. "Out, now."

"I'll be back."

"Yes? Do it right next time you come."

As soon as the door closed behind the woman, Granna sat heavily into a kitchen chair.

"How'd I do?" she asked.

"You were amazing! Is that really the law?"

She winked. "Do you think those numbskulls read the law? They just fill their quotas."

There was that word again. "Quotas?"

"For the work camps. They need man power, young power. So displace the kids and gather them up. Easy as pie, one, two, three, and you've got them. Right, Jonah?"

She was asking *him* for confirmation?

"I hope not, but it could be," he replied. "There is some logic to it."

"Do you know what logic is?" I asked him.

"How about common sense, then, Zeyya?" Granna interjected.

"That's it, I'm going for a walk." I needed air, lots of it. "Give me your account number and I'll go buy what I need, okay? I promise, only what I need."

"I don't know about this, Zeyya."

"Granna, I went shopping all the time for myself and for Mum and Dad. If you need anything, write that down, too."

She looked me right in the eye and when I held her gaze she nodded in defeat and scribbled some notes on a scrap of paper, handed it to me and gave me a skeptical look.

"No getting into trouble and be careful, Zeyya."

"Thanks, Granna."

"Have fun," she said.

I only needed my shoes and I'd be ready to leave.

"Have you seen my shoes, Jonah?"

Looking sheepish, he whistled and the Jo-Boy trotted up with both shoes in his mouth and dropped them at my feet. "Yuck! What the?"

"He had a good gnaw. I'm sorry."

"I can't wear those! They're totally slimed by dog spit."

Jonah reached behind him and brought his hands forward, offering me the Burmese sandals.

"You have to be kidding!" But he wasn't. My feet wouldn't fit into any of Granna's shoes and he didn't wear any, so off I went, the Burmese sandals flapping on and off the bottom of my feet. I hoped I didn't need to run again. I was down the block when Jo-Boy streaked up and fell into pace beside me. He looked up with liquid-brown eyes as if to say, I'm your safe escort. I glanced over my shoulder to be sure Jonah wasn't lurking there as well, but no—no Jonah.

"When he leaves, Jo-Boy, I'm going to miss you." Would I miss Jonah, too? I thought of his warm arm around my shoulder, and the sparkle in his eye as he lied amiably to the social worker. Would I feel safer if he was gone, safer when he wasn't there to draw attention to us? Would I?

I was almost to the store site when the Jo-Boy trotted off, and just where the dog had walked not a minute or two before, Alejandro fell in next to me. "Hey, Zeyya, how are you? How's your summer been?"

"Okay." No hugs exchanged.

"You stopped answering my Net Mail." Was it an accusation?

"Lost access," I said quickly. No point in reminding him I'd told him I didn't have Net time to answer much over the summer, or elaborating that fate had sealed off all hope of that when they Quarantined my parents and barred me from my life.

"What happened?" he asked. Seemed as if I was talking to an acquaintance, not someone I'd spent a year hanging with.

I answered with a lie. "Not much." I felt the tension of the moment ballooning between us.

Obviously, searching for something to talk about, he asked me, "Running track again?"

"Yeah."

"You sure don't have much to say to me, Zeyya."

"Sorry, it's just, well, see, things changed over the summer." Why couldn't I tell him what had happened? I should have been able to. Last year, I would have. We walked quietly, our hands hanging awkwardly by our sides. Last year, we would have had them locked together as soon as we saw each other.

As we entered the store site, he put his hand briefly on my shoulder and pointed at my feet. "Hey, what kind of shoes are those?"

"Uh, a dog chewed up my others," I said quickly, trying not to grimace.

"Sure! How about your homework? Does a dog eat that, too?"

"No, just my shoes."

"So, you have your list with you?" he asked when he finished what seemed like an obligatory laugh.

"Oh, shoot, I left it at home! Could we share?" My second lie of the day and it was so easy.

"Sure, yeah."

I glanced around quickly. Where had the Jo-Boy vanished to? I hoped he'd gone home, but I couldn't risk losing access to the school supply list to check on a dog.

"Zeyya, you aren't mad at me, are you?"

"Uh, no, no, why would I be?"

"I don't know, uh, maybe you, well, you thought, well, that I should have dropped by to see you, or something?"

"Let it go, okay? It was a bad summer, that's all."

He said a half-hearted, "Sure." How had things gotten so awkward between us in a couple of months?

We checked off things as we made out our orders and when we were finished, he said, "Okay, hey, I'll see you at school. Maybe we could go to a vid soon."

"Uh, sure, maybe after school one day."

He gave me a limp smile as we turned in opposite directions. I'd have to juggle lies to get away with hanging with him this year. Lies to him. Lies to Granna. Could I keep that many in the air? And even if I could, if

I wanted to stay at my school, I'd have to keep my head down, keep my eyes on the ball, keep the lies in the air, not look down, or I'd drop them all. It was an oxymoron: keeping my head down and my eyes up.

I waited to be sure he was gone. I still had to buy my clothes, but first I had to get a new order form so I could make a fresh list, because there was no way we could afford all the supplies Alejandro had gotten on Granna's budget. I kept the essentials, picked up a cheap coat, some warmer pants, two sweaters and the food Granna wanted. Lastly, I ordered shoes.

And of course, it was raining again by the time I finished. I stood under the overhang in front of the store waiting for the downpour to reduce itself to a slow drip when who should come bounding up, just as I caught sight of Alejandro again, but Jo-Boy with a few of his buddies. I wasn't going to let Alejandro see me with a Jo-Boy escort, so I ducked around the corner with the dogs on my heels. I got halfway home before the downpour came again, and had to wait it out under a covered walkway stop, squished between everybody else in the same boat. The shelter had leaked and soaked my shoulders by the time I shoved my way back out and walked the last blocks as fast as the stupid Burmese slippers would allow.

I dropped onto the front porch and thought about Alejandro—did I still want to hang with him? Maybe, but definitely not be his hung-girl. How the summer had changed me. Had my friends been transformed, too, and if so, in what ways? And what would Mr. Pompandow think of my concerto— which reminded me, I hadn't finished it and I only had a few days left. My heart sank. I was never going to have it ready in time.

The front door opened and without looking I knew it was Jonah because the Jo-Boy's ears perked straight up.

"So, you met a friend?" he asked.

"What? How did you know? You followed me, again, didn't you? I told you before..."

"Jo-Boy told me. Ask Granna, I was here the whole time."

"Right, Jo-Boy told you!"

Scooping up the packages, he stepped back through the door. A second later, a towel came flying at me and hit me in the head. "Dry off," he told me. I turned around, but he had already gone back inside.

Drying quickly, I stepped inside to a house cast in rainy grey reflections. Droplets slid down the window panes, dripping storm-cast shadows onto the walls. From the kitchen, the sounds of Granna laughing and Jonah's melodic voice caught my ear.

"I need to work on my concerto," I announced into the kitchen, where lights burned cheerily. "I'm going in my room."

Granna waved, but Jonah barely nodded his head.

"Are you mad at me?" I stopped to ask him.

"Go work, Zeyya."

Granna repeated my question. "Jonah, are you mad at her?"

He pushed back from the table. "I'm taking the Jo-Boys out for a run."

"In a lightning and thunder storm?"

He didn't respond, just clicked his fingers for the Jo-Boy to follow him.

"What'd you do to him?" Granna asked me.

"I'm not sure. I'm going to work."

I closed the door to my room. I'd never finish unless I worked every day until school started, and even then, it might be too late. I concentrated until Granna called me for dinner.

"Where's Jonah?" I asked.

She shook her head, plying my plate with food. "He'll come back when he comes back."

"What if he doesn't?"

"Isn't that what you wanted?"

I'd thought it was, but now, no, I didn't want it. The rain fell like bullets, the thunder growled while I played with my food, making mountains of my mashed potatoes and placing peas on the peaks.

Granna interrupted my games. "Will you stop that and eat your food? You're going to get too thin if you don't eat. No moping. Food in the mouth."

I absently chewed something. Why did I care what Jonah did? He could leave, he could stay, wasn't any matter to me. I chewed again. Potatoes? Peas? No difference to me. I swallowed quickly.

Next bite, a piece of chicken. No difference to me. Something rattled the door and I tensed? Jonah? Only the wind. The rain hammered harder on the roof and in the back of my mind, I admitted I was worried.

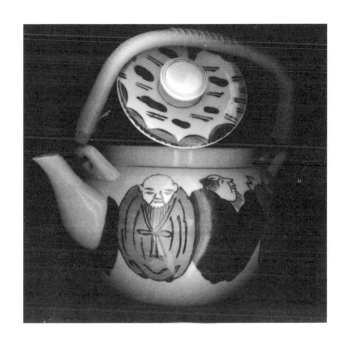

"Burmans heaved sighs of relief that the war was over,
that the Japanese were no longer masters of the country, and that
the British were back in Burma. After the liberation of Burma from
the Japanese, political trends moved very fast, and ultimately
Britain, under the new Labour Government, agreed to grant
independence to Burma."

India & Burma
W.S. Desai, Retired Professor of History,
University of Rangoon, 1952

December 19, 1958, Rangoon

 So little time for letters. I had a rare afternoon Tuesday. The wife of the first secretary of the Japanese Embassy had me over by myself and dressed me in a kimono (and even lovely Japanese underwear, styled like a kimono of sheer elaborately embroidered cotton) and an obi of gorgeous painted silk. She showed me how they drape the kimono and pad with the obi so one appears flat and it disguises the female figure. She also dressed her daughters in Japanese style. Mostly they wear Western clothes at home, in Japan and here. She had her girls do the Cherry Blossom Dance, played classical Japanese music and then the modern jazz equivalent. I was very flattered that she did all this for me.

 We were invited to an interesting affair at the Japanese Embassy last week—the showing of a Japanese film of the war period when the Japanese fought in Burma. The film was called "The Burmese Harp". You would have thought they'd have steered clear of such a delicate, ticklish subject—but they were so clever in what they did. The main character, a Japanese captain, finds a spritual life through music, and stays in Burma to honor and bury the dead.

 Our visit to Japan, plus the Japanese we've met here, have really impressed us with the great artistic skill and tremendous ability of the Japanese people. The phrase "cheap imitation" as applied to Japanese products arose because of the particular U.S. market Japan was trying to capture. Seen in contrast to the beautiful fabrics and designs we saw in Japan, it is truly dismaying. Ah, there is the dinner bell. Must go.

          More later—

          Blanche

Greater East Coast Metropolis: 2047
[Remember to register your new address if you move.
Any non-registered residents will be subject to prosecution
and internment as stated under the Rules of Security
and Public Health, Bill 321.0564.]

We both stayed up late, listening to the grumble of thunder followed by rain. Granna sat in the rocker, reading quietly. I sat on my bed with the door open and wrote out portions of my concerto. I was way behind, but after an hour, I got up and went into the living room to be with Granna.

"Well, here we are," I announced lamely.

"Yep."

I didn't want to think about Jonah. What did that leave us to talk about? School? Well, it was better than twiddling my thumbs and feeling guilty all night. "So, Granna, what was your favorite subject in school?"

"Mythology," she answered readily.

"Really?"

"Back in my day, it was the closest thing to fantasy we studied. It became my passion after Sis and I started school at Kirkam's."

"In Burma?"

"That's right. They housed Kirkam's in a sprawling colonial edifice shrouded by leafy spans of branches hung with swings. The classrooms were cool and dark with wide doorways that opened into wider halls." Her eyelids closed. "I can still see it when I close my eyes, still hear the quietness, still feel the loneliness. We had no formal classes. We sat at teak school desks working from manuals, each of us going at his or her own pace, with teachers who wandered by to inspect our work and check off that we were following the curriculum in the manuals. But there were no real classes. My teacher, a graceful Anglo-Burmese woman, no more than twenty, was taller than most Burmese. She wore Western clothing because she was half-British, and I liked her a lot, but I read mythology when I was supposed to be learning math and she never knew. I had a blue spiral bound textbook filled with line drawings of Greek goddesses and gods, and I mooned over the tales of Apollo, because he was so handsomely drawn." She smiled and opened her eyes.

"Sounds like it was nicer than my school." The only thing that hung over my school were the upper floors of the massive tower it was housed in.

"Maybe, but I didn't get to stay there. When Mommy and Daddy found out I didn't know my multiplication tables, they moved me to The International School, which met in a wooden house left by the British that sat on a plot of unshaded land on Kokine Road, and let me tell you, the fourth grade classroom on the third floor got really hot."

"Did you learn to multiply at your new school?"

"I can't remember, but Mommy and Daddy drilled me on my times tables, that I remember." Granna looked at the clock on the mantle. "We should go to bed. Lock the door."

"But...if..."

"Zeyya, it isn't safe to leave our doors unlocked without the Jo-Boys."

She went on back, but I stepped onto the porch, peering up and down the alley. No sign of the errant Jonah, not a Jo-Boy to be seen. I locked the door behind me, feeling guilty and uneasy.

Granna came in after I had crawled under the covers and kissed me as I pretended to be asleep. "I'm sorry, sweetie, I know you're hurting. It's hard to have everything turned topsy-turvy like this."

I didn't move. I wanted to tell her how scared I was. And I wanted to tell her I was sorry Jonah was gone, but I just lay there listening to the blood rush through the wrist I was lying on. Did she know I wasn't asleep? She kissed me again before she left.

Just as I rolled over, she came back. I snapped my eyes shut, but this time I was sure she knew I was awake.

"Here's a letter to make you laugh, Zeyya." She patted the bed and I heard the soft crinkle of old paper. I let it lie there a while, before switching on the light. It was a different handwriting. It was only a piece of a letter, a paragraph on a last page.

Sis and Susie have tried to continue their piano lessons, without a piano at the house. They practice and take the lessons at Kirkham's after school. The biggest problem is that the piano is badly out of tune, and some of the keys do not even play. The tropics is hard on instruments. The girls are already begging to quit. And since their musical abilities are hard to enhance, it is probably in the offing.

Love,

Jack

P.S. Susie's Birthday is coming. She's about to burst.

The postscript reminded me that my birthday was coming and that my parents weren't going to be with me. If Mr. Pompandow had the school orchestra play *Ethan*, my parents wouldn't be there for that either. I might never celebrate anything with them again.

I crumpled the paper angrily and tossed it on the floor, scooped it back up, started to unfold it, then in an uncontrollable pique of dispair and anger, twisted until it ripped. I kept tearing it, over and over and over until my rage exhausted itself. Tried to sleep after, but every time I got close to fading into dreams, I'd hear the out of tune plinks and plunks of piano keys warped by tropical humidity, playing this-and-that part of my concerto. At last I slept, to wake in the morning with a knot of old blue paper clutched tightly in my fist.

I let it fall from my fingers. What was I going to tell Granna? It was early, but maybe if I sat outside in the chilly air for a little, I'd think of how to explain to her. I opened the door. Someone was sitting on the steps. Jonah?

Rising, he said, "I need to use the shower."

He walked towards the door, but I was standing in his way. I gulped and said, "I missed you."

"I behaved badly. I didn't like you being with someone else."

"You were jealous?"

He shoved past me into the house.

"Wait, Jonah, I don't understand."

He ignored me, continued down the hallway without stopping. I heard the shower turn on. Granna was standing outside her door.

"He's back," I said, and went into my room, closing the door so I could get dressed in private. Jealous? He'd never shown any interest, had he? Then again, why would he, the way I behaved? Confused, instead of dressing, I lifted my concerto from under the jar of shells and immersed myself in work until Granna's brass dinner bell rang and she called out, "Breakfast, come and get it." The bell rang again. I took a few sheets of my composition with me.

Morning light streamed into the kitchen though the small window over the sink. Outside the sky was a washed out hue of blue, streaked by wispy-white clouds. Granna ate her daily soft boiled egg, dipping into it with white bread and sipping at strawberry tea, while I mulled over the last notes to a short section of my concerto that incorporated a viola.

Jonah came sniffing into the kitchen. "Tea! I've always loved the smell of the wild tea on the borders of our fields."

"Wild tea?" I asked, too embarrassed to do more than keep my eyes on my notations.

"What are you doing?" He peered over my shoulder, making the hair on my neck prickle. Why did he have to tell me he was jealous?

In a sweet, breathy whisper, he hummed the notes I was writing, until I put my hand hastily over my work. "Stop, please."

He retreated silently to a chair, as Granna poured him a cup of tea from a bulbous teapot, that was banded about its middle by pictures of portly, kimonoed blue men.

"Where is the pot from?" Jonah asked, picking it up, rubbing its warm belly with the palm of his hand.

"I got it out for you," Granna said with a smile.

"Why for Jonah?"

"Blue men," she said simply.

"Where's it from?"

"Japan."

"The place of tattooists is a place of blue men?" Jonah asked, turning the pot with his right hand and tracing a blue portrait on his face with a finger on the left. "I like this pot."

"Because it looks like you?" I teased, watching a pale pink finger nail, only stained blue at the cuticle, trace a plump little man. "Why isn't your fingernail etched?"

"I'll have it done when I return. I'm not fat like this man."

"But you're both blue." He made no response to my remark.

We sipped tea and ate in silence after that until I announced, "School starts day after tomorrow."

Granna nodded. "You'll have to leave early to get all the way there on time."

"By herself?" Jonah asked.

"No Jo-Boys, and you certainly can't escort me, okay?"

"But…"

"I'm not arguing this with you. I have to go back like nothing has happened or they'll send me to a different school. I have to do this alone."

Jonah glanced Granna's way and she nodded her assent. "She'll be safe. They don't grab people off the street. They take them from their homes so they can seal up the property. That's why the cop followed her that day, instead of just taking her."

"Why do they want to seal up people's homes?"

"Maybe they want the property for something or maybe it really is contaminated, who knows? Not me," Granna replied.

"And schools? Do they grab people from schools?" he asked.

Not that I'd heard about. But kids huddled together in small packs at schools, so we weren't such easy targets. Kids were unpredictable, volatile might fight back—well, I hoped they would. If they came for me, I would not go silently into the void. No way!

"May I send a Jo-boy to wait at the walkway stop?"

"Okay, okay, you can do that."

He gave me a smile. "I'm going to rest." He stood, wincing as he took a step.

"What happened to your feet?" I asked as I followed him to the sofa.

"I walked across some glass."

"Hey, let me see." He sat down and lifted his feet which he'd plastered with band aids, but blood was already starting to seep through them. "Do you need stitches?"

"They'll heal soon. I just need to put them up." He swung his legs onto the sofa. "I walked a long way."

"Without attracting attention?"

It had been night, he pointed out to me, and not many people were out. He'd stayed in the darker alleyways and along less well lit streets. He hadn't hit a problem until he walked across the shards of glass.

"May I suggest shoes?" I asked.

No. Okay, then what could I offer? More bandages? Some alcohol to clean the wounds? He rejected both, saying maybe later, but he really just wanted to rest.

His eyes closed almost instantly and began to move behind the lids in deep sleep. I tiptoed out and back to my room. Two days to work on the concerto. Two days! I wasn't going to make it and I hated to disappoint Mr. Pompandow. Maybe if I'd been more experienced, I could have done it, but now, it was going to be crap. All the same, I spread out at the kitchen table and tried. Granna brought me a cup of tea and apologized for not having a music player. It went along with no net.

"Granna, why don't you have any Net Tech?"

She whispered in my ear, "If you're not on the Net, they can't find you, now can they?"

"But your address must be in there."

She looked amused. "Could be, but before your social worker popped up, it'd been five years since I'd seen an official of any sort—not since

I disconnected. Even the geriatric social worker who used to come poking and snooping around every once in a while hasn't been by."

"But you have an account."

"Which I only use at store sites. Never have delivery."

She'd removed everything she possibly could by which they could standardly find her, short of her account for food and necessities. Was that why she was still ensconced in her little house? Could it be why she hadn't been Quarantined?

"That's why your father was so mad at me. He informed me I was ridiculous. He said I made it difficult for him and your mother to help me, to check on me, to have contact. *Contact?* I'd say to him. Contact was his coming over and sitting down for dinner and conversation, not a message over the Net. But he never understood. It got so bad, his way versus mine, that...well, you know. That's why he wouldn't live here with me."

My stomach dropped. Mum had lied to me about it. "Mum claimed it was the law that prohibited it!"

"It does, but how would the law have known? No Net, no law. He called me a criminal once. You didn't know?"

"Granna..." I could barely speak, had to clear my throat, had to concentrate. "Granna, how do you survive? No messages, no information, what, how...?" I ran out of questions but she answered anyway.

"It isn't bad. My world is finite, yes. It has clear boundaries, yes. If I want information, I go stand under a public Netcaster. It just means a little walk. If I want to see someone, I go see them, like Hank the holographer. We have supper out sometimes. I'm old. I don't need much anymore. And you seem to be managing just fine in my limited little piece of the universe."

"Yeah, but, I mean, well, it was okay during the summer, but school, I mean, I have to fill out forms with contact info and stuff. And I have to have a Net Mail address and..." I stopped mid-sentence. Maybe I just shouldn't go to school at all. It'd be easier, unless of course, then they'd Quarantine me and...Wait, wait, this was all just crazy.

"We'll take out a public Net Mail address. We'll just go check it every couple of days. A little less convenient but, no biggie."

No biggie? Yes, it was. It was big! It was... it might work. Anyway, I could tell by the set of her mouth there was no way to talk her out of it.

"Okay." What else could I say. I was really at her mercy. And what if she was right? What if taking yourself off the Net did assure your safety? What if nobody made an effort to do anything to or for someone off the Net. Was that greater or lesser safety? Did it mean that if enough time elapsed, people would forget about me, too? But the social worker assigned to me must have entered Granna's physical address back into the Net, mustn't she? And Granna had gone and made her mad, thrown her out. That couldn't be good.

"Tomorrow we'll do it," she said and ended the conversation.

Kalaw is the queen of Burma's beauty spots.

Nestling in the heart of the breathtakingly beautiful pine-studded blue Shan hills...surrounded by craggy slopes, with...entrancing walks, and roads gleaming like streaks of white ribbon... A tarmac road runs from Rangoon to the gate of Hotel Kalaw [which] has a first class tennis court, electric lights, modern sanitation, and hot and cold running water.

We are a tourist's haven.

Undated Advertisement, Hotel Kalaw, circa 1958

July 11, 1958

Rangoon

Dear Gertrude,

I'm so interested in your math curriculum committee. You know, we're using the Calvert System of teaching which has a curriculum that is one year ahead of U.S. schools in math. It's supposed to be patterned after Maryland schools. Sis, in Calvert sixth, learns what is taught at home in seventh. Susie is in a similar situation. Neither girl has had any trouble in moving ahead. You've heard me expound my own theory of teaching math in elementary school? The girls do miss the enrichment programs of school at home. Sis misses her science and reference reading, and Susie, who has such a lively imagination, finds school dull here. On the other hand Sis has used an Untermeyer anthology of poetry as a text and has been reading some of the classics as part of the curriculum. Also the English composition study is more advanced in its approach to sentence structure, parts of speech, etc. We'll have to have an extended talk about all of this when I have had a longer period of evaluation to see how the girls fit in back home.

Love,

Blanche

P.S. Despite the illiteracy here, the Burmese have many storytellers, who sometimes peddle stories along with food.

The Greater East Coast Metropolis: 2047
[All school children will report to their schools starting tomorrow.
Classes are expected to have declined in size due to the spreading
Quarantines. Despite the tragedy of Quarantine, reduced class size
should improve the quality of education and we expect all students
to return to school with a positive attitude and to take advantage
of the opportunity for a quality education.]

School. First day. I go. Nobody sees me. I'm invisible. Alejandro turns as if to wave, does wave to someone else, before walking through me. I am an apparition. I am gone.

I sat straight up and stared at my hands, expecting them to be translucent. Transparent. Like an apparition. But they were solid. I pinched myself. It hurt. Solid.

A dark day lay outside, barely reflecting any light. Had it already seduced me into ignoring my alarm and oversleeping? Wait, no, the alarm hadn't even gone off yet. I could be early to school, without anyone nagging me to get up. To the bathroom, back, combed at my hair, pulled it into the tightest knot I could manage, but couldn't contain all my stupid curls. Tried again. Better. Not perfect. To the kitchen. Quick breakfast, made a lunch, was ready to go.

The Jo-Boy and Bellisima stirred where they were curled together in the living room. Jo-Boy opened one eye, cocked one ear and ignored me. Didn't he see me? Had I truly vanished? Was I dead and just dreaming I was alive? I sat down in the rocker, but didn't rock. Nervousness overwhelmed me, making my stomach queasy again and my palms clammy. Did the dead perspire? Or maybe they evaporated. Why didn't the dog see me, come sniff me? Please. Please.

"Zeyya?" Jonah's voice.

"You see me?"

"Are you hiding?"

"You see me. Thank you!" I jumped up and kissed his cheek. "You're an angel."

"I thought I was a lunatic."

"No, I mean, oh, I had this dream. Nobody could see me and I thought, well the Jo-Boy ignored me, and..."

He took a finger and poked me. "You're still here, but it's only four in the morning."

"Huh? I thought the clock said five when I woke up."

"You read it wrong. You should go back to bed."

But I was all dressed, my hair was almost decent. "I'll just wait up."

He limped to the living room window and looked out. "You can still see the moon. It's full tonight. Come look at how bright it is."

He was right, it was a rare night. The full moon, usually lost behind haze, was seductively beautiful, giving off so much light it delineated scattered clouds, buildings, wandering shapes of dogs. "It's lovely."

"Like a cup of cow's milk," he whispered as he touched my shoulder. "Let's go on the porch for a few minutes to look at it."

"I'm not sure that's a good idea."

"You're afraid." He didn't ask. He had read me correctly, so I couldn't even deny it. I was afraid of stepping into the moonlight with him. He didn't seem alien any more. He didn't seem crazy anymore. That was the danger.

"No, I mean, you shouldn't, with your feet, I mean."

"Then sit on the sofa with me. Are you worried about school?"

A little scared—that I'd be discovered and sent away, that Mr. Jaster had gotten notification so that when I showed up he would call someone to drag me to another school, or somewhere worse, but I couldn't tell Jonah that. If I did, he'd find a way to follow me, or send his four-footed minions.

"Not really. I mean, everyone is nervous the first day back. You know, who's in your classes, what teachers did you get, stuff like that. You know."

He shook his head and his hair swayed. "No."

"Oh, come on."

"We don't go to schools."

"So how do you learn anything?"

"We explore the world or sit in meditation rooms and listen."

Not again. "Listen to your ancestors?" I stood up. "I think I'll lie down after all. See you after school."

Did I hear him ask, "Is it so impossible to believe me?"

I pretended not to have heard, tried to deny the answer, until finally as I arrived at school, I had to face it. The answer was no longer an unequivocal *absolutely*. Somewhere along the way, it had become possible for me to consider it. Did that make me crazy, too? I'd had enough on me to go crazy. What were the symptoms of insanity? Lying to yourself? I wasn't doing that yet. Not making sense? I made sense. Even Jonah made sense—at least he had internal consistency. Then again so did fictional literary characters.

"Zeyya!"

"Tracey, how are you?" We hugged outside the school.

"I'm back. The last year! Praise be! Praise be! Now I can get on with my life."

"Doing what?" I really wanted to know what she was so thrilled about.

"You know, uh, you know." She tipped her head towards a clutch of boys, including Alejandro.

"Which one?" I asked, truly hoping she didn't mean all of them. Last year a few girls had gone down to the cribs after graduation.

She smiled knowingly. "I've got him all picked out."

No more. I didn't want to know any more, but she blathered about it all the way to homeroom, which we always shared, which made it a pretty sure thing I'd be there this year, too. When Mrs. Rasha asked for my schedule I spoke my pre-planned lie. "I forgot it at home, Mrs. Rasha."

There was always someone who forgot their schedule, why not me this time? She gave me a copy. I had orchestra last period. My locker was near there so I could put my violin and still unfinished concerto into it and pick them up just before. Math was second and far away, and then there was lunch.

We left homeroom in a bunch. I listened but didn't chatter in with the other girls. PE was first. It was too early in the morning, plus I was out of shape. All I'd done all summer was hang out at Granna's and walk—oh, and run when I was being chased. Did that count as training? If I didn't get back into a routine, I wasn't even going to place in track this year.

Alejandro waved from across the gym. Was it to me? It could have been to any of the girls I was standing with. I looked out of the corner of my eye to see if anyone waved back. Three girls had their hands up in hesitant gestures. I decided not to be a fourth.

We ran laps and I wasn't much worse than anyone else, but bending over to catch my breath, I found myself thinking of Jonah who ran so effortlessly, without panting at all. Too bad he couldn't join our team. He'd be a star, but according to him, he'd never been to school, and having a seizure in the middle of math to learn from his ancestors was not going to cut it.

Alejandro walked over to us. I said hi, he said hi then hesitated as if about to stop, when Eileen stepped out, snuggled up to him, leaned up, kissed him. He looked at me as he kissed her back. I walked away, wishing, oh how I wished, that I didn't have to be near him all period, or see him. I knew one person who was going to be happy. Jonah.

In English, Alejandro sat next to me. I kept my stare straight ahead.

"You're mad at me, Zeyya?"

"You have to ask?"

He didn't answer, which made me madder.

"When you didn't answer my Net Mail, I figured you were done hanging with me, so I hung Eileen for the summer. I'm not going on with it."

"Have you told Eileen she was a convenient summer hung yet?"

"Okay, okay, I'm sorry, but look, how about coffee? You know, or I'll choke up for a pastry or even lunch. Just look at me, okay?"

I turned my head the tiniest fraction of an inch. "Explain to me what you want."

"I want you to be my hung-girl, go the whole way, the whole thing. Come on, Zeyya, you know you love me."

Did I love him? I couldn't answer my own question.

"Come on Zeyya, coffee. Give me a chance. After school, today?"

I wasn't so sure about it. I needed to get home. My parents would want to know all about school.

He pressed me. "They'll be at work, won't they? Don't make excuses, it's just a cup of coffee, for now."

I couldn't think of how to get out of it, and besides, I hated to admit it, but Eileen or not, I wasn't sure I was ready to let go of him. I primped in the girls room after last period, pulling my curls back into the bun and scrubbing at my teeth with a finger nail. I popped a little lip gloss I'd found in the bottom of my pack from last year onto my mouth. It felt thick and sticky, so I dabbed most of it off and that was all I could do before I met him.

The first thing he said to me was, "You seem different this year."

"Yeah? Why?"

"I don't know. Less sure, maybe? It's alluring."

My losses made me alluring? Or was he reading my nervousness as his idea of flirtation or standoffishness? Could he be one of those guys who wanted what he couldn't have?

"I didn't do it to be alluring."

We sat in the coffee shop and talked. He ordered coffee while we looked at the menu. I knew I should have left, but he was familiar and reassuringly oblivious to the dangers around us, like a child. I was about to order a pastry, thinking about hanging with him, maybe getting to be his hung-girl if he gave up Eileen, when a dog pranced in. I knew who it was in a flash, but nobody else did. The manager went crazy nuts, shouting and waving his hands. The Jo-Boy ignored him. Stepping diffidently around the tables as people pulled in their chairs, it walked straight at us. Alejandro pulled back, his chair legs squealing on the floor. The manager headed for the Net Phone and I knew that if I didn't act, this was going to explode into a major scene with cops everywhere chasing a wild dog.

"Hey, let's go," I said to Alejandro. "I have to leave anyway."

He started to stand, but the Jo-Boy growled deep in its throat. That's when I whistled and waved my arms towards the door, giving it a major frown and it left, but not before it gave me a withering look of reproach. What did Jonah do, shape shift into a dog so he could follow me around inconspicuously?

"Wow, that was—wow—I can't find the right word—impressive. Yeah, Zeyya, impressive!"

"Not really. I just have a friend who gets along with dogs and I've been picking up tricks." That was something of an understatement. That Jo-Boy would go back and report to Jonah. I knew it. I looked around as we left the café. No Jonah, at least that I could see. Was it possible he had an invisibility cloak? Or that he was a trained stealth spy who had gone rogue and deserted the corps?

"Hey, what are you thinking about?" Alejandro asked, taking my hand.

"Huh? Oh, dogs. Listen, I need to get home. See you tomorrow."

He dashed after me. "How about tonight? There's a party or we could go to a vid. I can pick you up."

"Can't go. I have work to do."

"No, you don't. There's never homework the first night."

"I have to finish my concerto."

"What? Hey, if you don't want to hang with me anymore, just so say, and we're over."

Protest, I thought. Explain, but when I opened my mouth, I didn't do it. Couldn't find the trust to tell him the truth. Last year, I'd told him everything, but that was before Eileen. And Jonah, I thought fleetingly before I banished the notion, reprimanding myself about being on the rebound.

"No answer? Okay, then, see you around, Zeyya."

I kicked at a piece of concrete all the way home, forgetting to hop a walkway. By the time I noticed, I was at the alleyway. I stared down it at the overflowing trash bins, at the shadows of the towers darkening everything. I looked behind me at the sky and the people walking by. I didn't want to live like this, ducking into dark alleys, telling cute guys I couldn't hang with them, hiding and lying. I stood there a long time before forcing myself to walk down to Granna's, forcing myself to put each foot on a step and open the door.

"Hello," I called weakly. "Hello?"

Nobody answered, but Bellisima came purring up to raise her back against my leg and rub. I put my stuff in my room and walked down the hall. Granna was asleep, curled under an afghan. Nobody was in the kitchen, but the back door was slightly ajar. I slipped through to find Jonah was sitting in the tiny backyard, his hands on his legs, with his eyes wide.

"How was school?"

"Don't you know? I mean your spy was there."

"He went on his own."

I laughed at him.

He uncrossed his legs and stood, shirtless in the chilly air, but at least was attired in pants. "I'm sorry if he disturbed you and your friend."

"See, you knew!"

He didn't bother to answer as he stuck his arms through his shirt sleeves. "I'm worried about Granna. She seems... I'm not sure she's well."

"What? Why?"

He didn't know. He sensed something was all he could tell me. Just a little something, but something. Would I watch and see if he was right?

I told him I would when she woke, but until then I had to work. He stayed in the yard and when I looked out the back door, he was in access mode, eyes rolled back, shirt off again, hands out. I watched for a few minutes, but there was nothing new to see, so I went back to struggling with my composition, trying to keep my mind away from Alejandro and also from Jonah. Mr. Pompandow had given me a month's extension on the concerto, but I still needed to work every day. It grew duskier while I sat at the kitchen table, not looking up until Granna flipped on the light.

"Why are you working in the dark?"

"Didn't notice."

She washed her hands at the sink with no sign of anything amiss. "I think I'll take you and Jonah out to dinner tonight."

"Why?"

"It's your birthday, isn't it?" I hadn't remembered? "Seventeen today, aren't you?"

She was right, of course, but the last thing I felt like was a celebration. She was already at the door, calling to Jonah before I could say no. She stopped, turned back to me. "How long has he been like that?"

"Huh? I don't know. A while."

"Any suggestions on how to bring him out of it? No? Too bad. Should I cook, do you think?"

"I'll help."

"So, school was okay? Nobody questioned you about being there?" she asked as we looked through the refrigerator for dinner. "I hadn't thought we'd be eating here. I do, however, have this!" She pulled out a big birthday cake. "Baked it today. Marble cake—your great-great-grandmother's recipe."

"Is it good?"

"How 'bout we find out. Want to forgo dinner and just have ice cream and cake tonight?" She looked at me over the cake.

"Yeah, it's my birthday! Why not?"

She pulled a gallon of chocolate, fresh churned ice cream out of the freezer. I grabbed bowls and plates. We sliced the cake, and dished the ice cream, and without further ado, we dug in. It was great cake. We cut seconds. I licked the crumbs off my fingers, considering thirds when the Jo-Boy jumped up and licked my ice cream bowl. "Hey, no!"

It backed off, lying down and putting its head forlornly on its paws, to look up at me with big eyes.

"Stop looking at me like that!" I instructed him.

"Here," Granna said, plunking a dish of vanilla ice cream on the floor for him. He brought his head up, his ears perked, but he kept his eyes on me.

"Okay, go for it," I said. His tongue lapped at the bowl rapidly.

I jumped a little when Jonah surprised us, saying, "How about me?"

"Sure, if you don't mind ice cream and cake for dinner."

"Does it make for a good meal?"

Granna smiled, before answering with, "Hmmm, hmmm good."

He sat and lifted one of his feet, pulling at a bloody bandage. "Uh, I think we should clean that up, again," I suggested.

"No need, Zeyya. It's healed, just a little tender."

"Right. See that, that's blood, Jonah."

"Not new blood." He stripped off the bandage and there wasn't a sign of a scratch. "We heal fast. I told you."

So how did I explain this away? He'd gone to a doctor while I was at school? I doubted that. What else? I couldn't come up with a single logical or believable explanation. What if he really could stay warm and heal faster than most people? What did that mean? My mind couldn't come up with anything.

"Let's go out," I suggested, standing up suddenly. "To a vid or something. It's my birthday, I want to celebrate."

"Not me," Granna said, "but I'll treat you two."

"And just think, Zeyya, I won't embarrass you as it'll be dark and no one will be able to see me." Jonah accompanied his comment with a grin.

The vid we chose was in a big room. About twenty couples were already snuggling into seats and the only places left were near the front. We were moving down the aisle when a hand reached out and grabbed me.

"Zeyya?"

"Alejandro?" Eileen clung tightly to his arm.

"Uh, this is, uh..." he said, uncomfortably.

"Yeah, I know." I pushed on down the aisle. Jonah was already sliding into a seat.

He leaned over and whispered, "Why do the girls lean on the boys?"

Who was that naïve?

"Hey," Alejandro whispered into my other ear, making me jump. I craned my head around. Eileen sat at their seats with a big bag of popcorn, her lips clamped tightly together.

"Shouldn't you go back to your hung-girl?"

"Who's this? I thought you had homework."

I glared at him. "I do. But I forgot, it's my birthday. This is my friend Jonah. Jonah, Alejandro."

Jonah lifted his hand in gesture of greeting as he stared at the vid screen. I jabbed him in the arm with an elbow. "What do you want?" he asked.

"For you to say a polite hello." Next instant, I wondered why it mattered to me, but too late. Jonah turned his head and awkwardly put out his hand. Alejandro, who had grasped the offering at the moment the screen lit up, illuminating both the room and Jonah, broke from the handshake as if he'd been burned.

"What's the matter?" I asked him.

"Nothing. I have to, uh, get back. See you later, Zeyya. Nice to, uh, meet you, Jonah."

"Why'd you do that?" I hissed at Jonah.

"You told me to."

"You timed it perfectly to embarrass me. I can't believe you're that jealous? Listen up, I'm not hanging with you, I'll never be your girlfriend, so quit being protective. I can take care of myself." I was really mad and moved in my seat as far from him as I could possibly get.

He sank into his seat and we sat through the whole thing in cold retreats, he in his, me in mine. When it was over, when I didn't move, he stood, then sat again. "Isn't it time to leave?"

"After everybody else. I know people here."

He looked at me for a moment. "I don't."

He was out of his seat and up the aisle before I could stand. Man, he could move. He really should have been on the track team. I saw him stop next to Alejandro, stand full face in front of him and shake hands with a wide smile. I saw Alejandro pull away, his face awash in an expression I couldn't quite read. I saw him look back at me and then at Jonah. We were exposed, no question.

They said something to each other and Alejandro laughed nervously, then moved on, Eileen yanking on his hand with a possessive, impatient gesture. Jonah walked back down the aisle to me. "There, I was more friendly to your friend."

"You shouldn't have done that!"

"Why not? Isn't it what you wanted?"

"No, I mean yes, I mean no... I don't know."

His expression was one of *I told you so*, but he didn't open his mouth. We walked home in silence, gathering Jo-Boys along the way who came quietly, responding to some silent call. No denying it. They were his minions and they heard him when I couldn't. Did the dogs talk to each other? Did one call to the other? Or did Jonah call them all?

Who was he? Whoever he was, it was better if people didn't see him surrounded by Jo-Boys. It could only get us into trouble. As surreptitiously as I could, I glanced over my shoulder to see who was watching, but all the kids had scattered, probably in fear of the wild dogs. I turned my attention back to Jonah to find Jo-Boys licking him, standing close, each one eerily awaiting a personal welcome and how-do-you-do as he greeted them like old friends.

"To the left is a huge sitting image of Buddha…In [an]
open space stands a banyan tree…which has grown from a sapling
Mahabodhi tree…planted…on 4th January, 1948.
Projecting beyond the base of the pagoda…are Tazungs [shelters]
in which are images of the Buddha…also figures of elephants
crouching, and men kneeling…images of lions, serpents, beloos, yogis,
nats or wahtudari (recording angels)."

The Shwedagon and Guide, ©1958
by U Aung Than

AIR LETTER

AEROGRAMME

March 9, 1958, Rangoon

Dear Mother,

The Shwedagon is very pretty, but also very dirty. Its golden spire goes up about 350 feet in the air. It has 4 entrances, north, south, east and west. We entered by the east entrance which has the most stalls and is therefore the dirtiest. We walked up about 100 steps, lined side-by-side with stalls. Then we came to a circular platform, at least a block in diameter. Along each side of this platform are small shrines, beautifully decorated with gold leaf, carvings, etc., each containing a statue of Buddha in every mood and every position. These shrines are erected by rich individuals, but anyone can pray at them. Rising above all, in the center of the platform, is the big spire, completely covered in gold leaf, with many diamonds laid into its point. There is no roof over the platform, although each individual shrine has a roof over Buddha.

The stall keepers live in their stalls, everyone barefooted. Despite the filthiness of the pagoda, I think what Justice Douglas said when he came in 1954 is perhaps the most evocative: "On the murky morning when I first saw it, Shwedagon pointed like a tongue of fire into the sky. At noon on a clear day it was peaceful and sublime; on a moonlight night, it had a mystic cast... Its moods are the moods of man; and yet its dignity, its plain beauty, its purity make it a symbol of the noblest things for which man has strived. I have seen sunsets and storms, glaciers and peaks, flowers and faces that have moved me more, but of all the things that man has created by his hands, the Shwedagon is the loveliest I have known." I can think of nothing to add to that.

Love,

Jack

The Greater East Coast Metropolis: 2047
[WARNING: Crime alert. Looting is occurring more frequently.
Please report any suspicious activity or individuals immediately.]

I brooded for hours each night about what might happen the next day at school—confrontation with Alejandro; exposure and subsequent expulsion; disappointing Mr. Pompandow, for despite the extension, I didn't seem to have enough time to finish the rest of the movements. Homework backed up into working on the concerto. Envy suffused me when kids discussed their plans for the weekends. My weekends were consumed with composing. Greater envy set in when my friends moved on to babbling about with whom they had already paired off for the annual costume ball, even though it wasn't until early November. To finish it off, jealousy set in when I heard Eileen bragging about the plans she and Alejandro had already made for costumes. I resigned myself to not going and tried not to listen.

At night, my dreams were filled with treble clefts, whole notes, half notes, quarter notes usually outlined in blue, dancing in the dark until one night I saw myself tattooed in musical notation—across my toes, my back, up and down my legs, down the bridge of my nose. That night I didn't sleep and the next day I felt stupid all day in classes. Mrs. Banaman asked if I was sick. Mr. Peebles asked me to stop and speak to him about my lack of class participation. Finally, Mr. Jaster called me into his office.

"Zeyya, what's going on here? It's only the first month of school and your teachers are expressing concern about you and your work. Do I need to call your parents?"

So they hadn't told the school anything. Nothing. I was safe.

"No, I'm fine, Mr. Jaster, really, just a rough month at home."

"And why's that?" he asked as he popped a disk with my student number on it into the computer.

"Uh..." Think fast.

He frowned as his eyes scanned the file. "There's a note here that our Net Mail to your family was returned as undeliverable.

"Yeah, we got a new address, public access. I can give it to you."

He looked up without moving his head, only his eyes traveling to pin with me with his stare. "What happened?"

"See, we moved, you know, last year and the new landlord provided us with Net Service, but the connection was really bad and unreliable, so we just quit using it."

"Uh huh, well, leave me the public address because we need to send your parents a few things."

"Okay, but they're out of town."

Now he raised his head, his eyes narrowing. He had eyes that the kids claimed could pierce thoughts. "Out of town?"

"They needed money." I hung my head sadly. "So they took jobs, you know, that paid well because, you know, the jobs aren't so safe, you know..." I let it all trail off. Not a bad acting job.

"So where are they?"

"Burma." Burma? I hadn't meant to say *Burma*. I was out of my mind. Granna said they didn't even call it that anymore.

"I see." Had he believed me?

"Uh huh, they had a tsunami that did a lot of damage. Cleanup jobs came available." Where had I gotten this ridiculous scenario? I was really in trouble now.

"And you're staying alone?"

"Oh, no, it's only for a couple of months. I'm living with my Granna. It's not that far from school."

He looked unconvinced. "So what's Burma like?" he asked.

"Uh, well, Mum says it's beautiful there. Tall palms. Tropical. Pretty undeveloped."

He nodded. "All right, but if you're still having problems, then I'll need to talk to your grandmother, okay?"

"Sure. Can I go? Otherwise, I'll miss Orchestra."

I was at the door when he said, "Oh, by the way, Zeyya, I heard Mr. Pompandow is interested in performing a piece you've composed."

"Yeah, well, I'm turning it in on Monday, so I hope so."

I rolled my eyes back as I left and said silently, *Thank you, thank you, Granna, for telling me so much about Burma. Thank you.* But what if Mr. Jaster wanted more details. Did I know enough? I was at the door to Orchestra when Tracey grabbed my arm. Had I heard about Alejandro?

"No, what about him?"

She took her finger and cut across her throat. "Quarantined!"

I started to shake. How was that possible? I'd just seen him.

"Hey, don't faint on me or anything."

I wobbled into class and sat down in the first seat that was empty, put my head down on my desk and closed my eyes. It was everywhere, stalking me. When I lifted my head, someone was standing in front of me.

Alejandro?

"I'm back," he chortled with a malicious grin.

Everybody was snickering. I stood up and swatted him across the cheek, hard. Now there was silence, not a sound in the room except for the door opening, Mr. Pompandow pausing to say something to someone in the hall, and then Alejandro announcing, "That smarted!" The whole class burst into laughter.

"Would anyone like to let me in on the joke?" Mr. Pompandow asked perfunctorily as he closed the door behind him. Nobody spoke. "Good, then let's get down to practice."

My violin hummed as I played. I lost myself in it, trying to forget the entertainment I'd just provided everyone, to ignore the fleeting realization that Alejandro had told some sort of vindictive tale about me to my classmates. Instead, I concentrated on wavering blue shadows and listened to the sounds of other instruments that sang in my head: melodic but unfamiliar, indefinable. I ceased playing before I realized that the rest of the class had stopped minutes before.

Mr. Pompandow was staring at me curiously. "Zeyya, you've been practicing." I hadn't. I hadn't picked up the violin more than a couple of times all summer. "Was that from your concerto?"

What? What did he mean? "No, I was following the music."

He shook his head at me very gently. "Are you okay?"

The most frightening thing was that the other kids weren't laughing at me. No whispers, no elbow jabbing and knowing looks. Give them a few minutes and they would undoubtedly think of something with which to taunt me, but until then, they seemed to be caught in a reign of silent awe. When the bell rang, Alejandro waited in the hall. Putting his arm around my shoulder, he announced, "Time for track practice." I shook him off angrily.

"What do you want? Huh? Leave me alone!"

I packed up my violin, grabbed my pack and headed down the hall, out the door. I wasn't going to track. Maybe the next day, but not today. I was going home. I looked around as I left, hoping for the Jo-Boy. No luck. People shuffled along, going to wherever they were going, and I—I was all alone.

By the time I got home, I had to stop on the porch to wipe at my face and sniffle up my tears. Granna wasn't going to know I was upset. I burst through the front door, calling out, "Burma time!"

Granna looked up from the rocking chair. "Pardon me?"

"I want to know everything about Burma. I mean, everything you can tell me."

She squinted suspiciously. "Why?"

"Because I told Mr. Jaster that's where Mum and Dad are for the next couple of months, that's why."

"Oh, Zeyya, you lied?"

I laughed, pointing out that she had lied to the social worker when she claimed Jonah was from Burma. So who was she to point a finger?

"Come on, Granna, details."

"I'm not prepared for on-demand reminiscing. Give me a minute."

I sat down to wait.

"Stop staring at me, Zeyya. Go put your things away, get a snack. I'll be ready by the time you finish."

I didn't budge. How long could it take to pick a story to tell to me? She never seemed to have trouble with it before.

"That's because I was free associating," she explained when I mentioned it. "Go. Come back in ten minutes. I'm not going to disappear."

Gave her twenty minutes before coming back, bearing a cup-of-tea-peace-offering. "I'm ready." She took a heavy breath and began. "This is a little forced, but I'll tell you about the Shwedagon Pagoda because it's the most famous sight in Rangoon, and the largest stupa in the city, with a spire shooting up hundreds of feet, completely covered in gold leaf."

She stopped. I waited. Nothing. "What else? There has to be more, Granna!"

"Zeyya, stop it!"

I thrust my face so close to hers that she shrank back against the sofa. "No, you have to tell me! I need to know or Mr. Jaster'll figure out I lied and they'll send me away!"

Someone grabbed me from behind and pulled me away. "Zeyya," Jonah's soft voice said, "stop! It's okay, it's okay." He drew me into his arms, pressing me against the tattoos on his chest. Did they writhe beneath my cheek or was I simply losing my mind? I pulled away.

"I'm sorry, I'm so sorry, Granna. I'm so scared!"

"Of what?"

I sobbed out the whole sorry story, of Mr. Jaster, of Alejandro's joke, of my accidental solo performance. "Granna, I have to know about Burma, so when Mr. Jaster asks, I can give him details. I have to know. Please, please!"

She rose with creaky sturdiness and moved herself to sit in the rocker, pecking me with a kiss on the top of the head before she sat. I leaned back into the sofa cushions as she spoke again. "Zeyya, it's hard to describe the Shwedagon. Maybe this other riddle, by Min Thu Won will help. Let's see, what was it? Oh—'Red gold radiance. Has the sun risen?'"

"What? I don't understand."

"No, I don't suppose you could. Early each morning, the pongyis emerged from the golden temple, cradling begging bowls in their arms."

"Wait, what's a pongyi?" I demanded, determined to get it straight no matter how disorganized and disconnected the telling was.

Surprising me, Jonah quickly supplied the answer. "A Burmese Buddhist monk."

How did he know? I turned to ask, but before I could, he supplied that answer as well. "I've been consulting with the aged ones."

"Is he right, Granna?"

"Yes. What else do you know, Jonah?" He shrugged. She picked up where he'd left off. "Pongyis wore saffron robes so bright as to be compared to the radience of the sun. Each morning they trooped from the temples, carrying black lacquer bowls to be filled with food for the poor. Round and black up against the deep orange, their shaved heads echoing the shapes of their bowls—that's what U Wun's riddle is describing. Anyone could enter a monastery as a monk whenever they wanted. Sometimes political leaders took sanctuary that way. That's where U Nu went when Ne Win came to power the first time."

"What else? I need to know as much as I can before I go back to school in the morning."

"Zeyya, I can't teach you all of it by then."

"Just try? Please. What else about pongyis?"

"I have a begging bowl somewhere. Mommy bought it at the Sule Pagoda, a smaller pagoda in Rangoon. All Burmese pagodas supposedly mimic the shape of the begging bowl. The story is that Buddha once turned his bowl upside down, put its stand on top of it and a staff on top of that and that's how Burmese stupas got their shape. The top of the Shwedagon's spire is encrusted in precious gemstones." She fumbled through one of her stacks of books and passed a coverless little volume to me. "Here, read this, begin on this page."

I held the book open so that Jonah could read along, but he shook his head. I raised my eyebrows. "Then I'll tell you what it says. Okay, here we go. The pagoda has different parts. A base that surrounds the stupa with sixty-four smaller pagodas on it. There are three terraces called something I can't pronounce.

"There's a bell that has a circumference of three-hundred-forty-four feet and is seventy feet high."

"Keep going," Granna insisted when I paused.

"The other parts are: an inverted begging bowl; a twisted turban, which is a series of embossed bands another forty-one feet high, with a circumference of ninety-six feet at the top. The Kyalan, the ornamental lotus flower, is thirty-one feet at the top. A bulbous bud-shaped spire with a girth of sixty-five feet, stands fifty-three feet tall. And the vane, almost five feet long and two-and-a-half feet wide, is hinged to the shaft."

I looked at Jonah and Granna. Like twins, they had their heads craned back, looking upward, as if seeing the pagoda.

I returned to the book. "Whoa, listen to this! The Seinbu, the Diamond Bud, crowns the vane. It's a gold sphere, ten inches in diameter, and inlaid with pieces of cut diamond and precious stones. To be exact, four-thousand-three-hundred-and-thirty-five pieces of diamonds."

"How did they get all that up there, Granna?" Jonah asked, his head now level.

"No idea." She looked at her watch. "I think we should have some tea and cookies and you should do some homework, Zeyya."

"I need to know more. Please!"

She ignored me, rising slowly, and I noticed that she wobbled until Jonah steadied her and then she was fine. He took a place on the sofa. "Zeyya, it's not good to weave so many lies. It will turn on you."

He was probably right, but I didn't know how to stop. If I owned up, I'd be sent away from my school and maybe from Granna. It was only a minor miracle that I had escaped so far, especially with him around.

"You may be right, Jonah, but I think it's already too late."

I went to do homework, trying to keep my mind away from the scenarios that played across it as to how I was going to get caught. Mr. Jaster would find me out. Tracey or Marilyn would let slip where I was living, bring a gang over, discover Granna had no Net or catch Jonah in the shower, blue but not from cold. I tried to shake the stream of narratives from my head. When I couldn't, I took a break seeking solace by rubbing Jo-Boy. When that didn't work, I sought out a snack, crunching on carrot sticks until blue fingers reached over my arm grabbing up part of my snack without asking.

"Hey, get your own," I yelped at Jonah.

"I paid for those carrots," Granna remarked, joining us and reaching for a helping for herself, so I got up and peeled more.

"I'm revived," Granna stated and, before I could blink, had plucked more Burmese reminiscences out of the air. "Things are brilliant in the tropics. The light, the colors, the sky, the dyes they use in fabrics, but the ugly and the terrible juxtapose themselves against the intensity of all that brightness."

I put more carrots on the table. "What do you mean, Granna?" Crunch.

"Patience," Jonah advised. Crunch.

Granna crunched, too, working her jaw before she went on. "The steps of the stupa are covered in betel spit and dirt, but you have to take off your shoes before you set one foot on a pagoda step. Mommy made sure we kept our socks on as a barrier between us and germs when we went to the Shwedagon. By the time we reached the platform that surrounds the stupa, Sis's white socks were black. I'd walked up on my tiptoes, so only my toes were stained."

Granna looked at me a moment. "So there we were, me, Mommy, Daddy, and Sis, climbing one-hundred-eighteen steps in all. I counted as we climbed—one, two, three four... Stands and stalls lined those steps, arraying toys and dolls, carved horse marionettes, ceremonial headdresses, tissue flowers, and candles to burn at the shrines when you got to the platform above. Oh, how I wanted a pink silk parasol and paper marionettes, a doll, flowers—I wanted it all."

"What did you buy?" Jonah asked.

"Nothing on that trip. I was too indecisive. I had to go back later." She cleared her throat several times. "At first, all I noticed were the toys, until I almost stepped on the hand of a living skeleton lying limply across the steps, arm little more than bone ending in outstretched fingers, reaching to us, imploring us for just a little contribution. A few kyats, even a pya. Anything. Just a little something. Anything at all. And he wasn't the only one. So many hands begged on those steps, so many reached out to us."

She looked upset as she spoke, moving her hands as if shaking something off them, turning her head as if she could still hear the pleas for food, for money. "Beggars with rickets-deformed legs and hunger-bloated stomachs crowded closer and closer, narrowing our passageway up the steps. I clung to Daddy, and Sis to Mommy. That's when it happened."

She cleared her throat again and took on a different voice. "It's a leopard."

"That's what I heard and what I said was..." She cleared her throat yet again, and this time the voice was that of a small girl. "Where? Where? Don't let it eat me!" Granna turned her head rapidly from side to side.

"Granna, are you...are you still here?

"Of course, I am, silly girl. I just want you to get the flavor of the moment." She went to the sink, filled a glass with water and took a sip. "My throat is dry—now where was I? Oh, yes!"

What was apparently the mother voice said in a slow drawl, "It's not a leopard, honey. It's a leper."

"There and there and there, they're everywhere! No arms, no legs!" Granna gingerly touched her own elbow. "They can't walk, they don't have toes or feet. No fingers either. Only stumps where limbs once were."

I felt my stomach heave, felt Jonah squeeze my hands, but Granna ignored my distress. "They sat on squares of frayed gray cardboard, scooting and leveraging themselves up or down the steps to new begging sites on whatever remained of their elbows and knees."

"Stop, Granna, please, that's sickening."

She picked up another carrot stick. Crunch. "Tell me when you're ready to go on."

I had to swallow before I could ask, "Why didn't somebody help them? Why didn't they go to a hospital?"

"No money. The only place they had to go to were the temples, like the Shwedagon. They believed they deserved their plight in life, that they were being punished for a wicked deed in another life. So they lived in the shadows of the Buddhas that lined the platform, large, small, sitting, reclining, watching their suffering with impassive expressions."

Jonah pronounced the obvious: "Statues cannot emote."

"Remember when I told you that Jonah reminds me of a Buddha, Zeyya? I meant physically. He's not diffident like a Buddha, and of course, there are no blue Buddhas." Her mouth tweaked up

"Isn't there more?" Jonah asked.

"Oh, my, yes, but Zeyya has homework and I'm getting hoarse."

I went in my room, sat on the bed. Didn't have too much left to do, if I could just keep my mind on it, could just concentrate. I needed to keep my grades up. I needed everything to look normal.

The house started to get dark before I came out. Granna was back in the rocker, dozing with her hands laid neatly across her lap. I touched her and she woke with a smile that faded as if something sweet had vanished.

"Do you want me to start dinner, Granna?"

"That would be nice. What time is it?"

"Almost six?"

"Is Jonah back?" she asked me.

"Back, back from where?"

"I sent him to get the holographs from Hank, but he should have been back long ago."

"He can take care of himself." I was unconcerned until I found the Jo-Boy under the table, but I didn't have time to think about it before Bellisima decided to claw the table cloth and bring it and the sugar bowl down on her head, which resulted in a wild melee of cat fighting red fabric with snarls and ripping claws, until she was tangled into submission. Miraculously, the sugar bowl remained unbroken, but the sugar was scattered to kingdom come, and as I discovered, was not easy to get off the floor or out of cat fur. To the shower went the squalling cat. The broom swept the floor. It wasn't enough. I still had to wet-mop it. By the time I finished, the sun had set completely and no dinner was begun, but I sat down to rest anyway.

Jo-Boy's ears pricked up. He rose, padding to the door, a small whine issuing from the back of his throat.

"What? The social worker again?"

Why wasn't he barking if someone was out there at the back door. Then again, I hadn't heard him bark for a long time. Jonah's voice came back to me. *There they never give voice like these Jo-Boys.* Okay, maybe Jonah had trained him. The dog scratched at the door. Maybe he needed to relieve himself. I gathered my courage and slowly pulled the curtain away from the little window in the top of the door. That was when I learned what the old saying *jumped out of your skin* meant. How long did it take for it to penetrate my terrified brain that the thing pressed against the glass was Jonah's blue etched face?

"Step back, get away from there and I'll open the door." He didn't budge. "Jonah, quit it, stop fooling around." No change. "Stay, Jo-Boy, I'm going out the front and around the back."

I dashed through the house, sending Bellisima flying for safety under the sofa. I vaguely wondered if she'd ever come out after the sugar, the shower and now my unmitigated dash through her territory. Night chill slapped my cheeks, but too late for a coat or shoes. My socks were caked with mud before I got more than a few feet. Granna's socks on betel-stained steps passed through my mind as I reached the back door.

He was slumped against it, unmoving. Unnatural. Like a dead body propped there. That couldn't be. A stiff couldn't stiffen standing up, could it? I made myself touch his shoulder. His body quivered. Good, not dead. I reached around him and opened the door, thoroughly expecting him to fall flat into the kitchen like a piece of wood, but he stood on his own, although he didn't move, didn't twitch. Nothing. I gave his shoulder a little nudge. Go, I thought. Nothing.

"Jonah, stop it, go inside." He might have been a statue until the Jo-Boy came up and nuzzled him, then licked his hand. He took a step forward, leaving me behind for a moment because I was scared. A few inches over the doorsill, he stopped, his face blank, his eyes focused somewhere, but not in Granna's kitchen. Where?

"What happened?" I whispered as I pulled the door closed and slid around him, afraid I'd spook him if I said anything louder or tried to make him moved further into the room.

I was about to get Granna, when he started saying, "No one, no one, no one." Over and over, a hollow mantra: "No one, no one, no one."

"What's wrong? What do you mean, *no one?*"

I pulled a chair to where he stood, offering it to him. All he needed to do was sit. He didn't have to take a step or pull it to him. Just sit. He stood. This was bad.

"Sit," I instructed. He did it. I knelt in front of him. "Jonah, look at me. What happened?"

"Inside, no one, no one," he repeated again.

Was that the remains of milkiness across his eyes? I heard Granna come in as the Jo-Boy laid its head in Jonah's lap. She circled him, eyeing him, but not touching. She tapped my arm. "Let's fix dinner."

"But Granna, what about Jonah?"

"Set the table, Zeyya. I'll make sandwiches. Put out three places."

She and I were halfway through eating our sandwiches in silence when Jonah shakily came and sat in the extra chair. His eyes had cleared, but when he sat, he downed a glass of water like it was a jigger of whiskey. One tossed-back gulp.

"Jonah, what happened?"

He looked at me blankly for a minute or two. "Is that what it's like?"

"What?"

"Empty. Abandoned."

"What are you talking about? Make sense," I begged.

He put his head down on the table and all the stuff in his hair clattered and clanked. Granna laid a shaky hand on his shoulder.

"Jonah," she said gently, "tell us what happened to you."

"Streets. Buildings. Shiny walls, all the reflections. Endless hallways. Soulless mirrors."

"Did you get lost?"

"Hank wasn't there. A back route home, following the streets behind buildings. In a garbage dump, heard something. A Jo-Boy thrown in to die."

"Maybe he jumped in to scavenge," Granna suggested.

"No. He told me." He hung his head. "Got him out, but he was dying. What to do? Look around. Duck behind the dump. Lay the Jo-Boy near me. Access the old ones."

In the street? He went into a trance in the street. Wisely, Granna didn't reprimand him. Instead, she urged him to finish. His next words raced out almost too quickly to be comprehensible.

"A man grabbed my shoulder, touched me, shook me, hefted me to my feet—me, still in access." He moaned a painful sound that made my scalp prickle.

"Did he hurt you?"

His body shook so hard, it took him several breaths before he could answer me. "He—full of nothingness, all alone, a wasteland—left in my access." He got up from the table, his food untouched.

We waited a few minutes to follow him. He was lying on my bed. He'd taken off his shirt and his chest was heaving, the tattooed portraits somberly moving with his sobs.

"Are you hurt?"

"No?" he asked uncertainly. "Empty."

Did Jonah feel empty or was he saying the man had been. "How'd you get away?"

He turned his face away from me. "He held me too long."

"Huh?"

"He fell. Don't know why. Maybe my access. He fell."

Granna's voice shook, but she asked, "Was he dead, Jonah?"

I wanted to deny all this, to say that someone couldn't die by touching someone else at the wrong moment. But this was Jonah, not your average Earthling. Tension behind my eyes rose as I made myself ask, "Was he a cop?"

Jonah said, "He still breathed," and I realeased a swish of air.

Granna sat on the edge of the bed careful not to touch him, her finger resting on the edge of her lip, clearly considering what to say before she spoke. "Jonah, humans aren't empty." He didn't answer. She shifted her body a little.

"Let's try it this way. When we moved into our house in Burma, my father's office supplied most of our furniture. The first thing they delivered was a chest of drawers, left in our driveway for us to put where we chose."

A story now? "Granna, do you think this is the time?"

She pointed at Jonah, who appeared to be calming down and continued. "Our servants were mainly fresh-faced young men from jungle villages. Our compound, surrounded by high iron fencing, was gated at the road against intruders. Across the front of the house ran a wide, yellow-green lawn, close cropped by machete. On the far side of the house was an abandoned L-shaped, concrete World War II bomb shelter, filled with old leaves, debris, probably a snake or some lizards, maybe rats... Uh, that isn't relevant, is it? Keep me on target here, Zeyya." How did I do that without knowing where she was headed? But I said okay and she picked up again. "For our young servant boys, our pukkah house must have seemed like—like going to an alternate dimension."

"Another world?" I suggested, barely syllabating out loud.

Granna nodded at me. "At the back of the compound, a row of reinforced steel boxes resting on concrete slabs served as servants' quarters. The main house looked more or less British in nature, but it really wasn't. The kitchen was way at the back of the house, set there to keep the heat away from the living and entertaining rooms. The stove was charcoal fed, as was the furnace, which had to be stoked before there was hot water for a bath, and which was also located in the kitchen, a dark, smoke-filled, windowless place."

Granna glanced up at me, put her fingers to her lips as if to say, just let me talk. She pointed at Jonah, whose eyes were open, staring at the ceiling. Were her words weaving a world for him, someplace for him to go, to escape whatever had happened, whatever he had done? I kept quiet.

"All the floors were solid teak, except for the pantry and kitchen areas where they were dark-red concrete. The servants shined the teak floors on hands and knees with dried coconuts halves. At the side door near the kitchen, ducks and chickens squawked and cackled, and on the walls and ceilings of the dining room, geckos clung, dropping their tails into our soup, onto the floor, the way babies drop food everywhere. Outside, our trim green lawns spread out to the edges of the jungle-covered hillsides on the other side of our fence."

"Your point?" I asked, wondering how this related to Jonah.

She gave me a withering look. "From the outside, our house looked a lot like the ones we lived in at home, just like we look a lot like Jonah."

Without warning, she ceased speaking. Had Granna actually run out of things to say, of points to stories? I hoped not because Jonah was still unresponsive.

She frowned. "Well...well, now that I've set the scene, let me return to the beginning." She cleared her throat. "Remember that chest they delivered? Daddy told the servants where to put furniture while Mommy supervised the unpacking. The chest was huge and the drivers who unloaded if off the lorry had left the drawers in a stack beside it. When Daddy told Nyuant Maung and Than Swe to put the drawers into the chest and move it upstairs, Sis and I stood in the middle of the driveway and watched. But there was a problem. They didn't know which drawer went in which slot or in which direction. They put the little drawers in the big slots, tried to squeeze the big drawers into the medium slots, experimenting with ever-failing combinations—sideways, upright, end to back, back to end. Sis and I, little devils that we were, didn't offer any help and ran off in boredom to see what was happening in the room that was to be ours. At last, they got the drawers inserted and moved the chest upstairs.

"It wasn't long before we heard Mommy calling, 'Come here, y'all. Look at this!'

"The drawers were in the chest, but they were all in upside down." Granna was grinning ear to ear, but I didn't get the joke. Her smile faded. "Don't you get it?"

"Yeah, I get it. They were dumb."

She threw her hands up and shook her head at me reprovingly, before she gave up and begrudgingly explained. "Zeyya, why would Nyuant Maung and Than Swe know what a drawer was for? They slept on bamboo mats, squatted flat-footed on the floor to rest. They had no chairs, no tables, no sheets, no mattresses, no bed frames. To store their possessions, they rolled what belongings they had into their mats, or lined them up along the walls of their quarters. And it worked just fine for them."

I glanced over at Jonah. He still lay with his face turned to the wall. Had he fallen asleep? Maybe we should tiptoe out. I pointed, but Granna, undetered, launched right back in almost without pause. "If they needed to move, it was simple. They bundled their belongings into a few yards of cloth, put them and their rolled-up beds on their heads and walked off down the road. They had no use for a drawers and chests, so how would they know a drawer needed to be inserted so it could hold things? They had done what they had been told to do—put the drawers in the chest."

She clamped her mouth shut. That was it? That was the whole story? I was ready to protest, but Jonah finally rolled over to stare at Granna.

Her lips parted and she finished with, "Jonah, do you understand? Just because Zeyya and I, the man who grabbed your shoulder, don't carry the voices of our ancestors in our minds, or weave our physical mementos into our hair, doesn't mean we're empty. We store our ancestral memories on tapes and disks, in books and on holograms and we keep our mementos in boxes and scrapbooks, and sometimes we put them into drawers. But you just carry them off down the road with you." She stood and smiled down at him. "I hope you feel better soon."

She beckoned me to follow her out of the room. As we left, did I hear him whisper, "Without memory, no one is complete."

That night as I pulled the covers up to my chin, I wondered, if Granna kept all those letters from her parents because it made her feel more complete.

"Northward of Mandalay…we enter a region of teak forests, mountains and…rice fields, well watered by…tributary rivers that come rushing down…towards the mighty Irrawaddy in the shining plain."

The Land and People of Burma
by C. Maxwell Lefroy

July 1958

Rangoon

Dear Nanny and Granddaddy,

Thank you for my present. I hope you are good. Ben in my class likes me. He says if I give him my chocolate milk from the Commisary he won't pull my hair. I didn't give it to him and he still didn't pull my hair. Judy says it's cause he likes me. I want to invite him to my birthday party, but he'd be the only boy, so I won't.

Love,

Susie

Jonah spent days that turned to weeks in mute mourning, rarely uttering a sound, never looking either Granna or me in the eye, until early one morning when he gently shook me awake into a storm-lit day. "Snow," he breathed into my dream-filled ears.

Stretching, yawning, it took me a minute before it penetrated my sleep addled brain that he had finally spoken again. I wanted more sleep, but I couldn't ignore him.

"It's too early." My half-awake words came out muddled.

Granna came to the door. "It snowed!"

"This early? How deep?" I sat up and rubbed at my eyes.

"Deep enough. I heard they're giving you a snow day from school before they melt it off the city. I let you sleep in, but it's time to get this show on the road. Jonah, go try on the parka I borrowed for you. And Zeyya, come help fix breakfast. You two are going sledding up on Manicot Hill—if you hurry."

Jonah smiled slightly for the first time since he had quit speaking. I jumped from the warm covers into the chilly room, pulling on socks and pants. A hefty baby-pink sweater lay across the foot of my bed.

"Where'd this come from, Granna?" I called out as I slid the warm wool over my head.

"It was your mother's." By the time I got my head through the sweater, she was in the kitchen, toasting bread and whipping hot chocolate into a froth.

"I didn't know you still had any of Mum's things."

"You don't want it?"

"Of course, I do! Thank you." I planted a kiss on her cheek and stroked the old wool.

"It should help keep you warm." She looked a little more bent over than usual as she cooked.

Jonah came out in his shirt and a pair of jeans Granna had bought for him. He slipped on a parka. It swallowed him out of sight, so that it looked as if the hood stood empty on the top.

"It's perfect!" Granna exclaimed. "I knew something of Matthew Mott's would be just right."

"Matthew must be a big man," Jonah commented, as he pushed the hood away from his face.

"He is. It's a perfect fit," she insisted again.

"Granna, it's way too big!"

"It hides his face, doesn't it? And if he's an alien, he doesn't want anyone to see him, does he? Now come eat," she instructed, having clarified the method of her mad thinking.

"You're not an alien," I said to him.

"No?"

We sat to eat, he still in the parka which billowed up even higher when he sat down.

"Have you ever been sledding, Jonah?"

"On polished tree bark, when the snow is thick enough." The voice floated ghost-like out of the jacket.

"Polished tree bark, huh? Well, around here you've got a choice of cast nylon Saucers or resin built Arrows," I told him.

"Do they go fast?"

"Oh, yeah! You punch in the speed, kick off and a computer does the rest. My Arrow is bright purple..." I stopped. Mine was gone, sealed up and out of reach. "Granna?"

She was at the back door, tugging something through it. "I don't have an Arrow. All I have is this—an American Flier," she announced, holding forth a wooden board with red runners and a long rope attached to it.

"What is that?" I asked.

"Polished wood, obviously. Do you have runners on yours, Jonah?"

"No, Granna."

"Okay, you two ninnies, I'll show you how to use this. You can both sit on it. The one in back puts his or her legs around the one in front. Whoever's in front is the one who steers by pushing with his or her feet." She put it down flat on a throw rug, sat on it, her legs extended, a smile spreading across her face. She hefted herself back up, saying, "Have fun, I'm going for a nap."

Jonah turned to me. "Do you want to go?"

"I'm not sure the sled will work."

"So, you don't want to go?"

"It's not that... Yeah, sure, I guess I'll go."

Bundled like a yeti, Jonah carried the sled under his arm as easily as he would have toted a feather pillow. A fog of white flakes spilled silence over everything. Trudging up the hill after him, I bent my head against the onslaught of wet snow and looked down at his footprints.

"Jonah, wait, where are your boots?"

"I don't wear shoes. I don't wear boots."

"Your feet are going to get frost-bitten!"

"No, they won't. They're warm."

I shook my head vigorously. "We have to go back and find you boots or at least shoes! Come on."

He stood stubbornly where he was. "Come, Zeyya, Granna wants us to have fun." He restarted up the hill so quickly that all I could do was run after him, jumping through drifts into his footprints.

The top of the hill was already coated with kids and parents. Jonah and I crammed onto the sled, me in front, him in back, his legs so long he had to bend his knees up. We waited for a clear path and pushed off with our heels. Sliding down a well packed run, the snow rushing by us, our cheeks burned red with cold. Leafless trees, limbs stark and tangled, loomed up more quickly than I anticipated. I felt Jonah pull back and jam his heels into the snow to stop us.

Ouch, I thought, as I remembered he had on no shoes. I glanced at his feet. Where they dragged, the snow had melted in tracks marking the paths of his heels.

"What the? Do you have heaters in your feet or something?" I'd heard of people augmenting themselves physically, not for warm feet, but who knew what people would try.

"Natural adaptation," he replied. "Let's do it again."

"What do you mean?" I said, running after him as he dragged the sled up the hill. "Come on, Jonah, explain."

"You won't believe me. Let's just have fun, all right?"

We swooped down the icy track again, dragged the sled back to the top for a third and then fourth go-down.

"Hey, Zeyya," my friend Marilyn called as we got ready for our fifth run. "What kind of sled is that?"

"It's from my grandmother's childhood," I explained, standing in front of Jonah to hide his bare feet. "This is my friend Jonah."

"Hi," she answered, trying to peer past the edge of his parka hood.

"See you later, Marilyn." I tugged at Jonah and led him off to get him out of prying eyesight.

Marilyn ran to stand with her newest boyfriend, reached up and kissed him, being sure to turn and wave as the kiss ended.

"Showoff," I murmured.

"Can we sled somewhere less crowded?" Jonah asked.

"We could try the next hill over. This is the traditional spot, but sure, let's go."

The next hill was eerily deserted. Laughing we climbed aboard the American Flier. Jonah flung back the hood, letting snowflakes catch in his dark hair.

"Let her rip!" I hollered as he shoved off.

Down the long, bumpy hill we flew, our bottoms bouncing. Down and down and down, our speed growing and the snow thickening with each foot we traveled. Jonah stuck his salmon-colored tongue out to catch flakes, snapping them lizard-like back between his lips. The wind picked up and shoved us from side-to-side, but nothing seemed to break our speed. My computerized Arrow would have compensated, but I had no idea how to stop the Flier.

"Jonah, we're going too fast," I yelled over the wind. Frightened, I turned my head to look back at him. His eyes were rolling behind blue lids. "No! No, Jonah! Not now! Not now!" But it was too late. The sled tipped, and as we flew off the sled and flipped through the air, a startling jolt welled up from under my ribs where our bodies touched, traveled up my neck and along the back of my head. Through blinding flashes of light, I saw the empty sled speeding down the hill without us, vanishing into a curtain of heavy snowfall. We landed, cushioned in deep drifts, Jonah's face near to mine, his eyes open and crystal blue.

"Your lips are blue like mine," he said softly, close to my ear.

"From the cold," I mumbled, feeling inexplicably nervous.

He blew on them with warm, wet air from his mouth. "Now they're almost pink," he observed and began to untwist himself.

When we got righted, we stood inside a deep snow-pit we had made when we fell. Jonah tried to put his arms on the lip of the hole to heave himself out, but the snow at the rim fell inwards on us. My mind flipped to a long-ago, once-only-trip with Dad to a beach, where we had dug a huge hole to make a sand room. We had slipped in easily, but to get out, we had packed the wet sand into steps. "How about this?" I asked and explained.

Jonah looked at me, I at him. We scooped up clumps of snow, patting them into place, me blowing on my cold mittened hands, Jonah ignoring his bare blue fingers. I threw a handful of white flakes at him. He responded in kind, hitting me between the eyes. Wham.

"I didn't hurt you, did I, Zeyya?"

"If I wasn't hurt when we fell, a snowball isn't going to do much to me. You're okay, too, right?"

"Yes, and I gained great apperception when I met your parents."

"What are you talking about?" Had he twisted his brain when we fell?

"When our velocity grew too great to stop the sled, I briefly accessed Uncle Martin for advice on how to stop it."

"And what did Uncle Martin have to say?"

"There was no time for advice. The impending danger was too imminent."

Yeah, big surprise in that one.

"You know, Jonah, it wasn't the time to go into a trance, but ignoring that, what did it have to do with apperception and my parents?" As if I knew what that meant.

"I was holding you."

"So?" I asked, growing tired of the game.

"So, there was no choice. I'm sorry."

"Look, Jonah, I don't know what you're sorry for. Could you speed up this explanation because I'm getting really cold?"

"We shared some memories."

"What?" I waved an icy mitten at him. "Cut it out. I'm not in the mood for a charade."

"You look a lot like Debra." Granna must have told him Mum's name, but for a second before I reasoned it out, it gave me a chill.

He turned to me and stroked my cheeks with warm, ungloved fingers.

"Where are your gloves?"

"Adaptation," he insisted, wiggling his bare fingers at me. "I thought your Dad would be taller."

That was an easy guess, considering how short I was. "If you're going to convince me, you're going to have to do better than that, Jonah."

"Later, maybe, when you're ready," he said softly.

"Right, okay, later."

He leaned over me and before I realized what he was doing, he kissed my blue lips with his blue mouth, his face so close to mine that the portraits were eye-to-eye with me. I started to push away, then changed my mind, but I accidentally flipped his hood back up over his head and snow poured out of it, showering us with clumpy wetness.

I spit snow from my mouth. "Sorry, I didn't mean to do that."

"Again then?"

"Uh, sure."

When we broke away, he asked, "Was my kiss as good as Randy Beamer's kiss?"

"What? How? Hey, that was in grade school for cripes sake, but how did you know about that?"

He gave me a knowing look, then quickly shook his head, scattering snow and water drops, his bejeweled locks clinking together the bits and pieces of his ancestors' lives, if he was telling the truth.

"Come on, answer, how'd you know?"

He only asked, without answering, "Again? A kiss?"

"Again? Wasn't that enough?" He looked hurt, and I wasn't willing to explain that it had been too inviting. I touched his arm and, almost without thinking, asked. "Want to go to a dance with me?"

"Wouldn't I be too conspicuous?"

"It's a costume ball. Your tattoos'll be the perfect costume. Do you want to go?"

He nodded, turned without warning to kiss me again before furiously going back to packing snow. "By the way, Zeyya, how old was Randy Beamer when he stole that kiss?"

"Nine," I whispered, wondering how he had known Randy's name when I barely remembered it myself.

" ...such is [the children's] physical grace...that they make all simple exercises and rhythm...a feat of the utmost beauty."

Ethel Mannin, British Novelist, early 1954
Mandalay School of Fine Arts

The first record of Burmese dance is in 800 A.D. The songs of that time were Buddhist, but the dance was flavored by Indian influences. Over the years, the movements of marionettes, and the Thai Yodaya style blended into Burma's dance. The plots of some of the story dances (zats) are based on the Indian Ramayana tales; others are taken from Burmese history; and still other plots are drawn from the early life of Buddha.

June 4, 1958

Rangoon

Dear Mother,

You should see your youngest granddaughter in a Burmese golden cardboard headdress of the sort worn by a little girl at her ear-boring ceremony. I took pictures, but can't get my color slides developed until we get back to the U.S. Jospehine gave Susie the headdress to do her Burmsese dances in, and also many, many trinkets. She gave Sis a doll and many trinkets. Sebastian brings Susie chains of jasmine flowers to drape in her hair every day. They give off the sweetest perfume. Sis thinks the Burmese have the best customs. Here, the younger sister waits on the older sister hand and foot. Despite the custom, Susie simply won't participate.

I have written to you before about the political upheavel going on. During WWII, the various political parties combined to try to win independence for Burma. The coalition was called the Anti Facist Peoples' Freedom League—AFPFL. It has persisted to this day, but now there are two wings which are breaking apart. There has been a lot of name calling and a special meeting of Parliment has been called for tomorrow to decide the issue. The present Prime Minister accuses the other side of being dishonest, and the other side accuses the Prime Minister of using Gestapo tactics, which we don't see, but there may be some truth to both sides. We'll be watching the outcome curiously.

Love,

Jack

The Greater East Coast Consolidated Metropolis: 2047
[If you are a legitimately registered voter, please be sure to update your address. You may not vote in a district you have left. Many important issues are on the referendums for the next bi-monthly votes. Please re-register.]

[Warning: Re-registration at new residences for voting may result in Quarantine. We are noticing a direct statistical correlation. WARNING: Please Beware]
Subterranean Net site

We walked down the hill until we spotted the sled covered by an icy layer of snow, it's red runners crying out in distress where it had slammed forlornly against a spindly sapling. We gathered it up, amazed that it wasn't even scratched and trudged back. Jonah took the sled rope in one hand, clasped my hand in the other and hauled us up the hill. As we came to the top, he shook the hood free of snow, before yanking it back over his head. Kids were still sliding safely down the neighboring hill.

"Let's go home," I suggested.

"Sure. Hop on. I'll pull you."

The sled sailed along smoothly. He sped up, slowed down, made serpentine curves, until I scooped up another mitten-full of snow and smacked him with it. Our laughter cut across the muffled streets. Granna stood at the window as we arrived at the house. She flung the door wide and ushered us in. "You're soaked through, blue with cold!" she exclaimed.

"Well, I'm blue from the cold. Jonah is just plain blue, Granna."

"Hot showers, both of you. I'll make tea."

Jonah shed his already soggy clothes and ran for the bathroom, while I tugged off boots, gloves, hat, coat, still stiff with encrusted ice, until I got down to brittle pants and shirt.

"Can I use your shower, Granna?"

She nodded. I scurried down the hall. As I passed the other bathroom and heard the water of Jonah's shower, I had a vivid flash of him running on a dry river bed, Jo-Boys trailing behind him, Jo-Boys streaking ahead of him. He bent to pat the dogs, whispering to each one. The mirage dissolved, leaving me in the hall.

Back into the kitchen, dry and warmer after the shower, soup steamed in bowls on the counter. Jonah, still mopping at his hair with a towel, had wrapped a small blanket longyi-style around his waist, but wore only his tattoos across his chest, over his back, down his arms.

"Aren't you cold?" I asked him.

"No."

"Natural adaptation, right?"

"Yes."

"You two looked like cats a Jo-Boy dragged in," Granna commented. The dog's ears pricked up at the sound of its name. "We came home drenched like that from the Water Festival at Burmese New Year. What's your explanation?"

"We got tipped into a deep drift," Jonah explained.

"Was it fun?" She didn't wait for an answer. "That sled is an heirloom. Sis and I took turns riding it with our Daddy, and your Mum rode it with your grandfather. I offered it to your father for you, Zeyya, but he got you the Arrow."

I had a brief flare of anger at my father before I took comfort in the image of Mum on the sled, clasped in my grandfather's arms. "Can I have the Flier for my kids, Granna?"

Her mouth raised itself into a happy arc. "And how about you, Jonah, will you let me give you some things to string into your hair?"

"You wish me to add you to my heritage?" he asked.

"I thought of it as bequeathing you a remembrance of me and Burma."

The bells by his ears tingled lightly as he fingered them. "I'd be honored to accept your gift."

She plunked a wooden box down in front of him as she flipped it open. Inside, buttons and charms carved from mother of pearl and ivory gleamed against the wood. Chains of elephants hauling logs, boats full of fishermen, spread-tailed peacocks, people obviously dancing lay in pools of their own reflected light. I fingered a strange beast I didn't recognize.

"That's a chinthe, a leogryph. It guards the gates of pagodas, saying goodbye when visitors leave, keeping bad spirits out to begin with."

I put the half-lion beast back in the box. Jonah picked out all the elephants and I watched blue reflections from his fingers sprinkle themselves over the mother of pearl. Then he picked out a dancing figure and let it hang near his bells.

"Granna, can you teach me to dance like this?"

"Only if you can stretch your fingers backwards from the joint where they meet your hands. Yes, like that, that's good, Jonah, very good! Now the thing to remember is that this particular Burmese dance was influenced by marionettes, so every time your hand moves in one direction, your head has to follow, as if hands and head are connected to one string. Like this." She showed us, bending her knobby hands in the requisite fashion.

"Granna, do you think you should be dancing?" I asked nervously.

"We won't know until I try. I was never rhythmical, but I was always agile. I might be the most flexible dancer from my Burmese dance class."

"Wouldn't everyone from the class be almost one-hundred, or maybe older?"

"That's a point, Zeyya—not much competition in that. I might even be the only one left. Back then, when I think about it, our teacher must have found all of us a frightful lot. Five little awkward American girls in sleeveless shirts and shorts, standing around trying to imitate her grace as she danced in silken longyi and sheer angyi to the rhythm of a putma drum."

"Can you teach me before the dance at Zeyya's school, Granna?"

"What dance at Zeyya's school?"

"What?" I asked almost simultaneously with her. "Oh no, no Burmese dancing at my school!"

Granna bypassed her first question to ask me, "Then what dance are you going to teach him to dance?"

"The only dances Zeyya knows are things like Line-Spasming," Jonah announced before I could answer.

"Burmese dance is better than that," Granna said with a laugh.

"Line-Spasming is the *in* thing, Jonah."

He made a face.

"I'll teach both of you," Granna offered.

"No way!" I turned to Jonah. "How did you know about Line-Spasming? Do they do it on your world?"

He smiled and I felt the jolt as we fell again.

"No harm in having choices," Granna insisted. "You can teach him your dances and I'll teach him a Burmese dance. And by the way, what dance are you going to?"

"The annual costume ball at school. And his tattoos are his costume," I explained.

"And what are you going as?"

"Uh, I've got..." I stopped. My costume was in Quarantine. I had nothing to wear.

"I have the perfect solution," Granna announced excitedly. "After I teach you to dance, you can go as a Burmese dancer, Zeyya."

"I'm not going as someone from Burma!"

"But you could say your mother and father sent the costume to you," Jonah suggested.

"No!" The dance was rapidly becoming a nightmare.

"Zeyya," Jonah said, following me as I fled into the living room, "I know you wanted to go with Alejandro, you as Guinevere, he as Lancelot, but you can't do that now, so maybe Granna has a good idea."

"I'm not going as anyone from Burma," I answered weakly just as Granna came in, little wooden clappers in one hand beating out a flat cadence. A peaked hat encrusted in gold paper and sprinkled with metallic glitter, small wings sprouting from the sides, perched precariously on her head.

Granna chanted in a creaky voice. "Top beato beaa, top beato beaa, beaa beaa top, beaa top, beaa top!" Still chanting and beating the clapper, she pushed her feet out, heel first, toes up, turning her head from side-to-side as first one foot, then the other followed in like step—heel, heel, heel. Slowly, she lowered her body towards the ground and just as she got down to where I was sure she would slip, managed to shakily raise herself back up.

Jonah had moved behind her, following along with his feet, while protectively keeping his hands out, clearly expecting her to fall.

"There, now you both know how to do it," she proclaimed as she completed a last series of movements before plopping the golden hat onto my head. "This is part of the costume, if you want to borrow it."

"Actually, well, uh…" I ran out of stammers and just stopped speaking as I looked at her expectant face. "It's lovely, Granna, uh…"

"If you have another idea, why that's fine, Zeyya," she said magnanimously, but with obvious disappointment.

Jonah looked reprovingly at me as Granna left, the hat hanging loosely from her hand.

"Granna," I called, catching up to her. "It's just, you know, well…"

"I understand, Zeyya. It's alright. I want you to be happy."

"Let me think about it, okay?"

"Just let me know."

I went into Mum's room and stared into the mirror. Jonah came in, reached around me and strung a little elephant in a lock of my hair. I watched him in the mirror as he left the room, then fingered the strange charm as I imagined myself blue faced, a touch of pale line lying near my ear.

Burmese Phrases

English: Good Morning, Good Afternoon,
        Good Day, Goodnight
Burmese: Closest Equivalent—"Nay kaung yai-lar?"
        or "Mar-bar-ye-la?"
        Meaning "How do you do?"

English: Good Bye
Burmese: Closest Equivalent—"Thwa lite par own mai"
        Meaning"Please excuse me for leaving."

English: Mrs./Madam
Burmese: Daw or Daw Daw

English: Mister
Burmese: U [for elderly gentleman]
        Maung [for young men]

October 27, 1958

Dear Mama.

Both girls went to Halloween parties and both won prizes for originality for the costumes I made. Sis and her friend went as a señorita and a toreador. Sis wore my old white pique evening dress and I attached a tiered slip of hers as the ruffles around the bottom and a slip of Susie's served as the mantilla on her head. She wore a scarf of mine and carried a Japan Airline fan. She was darling. We lent her friend a black bolero and fancy pants. Her mom had a sequined tie for her collar and used one of her dad's red ties at her waist and a red apron as the bullfighter's cape. They were so cute, and their friends didn't even recognize the masked "couple".

To one party, Susie wore a full black slip of mine, an orange crêpe paper top hat and sash, and carried a crêpe paper covered cardboard piece on which I stood all of her paper dolls that had costumes. On her hat was a sign— "Miss Halloween Parade"—and on a corner of the board base was a street sign "Main and First." She was so cute, and we took pictures. To the other contest, she went as a Red Cross nurse. Of course, the leaves are all still green here, and children don't go from door to door collecting candy. Burma has no equivalent to Halloween, but they have many spirits in the form of many, many "Nats". Must go say goodnight to the girls.

Love,

Blanche

Greater East Coast Metropolis: 2047
[As the nights of School Celebration and Balls approach, we
issue our annual warning of caution. Do not go to Celebration
alone, stay in groups, remember, many of the homeless
and displaced wander the streets these days searching for
sustenance, money and clothing from any vulnerable sources.]

By the next morning, they had turned on the under-street heaters
to clear the roads and walkways. My arms were tired and bruised from our
flying fall into the snow and I wanted to stay scrunched into the toastiness
of my covers, but the brief school holiday was over. Lucky Jonah—he could
sleep in without consequences.

Granna padded around the kitchen in soft-soled slippers and her fuzzy
robe, her snowy hair released from its usual braid to cascade down her back.
"Good morning. Toast at your place." I sat. She sat across from me, staring
until I looked up.

"What?"

"I'm thinking of getting a family portrait tattooed Jonah-style in
the middle of my forehead." She slapped a handful of old photos down
on the table. "Which one should I choose for it? Here's one of Daddy
in his swim trunks. Or Mommy in her oh-so-perfectly-ladylike pose, skirt
spread precisely across her legs, fanning onto the sofa? Or this one of my
grandfather? Oh, oh, here's U Tun Kin and his daughter!"

"Someone in our family was named Ew?"

"U—spelled with just the letter U. It means mister in Burmese.
He wasn't part of our family. But see me? That little girl? Those flowers
hanging in my hair are jasmine. You should smell jasmine! So sweet, so
sweet!" She breathed in deeply. "When I was nine, I wanted to name my
future daughter Jasmine." She placed the old photo gently on top of the
others. Before I could look at it closely, she exclaimed with delight, "Oh,
lookie here at this one! It's the snake and the tactoo!"

I looked up. "There's no tattoo in that picture!"

"Not tattoo! Tactoo—a kind of lizard. Look at him, he was a big
one!" I looked but the picture was so small, I could barely distinguish the

252

lizard from the snake coiled around it. "We had eleven poisonous snakes in our compound and nine that weren't poisonous, not that I could tell the difference by looking at them. This one wasn't dangerous, but see the servants' legs, there? They were at the ready with machetes, not taking any chances." She rubbed the photo with the ball of her thumb. "Everybody was nervous. Two days before, the durwan had killed a snake that had crawled onto Than Swe's head while he was sleeping."

"A snake?" My skin crawled.

She tapped the photo where it lay. "This is a picture of a fight to the death."

"The snake won, right?"

"Don't be so sure. Tactoos are wily. Of course, snakes are stronger. Of course, lizards are slippery."

"Okay, okay, what happened? Come on, just tell me."

"Daddy ran, got his camera and snapped picture after picture after picture of the two combatants."

"Granna! What happened to the lizard? Did the snake eat it? Wait, don't tell me, I don't want to know!"

Granna picked up the picture and waved it in front of my nose. "Zeyya, you have to let me tell you."

"I'll throw up, I swear it."

"There's nothing to throw up about. Snakes swallow their food whole. No blood, no gore—it's very clean."

"Granna," I protested, "stop!"

"Just trust me—you'll like the ending." She patted my shoulder and continued. "The snake wrapped itself around the tactoo and after a whole lot of tail thrashing, the lizard went limp."

"See, I told you so!"

"Shush up, let me finish! The snake unwound, ready to devour its victim, but the minute it loosened its coils, the wily Tactoo, who had only been playing possum, sprang into action and ran for the jungle."

"It escaped?"

She nodded. "But the servants chopped the snake up with their machetes anyway, for good measure."

I raced for the bathroom. By the time I came out, Granna was telling Jonah about another snake, a king cobra living in the banana tree in their side yard. I didn't listen. I went in another room until she came looking for me.

"You weren't serious about getting a tattoo, were you, Granna?"

"No. Come on, now, come finish your breakfast or you'll be late for school."

I munched on my toast, staring at the photos that were turned face up on the table. I pointed. "Who's that?"

"No time, now. You have to hurry," Granna urged. "And don't come in looking like you've been hit by a fire hose again. No frolicking in the snow today."

Out on the hills, the bare tree limbs were still hung with a lacy crust of ice that blurred their lines to featheriness in the unnatural cold snap. Out on the hills, the sun reflected blindingly off the snow, but the streets were warm and dry underfoot and not a speck of snow or ice remained on them anywhere. The city was never allowed to stop for long. School was abuzz between the snow holiday and the impending dance, and everyone had a hard time paying attention.

Last period, Mr. Jaster came into the room. "I'm subbing for the day."

Whispers floated from kid to kid. Mr. Jaster? He didn't know anything about music. Where was Mr. P? Finally Tracey raised her hand and shouted, "Where's Mr. P?"

"Uh, he didn't come in today."

"We can see that," someone snickered.

"Quiet down. I found a quiz he planned to give." He passed it out. "Please do your best."

"Is he coming back tomorrow?"

"I hope so. Now please, quiet down, pick up your pencils and begin."

I nibbled on the eraser as I read the quiz. This was old. We'd done it two weeks ago. What was going on? I filled in the answers and turned it in. "Where is he?" I whispered.

He evaded answering by countering with, "Is there any news from your parents?"

"Some. Mr. Jaster, what happened to Mr. P?"

He wouldn't meet my eyes.

"Quarantined?"

He didn't answer, but he didn't say no either. My stomach sank. Mr. Pompandow? Gone? I ran from the room and into the girls bathroom where Marilyn was brushing hard at her hair, muttering at her reflection, "Got to look good for Willie."

I slammed a stall door and sobbed. Gone? Taken?

"What's the matter, Zeyya?"

"Leave me alone," I managed to say. It wasn't until I was washing my hands and face, and rinsing my mouth out from the tap that I remembered, Mr. P had my only complete copy of the concerto.

I started for home, my head low, asking myself what I would do if they came for us. Run? To where? Did Granna have enough money to bribe them to leave us alone? Did they take bribes? Who was the famous 'they'? Was I safer on a road crew? But they wouldn't be likely to want a smallish girl on a crew. What good would I be digging ditches and laying walkways? I wiggled my fingers to break the train of thought, but I couldn't get rid of the numbness that was crawling from my fingertips up my arms, or the tears that kept welling in my eyes. Mr. P!

A collection of Jo-Boys, who waited for me a block from the school, sniffed at my heels all the way home. Jonah was standing on the porch in the cold. As soon as they saw him, the Jo-Boys broke into a yowling cry. Granna came running onto the porch, umbrella ready in hand. As soon as they saw her, they sat where they were and silenced their voices, tongues hanging out.

"That's better," she admonished them.

"How'd you do that?" I asked glumly.

"I have absolutely no idea."

Jonah bent down, went from Jo-Boy to Jo-Boy, whispering to each one, reassuring them I supposed. He looked up at me. "What's the matter, Zeyya?"

"Mr. Pompandow was taken." I burst into tears.

He straightened up. "I'm sorry!"

I wiped at my eyes. "He has my concerto."

He wrapped me in a gentle hug, which made me cry harder. I pushed away and ran into the house. Nobody was safe, no place was safe, they'd find us, too. It was only a matter of time. They'd come in the night, they'd seal the house and even if we found a place to hide—in the basement, in the attic, we'd be sealed in, with no way out. We'd die inside when our food ran out. I kicked the nearest thing to me.

"Zeyya! Don't kick my furniture. It isn't its fault."

"Why? Why do they take people?"

Granna shook her head. I looked to Jonah. He didn't answer either. At last, as if from far away, I heard Granna say, "Something always comes for you, Zeyya. Nobody lives forever."

"Except in memory," Jonah said.

I shuffled towards my room. "Not now, please, Jonah," I whispered, closed my door and lay down in the dark.

<table>
</table>

Thiri Pyanchi U Hpu

and

Daw Khin Myint Myint

request the pleasure of

Mr. & Mrs. **Jack Steiner's** company

at the reception to be held on the occasion of

the marriage of their son

Maung Myint Hpu

to

Naw Jennifer Dwe

daughter of

Dr. S. M. Dwe & Daw Sein

on Sunday the 15th. February 1959

between 11 a.m. and 1 p.m.

at the "Strand Hotel"

Rangoon.

ထိမ်းမြားမင်္ဂလာဩိတ်ကြားစာ

ရန်ကုန်မြို့၊ ကြည့်မြင်တိုင်အောက်လမ်းအမှတ် ၅၁၅ နေ
ဆရာဝန်–ဦးဌေး နှင့် ဒေါ်ဝိန်တို့၏သွေး

နော်ဂျင်နီဖာဒွေး

ကို

ရန်ကုန်မြို့၊ ပွတ်တလစ်လမ်း၊ အမှတ် ၉ နေ၊
ဓမ္မယာကျေးလက်ကြီးပွားတိုးတက်ရေးကော်ပိုရေးရှင်း
စပါးဌာနအမှုဆောင်အရာရှိချုပ်
သိရိပျံချီ–ဦးဖူးနှင့်ဒေါ်ခင်မြင့်မြင့်တို့၏သား

မောင်မြင့်ဖူး

နှင့်

ဒိဘတို့ဝတ္ထရားရှိသည့်အတိုင်း၊ ထိမ်းမြားမင်္ဂလာပြုလုပ်မည်ဖြစ်ပါ၍
၁၃၂၀ ခုတပို့တွဲလဆန်း ၈ ရက်၊၁၉၅၉ ခု–ဖေဖော်ဝါရီလ ၁၅ ရက်
တနင်္ဂနွေနေ့နံက် ၁၁ နာရီမှ ၁ နာရီအတွင်း
ကန်းနားလမ်း "စထရင်းဟော်တယ်" သို့မင်္ဂလာညှည်ပွဲ
ကြရောက်ချီးမြှင့်ပါရန်–လေးမြတ်စွာ
ဩိတ်ကြားအပ်ပါသည်၊

With us, family ties are always very strong…most Burmese
have a warmhearted desire for as many relatives as possible,
including cousins and in-laws. Our word for "relative"
has the same root as the one for "friend".

<u>People of the Golden Land</u>
by Daw Mi Khaing
Perspective of Burma
The **Atlantic** Supplement, 1958

*(DECEMBER 1957) **FIRST DRAFT ITINERARY:***

For Mr. and Mrs. Jack Steiner and daughters,

Susannah and Louisa

Sat. Jan 31,1958: Lv Wash, American Airlines #201
(DC-6) 7:10 pm, arrive Nashville, 9:00 pm, non-stop.
Visiting grandparents

Fri Feb 6,1958: Depart Nashville, Eastern Airlines
#260 (Convair) 12:30 pm,arrive St. Louis 2:08 pm,
non-Stop Visiting Mrs. Steiner's sister

Sat, Feb 7,1958: Depart St. Louis, TWA # 95
(Jet Stream) 4:10 pm, arrive Los Angeles 8:37 pm.
Visiting Mr. Steiner's brother. Staying in Statler
Hotel

Sun Feb 8,1958: Pan Am #833 (Super Strato Clipper)
Two Berths 11:59 pm, arrive Honolulu 8:50 am. Sun,
Feb 9th to Wed Feb 11th: Edgewater Hotel, Honolulu

Wed. Feb 11, 1958: Depart Honolulu Pan Am #5 (Super
Strato Cruiser) 9:45 pm. Arrive Tokyo Friday Feb. 13
at 12:15 pm after crossing International Dateline.
Fri. Feb 13 to Saturday Feb 16: Imperial Hotel, Tokyo.

Sat. Feb.16,1958: Depart Tokyo JAL 705 (DC-6B) 11:59pm.
Arrive Hong Kong 7:14 am. Sun. Feb 16 to Wed.
Feb 19: Peninsular Hotel, Hong Kong.

Wed, Feb 19,1958: Depart Hong Kong. Pan Am 11 (Super
onstellation) 10:55 am. Arrive Bangkok, Thailand
2:30 pm. Wed Feb 19 to Friday Feb 22: Metropol Hotel
in Bangkok

Sat Feb 21,1958: Depart Bangkok, BOAC 793, 8:40 am.
Arrive Rangoon, Burma 9:50 am

Greater East Coast Consolidated Metropolis: 2047
[New strain of influenza is sweeping the city. Pills available
at local sanitation stations. Easy to take. No side effects.
Instant and complete relief.]

"I'm not going back to school. I'm sick," I announced at breakfast the day after they Quarantined Mr. Pompandow.

Granna stuck her chin into my face. "You're going, Zeyya!"

"Why bother? They might as well just come and take me now."

"Oh, for goodness sake!"

"There's no point to going back."

"You'll miss the dance, Zeyya. Isn't it day after tomorrow?"

I gave her a dirty look. "I'm not going back."

She shook her head. "Then I'll have to call the social worker and tell her you're a drop-out."

"What? You wouldn't do that!"

She didn't answer. She plopped a bag lunch on the table and said, "You're going."

Something in the way she said it made me pick the lunch up and sulk off to get ready. I stuffed everything except my violin into my pack—no point in bringing it. By the time I got to school, the bell had rung and I had to run without going to my locker to make it to PE on time. Tracey and Marilyn were waiting by the door for me, shifting nervously, foot-to-foot.

"What's wrong?"

"Half the school is out. Nobody knows why."

"Protesting," Tracey said, "I bet."

"Quarantined," Marilyn guessed.

"The flu, maybe?" Alejandro came up and suggested.

"Just get in your gym clothes," I told them. Whatever it was, we weren't going to solve it. I ran laps most of the period. We had a meet in less than two weeks and I was still out of shape. But that matched the world. It was out of shape, too. Warped. Pulled. Distorted. I showered quickly. Nobody liked the showers at school. No privacy. No chance to enjoy the water or let it really soothe sore muscles. All we did was dash through the prickly drip, covering ourselves as best we could. I was in my underwear, clothes, grabbing my backpack and out before the dismissal bell even rang. Each period brought me closer to orchestra, closer to dread. And then it was time.

Of the kids who were there, no one spoke. Someone had pasted a holo of Mr. Pompandow on the board. We were all early, sitting in memorial silence to our teacher until the door opened and the secretary came in.

"Your sub is late. Mr. Jaster asked me to hand out a few things we found in Mr. Pompandow's desk. Please come up when I call your names."

I slumped into my seat. The stack of papers was slight. I watched the sheets pass from hand to hand.

"Zeyya."

She handed me a thick brown envelope. I peaked in. My concerto! Hugging it tightly, I breathed a sigh of relief. The woman left and we sat in continued silence. We were in mourning. The minutes ticked by until at last, we all just got up and left, huddled close to each other, arms linked, one to the next. Tracey on my left clutched me tightly. "It isn't right," she murmured. When we got to the door, the chain of hands broke and we scattered, each to go home—to what? To wait for the pounding on our doors, the inevitable yellow tape? But not everyone was taken. And did we know for sure that Mr. Pompandow was quarantined, or had he simply not shown up for work? Maybe he'd escaped. To where? Burma?

By the time I got home, all I wanted was to open the envelope that lay between the books in my backpack. I went in the back door, hoping that Granna wouldn't be in the kitchen. Jo-Boy and Belissima looked up at me as I snuck in and quietly sat down. The envelope burned in my hands. On the front was a note. "Better. Needs a little more work."

That was fair. Mainly I wanted to know that it was all there. While I spread it out, Jonah came in. "You got it back?"

"It was in his desk. They returned it to me, but the last movement is missing."

"That's okay."

"No, it isn't. I'll never remember how it was set up."

I got up to get a drink, but a sound made me swing around. Jonah was humming the end of the concerto, each part separately from the other: oboe, viola, drums, triangle, the wail of the horn.

"How? No, no, don't tell me! Just do it again. I'll write it as you hum. Then you can explain."

We worked for a long time, ate sandwiches for dinner, and worked on it after Granna said her goodnights. It was tedious, but when we were done, there it all was, restored to its original composition.

"Now," I said, turning to him, "how?"

"Promise you won't be mad? Okay, then, I looked at it when you were gone one day, but I couldn't quite hear it, so I went to Uncle Lem and he, uh, 'hummed' the parts for me. Once something is shared in access, it is never forgotten."

I shook my head, sending loose strands of my hair across my face. "You know what, I don't care. I really don't. Thank you."

"You believe me?"

"It doesn't matter." I kissed him on the cheek. "Thank you, that's all."

"But..."

"No, I don't want to ruin this! I'm going to bed."

Sleep. Welcome sleep. Dreams. I couldn't remember them in the morning, except that music had filtered through them, rising and falling with my rise and fall of consciousness.

In the morning, as I walked to school, my hair whipped at my face and thunderheads flew across the sky, and although the clouds had vanished by the time I got to school, the wind still howled, tearing at whatever got in its way, blowing us into the building, our hair tangled, our cheeks ruddy, forcing us to rearrange ourselves before we started the day. Everyone was excited about the dance and chatter filled the halls. Not as many kids were out sick with colds, which was all it had been. Only in orchestra did Mr. P's presence hang on. Everywhere else, he was already a flickering memory.

"So do you have someone to hang with at the Ball?" Tracey asked. Marilyn was standing near her, Willie virtually growing from her side.

"Uh, yes, but a costume—that I'm still working on."

"Who're you coming with?"

"The boy you met when we were sledding, Marilyn. Jonah."

"Oh, yeah Well, does he have a costume?"

"Absolutely," I said readily as I parted company with Marilyn, thinking to myself, he can come as himself. I spent the time on the way home mulling over what I could be. It was too late for anything elaborate. I nearly tripped over Bellisima stretched out on the first step of the porch in a single patch of sunlight.

"Sorry." She arched her back so I rubbed the spot above her tail which made her purr with delight. Straightening up, I found Granna at the door, holding it for me.

"Was school better today, Zeyya?"

"I guess. Granna, would you be upset if I fake tattooed myself and went as Jonah's mirror image to the dance tonight?"

Without a word, she let the door close behind her and disappeared into the house. Almost immediately, Jonah appeared at the door, munching crackers, encouraging Jo-Boy to lap up the crumbs with its tongue. He thumbed back the way Granna had gone. "I think she's upset."

I was about to capitulate and tell Granna I'd go as a Burmese dancer, when she reappeared clutching a stack of photos and holographs, a package of blue pens and eye-liner pencils, and a shoe box.

"Come on, you two. You've got a lot of work to do."

We hurried after her into my bedroom.

"Sit on the bed, Zeyya. These," she said, patting the photos, "are your ancestors. Now then, Jonah, will you do the honors?"

"What?"

"Zeyya wants to be tattooed for the costume ball. Here." She thrust the blue pens and the eye-liner pencils into his surprised hands.

"I'm not a scriber. What if I make a mistake?"

"It'll wash off," Granna assured him.

"But your ancestors will be offended if the likenesses aren't true," he declared.

Granna said, "I promise they won't be. You'd better get started."

"Is there time for me to cover her?"

"Here now! Only the hands, face and feet. Keep your paws off the rest of her, and while you start that, I'll string her hair." I heard her mutter under her breath, "And chaperone."

She lifted the lid off the shoe box, which brimmed with jewelry. Old rings inscribed on inner surfaces with dates of marriage. Silver pendants. Loops of gold earrings. Glass beads from broken necklaces. Each time she knotted one in my hair she announced what it was. "Mayan face. Aztec sun calendar. Venetian glass bead. Mexican turtle. Chinese panda. Antique citrine drop. One Peruvian gold earring. You're wearing my life history, Zeyya—don't lose any of it."

"Better for her to wear it than for it to be hidden in a box," Jonah said as he picked up a photo. "Which is the eldest person among these?"

"Him." Granna pointed to a peeling metal plate. "That's my great, great, great grandfather Samuel."

An intense-eyed, white-haired gentleman with a long straight nose and high cheekbones, emphasized by the tight horizontal line of his mouth, peeked from behind the flaking surface.

"He's first then," Jonah said. I felt the pencil begin, sharp lines, short strokes. He drew in the very center of my forehead. "The oldest always goes here," he explained. "Now who's next?"

"Does it have to be chronological?" Granna inquired.

"No."

"Then here's Sis." Granna pointed out a dark haired girl with eyes like coals and white skin, standing beside an older woman. "And that's my mother with her on our lawn in Burma. Look how civilized that lawn looks."

"Very nice, Granna."

"Nice? That shows how well you've been listening, Zeyya. Snakes? Wildcats? Chimpanzees? That's nice?"

"Don't move your mouth while I draw on your cheek," Jonah instructed when I started to speak.

He frowned at me sternly when I tried to keep my mouth immobile at the same time I slurred out the question, "Chimpanzees?"

"You stay still and I'll tell you about it. Our servants got a chimp from the servants of the German family who lived one house below us on the hill. Sis and I had always thought chimps were like Cheeta in Tarzan. Oh, you two probably don't know who Tarzan is, but that's a longer story. Got to watch those references with your generation. In any case, we thought chimps were cute, clever, mischievous, and almost human."

"What does a chimp look like?" Jonah asked.

I rolled my eyes because it was the only part of me I was allowed to move, but Granna answered unphased, "Hairy." She paused, closing her eyes as if to look at something. "Big. When it stretched it was nearly as big as nine-year-old me. And it smelled—musty yucky." She crinkled her nose up. "The servants chained it to our flag pole, which made it race frantically first in one direction, then the other until, each time, the chain brought it up short."

Granna chatted on as Jonah drew on my face in what felt like ever increasing detail. "It spent most of its time racing round and round that flag pole. Round about one way, then round about the other."

Jonah winced. "Why didn't you set it free?"

"Me? Oh no, I wasn't going near it! That chimp hissed, snarled and spit. It hit Ba Kyi square between the eyes with a glob of spit when he got too close." She stabbed at the middle of her own forehead with her thumb. She stopped talking for a minute when Jonah picked up a new photo, then her face lit up and she asked, "How about a drawing of the chimp on her arm some place?"

"Only ancestors," Jonah answered, much to my relief.

"Darn it."

"Do you have a picture of it?" I asked while Jonah chose the model for the next tattoo.

"No. Never got a chance to take a snapshot. One day it was gone. I knew something was wrong because I didn't wake to the chain clanking up against the pole. Josephine told us a wild cat ate it in the night, but I knew that couldn't be right. Daddy told us later that he'd made the servants return it to the Germans."

"There, " Jonah said, stepping away from me, "your sister and your mother, Granna. What do you think?"

"Are you done? It tickles when you draw," I complained, but Granna was crossing in front of me, looking at me from all sides.

She put her face up to my cheek where Jonah had just drawn. "Sis? Mommy? You look so real!" she addressed them, almost touching the lines. I saw water gather in the corners of her eyes. "I'm going to lie down. Call me when you're done. Here's a picture of Daddy, and here, of Mommy's father and there's my Daddy's daddy. I'll be back," she said, tapping the three photos. She wiped at her right eye with one fingertip.

Jonah's eyes never left the drawings as he worked. It seemed to be taking forever and my mind began to wander. I found myself in Burma, a pastiche of palm trees and blue skies, golden spires and longyied young men, tubular skirts pulled through their legs as they leaped across green lawns chasing cane balls. The image blurred, faded to blue and congealed into the image of a small boy sitting calmly before a blue-faced tattooist. Expressions played across the child's face while the tattooist murmured, "Maria, Harry and now Elija." I could see several pairs of eyes already in place on the child's face, Maria's in the very middle of his forehead. The child's blue eyes blinked and stared full-on into mine. I felt the pencil begin to draw across my eyebrows, as I saw the tattooist's hand on the eyebrows of the child.

"Zeyya," Jonah whispered very quietly as I opened my eyes, "you're beautiful!"

"Maria," I murmured, reaching out and touching a tattoo.

He nodded. "Yes, but come, look at my handiwork. See how you like it."

I rose slowly to the mirror. Staring back at me were faces I didn't know, covering the one I did. "Wow, what a great mask!"

"I'll do your hands and then we'd better get dressed. It's late."

"No one will recognize me, Jonah."

Granna called to us from down the hall. "I'm up, Jonah, Zeyya! Oh my, I've slept too long. I'll fix a quick supper."

"Sure," I called back, "but don't come in. I want to surprise you."

Jonah drew tiny faces and bodies on my hands. Across the palms, old faces appeared that wrinkled and laughed when I bent my fingers. "Oh, this is perfect!" I cried and kissed him on the cheek. He shifted slightly to kiss me lightly on the lips.

"Enough now, go get dressed, get ready, go!" I flung open my closet and my stomach fell. I had nothing special to wear with my new face.

"Zeyya, I won't come in, but I have something for you. It's hanging on the doorknob," Granna called through the closed door. I heard her footsteps retreat down the hall as I cracked the door and reached around for whatever she had left. I tore off the paper that covered the hanger and in my hand shimmered a gold jacket woven in luxurious silken threads. Underneath hung a golden blouse and a loose-fitting pair of matching pants.

"Granna?" I yelled down the hall without coming out.

"What?" she yelled back.

"Where'd this come from?"

"Mommy bought the material in Japan and had it made up by a Burmese tailor who lived on a narrow street of tilting teak huts. When we went to pick it up, little children ran to us, laughing and chortling, their palms out for money, while bigger ones toted half-naked babies on their swung-out hips." I could hear her voice approaching me as she spoke. "One last thing." She handed me something through the crack in the door. My hand closed around a strand of gems, set into a delicately undulating wave of silver. At the peak of each wave dangled a gemstone of a different color.

"Daddy had that made in Burma for his and Mommy's nineteenth anniversary. It's yours now, Zeyya." I heard her shuffle off down the hall before I could answer. I dressed, sucking in my breath when I looked in the mirror. I no longer recognized myself.

"We Burmese throng the movie theatres and…sit up till dawn watching an all-night pwè. Music and dance are part of our frequent festivals and family celebrations. But the truth is that the world of Burmese entertainment is now going through a period of rather chaotic transition. Our old theatre traditions are being discarded or watered down— and what is taking their place has yet no clear direction nor much artistic quality."

Burmese Entertainment
by U Myo Min
Perspective of Burma
An **Atlantic** Supplement, 1958

Rangoon, Sunday, May 8, 1958

Dear Mama,

We haven't had mail in weeks. The political situation here has everything in confusion and little gets done. Last night, Sis and her friend Sheila had a Rock-and-Roll dinner dance at our house. I made up this verse for the invitations:

> Your passage is booked,
> Your dinner is cooked,
> All aboard the Rock-and-Roll Ship!
> Travel at a fast clip
> Have a grand trip
> All aboard the Rock-and-Roll Ship!
> Embark at 58 B Golden Valley Road
> at 6:30 p.m.
> Disembark at 10 p.m.
> RSVP To Captain Louisa(Sis) or First Mate Sheila

They had twelve guests, multiplication dances, broom dances, statue dances, etc. Here the boys are expert dancers and Sis is the second best girl dancer, so you know the girls aren't so good. I think they had fun, but it probably cost us $15 American—PHEW. Next time they don't eat, just dance. I hope you get this letter. Who knows, with the mail as it is. Perhaps, you will never see it. But, if you do, could you share it with the rest of the family.

Love,

Blanche

The Greater East Coast Metropolis: 2047
[As the need for more housing increases, the Metropolis
must once again weigh the wisdom of retaining green space
between the original boundaries of cities. Is it necessary to
continue to observe antiquated demarcations of territorial
and historical borders? Some say aye, but we say nay.]

Oddly detached from reality by my costume, I walked slowly, slowly
to the kitchen. Two candles flickered on the table, and the unearthly hue of
Jonah's blueness, heightened by their glow, sent ghostly fingers running up
my arms. Granna rose from a chair, walked around me once, twice, came
up to my face and whispered, "Sis? Daddy? It's really you? Do you remember
the night you took us to the pagoda, Daddy? Do you? Remember how
the blue incense they burned twisted itself into the night sky? Remember
looking through the blue haze at the little golden-robed boys waiting to
be initiated into the priesthood, their faces so solemn. Do you recall the
huddled, twittering girls, drawn together by the ropes of blue smoke, tighter
and tighter? Do you? And do you remember the pongyi who handed me
that huge banana leaf fan to push the hot air away from us in the steamy,
heavy tropical night? Remember how they shaved the thick black hair off
the boys' heads, down to the skin until their polished scalps shimmered in
the moonlight? Remember how they draped the boys in the saffron robes
of priesthood, all those small nine-year-old boys? And the girls, dressed in
their finest, pushed forward for the ceremonial ear boring that declared
them women, ready for wifehood? Many married by fourteen, many dead
by twenty-eight. And Sis was already thirteen. Do you remember?"

"Granna," I said gently, "it's only a bunch of drawings."

"Oh," she said, "I thought it was my life. Is it, Jonah, only drawings?"

He didn't answer.

She walked up to me again and stared at each face. "My whole
family, my life, so small now, my life, my family. Take good care of her,
Jonah—I don't have much left." She shuffled slowly from the kitchen.

I couldn't shake the look on her face as we walked to the Ball. I bit
my lip and kept my eyes on my feet.

276

"What's the matter, Zeyya?" Jonah asked.

"Nothing, well, actually, I mean, did Granna seem different to you just now? The way she spoke to her family? I mean, did she seem..." I let it trail off.

He put his arm around me comfortingly. "It was just the effect of the drawings. They're powerful images."

"Maybe we should go back, Jonah. I'm not sure she should be alone."

He stroked my artifact-woven hair. "You don't need to worry. Memory is comforting." He guided me forward, reminding me of how beautiful I looked, promising me that Granna would be fine.

I hoped he was right, but I didn't have much time to think about it before we began to see other kids on the street. For Costume Ball Eve, a long-standing tradition at schools across the Metropolis, the streets were illuminated citywide late into the night. Air lights burned, floating above the walks all the way to my school auditorium. Some people were dropped off by fancy solar limousines. Others strolled in giggling groups. I was glad to be walking so I could see it all, reluctantly admitting to myself that I was also glad to have Jonah by my side.

"Who's that?" someone called out, pointing at a costumed figure sporting a plumed hat that stood close to four feet tall.

Jonah clasped my hand tightly. We saw Alejandro and Eileen strut by wing-in-wing, sequin-sprinkled feathers conspicuously plastered to flesh-toned skin-tights and all I could think was how much better our costumes were than theirs. I saw Jeremy saunter up as an Old West cowboy, all in black vinyl, belt studded in glass gemstones, an antique pistol slung into his waistband and authentic yellow-ochre leather boots on his feet. Wilamena and her hung-guy were a dragon, he the tail and rear paws, she the front half and wings. When she pressed a button the wings flapped. Pinky came as a glistening dragonfly. Marilyn was a queen in red silk and jewels and Willie was King Midas with a golden face. The glitter and display filled our auditorium-turned-ballroom until it was so crowded I thought it would boil over into the street.

"Who are you?" Pinky asked, putting her face right up to mine and jingling my hair with one finger. "Do you even go to school here? Or are you a crasher?"

"It's me. Zeyya. And this is my friend Jonah."

"Zeyya? Really? You guys are ever-awesome. Maybe you'll win the grand prize."

"Thanks, Pinky. See you later."

The music came up on the all-arounds. Kids paired off to do the Shimmer. Jonah stared, his eyes bright and blue, glowing cat-like in the dimmed lighting. "I could do that, Zeyya, but why would anyone want to?"

The next dance was slow and kids mainly clenched and swayed on the floor. "Okay, let's try this," Jonah suggested, but by the time we inched our way onto the floor, the music had slid into a Buzz-Buzzman and Jonah and I were trapped among flying arms punctuated by punching, balled fists.

Jonah put his arms around me and I could hear a purring rumble in his chest. We stood like that, surrounded by wild motion, frozen until the music finally paused. I shoved Jonah off the dance floor, but our seats were gone and the music was slow again.

He reached to me, pulled me into the sway of his body. We danced where we stood, he bent over, me on my tiptoes, our cheeks touching and sometimes our lips. In the background, over the real music, I started to hear notes to a new composition. It was lilting, peaceful, floating above the slow-waltzing bodies. The lights came up for a time out and everyone stood about blinking, except Jonah. His eyes were already focused, startlingly alert.

"Let's go out for some fresh air, Zeyya."

"Sure." I took his hand.

Just before we got out the door, Mr. Jaster grabbed my elbow. "I almost didn't recognize you, Zeyya. How are your parents?"

"Uh, fine."

"Are they coming home soon?"

I lied quickly, trying not to blink, trying to make the lie sound authentic. "They're helping put new gold leaf on the Shwedagon Pagoda. And then they've been asked to help treat the lepers."

"Interesting. You know what I got today? Transfer papers for you. Your parents were Quarantined last summer."

"Huh?" I was actually surprised that he didn't believe me. I had practiced the story so often in my mind, every time I saw Mr. Jaster in the halls, that I'd begun to believe it myself. They were in Burma, not in Quarantine.

"I talked to your social worker today. It's quite a little hoax you've pulled."

"I can explain. Please!"

"I'm sure you can and I'm sure you will, Monday in my office. Don't be late." He started to walk away, but turned at the last minute. "How'd you come up with Burma?"

"Her grandmother told us about it," Jonah replied.

Mr. Jaster turned his head towards Jonah. "Who are you?"

"A family friend," Jonah remembered to say.

"And you know about Burma, too, family friend?"

"Granna has been relating her childhood there to us."

"Unlikely, family friend. I looked it up. It hasn't officially been called Burma for over half-a-century, and very few ever traveled there. Is your grandmother okay, Zeyya?"

"She did live there!" I insisted angrily.

"We have a lot to discuss on Monday," he warned sternly as he stalked off.

"I want to go home now, Jonah! I should have told Mr. Jaster the truth right away. I should have known I'd get caught." I pushed my way through the crowd and dashed outside, gasping in the cold air over and over to try to clear my head, but still I felt like I was drowning. If I was lucky, I'd get transferred to a trade school or sent to a work crew and if I wasn't— Quarantine.

"Zeyya, wait!" I heard Jonah's call as I ran off, jumped a fence and headed towards the snow zone. "Stop!" he cried behind me. "Stop."

I picked up my feet and sprinted. I could hear his feet pounding behind me, then crunching in perfect unison with mine as we hit the crusty surface. His hand grabbed my elbow, my feet went out from under me and we fell together into the snow.

"Zeyya, Zeyya," he said, holding my face softly in his hand.

I slapped at him. "Don't touch me! Don't you get it? They're going to take me away. Don't you understand? I lied about my parents, about them being in Burma so I could stay at my school. Now, if I'm lucky, they'll train me to scour sewers."

He laughed. "You?"

"Okay, then I won't be so lucky and they'll use me for medical experiments. There's rumors of that, you know?"

"We won't let that happen." His voice was eerily calm.

"And how is an old lady, living half-in and half-out of her past, and a guy who claims he's from another world going to prevent it? Do you have money to pay someone off? Does Granna know somebody with influence?"

"I'll protect you, Zeyya."

"How? You're probably the craziest of us all. Nobody is going to listen to you. Who'd believe you about anything? Ever?" I began to laugh, tears streaming down my face. "The world's gone nuts. How did this happen? Last spring, I was living like billions of other people on the planet. Now I'm living with my anything-but-average grandmother, a bunch of dogs, a cat, and a crackpot."

"Is that me?"

"I'd run away, if I had someplace to run to."

I choked back tears as he put out one finger and began to trace a picture on my cheek. He fingered a tear on my chin. I was exhausted and despite myself, leaned into him, searching for reassurance, for some small bit of security.

"Tell me about your ancestors," I begged. "Tell me about the cluster of bells." I jingled them with my own finger so that their clear notes spread across the snow-covered hills.

"My mother had a voice so sweet that it carried on the wind like a bell, but at night, instead of singing she'd hold these in her hand and ring the notes to a lullaby as I fell to sleep." In a sweetly mellow voice, he sang a melody I'd never heard. Then he switched the tempo and was humming one of my pieces that had been sealed with everything else into our Quarantined apartment.

"How did you...?" I tried to ask, but he put his finger to my lips and spoke again.

"She sang to me until I was eight, when she died. My grandfather tied the bells into my hair the day her face was scribed on my stomach."

"Why there?"

"All mothers are scribed near the womb."

"Oh. And this?" I asked quickly, touching a copper loop tied behind his ear.

"Grand Auntie Lucinda's bracelet? Her memory rattles on like a parrot. My whole family knows you need a lot of time when you access her, but if you pay attention, she's pretty interesting."

I pointed to a steel nut and bolt that hung as a single unit.

"Charlie, an engineer of bridges and towers made of thin metal and glass that still span lakes and rivers. And this," he added, touching a tiny instrument completely unfamiliar to me, "is Vanya, a space vessel engineer."

"Uh huh. That one there," I said, hurrying past Vanya to what looked like a piece of cartilage.

Jonah frowned. I thought he was going to return to the space vessel comment, but he didn't. "The spine of a creature we use as a fishing lure. My father helped me find it when I was three, just before his death. It's polished because I rub at it a lot."

"How'd he die?"

"On an exploration trip in deep winter. The men had walked onto a frozen finger of water. An ice flow broke off and carried him under as it sank. My mother never recovered."

"I'm sorry."

"It was long ago." His fingers drifted back to the small artifact in his hair.

"Jonah, tell me the truth. Where are you from?"

"Not here." It was simple and obtuse, like Jonah.

"Come on, don't you trust me? I promise, if you're from this planet, it doesn't matter. Truly."

He dipped his head, hair clattering slightly. "Zeyya, when you want knowledge you don't have, how do you get it?"

"Search for it on the computer."

"And what does that give you?"

"Information."

"When I want information, I go to my ancestors. The longer my ancestral line, the more knowledge is available to me."

"But it isn't factual information, is it?" I wiggled my wet fingers, my teeth beginning to chatter.

"Who is to say what is fact? New discoveries change what we think of as fact all the time, true? But our ancestors give us knowledge, flavored by history and wisdom, like what Granna is giving you."

"Except Burma doesn't exist anymore, so what good is the flavor? Let's go home, I'm cold."

"Zeyya, why can't you believe me?"

"I want to, but so far, you haven't told me anything I can verify."

He scowled. "Verify?" His lips clamped together, opened, closed, opened again before he spoke. "I shouldn't have come. I only wanted to take a peek at your world, but then my vessel...it's repairing itself."

My eyebrows went soaring up. "Repairing itself?"

He nodded his head in a hard yes, and a symphonic clatter rolled out over the snow. "No matter what I tell you, you won't believe it, will you?"

"Nope, probably not, but I do admire how you've imagined your world. It's a lovely dream."

"Zeyya, my imagination is not that good."

"Okay, okay, let's go home now. I'm tired, cold, and enough is enough."

"Please believe me!" he pleaded.

"Jonah, you're a nice guy. You don't have to pretend, you don't have to make up glamorous stories for me to like you."

"Look at me," he said, pulling me back towards him, holding me tightly at arms' length, his face dressed in a serious expression. "My world exists. It's a place of carefully weighed goals. Everything is decided for balance. My grandfather was a mapper. Our world is full of deep valleys and craters. To map it, he needed to be able to travel safely. He accessed Vanya to help him design a glider, powered by solar energy, organically fitted to repair itself if damaged. To gather the rest of what he needed, he went from person to person, gathering information which they gathered from their ancestors, until he could build his glider."

"So everybody gives away their secrets for free?"

"There are no secrets."

"Paradise, huh?"

"No, not paradise. There are many dangers. There are always dangers and risks in life. Do you want to hear more?"

"Sure, go on."

"For years, my grandfather flew on the fingers of the sun, discovering places we didn't know about. Valleys full of fruits, craters of lava spume, hot springs, fishing lakes. Dim gray-green plains, craggy mountains, red towering buttes, snow fields covered by layers of permafrost. We spread his maps across the walls of the cliffs in beautiful hues, and since then, every three years there is a festival to repaint them, and add to them."

Jonah brushed the details of the maps onto the canvas of my mind until I could see them, as if I'd been to this place he claimed to be from.

"Zeyya, you're smiling. What are you thinking?"

"That you can paint magnificent pictures and weave phenomenal tales of fantastical places. Keep going."

"Yes?" His blue lips curved upwards, his hair clanged, his voice continued softly. "When I was twelve, my uncle took me on a trip. We traveled the rivers, portaging when they were dry, running rapids when the rains bloated them with water or the snows melted endlessly into them."

"Was your uncle a cartographer, too?" I hugged my arms to try to get warmer.

"Let's go home. You're cold."

"You might as well finish," I said, surprised at how much I wanted to hear the rest. It was lovely to imagine his world. "Please."

"No, he wasn't a mapper. We went to search for new plants and animals. He taught me to draw what we found with tiny, fine-pointed pens he devised. He taught me how to tint the pictures with dyes from the plants themselves. When he died a few years ago, he left me his pens and journals."

"Can you show them to me?"

"They aren't with me."

"So your vessel, when it's fixed, then what? You just vanish back into space?"

"I'm not thinking about that right now. Right now, I'm being with you, here with you." He was slick, that was for sure. What girl wouldn't like to hear that, but it wasn't going to do him much good, even if it was true, because they'd be taking me away soon.

"You're right, I'm cold. Let's go home."

"Zeyya, I know you're skeptical, but please, please, believe me, trust me." He reached out to stroke my hair, but I pulled my head away. "I didn't mean to find anyone here I cared about. What can I do to convince you?"

It was hard to keep my distance when he put it that way, when his longing was so palpable I could taste it, smell it. It was nice to be wanted, I needed that so badly. Inexplicably, a picture of his world came into my mind, like a reflection on water, clear and sharp, until small movements of things hidden underneath rippled the surface, separating it from my reality.

"I'm not pretending, Zeyya. Do you believe me?"

I couldn't say no, yet accepting what might be some gentle madness still terrified me, so I only replied with, "Help me up, Jonah, my knees are numb."

He picked me off the ground and as he did, I fell against him and our bodies touched through the wet, clinging fabric of our clothes. A lightning jolt shot through my head as we pressed closer and closer and fell into the snow, entangled, laughing, pressing closer still, shedding our clothes, anticipation rising despite the cold, then a clouding as if the world was covered in a web of milkiness. People I didn't know seemed to be tramping across my mind, speaking in rapid-fire words I could barely comprehend, yet which seemed familiar in cadence. Anger, regret, fear, love, passion, greed, pain walked through my open mind, digging into its folds and convolutions until my back arched and I heard two cries in perfect synchronization, and fell out of Jonah's arms into iciness, imagining my body fading away into the snow, swallowed by whiteness.

Startling.

White.

Endless

White without imprint.

Unbroken by our cries.

Silence in the mute night.

Fruits in Rangoon Bazaar:

Bananas, Plantains, Cocoanuts, Citrons,
Lemons, Limes, Tiparee (Cape gooseberries),
Guava, Jack Fruit, Muskmelons, Oranges, Papayas,
Pomelo, Sweet Limes, Rozelle Pods, Tamarind (half
ripe for curries), Tamarind (ripe for chutney and
sherbet), Bael Fruit, Kawanda, Mango, Marian,
Pineapple, Amrahs, Custard Apples, Guavas,
Durina, Mangosteen, Pomegranate, Rambosteen,
Karwanda

Vegetables in Rangoon Bazaar:

Beans (long), Bean Sprouts, Beets, Brinjal (eggplant),
Cabbage, Coriander Leaves, Cucumber, Garlic,
Green Chilies, Green Onions, Karela (bitter gourd),
Lady Fingers (Okra), Lemon Grass, Lettuce, Mint
(poorest in rains), Onions, Potatoes, Pumpkin, Rabbit
Greens, Spinach, Stone Pumpkin, Sweet Potato Greens,
Tomatoes, Vegetable Marrow, Yams, Arrowroot,
Chinese Cabbage, Coriander, Indian Corn, Drumstick,
Garlic Budds, Jerusalem Artichokes, Knol Kohl,
Mustard (white and green), Snow peas,
Turnips, Booth (White Pumpkin), Green Mangoes,
Green Marians, Bamboo Wah Bho, Frilly Beans,
Ginger, Snake Gourd, Ribbed Khain-oo (gourd),
Rozelle Leaves, Tapioca Root

An Every Day Burmese Meal:

Hingyo Broth (Fish broth)
See-pien (Curry with oil)
Vegetable Fry
Balachaung (to be eaten with mixed raw vegetables)
Rice

from *Rangoon International Cookbook*, 1956
Published by Woman's Society of Christian Service

Sami's Curry

1 pound meat or chicken (ground or pieces)

2 grated cloves of garlic, mashed

1 tsp. fresh ginger or ½ tsp. ground ginger

1 tsp. onion grated

1 ½ tsp. salt

¼ cup tomato juice

1 tbsp. oil

1 bay leaf

¼ tsp. chili powder

Pour 1 cup boiling water over 1 can or 1 ½ cups grated cocoanut to get cocoanut milk strained, of course. Put oil in pan. Heat. Add onion, garlic, ginger, and chili powder, salt, and Bay Leaf. Fry slowly 5 or 10 minutes. Add meat, tomato juice and cocoanut milk.

Simmer ½ hour. Serve over rice.

Greater East Coast Metropolis: 2047
[Raids on Celebrations yield caches of Exuberants.
Snap-up particularly prevalent. Many arrests.]

We plucked our clothes out of the snow, which I didn't remember removing, pulled apart the wet fabric and dressed. We were soaked and I, at least, was cold, but when I thought about being a hung-girl, about being scared, a comforting voice tickled the back of my mind. White oblivion dangled in front of my eyes, clouding my focus, and even when it began to fade, I felt little more than a wisp of whom I had been before the snow.

Everything muffled.

Everything hushed.

Jonah too looked shaken, tipping his head to one side, then the other, neither of us speaking until at last, as from a great distance I heard him whisper. "I need a few minutes, just a few is all, I promise, Zeyya."

He squatted without warning on the sidewalk behind the school, palms up on the tops of his knees while his eyes rolled back. I looked around desperately as I saw three or four kids sneaking towards us, cans of Snap-up and All-High in their hands.

"Hey, what the?" one said. "What's wrong with him?"

"Nothing! Just like you aren't out here getting high," I replied quickly, as firmly as I could.

"But..."

"Zeyya," Marilyn said, clarifying out of the dark. "Why are you all wet?"

"We fell in a drift." It was only a half-lie. "Why are you using Snap-up?"

She looked away, embarrassed, then turned to the boys. "We didn't see them," she instructed. "Come on, let's go somewhere else."

I felt, more than saw, Jonah rise next to me. "We can go now, Zeyya."

"Who were you talking to?" I asked, curious as to whom he'd picked this time.

"I'm not sure. Your ancestors are pretty muddled. That's how most first generationers are."

"My ancestors? Can this wait?" I asked, my teeth chattering loudly. "We have to get our coats and go home before I die of hypothermia."

He cradled my icy hands in his warm ones. "Of course."

An outpouring of kids announced the end of the Ball. Fighting the flow, we managed to get inside. Our coats were the last on the hooks.

"How did it get so late?" I asked.

He just looked at me with limpid blue eyes that answered all without a word, before putting his arm around me as we left.

Mr. Jaster stood on the sidewalk outside like a guard dog.

"Goodnight," Jonah said to him.

"Just one moment, Zeyya, please. You're white as a sheet," Mr. Jaster remarked.

My frustration and fear returned in a nauseating wave that wiped away the last of the white mist over my eyes. "What do you care?"

"I'm sorry about your parents. You're an excellent student whom I'd like to keep. You should have come to me with the truth."

"Would the truth have helped?"

"It may not be too late. I'll do my best to keep you here. Just be straight-up with me from now on."

I managed to mutter a thanks, but I knew it was too late. Soon, someone was going to scoop me up and haul me away, the only question being to where. There was nothing Mr. Jaster was going to be able to do, or Granna or Jonah, who might actually be living in an extended fantasy, anyway.

"Goodnight, Zeyya," Mr. Jaster called after us.

Jonah hurried me on, his hand reassuringly guiding me from where it rested on the small of my back, but neither of us spoke nor looked at each other. What had I done? Halfway home, a pack of Jo-Boys brushed up against us. "I'm training them," Jonah said, breaking the silence.

"For what?"

"For you, for Granna—to watch over you, to keep you safe."

I didn't have the energy to point out that we were never going to be safe. I was exhausted, I wanted to sleep, but when we got home, I paused at the porch steps.

"Do you think Granna will still be awake, Jonah? What will we say to her? Do you think she'll guess? About us?"

"I hope not to both."

We tiptoed in. The kitchen light burned brightly, but the rest of the house was dark.

"Wait here, Zeyya. I'll get us towels."

On the kitchen table was a note written in Granna's shaky hand-writing: "Pot of chocolate and cookies in the warmer."

I punched in heat-up as Jonah returned with towels. He rubbed my hair, then offered me a warm washcloth to clean my face.

"No thanks, I want to keep the drawings."

"Too late. They smudged in the snow, Zeyya." When I finished, he handed me my violin. "Will you play for me?"

"Not now, Jonah."

"Then can I play for you?"

He picked up the gleaming wood without waiting for my permission, the bow dangling from his fingers while he leaned pages to my concerto against a wall where the paper bent gently. Bringing the bow across the strings, perfect, plaintive notes sang from the violin into the quiet house. Suddenly, I was sobbing against Jonah's chest, forcing him to lay the violin down as I clung to him.

"Don't cry, please. Don't hate me either," he whispered by my ear.

"Why would I hate you? I'm not crying about what we did. I'm scared, really scared!"

He pushed me back, looking into my eyes. "I didn't mean to make love to you—I shouldn't have."

I blinked. "I think it was a mutual decision. We hung each other, you know?"

He looked away from me, his pinkish tongue touching his lips, only to retreat behind blue teeth before he spoke again. "But what we did has biological consequences."

"Sure, we were impulsive, I could get pregnant."

His eyes looked moist. "There is no reversal of this choice."

"Yeah, it's a little late for that, but I think you're taking this a little too seriously."

"Perhaps you don't understand. I can share total access with one, only one, sexual partner."

"Okay—just one moment—wait, you can't mean you thought, I mean, even if it's true—I mean, me? Why?"

He stated unequivocally, "I love you."

Oh, how I hoped he was a lunatic trying to manipulate me and that this wasn't true, that he hadn't risked everything on me—me, who was most probably going to be dragged away by the authorities shortly, any moment now. Me, who might not have a future, much less be able to make a commitment to anyone at this moment in my life. Oh, how I hoped he had created a magnificent illusion and wasn't telling the truth.

"It's a consequence of our evolution." He looked at me with such sincerity it made me want to wail. He believed what he was telling me, and it was so beautiful it hurt: he, a prince from a kingdom of perfection, had cast his lot with me, at best an imperfect peasant whom he wanted to take home for a happily ever after.

"But Jonah, I don't..." I stumbled into silence.

"Remember when I stopped outside the school? The ancestors informed me you might not be ready for the commitment. If only I had known before we..."

"We got hung?" I interjected.

He dropped his face so I couldn't be sure, but I thought I saw tears. "Jonah," I moaned, taking his hands in mine, "I don't know if I'm ready. My life is already so confusing. And I don't really know who you are, or what, or what might be wrong with you." I let my arms drop away, sobs welling out of my chest, unable to meet his gaze, unable to face him any longer, and tore into my room.

I slept as if I had died, not awakening until well past noon, when Granna finally came in with a tray of eggs and tea, asking, "Late night?"

"Yeah," I mumbled, my tongue still thick with sleep.

"Jonah has been accessing for two hours. I'm worried about him. I thought of calling Medical Emergencies."

"No, Granna, no! Don't ever do that to Jonah! They'd take him away for sure. I'll go see him."

"Remember, no touching," she remonstrated me, trailing right on my heels. I wasn't sure *no touching* mattered any more as far as I was concerned. "My, oh, my, life was simpler when it was just me."

"I'm sorry, Granna."

"Well now, what were my choices? To kick you out? To leave Jonah on the street? But I do hold you responsible for that cat!" She grinned.

I walked around Jonah, looking at him from all angles, hoping for a clue as to what to do. He sat in the middle of the living room with nothing on except a blanket Granna had flung over him. His face seemed bluer than ever and the eyes of the portraits had silvered over. His hands were clenched, opening and closing, more and more rapidly; slowing, stopping, opening again at an ever increasing pace until a spasm took him and the process started over.

"Zeyya, stop circling him like he's prey. Sit down." I didn't want to, but she looked at me sternly. "Now, sit beside me, young lady, and we'll wait together until he comes out of it."

I remained standing, deliberately staring at Jonah while I asked her, "Granna, tell me what I'll miss if I get Quarantined."

Had Jonah blinked?

"Falling in love—it'd be a shame to miss that, Zeyya."

I felt her eyes boring into me, but I kept my eyes on Jonah. "I haven't missed that, Granna."

"That's what I thought."

"What else, Granna? What else am I going to miss?"

"Silly goose, you aren't going to get Quarantined."

"You don't know that! What else?" I demanded.

"Well, if you insist—I suppose, the pleasures of having children, although they bring great responsibilities with them." She was watching me closely.

"To you?"

"To me, but even more so to our second cook, Sami."

I circled Jonah one more time, staring at all the faces on his body. I knew their names: Vanya, Maria, Harry. Lavenia, Marcus. Every face had a name and I knew which name belonged to each portrait.

"Jonah," I whispered into his ear. "Where have you gone? Please, come back. Who are you talking to? Please, don't leave me. I believe you! Come back, play my music with me, hold me, kiss me, touch my cheek."

He spasmed, as his fingers began to open and close, open and close.

"Zeyya, come sit beside me," Granna called again. She pulled an afghan over us as I crawled in to sit next to her on the sofa.

"He must be accounting to all those faces for something. Do you know anything about it?" I laid my head on her shoulder and she patted my hand. "You know Zeyya, if you are responsible for this in some way..."

"Don't say that, Granna! Don't."

As we sat huddled close, all I could think of was how I should have told him I'd be his hung-girl forever. I loved him, but forever was ominous and hung-girl seemed an infantile commitment. In desperation, I said, "Granna, tell me about Sami. Please, anything to keep my mind off Jonah."

"All right, let's see. After Mommy and Daddy caught Josephine and Sebastian stealing from us, they fired them, which meant my mother had to do all the shopping and cooking. My mother was a great cook, but bartering at a Burmese market for food was not one of her skills, nor was slaughtering chickens for dinner."

"Yuck!"

"Yes, but if we wanted dinner, someone had to do it. So they hired Sami, a short, trim, squarely built Indian cook who had lived in Burma since the War. Sis and her teenage hoodlum girlfriend immediately raided his cookie jar and after only one short week, he learned to be on guard against those two varmints. In Burma, our oven was a tin box heated over a kerosene flame. To bake in it was more than an art—it was a feat, which Sami performed with what looked like magical ease. His chocolate chip cookies rivaled my grandmother Sadie's famous batches.

"You look a lot like Sadie, you know, but without the red hair. You got stuck with my hair, my dear."

"What do you think Jonah would look like without those tattoos?" We looked over at him simultaneously.

"Hard to imagine," she replied.

Looking away, I asked, "Go on, what happened, with Sami?"

"Sami quickly tired of finding his cookie jar empty. Chocolate was expensive for Madam and baking was a time consuming project for him, the fruits of which Sis and her friend Martha seemed to devour in single sucking gulps."

"Cookies," I murmured.

"Should we go make some?"

"Now? Maybe later." I didn't want to leave Jonah like this. "Tell me the rest of the story, please, Granna."

She gave me a little hug. "The day came when Sis and the overly tall Martha, who could also suck spaghetti strands off a fork without getting a single drop of sauce on her face, finished off a whole batch of cookies in fifteen minutes, and that was the day Sami took action. The next time he heard Martha was coming over, his eyes twinkled and he hummed to himself. Sure enough, as soon as Martha arrived, she and Sis headed for the pantry where Sami kept his cookies.

"'Where are the cookies, do you know, Susie?' Sis asked me.

"'No,' I answered and kept on playing with my dolls on the dining room table.

"'Come help us look, Susie,' Sis demanded.

"We scanned the shelves until Sami came padding up in his Burmese slippers and white Western style shirt, a smile plastered across his face.

"'What is it you girls are doing in my pantry? Shoo. Out of there!'" Granna said, imitating the deepness of a man's voice.

I took a quick glance at Jonah before she went on, but he sat as before, the unchanging blue Buddha, his eyes still rolled back, lids still closed.

"'We're looking for cookies, Sami,' Sis said, not budging an inch.

"'What cookies would those be, Miss Sis?'

"'The ones you just made,' Martha stated, standing staunchly next to Sis.

"'Oh, those cookies. Aren't they here?'

"'Nope!'

"'What? Did you young missies eat them all already?' Sami asked with faked dismay.

"'Not us, Sami!'

"'Now, I know you and Miss Martha. You two girls have eaten all those many cookies and I am not baking again for several days! Now I must tell Madam there are no cookies for her luncheon party. How could you?'

"'It wasn't us, Sami, really!' they insisted, backing into our dining room, past me, escaping at double-time up the stairs.

"As soon as they were out of sight, he began laughing as quietly as he could. Still chuckling, he went into the pantry, pulled out a rice tin from behind the pans, the pots, the tiffin carriers, the flour, the sugar, and spices that lined the big floor to ceiling pantry between the dining room and the kitchen. He held that tin out to me and I helped myself to two or three cookies. Sami beamed at me proudly. 'Our secret, Miss Susie.'"

"Did you ever tell Sis?"

"Never!"

I giggled despite myself, before my eyes were drawn again to Jonah. I felt a chill run up my back. He was rigid now, his hands opening stiffly backwards. How long could he go on? Where was he? With whom? Were they telling him I was a mistake, that he should leave me?

I slid my eyes away from him. "Granna, did Mum ever, well, did she ever bring home a boy you didn't approve of?"

"She married him."

I was startled. "You didn't like Dad?"

"Nope, not one little bit, and you know what, he didn't like me one little bit either. But, over the years we came to accept each other. Or maybe, it was just me who accepted him. I think I was a little too wild for him." Her mouth tweaked in a slight smile.

There was one thing about Dad that was true, he was a stickler for the rules, but I loved him, and it had never occurred to me that he and Granna didn't liked each other. "He sent me to you," I told her because I couldn't think of anything better to say. "He dropped a note on the floor for me, by our door. Did you forgive Mum for marrying him?"

She looked at me with her head tipped slightly and the edges of her mouth turned up. "Of course, she was my daughter. Besides, look what came from that union." She pointed at me.

Maybe there was hope. Without meaning to, I muttered, "I hope Jonah's people don't reject..." I stopped myself in mid-sentence.

"What's that?" She had narrowed her eyes. "What about Jonah's people?"

"Granna, if you make a mistake, I mean, what if you do something that has consequences you don't expect? What happens?"

"Depends on the consequences. Look at what happened to Sami."

"Because he hid the cookies?"

She laughed. "No, no, not because of the cookies. Because he had two wives at the same time!"

"That's illegal, isn't it?"

"That's what Daddy asked Sami. 'Not in Burma, Master,' is what Sami told Daddy. 'There is no divorce in Burma, Master.' Seemed that during the War, Sami couldn't support his family in India, so he came to Burma looking for better opportunities. But he never got enough money together to bring Indian Wife-Number-One to Burma. So eventually, he married Burmese Wife-Number-Two. Meanwhile, back in India, Wife-Number-One scrimped and saved until she had enough money to bring herself and her children with her to find Sami in Rangoon. So there he was, with two wives and two sets of kids to support."

"Uh, how'd he manage that?"

"All I know is he lived with Burmese-Wife-Number-Two, who had just had another baby when Indian-Wife-Number-One showed up, and that Mommy and Daddy got Indian Wife-Number-One a job with some people they knew. Now what consequences do you have to deal with, young lady?"

"It's nothing, Granna," Jonah said, fortuitously refocusing at that moment, his eyes still milky from access. He looked at me and smiled slightly as he pulled the blanket tightly around himself. How long had he been back?

"Uh huh?" Granna said skeptically. "Well, this discussion isn't over, but right now, Jonah, I think you need some food."

"What he needs are clothes," I pointed out.

"I'm still drying the ones from last night. How do you two keep getting so soaked?" she asked as she went into the kitchen.

Jonah slipped his fingers between mine. "I'm as confused as you are," he said, "but I want, I need, I must be with you."

All I could do was squeeze his fingers. I couldn't bear to point out it was out of our hands.

So soon the fires of war were to burn up,

not only the show and tinsel of Burma,

but things more solid and golden…

December 8th fell soon after the full moon of Tasaungmon…

and laid a blight upon the whole country.

Destruction was so swift, so sudden."

From *Burmese Family*

by Mi Mi Khaing

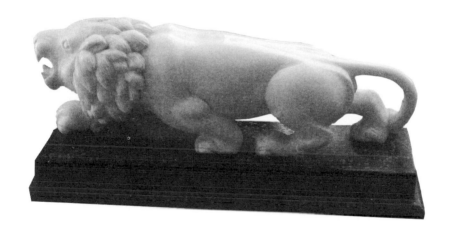

Saturday, August 9, 1958

Rangoon

Dear Mama,

I made a present for Mary, Josephine's 15-year-old niece, whom they've adopted. Mary is a nice girl tho' completely illiterate. Her clothes are truly ragged and her birthday is Monday, so I got her Burmese sandals and made a skirt, as you can't buy anything ready-made here. Josephine helped with the basting and cutting. I'm having Sebastian make her a cake and freezer ice cream. We won't even hide the preparations, as she'd never dream we'd do anything for her occasion.

Josephine's sister was born in Rangoon and lived here until the Japanese conquered Burma during WWII. Like Josephine and Sebastian, she and her husband fled to India—on foot. She was pregnant with Mary, who was born upon her arrival. Mary's mother has been stranded there ever since, but her husband deserted her and brought Mary back to Burma, then neglected Mary, so Josephine took over. Life can be cruel sometimes.

Love,

Blanche

Greater East Coast Metropolis: 2047
[There are more unconfirmed rumors that Quarantine
victims are deported to camps in the Cold-Lands. This
would indeed be a convenient way to alleviate the
overcrowding and social unrest of our cities due to
flooding and spreading environmental change. The
conditions and locations of these camps remain undisclosed,
if they truly exist. The possibility that these rumors are simply
the wishful thinking of the relatives who have lost family to
Quarantine cannot be ignored. And certainly some deaths
can be confirmed, but the nature of the disease that
Quarantine seeks to prevent remains ominously unrevealed.]
Subterranean Net Site

By four, I was ready to sleep again, but Granna had other ideas. "Let's go pick up the holographs."

"Oh, yeah." I'd forgotten about them, but I didn't feel like going out. I only wanted to sleep. "I'm kind of tired, why don't you and Jonah go on and go?"

Jonah agreed, but added a codicil. "Jo-Boy will stay with you. Maybe several Jo-Boys, if they want to."

Granna chuckled. "I swear you talk to them, Jonah!"

He probably did. As soon as they left, I lit a synthetic fire in Granna's fireplace and stared into the artificial warmth. I wanted to think, but instead I found myself succumbing to the seduction of the heat and flickering blue flames. I felt my eyes roll back as they did when my dreams began.

Dream Mum: "Zeyya, we left you a message."

Dream me: "I got it. I came to Granna's."

Dream Mum's lips in a gentle smile: "Don't mourn me. Remember me. Call me when you need me."

Dream Dad speaking clearly, as if next to me: "Or me. I'll be there the day you marry. I'll be there when your music is performed."

I reach to touch them, sniff to smell them, but I can do neither.

Dream me: "Are you dead?"

One of them: "Everyone dies." Which one?

Dream me: "No! Please! No!"

Dream Mum: "I'll be here always."

Dream Dad, voice fading away to a raspy whisper: "I'll be here."

Dream me: "Wait, wait! You have to tell me what to do about Jonah! Wait! Please!"

But they were gone, and Jo-Boy was licking me. I wiped at my eyes which were stiff with sleep. "Hey, boy, are Jonah and Granna back?" Rubbing my arms, I stood and went to get a sweater. Jo-Boy and I were the only ones home. "What do you think, huh? A snack for you and me? Jonah's a good guy, isn't he? Pretty amazing, this mess I'm in. What do you think, huh? I wish I could truly talk to Mum and Dad, but maybe they'll be back soon, huh? You think? In the meantime, I wish I could access all you Jo-Boys and see what you think of Jonah. You might be smarter than me. That wouldn't be hard, huh?" I blathered on and on.

After my snack, I washed my face at the kitchen sink and when I looked up, a man was staring in the window above it.

"What do you want?" I called through the glass as boldly as I could.

"Is Susannah home?" he called back. The tip of his tongue flicked out, then pulled back between pointy little teeth. I thought of one word. Snake.

"What do you want?" I asked again, nervously.

"No, huh? Not home? Can I come in?" A quick little smile pricked his cheeks.

"No! Mum taught me never to let a stranger in." Fear was making me flippant.

"But Susannah knows me."

"Come back later!" I said.

"I'll wait," he said tersely. A few minutes later I heard someone settle into a chair on the front porch. When I looked, it was him, puffing contentedly at a pipe, seemingly unaware that it was cold out.

"Jo-Boy," I whispered, "can you call to the other Jo-Boys? Can you get them to come? Can you get them to warn Jonah that man is here?"

He thumped his tail happily and put his head down on his paws.

What was I thinking, talking to a dog like he understood me? But I had to do something. "Jo-Boy, if this guy sees Jonah, the gig is up." His ears went up and back down. "Yeah, you see?" He raised his head.

I tapped on the front window, calling through it. "Can't you tell me? I'll give her a message."

"Not this one. It's official," he answered.

At that moment, there came Granna, surrounded by Jo-Boys, no Jonah in sight.

"Thanks, that's the way to go," I whispered to the Jo-Boy who had moved to my side as I scratched him behind the ears.

"What do you want this time?" Granna greeted the man cantankerously, but familiarly. So he did know her. "How many times do I have to tell you? I'm not moving into a retirement protectorate so some developer can gobble up my property."

He smiled for the third time since he had appeared, as if relishing a triumph. "You may feel differently, Susannah, after I tell you why I've come."

"Don't call me by my first name, you presumptuous little upstart."

"Fine, we'll be formal. Mrs. Smith, I've come in my official capacity as your geriatric counselor to inform you of the Quarantined deaths of your daughter and her partner."

I saw Granna stagger as I dashed out the door, tears streaming down my face, all my fear exploding into anger. "Why'd you take them? Tell me why you Quarantined them? What did they ever do to you?"

"I had nothing to do with their Quarantine," he said, putting his hands up in front of him as I got closer.

With a flash of insight, or maybe insanity, I yelled, "Whoever you work for wanted Granna's land, so you arranged to hurt her. You did it! All of you!"

"I'm a geriatric social worker, assigned to your grandmother. I wasn't concerned with her family!"

"Yeah, sure!" I was almost growling like a Jo-Boy.

"I'm sure they were sick." He spoke with an indifferent calm, although the edge of his eye was twitching.

"No, they weren't. I would have known. Why'd you kill them? Tell me the truth!" My fury drove away my tears.

He shook his head, but I saw the side of his mouth crook up just a little bit. "I've told you, I know nothing. I'm only the messenger. I wasn't involved in their deaths."

"Liar, liar, pants on fire," Granna chanted shrilly as the Jo-Boys encircled her again, like a pack protecting the young.

"Leave, take your lies and leave!" I heard myself bellow at him. "Get lost!" The Jo-Boy next to me rumbled a warning from deep in its chest.

The man dropped a packet on the steps and sneered. "I'll be back with your social services agent, girl. There's the issue of your custody now, and that I may have some input into." Glancing at all the Jo-Boys coalescing around Granna and me, he shook his head and muttered as he scurried away, "I'm not paid enough to face a pack of wild dogs."

Jonah came around from the back of the house at a clip, the inside Jo-Boy already at his heels. He picked Granna up in a single swoop and carried her inside. I eyed the packet. Forcing myself to pick it up, I carried it inside, hanging like a dead rat between my thumb and forefinger. Jonah was already putting tea water on the stove.

Granna sat with her head in her hands, muttering over and over, "Nyuant Maung came back, Nyuant Maung came back." Over and over. "Nyuant Maung came back."

"Granna?" I bent over her. "Granna, please, please, I need you!"

She ran her thumb down the side of my face. "Yes, darling, I know, but I'm old, so old and such a shabby excuse for a grandmother."

Jonah poured three cups of tea. Granna's sat untouched.

"I don't understand, Zeyya. Why didn't she come back? How is it she didn't come back?"

"I don't know, Granna." I made no effort to stop the tears that dripped down my face, except to sniffle when I had to.

"I'm going to lie down," Granna said, and tottered down the hall, using the walls for support.

"Oh, Jonah!" I sobbed, holding onto him tightly. "The walls are tumbling. Everything is broken!"

I cried into his chest until his shirt was soaked. He stroked my head, at last saying ever so gently, "These papers? They tell you that your mother and father died of advanced Darwin Quarantine Syndrome for which there is no known cure."

"That's a lie! They can cure everything: the flu, heart disease, the common cold, even dementia. They found a cure for leprosy a hundred years ago. They can cure this new disease, they just don't want to, or else it doesn't exist!"

"I'm sorry, Zeyya."

"Maybe they aren't really dead." I started to shake all over. "Don't leave me, okay, Jonah? Never leave me. Promise!"

"I won't ever leave you, but Zeyya, that man—we need a plan. Maybe your mother or father has an idea?"

I jerked away. "What? What are you talking about? They're dead!"

"I thought perhaps you'd spoken to them, Zeyya."

"After they died?"

He was watching me expectantly. My stomach spasmed as I thought, My dream? Without a word, he nodded, his eyes holding mine as he did.

"Stop that, Jonah! Just stop, stop, stop. Not now. How can you play games right now?"

He drew away from me. "You don't believe me? After everything, still you don't believe me?" He stood up. "By the way, the holographs weren't ready yet. I'll be on the porch. Jo-Boy," he called and left me in the cold, disquieted kitchen.

In Rome, May 1956, more than two hundred delegates from fifty-one nations presented reports to an International Congress on Leprosy, the oldest known disease in the world. In recent years, cases of leprosy had increased. In Burma alone, where two thousand cases were reported in 1951, thirty thousand cases were reported in 1956. Treatment had improved by the mid-1950's, making recovery possible, but in many underdeveloped nations, such as Burma, it was still hard to get those treatments to the people who needed them.

Partially based on an article from
Time, May 7, 1956

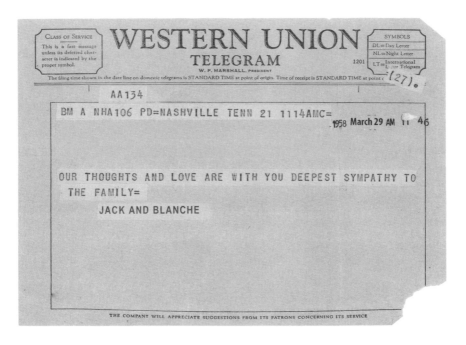

WESTERN UNION

TELEGRAM

W. P. MARSHALL, PRESIDENT

1201

The filing time shown in the date line on domestic telegrams is STANDARD TIME at point of origin. Time of receipt is STANDARD TIME at point c

(27).

AA134

BM A NHA106 PD=NASHVILLE TENN 21 1114AMC=

1958 March 29 AM 11 46

OUR THOUGHTS AND LOVE ARE WITH YOU DEEPEST SYMPATHY TO
THE FAMILY=

JACK AND BLANCHE

March 30, 1958

Dearest Mother,

Your cable arrived yesterday which explained why we hadn't heard from you recently. We are very sad that we can't come to Nashville. We hope the rest of the family has been able to come home. I imagine you're all together today, and am sure that is some comfort. I know what Aunt Sara's passing means to you. The girls were distressed when we told them, but of course, did not understand how miserable her last weeks had been. Even that knowledge must only slightly ease the loneliness and sorrow her passing causes. She will be greatly missed—people of her intellectual force and interests are so rare. I hope our cable is there, but I wish we could be with you, too.

Your news of the bombing of the Jewish Community Center was shocking. It even made the Rangoon papers, which invariably carry news of violence, in particular in regard to desegregation. Other news, unless it contains foreign aid data, rarely gets printed. I hope there won't be any further attacks. It is hard to believe that the bombing is related to the Civil Rights Movement, but it sounds as if it may be. We are thinking of you. Please write as soon as you feel able.

Love,

Blanche

Greater East Coast Metropolis: 2047
[We are disturbed to hear that the Quarantine Squads
have been renamed among the populace as the
Death Squads. This is a dangerous misnomer, and anyone using
it shall be prosecuted to the fullest extent of the law.]

I fell asleep, sprawled at the table and woke to the crash of a cup as it fell, cold tea drops splattering, shards of cup skittering right and left across the table and the floor. I wiped and swept up the mess. The house was still, with only the first gray fingers of morning creeping through the windows. I rubbed my eyes and went to check on Granna. She slept soundly on the bed, surrounded by letters laid out over her like wildly scattered quilt squares, decorated in small scrunched writing on brittle, sky-blue paper. I picked one up.

August 7

Dearest Helen,

Than Swe, our house boy (bearer sweeper) is a stolid, phlegmatic boy in contrast to Susie, who is a whirlwind little girl with energies bursting out in much wasted motion and many words. When she sits at a table, she can't stop talking because after all, sitting is such a quietness in itself and she never compounds quietness. At times our family seems like a candle in a candlestick, and Susie the flame that's always moving, burning brightly, and wearing the rest of us down. Her attitude towards sitting was never more apparent than in her reaction to French lessons: "But Mommy," she wailed, "all you do is sit around and learn words."

August 24

Dear Mother,

Nyuant Maung, our day durwan was away and our substitute durwan, Te Aung, needed fluid for his cigarette lighter. While smoking his cheroot, he crawled under our jeep and tried to break the fuel line so he could put petrol in his lighter. Pabrinard, the gardener, saw smoke coming from the garage and roused us all. Te Aung was not yet successful and had only sizzled a little grease, so our garage didn't explode. Te Aung left and Nyuant Maung returned, but things are not as they were. We have worried for some time at Nyuant Maung's gradual transformation from a young, oval-faced, clean-cut lively boy to a slow-moving creature. Upon his return from the jungle, we were struck by his puffed, distorted face and darkened, thickened skin, pulled tightly across a leonine face. It almost seemed another head had been placed on his body and after his absence and return, the change was very pronounced. At first, we had wondered if he had been taking dope. We had questioned a doctor who had given us vitamins for him and he seemed to improve. But on his return, our servants at last broke their silence. 'Master, Nyuant Maung has bad disease, like people with fingers falling off.' I thought they must be wrong, but we sent him to another doctor who was not as hasty in his judgments or tests. After a week of waiting, we learned Nyuant Maung was one of Burma's many lepers.

I paused in my reading. It nagged at me. It didn't make sense. Way back then, they had cured Nyuant Maung of a disease that made his fingers, his toes, his feet fall off, but they couldn't save my parents from Darwin Q. Syndrome? A shudder went through me. I wanted to wake Granna, to demand an explanation that made sense, but she looked so pitifully small, so overwhelmed amongst the blue sheets of paper that I just read on.

After spending many hours persuading him not to run back into the jungle and hide, we have arranged for treatment for Nyuant Maung. We gave him money for it, read about leprosy and realized he'd had the lion-like look for a long time. We were frightened until we found out that the risk of contagion for those over five is slight, although the incubation period is up to forty years. Neither we, nor our servants, had tiny children. We had thought our servants trusted us, but their fear of telling us their suspicions earlier made us realize they had been servants, taking orders, for far too many years.

I had to know what had happened to Nyuant Maung, but the trouble with letters was they were written as things happened. Nothing was complete. The plot unfolded like life instead of a novel. I pawed through, but couldn't find the end of the story.

I gathered the letters into a disorderly stack and in the process uncovered my grandmother. I looked at her lying there in the dreary light and thought how much she looked like one of the faded, antique photographs she hoarded.

"Granna," I breathed into her ear, "Mum's not really gone. I carry her around the way you carry Burma—I can hear her the way you can see Burma."

I turned to go. Jonah stood in the doorway of the room, a blue shadow against the light behind him. I put my finger to my lips, rose, and closed the door softly with nothing more than the sound of a small click. He followed me into my room and when I sat on my bed, he sat next to me, hands in his lap.

I looked at my palms as I spoke. "I'm sorry, Jonah. I wasn't fair, but all I can think about right now is Mum and Dad." I clenched my fingers to keep back a new onslaught of tears.

"I only thought you might have accessed one of your parents," he said, brushing my curls gently back from my face. "It can be comforting."

That simple, feathery touch made me shiver, both with desire and relief, as I made myself admit, "It wasn't access, but I did dream about them, as if I was really able to talk to them."

He pressed nearer and I lay against his shoulder and calmed myself in the serenity of his presence, until a Jo-Boy let loose with a howl that shattered the moment. Someone was rapping on the front door. Shakily, I peeked out. It was Marilyn.

"What are you doing here at this hour, Marilyn?"

She looked awful, her hair hanging in strings, glitter stuck to her cheeks in goopy clumps. "Can I come in, Zeyya? I can't go home like this."

"You haven't been home since the Ball? Where have you been? Your parents must be frantic."

316

She shook her head. "I All-highed out with Willie and a couple of guys. You know, I'd do anything for Willie. I can't remember too much of it. I woke up in the middle of a walkway with an empty contraceptive tube in my fist." She sank down onto the floor. Her eyes were glazed, her lips purpled, skin splotchy.

"Come on, Marilyn, it's been two days. Get up, go home, face your parents. I can't believe you did this with Willie!"

"But he loves me, Zeyya."

"Yeah? He left you passed out on a walkway—how's that love, Marilyn?"

"Oh, Zeyya, you don't understand. You've never been in love."

"Go home! I've got enough problems without adding yours."

"Is that Jonah?" she asked, looking past me, to where he sat in the living room, mainly clothed in tattoos. "I can see what you two have been up to. But I suppose your grandma's too old to notice. Lucky you."

"Be glad you have parents," I snapped at her.

"Oh, come on, tell, tell! Tell me everything about you and Jonah." She tried to smile sweetly, but only managed to distort her face more. I tried to remember why was she my friend.

"Go home, Marilyn, now!"

She ignored me. "He hasn't washed up yet, either?"

I glanced at Jonah. "It won't come off," I said truthfully.

"Oh brother, are his parents going to be mad! I'll see you at school." She hopped up off the floor, trying to whistle as she left, but her lips were too swollen for much success.

I turned to Jonah and grimaced. He put his arms around me, kissed me lightly. "Come on," he said, pulling me out to sit on the porch with him. We huddled under a blanket, his warm bare toes next to my slippered ones, his warm, blue fingers intertwined in my plain, cold ones. I leaned my head against his shoulder again.

"I'd never leave you unconscious on a walkway," he vowed, rubbing the inside of my palm.

"Jonah, you really love me, don't you?"

"How can you ask that?"

"Because, I'm afraid you'll leave me, not on a walkway, but just walk off to wherever you came from."

"I can't walk there," he said with a little laugh before his face got serious and looking right into my eyes, he swore, "I won't go anywhere without you. Where you go, I go. Where I go, you go."

"You haven't known me very long, how can you promise that? How can you be so sure?"

"I love you, Zeyya."

"Yes, but..."

"Even if I want to, I can't leave you behind. Every time I sit like Buddha, you will be there, your music will sing to me, your voice will speak to me. From now until I die, you will be the first voice I hear when I speak to my family."

His belief was frighteningly simple. Unquestioning. And me, what did I believe? I still didn't know, but I acquiesced in one way.

"I want to get Mum's portrait scribed on my belly."

"Are you sure?"

"Yes, I'm sure. We can go today, if Granna is feeling better." We stood, we kissed, but that was all because who knew when Granna might wake up.

"Today, if she feels okay." He placed a warm hand on my stomach, precisely where the portrait would soon be scribed, and kissed me again.

"The true development of human beings involves
so much more than mere economic growth. At
its heart there must be a sense of empowerment
and inner fulfillment."

Aung San Suu Kyi, 1994

"One seeks greatness through taming one's passion.
And isn't there a saying that 'it is far more difficult
to conquer yourself than to conquer the rest of the
world?'"

Aung San Suu Kyi, 1997

AIR LETTER

AEROGRAMME

Dear Mama,

Yesterday afternoon, Jack and I took Susie and Sis with us to the golf club and they walked as we played. We let them put balls on the putting greens and putt. We had given Sebastian and Josephine the day off, as it was their 18th wedding anniversary. She cooked us an Indian curry as a treat and it was wonderful. If only I could capture that seasoning, I'd be the best party-giver in Washington, DC when we return.

Today the Burmese Parliament meets and Monday they select the Prime Minister. On the golf course (we play at Burma's equivalent of Ike's Burning Tree) yesterday, we saw the Commander-in-chief of Burma's army playing—with an armed escort carrying machine guns! It was so odd, a bit unnerving, to see him and his party trail after their balls in the unpatterned fashion of golfers, and at the same time to see the rigid, disciplined, bee-line march of the armed escort. Then, unexpectedly, General Ne Win stopped to greet us and effused over the girls being on the golf course with us. It was very strange indeed.

Josephine and Sebastian insist that Susie catches onto some of what they say in Tamil, and insist that she has learned to sing a Hindustani popular song correctly, tho' she understands not one word of it. Both languages are spoken in India and wherever many Indians are, including here. Tamil is also one of the two controversial languages of Ceylon, you know.

Much Love,

Blanche

Greater East Coast Metropolis: 2047
[Resistance to Quarantine is a crime against your neighbor.
The greater good is always the best road. With this in mind,
the legislature passed a bill today to raise taxes to pay for
the cost of Quarantine and other public mental and
physical health programs.]

Granna woke, bundled herself up and insisted that we drag the rocking chair back out onto the porch so she could sit there.

"But it's so cold," I protested.

She waved her hand around her bedroom. "I don't want to be in here. Out there, I can travel beyond the street, can rock myself to far away places. Out there, I can go anywhere I want to. So no arguments about what's good for me."

Jonah came out with a huge load of blankets that he wrapped around her, tucking her in so that only her face and gloved hands were free to move.

"Where do you go when you rock?" I asked, sitting next to her on a cold metal chair.

"To the movies. All those walls are my vid screens." She lifted her head a little and flipped her hand at the blank faces of the towers, released a little sigh, then another, at last expelling a running monolog of rememberances. "There goes Jenny Aung Nwè with her baby." She turned her head a little more. "She's a plain, overly shy, young American woman who came to Burma for the love of her life and a lie. She met her husband in the U.S. while she was getting her education degree at some fancy school and he was taking some course work or the other. Romance flourished. No one had ever asked her out before, much less courted her. He spun quite a fairy tale for her: he, the wealthy but lonely businessman, living in an elegant but empty house in Rangoon. When he asked her to marry him, what could she say but yes? She packed herself up, along with her shiny new degree and went to Rangoon to discover the lie. He was a widower, living in a small teak house, without running water, with several children from a previous marriage. Perhaps she had no way home. Perhaps the lie was better than being alone. She stayed and became our teacher."

324

"What happened to her?"

"I don't know. Wait! Look! There's Sis, giggling and carrying on with Lisa and Martha and The Scoon Goon. There—" She pointed this time. "I can see Daddy jumping into the pool, swimming faster and churning up more water than anyone we'd ever seen, except maybe Johnny Weismuller in the Tarzan movies. I got my Shrimp Certificate for Advanced Beginning Swimmer at the Kokine Swim Club. There, that's Prime Minister U Nu and his wife, and there, General Ne Win who took over everything and made all the foreign nationals leave."

She was smiling as she said, "Don't worry, Zeyya, I'm not crazy. I've been watching my homemade vids out here for years without any harmful effects. Until you and Jonah came to live here, what else was there for me to do?"

Something in her expression made me cringe. Resignation? I grabbed her hand. "Granna, do you see Mum up there?"

"I see everyone. Your Mum, your Dad. My Mommy and Daddy. My grandparents. Everybody. No one can censor my moving picture shows. No one can turn off the projector—except for death. That's when the light goes out."

My throat got stuck as I desperately searched for the right thing to say to keep her from giving up. "Granna, you have to let me watch with you, please! Okay?"

"Watch with me? I've never had anyone do that before." She leaned over, tilting stiffly through the blankets, and planted a wet kiss on my cheek.

We sat for an hour, she speaking into my ear, Jonah bringing us hot tea, eavesdropping when he could, then moving out of earshot, leaving us in my grandmother's world. At last she was tired and asked for help to unwind from what she had nicknamed the *mummy blankets*. I helped her inside.

"Granna, Jonah and I were thinking of going out for a while, is that okay?"

Relief swept me when she said as if everything was normal, "Dinner will be late tonight." She squeezed my hand. "Have a good time, darling."

We walked arm-in-arm until we got on a walkway where we switched to fingertip-to-fingertip. Jonah had buried his face in the parka and agreed to gloves and socks.

"Hey girl, your boyfriend forgot his shoes," a six-year-old yelled as he tugged at my sleeve.

"I know. He hates shoes."

The kid made a face and I heard him telling his mother, "That guy doesn't have on any shoes."

I was relieved to get off at the next stop. The tattoo shops were clustered in an unsavory section of the city. The buildings wavered precariously this way and that near the top stories, too tall for their own structural engineering. Many people wanted to raze the area, and frequent proposals for better land usage were posted on Netcasts. Some people claimed that Darwin Q Syndrome had originated here, and although there was no proof to that effect, the rumor persisted.

As soon as we stepped onto the street, Jonah shrugged out of Matthew Mott's oversized parka and slung it over his arm. The first shop we tried was *Pictures Galore*. The tattooist, a middle-aged pouchy woman dressed in a skimpy metallic outfit, eyed Jonah hungrily. I gave her a dirty look as I yanked him out onto the street.

We passed by several more shops until Jonah pointed out a small store, simply called *Tattoos*. A girl about my age called into the back and out hopped a lively old man with what must have been a new set of eyes, surgically enhanced by special lenses. He ignored me completely and went straight to Jonah.

"Son, those are spectacular works of art you're displaying."

Jonah smiled broadly, nodding at me—this was the one.

"Even did your teeth? That is out of this world!"

"You'd better believe it," I said, "but it's me who wants a tattoo."

"You, huh? What kind of tattoo? I don't do kinky work, especially not on young girls. I purely don't approve."

"I want you to scribe a portrait of my mother on me." I handed him an old holograph Granna had stashed with the pile of ancestors. Mum was young, maybe my age, her hair long and shiny, her smile rosy, her eyes even glittered slightly.

"Scribed, huh, like a drawing instead of a tattoo? I can try, but the expression your friend has in his is going to be a push for my talents, if you can call them that."

"Please, grandfather, it's important to her—her mother just died," Jonah announced.

"Sorry, Miss. So you want to immortalize your mother? That's unusual. People up top do that kind of work sometimes. For the number and quality your friend here has—that would cost a bundle! There is a guy," he mused, "he's the best. Joseph Peabody. Do you know him, son?"

Jonah shook his head. "No, I don't."

"Okay, but don't expect me to tattoo your girlfriend with the likes of what you have there. Where do you want it?" the tattooist asked, turning the conversation back to me.

"I'll help scribe her," Jonah volunteered.

"Are you licensed? No? Then you won't help in my shop, son. I still have ethics. Just decide the placement while I get ready, Miss."

"On my stomach," I said firmly. "Will this hurt?"

"Hurt? Used to be it was painful, but not anymore," the old man reassured me. "In the old days, whether it hurt or not, sailors got tattoos that declared sweethearts in foreign ports, and bikers got tattoos to declare membership in a gang." His eyes took on a slightly distant look, which disturbed me. I wanted him to concentrate. He seemed to shake it off as he continued with, "And in the 1930's and early 40's, they tattooed numbers on prisoners to identify them in Nazi Germany. But you're too young to know about that."

"I've studied it," I said. "It was a long time ago."

"More than a hundred years." His eyes glazed over a little.

"How old are you, grandfather?" Jonah asked, obviously fascinated.

"Humph, don't ask, young man."

"He's one-hundred-and-seventeen," the girl from the front room proclaimed. "I'm his great, great, great granddaughter."

"She's a lot more proud of my age than I am."

She winked from the doorway where she had spoken and vanished back into the front of the shop.

"You're older than my Granna."

"I'm older than most people due to the miracles of modern-day medicine."

Modern medicine could restore our bodies and extend our lives for so long, but couldn't cure the Darwin Q Syndrome? "What do you think about Quarantine?" I asked.

"Me? I feel guilty, Miss."

"Huh? Why?"

"Lie right there on that table. Pull up your shirt. I'll just wipe you down and we'll be ready." He whistled as he dabbed at my belly.

"Why guilty?" I asked again as my stomach tingled.

"Because, if people like me didn't live so long, as more and more people got displaced, they wouldn't need to reduce the population. Maybe no more Quarantine. Now, don't talk!"

Nobody my age questioned the reason for Quarantine. Did all old people think the Darwin Q. Syndrome was a contrivance? Were they all paranoid, was paranoia contagious among the elderly, or did age give them the perspective to see the truth? "They didn't do this kind of thing when you were growing up?" I blurted out.

"Shssh, now. Your boyfriend can talk, but not you."

The needles tickled as they left their stain on my skin. The tattooist glanced from the holo of Mum to my tummy, back and forth, back and forth while Jonah looked at a chart in a frame.

"What is this?" he asked.

"Thirteen generations of my family tree." The tattooist didn't even look up as he answered.

I watched as Jonah's eyes climbed the family tree and crawled across its branches. "There are many more limbs on the tree before the early 1940's."

"You're an observant one. Yes, a lot of us died then."

"Empty," Jonah said so softly I didn't think the old man heard him above the ditty he was whistling as he worked. Nobody spoke. The song carried through the workshop. The furniture was dusty, the furnace whispered, the old clock on the wall was a real ticking clock. I listened to it keep its own rhythm under the whistled melody until I combined the sounds into a new composition. Music. Just like Mr. Pompandow had said. All around me.

An hour passed before the tattooist stepped back. "You must have inspired me, young man. That's the finest work I've ever done," he announced. "When you see Joe Peabody next, tell him Abraham Brankovitz said hello, not that he'll know who I am. But do me a favor and show him this work on your girlfriend, okay?"

"I don't know Mr. Peabody," Jonah insisted.

"Sure looks a lot like his work," Mr. Brankovitz mused again.

"You mean there are other people tattooed like Jonah?" I asked, holding my breath for the answer.

"Not exactly like him. Here, let me see your wrist, son." He turned Jonah's hand palm up. "Well, I'll be, I'd have sworn that Peabody would've signed it right here on your wrist. Instead there's just this little scar. Is that where an interface used to be?"

I preempted the question defensively with an answer. "It's dangerous to get an interface removed and expensive, too."

"Anyone who could afford all those tattoos could afford to have an interface removed," the old man insisted.

"Stop!" Jonah snapped. "I told you, I don't know Mr. Peabody and I never had an interface. That's a snake bite puncture."

Abraham Brankovitz laughed good naturedly. "Snake bite? Where would a fellow like you have gotten a snake bite? Haven't been any in the East Coast Metropolis for longer than you've been alive. Good try, but no ring. Got any other explanations?"

"Have you ever talked to your ancestors?" Jonah asked in a change of subject.

"I see, we're on a new topic. No, I haven't. Not recently. They're all dead. I'm the last of my generation."

"I will tell my descendents of you," Jonah said, "and you will be remembered by them forever."

"Thanks, young fellow, that's a real nice sentiment. I appreciate it and no charge for the tattoo. It's been entertaining and a pleasure to help you two out. And young man, you're good, really good."

After the warm dampness of the tattoo shop, the cold hit me hard. Jonah insisted we get hot buns in a sleazy store front. While we waited, *Joseph Peabody* ping-ponged off the walls of my mind. Did Jonah know him? Was this the explanation? Was he, afterall, a rich boy slumming?

As if he knew what I was going to ask, he answered my unspoken question. "Zeyya, I don't know a Joseph Peabody. A scribe must be a member of your family. It's an honor passed from generation to generation."

The bun was delivered into my hands. Doughy sweetness and my unease about Jonah combined to make my stomach cramp.

"Jonah, you're giving me a stomachache. Tell me the truth! Why are you here?" I couldn't look at him as I asked. I didn't want him to be from here. I didn't want him to be suffering a gentle madness.

"Because I fell in love."

It was so plain, so absolute the way he said it that it plucked all other possibilities out of my mind. The day was bright and out in the two-mile zone the snow had melted.

"From the ascendancy of the Buddhist Kings (1057-1824)…

onwards to more than four decades of military dictatorship,

this central landscape [of Burma] has been continually recruited

to the tasks of resistance, rebellion, memorialization, and nation-building."

Monique Skidmore
Introduction to *Burma at the Turn of the 21st Century*
©2005 University of Hawai'i Press

December 11, 1959

Dear Helen,

I should have finished this appallingly disorganized letter long ago, but much has happened very fast! The new Burmese military government cancelled contracts with our firm & another larger one. Also with some Yugoslavs and it ousted some Japanese businessmen. We don't know if the aim is to eliminate all commitments of the U Nu government or if there is an anti-foreign drive—maybe both motives exist. Since Jack had an extension of his leave of absonse from his job at home, our situation is complicated and we will either travel for 5 ½ months before returning or we will come back in six weeks from when we leave.

Lillie and Jim Lester will stay longer than we, as they are here with a different company, but it will be a shame if the research Jim's been doing is all for naught. He's been experimenting with making paper from shredded bamboo. We went on a tour of his institute and saw them making pottery, making charcoal, tanning leather and blowing glass, etc. The idea is to introduce these industries here, using local substitutes in processing. For example, they're trying local barks in tanning hides. There's also a pharmaceutical lab experimenting with using Reserpine, amongst other local plants. Reserpine has tranquilizing effects learned from Indian (of India) mothers, who give their babies the roots to chew to stop their crying and make them sleep. But it is likely the Lesters will be leaving not too long after us. Hopefully, we'll see them in the U.S. as they are good friends. Must go now.

B.

P.S. Daw Thin Min brought longyis & angyis (Burmese blouse) for us to put on over our clothes. I had on a full skirt and petticoat, and hence look like a tub in my striped silk longyi in the photo Jack took.

Greater East Coast Metropolis: 2047
[There is a shortage of cemetery plots. Alternative
arrangements can be made by logging onto Deathweb.net.
For those whose religious beliefs prohibit cremation,
piled gravesites may prove an option. Underwater
cemeteries are also under consideration. Please choose and
make preparations for you and your family. ***Quarantine
victims are required to be cremated.***]

"Granna?"

She whistled as I tried to talk to her. She had been whistling non-stop since the afternoon we had returned with Mum tattooed on my belly.

"Granna?" I tried again. "Please talk to me."

She continued whistling along in some distantly familiar tune until she spoke, taking me by surprise. "Zeyya, people can't come back as bugs."

"I know, Granna."

"Too bad, but if we could, I'd come back as a dragonfly." She returned to whistling.

Granna, don't give up now, I begged silently, but she whistled on with a little popping of her lips and when she stopped on the last pop, she announced, "I'm moving. Might as well, they'll move me anyway, or Quarantine us all."

"No, Granna, don't! We'll be okay."

"I can't risk having them take you."

"Then I'll come with you!"

"To a retirement protectorate? I don't think you're old enough." Oh, Granna, I moaned to myself, but she was whistling again. She stopped the tune in the middle of a note. "You sell everything you don't want. I won't need it. Make the shops give you good money for it. You may need the cash."

"Granna, give me a few days! I'll think of something."

"So you have a plan? No?" She shook her head.

"I told you, I'll think of something!" I insisted desparately.

"Zeyya, I'm too old. Everyone is gone. Mommy. Daddy. Sis. Your mother. No one should outlive their child. I can't go on like this."

The whistling began again.

"Granna!"

When she spoke again, it was almost too calmly. "We don't always get what we want. And pretending doesn't make it so. I wish we could stay together, but at least you have Jonah."

"Jonah?"

"I like him, I like his sense of imagination, and you two love each other, don't you?" She whistled between the words in short puffs.

"Granna, do you believe what he claims?"

"I want to believe him, Zeyya."

"But you don't?"

"I don't think it matters if I believe him or not. I believe in him, that he is kind and will take care of you. As long as you love each other, maybe that's enough." With a deep breath she blew more notes out, this time wildly off key, some of the sounds no more than air blown between her teeth.

"What's wrong with her?" Jonah asked as he came into the kitchen with a hammer and nail in hand.

I dragged my fingers through my hair. "She's given up. She's selling the house."

"No! That's not right, that can't be. I just fixed the shutter for her," he cried out, as if that was reason enough for it not to be true.

Shrugging, I told him, "She's doing it anyway. I'm going to a store site for a few things. Will you stay with her?" I swiped at a tear as I left, barely noticing which way I was going. Halfway back with a carton of eggs, a quart of milk, a loaf of bread and carrots, I stopped under a public Netcaster, waiting to catch a walkway back. I didn't pay attention until the Caster's words penetrated my grief stricken brain: *Wealthy Teen Found. Jeremiah Haynes, son of Net Czar, Tim Haynes and heiress, Miriam Marston Haynes has*

been found basically unharmed, after living for three months in the Two Mile Zone.
Ragged and marked by several self-inflicted and badly infected tattoos on his hands,
young Haynes remains convinced that he was living in a Safe Zone community
where Darwin Quarantine Syndrome does not exist. He is receiving treatment for
Associated Quarantine Stress Madness.

I didn't wait for the walkway. I walked. Dazed, the words of the Netcaster replayed over and over in my mind.

Madness? Rejection of reality? Tattoos?

Jonah?

He sat near Granna, both dosing peacefully. His eyelids fluttered open and he smiled at me. "You're back. Good." I sat down heavily, leaving the packages on the floor by the door. "Are you okay, Zeyya?" I couldn't answer. "Zeyya, please, talk to me. What are your plans?"

"Granna says to sell everything. All these things hanging in my hair." I touched them gingerly, thinking how I hadn't intended to leave them there, but that it had just felt right after the night of snow with Jonah, and then the tattooing of my stomach. "All the books. The letters. The clappers. The dancer's headdress. The pictures." I muttered the list off unhappily.

"And me, what does she want me to do?" he asked warily.

"Take care of me."

"I always will." His promise made my stomach turn over uncomfortably. What if his belief in being from another world was a form of Jeremiah Haynes' madness?

I took a deep breath. "It's truth time, Jonah." Another breath. "I love you, too, but, well, I mean, if you're a rich boy with Quarantine Stress Syndrome, you might not be able to take care of me always. Come clean. Did Joseph Peabody tattoo you?"

"It's called scribing,. And you've heard the voices, too, Zeyya. You know I'm not lying."

"You've got a great imagination, nobody can deny that, and I know you love me, but is that enough, Jonah? Love? Is it?"

He tried to kiss me, but I turned my face away. "I know you believe you hear voices, but me, maybe I just needed to hear something, wanted to believe in anything other than what was coming, what has come."

"Zeyya, don't!"

"Can you prove that you're from another world, that you aren't deluding yourself? Can you? No? That's my conundrum, Jonah."

He managed to enfold me in his arms. "I'm sorry about your mother. I'm sorry Granna is giving up, but if you love me, even if you don't believe the voices, trust me!"

I pulled away from him. "It's a simple yes or no answer. Is your world a lie?"

"No!" His eyes were cloudy with tears that I knew matched my own. "It's real."

I turned my back to him so that he couldn't see me wipe at my eyes. Questions without answers filled my head, tongue-tying me. His claims had to be fabrications, didn't they? They couldn't be true. But what if they were? Could he really come from an idyllic paradise? From Utopia? Or was he homeless, with nowhere to go? What then? What would happen to him if I sent him away? What would happen to me if I went with him? Back and forth my thoughts flipped, back and forth between answerless questions, until it felt as if my brain was being torn apart. "I have to start sorting what to sell. You—you'd better go home, wherever that is, before you get me in more trouble."

"You want me to break my promise to stay with you?"

"It was a childish request and a childish promise. If you're still here when they come for me, it's going to make it worse. They'll investigate you, and if you're suffering from Quarantine Stress Madness, they'll throw you into a mental facility and me into Quarantine. Go home. Stay away from me. Be safe."

"And you? What will happen to you, Zeyya?"

"Me? Not much. I'll hear compositions in my head while I dig ditches, I'll hear them while I sleep, but nobody else will."

"At least let me help you close up the house before I leave," he pleaded. "Let me stay with you a little longer."

"I can do it without you. I told you, go home!"

"Zeyya, don't send me away! Once I go home, I can't come back."

"No!" I burst out. "Go! I can't have you here. When you're here, I can't think!" I sat down on a stool, my head in my hands. "Go, Jonah, go back to your family in their fancy penthouse tower. Go now, please, before you get us both Quarantined." I wept unabashedly as I spoke.

His voice stammered, fading to little more than a breath of sound. "My parents don't live in a tower. They're dead."

"Give me proof, oh please, give me something, anything undeniable and I'll gladly believe."

He spoke sadly. "I can't give you any more than I have."

"Oh, Jonah, I wish your world was real, I truly, truly do, but it isn't, is it?"

With his head bowed, the eyes on the tattoos dimmed as he acquiesced. "I'll leave, but Zeyya, I'll never stop loving you."

Emptily, I heard my voice speak in dull, heavy words. "But love isn't enough to save someone, except in a fantasy. And this is reality. This house. The Metropolis. These streets. These towers. Quarantine. This. Not living together happily-ever-after in paradise."

He stood in front of me, his eyes downcast and spoke. One word: "Please." Then, "We can be happy."

The preternatural calm I'd been feeling cracked and I wept as I shouted at him. "How are we going to be happy?" I frantically yanked trinkets from my hair. I tore out a gold wedding band, threw it, and hit him in the eye with it. "You won't even tell me where you're really from." A pearlescent Burmese dancer went flying. "Because you don't trust me." A teeny elephant. "I wanted my parents back." An Aztec sun calendar. "Granna promised they'd come back because Nyuant Maung did." A chinthe. "But they didn't." A green glass bead. "They died." A cameo. "Dreams die, too. Mine all have. It's all over! You. Me. Finished! Just leave so I can get on with my miserable future." A pearl drop, an ivory earring. "Go home to your family." The more I tore from my hair, the more it hurt, as if I was ripping pieces of flesh from my body.

"It doesn't have to be over!" The plea in his voice breached my walls, threatened my decision. No—he didn't belong in my life.

"I can't do this. I can't go with you." I said as firmly as I could.

Watching me, his blue eyes suddenly clear and penetrating, he whistled a single note and the Jo-Boy came to his side. "I have my answer, then. Goodbye, Zeyya." He opened the door without looking back, and he and the dog trotted down the front steps.

I fell onto my bed and cried. Drained, dull, my legs and arms leaden, I dried my eyes and began to sort through papers and books, clothes and household goods, soon just dumping stuff to be sold into boxes, stuff to be thrown out into others. It took days that lengthened into weeks, and all the while, Granna rocked away on the porch. As soon as Jonah was gone, the Jo-Boys vanished, but Bellisima the Terrible still stalked the house, mewing loudly, walking atop the piles of boxes as they grew, or rubbing against Granna's legs, begging for a scratch she never got. A musical dirge began to play in my head. I titled it *Lost*. Granna whistled and rocked while I worked, and her whistling wormed its way into my dirge, a strange airy sound I imagined as music blown through the teeth of a comb in harmony with the cat's pleading cries.

Out of the corner of my eye—was that the shadow of a blue ghost?

Blink.

It was gone.

The social worker came, interrupting my musical elegy, bringing the papers for the trade school to which I'd been assigned. It could have been worse, but Mr. Jaster had vouched for me, so they were sending me to learn how to repair small machines. I didn't bother to see where the school was. It didn't make any difference. I worked like a fury during the day, cried myself to sleep at night and threw up in the mornings. Granna rocked until the day they came for her. It was after lunch, when I saw the air van pull up. It was full of old, white-headed faces, staring solemnly out the windows. I helped Granna to her feet, giving her one arm, snatching up her suitcase with the other. Bellisima wove between our legs as I guided Granna slowly out the door. The driver helped her into the bus and I saw her sit at the window, saw her turn her face towards me. Was that the hint of a smile at the corners of her mouth or a trick of the light? I couldn't bear to watch them pull off and hurried back into the house.

I sat down at the kitchen table and buried my face in my hands, ready to cry, but before I could shed a single tear, I heard footsteps outside and then an insistent pounding on the door.

"What do you want? Isn't this enough?" I flung the door open, the first wet trickle running down my cheek.

"Miss, it's your grandmother, she's had an attack. I think you'd better come."

I raced down the steps, nearly bowling the man over. "Granna!" I cried as I ran down the aisle of the bus. Her head was tipped strangely, but her eyes were wide and open. I kissed her wrinkled cheek. "Granna!"

"I will be the dragonfly with the purple wings veined like lace," she mumbled thickly, but clearly.

"You can't die," I sobbed.

"I'll be back, Zeyya. Nyuant Maung returned." Her words were ragged but her eyes clear, as she faded away in my arms.

The man pulled me away and when they drove off, after promising a stop at the morgue, I sat in the rocker in my bare feet and pumped and pumped until I fell asleep in the cold. A Jo-Boy's rough tongue woke me as Jonah said, "Let's go inside, Zeyya."

I stumbled to my feet. Jonah! I flew into his arms and let him run his warm fingers through my hair, accepted his kisses gratefully, until he said, "She will return to you and ask to be scribed upon your forehead."

I pulled away. "She's dead. My parents didn't return. Neither will Granna. Don't make up a fairy tale for me as if I'm a child."

He cocked his head, his festooned locks hanging off to one side. "Granna would want you to come with me." His face was close to mine, the portaits too clear, too real. Had one of those faces frowned at me?

I stepped back, my knees shaking. "Jonah, I can't. You shouldn't have come back. Go home. You'll find someone else."

"Zeyya, we belong with each other."

"You and I can't be a 'we'. I'm going one place, you're going another, so don't do this. Don't make this harder than it is. I'll be fine."

"Maybe, but how will you take care of the baby by yourself?"

I laughed. "*The baby?* What have you concocted now?"

"You're throwing up for a reason, Zeyya." He looked directly into my eyes and I had to blink and back away. "Come with me. Please."

"A baby? That's beneath you, Jonah. I'm throwing up because I cry all the time and because I have a weak stomach. You know that. I'm going to spend my life repairing machines and it's tying my stomach in knots."

"Come with me." He reached out to touch me, but I slapped his hands away. If he touched me, I'd cave in. "I can protect you, Zeyya."

"No you can't and I can't survive losing anyone else I love."

"You won't lose me. Let me take you home with me."

"Take me home? Okay, the truth, tell the truth—where's home?" I put out my hands on my hips and waited, but he didn't budge. His eyes were fixed on the boxes I had stacked on the porch marked *For Sale* or *Trash*.

"All of it? You're getting rid of all of it? You can't! You promised you'd take your children sledding on the American Flier. You can't sell it! Or the necklace! And what about the letters? You have to keep them! Please, you have to reconsider."

"It's none of your business."

"If you sell all of it, how will our child remember it's heritage? There will be nothing left."

I moved to the door, stepping just inside before I took a deep breath and forced myself to reply. "Granna told me to sell it. Goodbye, Jonah." I closed the door in his face, just to end it, but the Jo-Boy was inside nuzzling Bellisima, and started howling.

"Oh, for heaven's sake," I said, trying to keep the tears back. I opened the door and Jonah was waiting there.

"Zeyya, I'll wait on our hill for a few days. It's going to snow again. You can smell it. Hurry."

Then he and a pack of Jo-Boys loped off. "I'll wait for as long as I can," he called back over his shoulder before he rounded the corner.

I stood, humming my dirge.

Dry-eyed.

Trembling.

<u>Reincarnation</u>

1. It is an uninterrupted chain of truth that moves from life to life

2. At death, each life passes into a new life, and the next life is determined by actions from the previous one.

3. Buddhism is neither a religion, nor a system of worship

4. There is no dogma, no supreme being, no savior, nor does a Buddhist carry out the will of a god.

5. Buddhism is a serach for personal truth.

Compiled from various readings on reincarnation

February 30, 1959
Rangoon
Dear Mother,

It seems impossible that we are leaving in a month. This has been the experience of a lifetime! Blanche says she will never again laugh at the idea of reincarnation, which before we came was so alien to our culture as to seem absurd to us. No longer. We have been changed in ways that will affect us for the rest of our lives. We will never be the same. Susie swears she will wear her longyi and angyi to the first day of school back home. Sis promises to write her gang from Rangoon at least once a week.

As for me, going home seems like it will be a reincarnation—new lives, connected to our old and yet so altered as to seem we are being reborn.

Love,
Jack

Greater East Coast Metropolis: 2047
[Flash: We have been labeled a subversive publication.
We are not. We are attempting to offer news and
editorials that would otherwise be unavailable to the
public. Our goal is merely to encourage questioning
and reevaluation of our world. Change is up to the
individual who reads our reports.]
Subterranean Net Site

I dreamed of Granna in Burma.

I am eight years old and we are all sitting at a long dining room table in a room where small lizards crawl up pale yellow walls.

"They're called geckos," Granna says. "They walk the plaster walls of the Pukkah houses." A lizard tail falls into my soup bowl. I look up and a tailless lizard is crawling across the ceiling.

"They do that a lot, but at least snakes don't like to eat geckos. No snakes inside the house, only scorpions. Mommy got chased by a pair the other night when she went into the pantry for a glass of water. You can't drink it from the tap. Or even brush your teeth with it from the tap. And if you want hot water for the bath, you have to get them to fire up the charcoal furnace in the back of the kitchen. Mommy was warned by the sound of scorpion tails on the concrete floor in the kitchen. Clickity, clickity, clickity behind her. Do you believe, Zeyya?"

I shake my eight-year-old head up and down enthusiastically.

"Good! Do you want me to tell you about going to school?"

I don't, I don't like school. It's a scary place. This time I shake my head no, and the long, uncaptured hairs in the top-knot that magically appears on my head swing wildly.

"Come, you'll like school here. We only go until 12:30 and it's such fun every morning!" Suddenly Granna is eight, with short hair and bangs. "See that green Jeep outside the window? It belongs to Daddy's office, but I get to go to school in it every morning, that is, after the driver gets it started. It never starts when he turns the key, but he's got it covered. He pushes the car to the edge of the drive and the durwan swings the gates wide. That's when I hop in the back seat and he closes my door, opens his, reaches in, releases the clutch and shoves the car through the gates and down the hill."

We stand, looking through a pair of wide iron gates, down a steep hill. Behind us, a tall white house looms. "58 B Golden Valley Road," Granna announces. "The road dead ends into our driveway. We're the last house at the top of the hill."

We step to the side as a jeep comes flying past us, down the hill, the driver racing right beside the vehicle. The driver leaps into the front seat, slams the door and pops the clutch. The engine springs to life and the car is gone.

"See, it'd be fun to go to school here. Wouldn't you like to start your days like that?"

"Oh, yes!" I hear myself cry.

"I wish I could live here forever." Granna shifts again as her voice deepens back to her adult tone. She faces me full on, her face old and crinkled, her dark eyes staring into mine. "Zeyya, it's all there in the letters and the books. You'll see! I saved it for you."

I awoke with a start and before I could even think, I stumbled to her room, opening the nightstand where I had last seen all the letters neatly folded and banded, all the old envelops and airmail forms with their obscure postmarks. I had been planning to throw them away, but had forgotten. I sat down and stared at them, picked up the first one, then the second, reading them one after another.

The house was cold and quiet and empty, yet the more I read, the nearer 58 B Golden Valley Road came. By the third letter, I could hear the sound of a voice as I read. It seemed close, familiar.

April 26, 1958
Dear Louis,

Do you remember the car we bought to come over here? Well, the thing is the brightest, largest and most conspicuous car in Burma—at least in Rangoon. People tell me that it will sell easily when we leave, because it's yellow, which is the color of happiness, but I feel funny every time we ride in it.

Yesterday, Susie saw a papier mâché doll she liked, but had to look at all the stalls in the Schwedagon before she made up her mind. By the time she decided, the stall was closed so we took her back today to get the thing. It is a large, green, loud, ugly doll, but Susie loves it.

I saw the flash of green I had compressed in the trasher yesterday and felt a flash of fear. What had I done? What else had I tossed aside in my grief and anger? Had I callously thrown out Granna's childhood? I rifled through the letters.

Dearest Mother,

About two weeks ago we had a week's holiday for the Water Festival. It marks the new year, and is sort of like a gigantic Mardi Gras, with the chief activity being to throw water on everyone and everything instead of throwing dubloons. A group of Americans and a few Canadians decided to rent a truck with sides so as to venture out into the streets safely without getting too wet. Everybody met at our house, dressed in bathing suits and shower caps. But the truck's sides proved to be only a few strips of wood and nothing had prepared us for being blasted with fire hoses. We came back a much bedraggled lot.

I knew the voice that wrote. It was Granna's father, so real, so down to earth, writing his own mother about something as distant and removed from her reality then as it was from mine now, and yet so rich, so vivid for both of us. I hopped to the next letter, expecting him, but this one was in a child's hand.

Dear Gwammy,

How are you? We are all well here in Burma. Here in Burma Sis made friends with Mary, the niece of our cook and nanny. She is 15 years old. There is another girl named Sylva, the cook's and nanny's daughter. She is 13 years old. About 2 weeks ago, we went to the Shwedagon. Sis got some ivory charms and I got a big, beautiful doll with green clothes painted on her. The Shwedagon is made out of gold leaf. It is the biggest pagoda in Rangoon.

Sometime in May, Sis is giving a party. Sheila Henie is helping her. I'll have my birthday party in July.

Love,

Susie

P.S. Sis helped me with the spelling.

Then, added in type at the bottom of the page:

Mother—I'm adding to Susie's letter. The work out here is slow and I really don't know how to solve the problem. The Burmese have a philosophy which contains several points that make it difficult for them to move faster. The first one is a concept of personal culpability for even an honest mistake. One can be thrown in jail for making a mistake. Therefore, their tendency is to try to keep from making a decision so they won't make a mistake. The second point is that big executives don't do physical labor, even clerical work. Therefore, the way to prove one is a big executive is not to do any more work than is absolutely necessary. The last is that culturally it is incorrect to tell someone no, so it's very hard to tell what they will really do.

I didn't like the typing. It was cold and distant, and muffled my great-grandfather's voice. I paused, but Granna's collection of letters demanded to be read. Now I couldn't put them down, as if she and her family were talking right to me. I could hear the sounds of their voices as I read on, just as they had sounded in my dreams. First the deep sonorous tones of Granna's Daddy, then Mommy's soft Southern drawl and even Sis's howls of indignation at her tag-along little sister. The letters were taking on lives of their own.

Dear Mama,

A lazy Sunday afternoon. This morning we went to our first Burmese wedding, which was like no wedding we've been to. It was held in the auditorium of the city hall. The stage of the auditorium was decorated on the sides with yellow-gold drapes, and the back of the stage was draped in a pale blue backdrop studded with silver stars. The significance of yellow in Burma is joy and blue represents the sky. Two large, hand-wrought silver bowls filled with flowers and a golden peacock surrounded by green vines sat in the center of everything. The bride and groom, their parents and attendants sat spread across the stage. To one side was a microphone with two officials speaking in Burmese, of course. Throughout the ceremony, a vocalist and a full orchestra of Burmese instruments accompanied the service in chants and tonal chords. To our ears, the chanting was out of tune and nasal. The climax of the ceremony came when the bride's and groom's hands were united in a bowl of water before the couple descended from the stage to receive congratulations. The bride and groom did not know each other before the wedding—the selection was arranged by the parents. Sis says she's picking her own husband.

I pushed on, barely stopping, more and more pulled in by the voices of my ancestors calling to me. If only I could talk back to that deep voice I imagined while I read the letters, could ask my great-grandfather what to do. I could almost feel him holding Granna in his arms, holding her hand as she fell asleep each night to a story, or to Kipling's poem set to song:

> On the Road to Mandalay,
>
> Where the flying fishes play,
>
> And the dawn comes up like thunder out of China cross the bay.
>
> There's an old Moulmein pagoda,
>
> Looking eastward to the sea,
>
> And a Burma girl a-waiting and I know she thinks of me.

For the wind is in the palm trees and the temple bells they say:

Come ye back ye British soldier, come ye back to Mandalay.

Oh, Granna, I moaned, I promise, I'll remember it all. I'll hold Sis and Nyuant Maung, Than Swe and Sami forever near to me. I promise, the Shwedagon will always soar in my memory. Thank you, thank you!

Tears were running freely down my cheeks as my eyes skipped to the last part of a letter. They were packing up, leaving, going.

The packers have been here for two days and will be here two more. They're either Chinese or half-Chinese/half-Burmese, and are meticulous. They're using paper and wrappings that came into Burma on shipments from elsewhere, as such material is not available here. They wind strips of paper around all the furniture, as if they're caning a chair arm or purse handle. We actually enjoy watching them. I'm afraid they'll adopt Susie. She has been notoriously successful at communication and making friends across the language barriers. At the last minute, she dragged her Daddy to the Shwedagon to buy a huge papier mâché owl, covered in metallic gold paper. I hope it fits into the sea crate. In Burma, the owl is lucky, not wise, so maybe it will watch over our shipment and get it back to the U.S. safely.

Blanche

I stopped reading and just skimmed the letters. I could feel myself racing through the years, but couldn't stop, couldn't put on the brakes. Something drove me faster and faster. My eyes ran across handwriting that told of bamboo hula hoops and come-as-you-are parties; about secret hiding places and white ants eating away parts of the Pukkah house and servants roasting the big, juicy white ant grub-queen as an edible delicacy.

I wish y'all could see this city. Its natural beauty is great. There are lakes in the middle of the city and many trees of magnificent

height and girth of trunk. The "Flame of the Forest" is my favorite. It's
covered with bright, red, large orchid-like flowers and the tree itself has
the graceful shape of a larger mimosa.

I could almost see the trees and the water buffalo, vaguely real like a distant memory. I could hardly wait to read the next letter and the next and the next. It was as if I was putting the last, lost pieces of a treasured puzzle into place. Had Granna shared these letters with my mother? Had my mother had a chance to know her grandparents? Had I become my ancestors' last chance to be remembered, just as Jonah claimed he had become his family's last hope?

I caressed the paper of the old letters, fragile like the skin on the backs of Granna's hands. "I can tell from the handwriting who is speaking in each letter, Granna," I said to the empty air. The letters weren't anonymous anymore. Each one, each word had become imbued with personality, with sound and texture. If only I could squeeze the people from the script, hold them, smell what they had smelled, know them as Jonah appeared to know his ancestors.

I felt into the back of the drawer, but there were no more letters to read. I wanted more, but that was it. It was the end. I lay down on Granna's bed and closed my eyes, expecting to see her again, but all I did was fall asleep. When I awoke, it was deep into the night. Instead of Granna, I was left with the taste of a dream about Jonah, and the sound of his voice saying, "I'm waiting. Hurry!"

I got up and frantically pawed through all my boxing work, sorting out Burma and family pictures, gathering letters, one-by-one by their dates. Each time I touched one, I heard voices reverberating in my mind, the faint whispers of their sentiments and sounds. Ba Kyi, Than Swe, Granna, Sis, Sebastian, Josephine, Daddy, Mommy, Sami. I clumsily knotted the jewelry back into my hair and zipped up the passports, the books and magazines into plastic pouches for safe keeping.

I called coaxingly to Bellisma, grabbed her up and dumped her into a box I'd punched air holes into, piled everything on the American Flier, with Bellisma and my violin as the crowning stars. I put on my mother's sweater, made sure I tied everything in place securely and dragged the sled out onto the glazing of ice that was falling, tinting the rising morning a silvery grey. I pulled the sled to the holography shop, pounded loudly on the door until a sleepy-eyed Hank appeared.

"I've come for our holographs," I told him

"Couldn't you have come at a better time? Where's Susannah?"

"She told me to tell you she'd send the credits for your work, and asked me to see if you wanted this antique camera. She used it as a child in a far off country, and I think there's still film in there." I handed him the camera labeled *Brownie*.

"Gee, thank her for me. This is great!" was his response as we exchanged gifts. That was how I viewed it, for I knew I'd never pay him.

Pulling the sled was heavy work and my muscles ached. It had been more than two months since that night in the snow with Jonah. Was it too early to be able to feel a baby kick yet? Afraid I was going to throw up, I felt for Mum's portrait, safely covered under my coat, as if holding my stomach would settle it. Was there an ever so slight, soft swelling beneath her face?

I stopped as I crossed into the park zone and looked back at the squared grid of the city, then looked at the clouded hills and shadowy trees around me, breathed in the sharp smell of cold air. The morning was dark, except for a growing reflection off the ice. Why hadn't I gone to a doctor to be sure I was pregnant? I could still go, confirm it, but what if Jonah didn't wait that long? Going back might condemn me to repairing machines for the rest of my life and I wanted more, lots more. I wanted to compose, to have my music performed, to pick wild tea and run with Jonah on the dry river beds, to see the great maps painted on the cliffs. And I wanted Jonah. To hold him, to touch his hair, to see his blue-toothed smile, to run my fingers over his blue ancestors.

My stomach spasmed. What if he was already gone? What if I never saw him again? I sank to the ground, barely holding onto the rope of the sled to keep it from sliding down the hill and out of my grasp. A tear dripped coldly out of my eye to freeze on my eyelash.

"Zeyya?" Jonah stood up out of the snow like a blue ghost. "Zeyya! I'd almost given up!" His tattoos glowed metallically in the dim daylight as I rose into his embrace. "Old Asha will scribe you. We'll put Granna right there." His finger brushed my forehead. "She'll be beautiful."

"I'll have her scribed the way she looked as a little girl in Burma." His breath caressed my earlobe, the edge of my jaw. "I've missed you so it hurt! I don't care who you are anymore, but Jonah, promise me, even if it turns out you are a crazy rich guy out slumming, you'll stay with me."

"Always, Zeyya. You'll be safe with me."

"And my music, will they like it where you come from?" Ice was forming on my eyelashes and I had to blink to see him clearly.

His laugh hit a familiar note of music. "We'll play it for our baby, we'll play it for everyone." He held me close. "You're safe."

Safe? Yes, if his world existed, we'd be safe. But even if it was only make believe and we ended up hiding out in the Metropolis, moving from one empty cockroach-ridden building to another until they caught us, at least we'd be togeher. Always.

I shuddered. It was getting colder. The ice had ceased falling, leaving an unbroken sheen on the long hill. Far below us the city lights faded into newborn daylight. My eyes traveled back up the hill to a single blue letter that had fallen off the American Flier and lay tattooed on the emptiness.

"Oh, Jonah, I lost one," I cried. "Hold the sled."

I scrambled and slipped down the hill and scooped the letter into my hand. Tiny ice crystals slid across the inked printing on the face of the paper. I shook them off, the way I had shaken the bugs from the note Dad had left dropped by our door.

10 August 1959

Please excuse us for having a scribe to write this in the English

Dear Sir and Madam,

I am very glad for receiving the letter from Sis and Susie dated 10th July. I wish to let you know that I worked a month only in the job you have found for me. Because, they said that the baby was frightened of me. At present I am not going to school. Moreover I want to say that I miss you all very much. Ba Kyi also is missing you all. Will you not come to Burma again? We are very much expecting you all. We both are speaking about you every now and then. When we hear the noise of the plane, we both had tears come out and are looking for the plane. Even while we are working, our mind is not in the work.

When you come, you will meet all your obedient servants. We shall never forget you all. I hope and pray that you all are well, safe and sound.

I am safe here by the grace of god and hope you are the same.

Sans,

Than Swe

The plaintive voice in the letter whispered to me. I took a deep breath. Watch for me, I whispered back. I'm coming. I'll find you. Wait for me in the shadows of the Shwedagon. I'm coming.

The day had lightened. At the top of the hill, Jonah held out his hand to me. His hat was gone. Sewn and tied onto his clothes were bits of paper, little tools and pieces of brick-a-brack. Jo-Boys, their wet breath turning to mist in the cold air, milled impatiently around his bare feet. When I reached for his blue hand, it was warm. Natural adaptation.

Mum, Dad, Granna? I listened for their voices expectantly. Nobody answered. Weren't they supposed to speak to me?

"Ready?" Jonah asked again.

Where were they? Why didn't they answer?

"Zeyya? Are you coming, Zeyya? We need to go."

I inhaled and wet my lips with my tongue.

"You must make a decision, Zeyya."

I stood, waiting for the voices to tell me what to do, but they were silent. Tears gathered in the corners of my eyes, but I was frozen, unable to say the words I wanted to. Jonah ran the edge of his thumb under my eye, catching a cyrstal teardrop before he took a step backwards, turned and started to walk away over the hilltop.

My eyesight blurred, woozily coating the world in whiteness. Someone was whispering to me. It was Granna. "Zeyya, I'll be the dragonfly on the tip of the Chinthe's nose that guards the Shwedagon."

Even before the milkiness vanished, I was yelling, "Wait! Wait, Jonah! Are there dragonflies where you live?"

He stopped, turned. "Dragonflies?"

"Yes, are there?"

"There is a lake my uncle found in a tiny hidden valley below the cliffs where they skim the water like ice skaters."

"Real dragonflies, like the ones here?"

"Yes, real dragonflies, much like the ones here."

"I'm coming, Jonah."

He came back, bent down, and kissed me before he took the rope on the sled and helped me pull it over the crest of the hill. A golden spire of sunlight cut through the gloom. Below us the ice glistened and the Jo-Boys ran wild in the early morning light without a single howl or bark. Jonah whistled and they came running as we left the city behind.

PICTURE GUIDE

Line of Buddhas, unknown location, 1976
p.3

Palm tree, Rangoon, 1958/59
p.4

Burmese orphans, Rangoon, 1958
p.13

Shan drummer and dancer from Burmese postcard
bought in 1958/59
p.15

Kokine Swim Club, Rangoon, 1958/59
p.16

Burmese lacquer tray collected in Rangoon, 1958/59
p.25

Kambawza Palace Hotel, 1958,
p.26

View from 58 B Golden Valley Road, Rangoon, showing bomb shelter in compound and looking down the hill at the home of neighbors, 1958/59
p.35

Indian malis (gardeners) cutting the lawn of the Kambawza Palace with machetes, Rangoon, 1958
p.37

Burmese Postage Stamp
p.38

Mortal combat between snake and tactoo, in the drive of 58 B Golden Valley Road, Rangoon, 1958/59
p. 45

Temple at Pagan, Burma, 1976
p.47

In sari, 1958
p.48

Moona, the 2nd nanny, Rangoon, 1958/59
p.61

Reclining Buddha, unidentified site, Burma, 1976
p.62

Advertisement in Rangoon International Cook Book,
the Woman's Society of Christian Service of the
Methodist English Christian Church, Rangoon,
Burma, (1956 uncopyrighted edition)
p.77

Bamboo chinlon balls, collected in Burma, 1958/59
p.79

Portion of an advertisment for Rowe's department
Store, in Rangoon International Cook Book, the
Woman's Society of Christian Service of the Methodist
English Christian Church, Rangoon, Burma (1956
uncopyrighted edition)
p.80

Basha hut with the University of Rangoon on the other
side of the bridge, 1958/59
p.91

Sebastian, Josephine, Mary Sylva, Dak and two
undentified girls, Rangoon, 1958
p.92

Burmese Village on the way to Pegu, Burma, 1958/59
p.109

Padaung women, from a Burmese greeting card, 1958/59
p.110

Karaweik Restaurant, mimics royal barge, based on water
bird from Indian prehistory, with many tiered pagoda on
top, Kan Daw Gyi Lake, Rangoon, 1976
p.125

Shwedagon Pagoda, Rangoon, 1958
p.127

Peddler at front gates of 58 B Golden Valley Road,
Rangoon, 1958/59
p.128

Hand carved wooden elephant and chinthe collected in
Burma, 1958/59
p 139

Shrines on the platform of the Shwedagon Pagoda,
Rangoon, 1958/59
p.140

Burmese coolie hats collected in Burma in 1958/59
p.147

Starving Buddha, unidentified location, Burma, 1976
p.149

Coconut pickers, Burma, 1976
p.150

Group picture in Burmese village, 1976
p.163

Class picture at the International School on Kokine Road,
Rangoon, 1959
p.164

Tea Pot bought in Japan
p.175

Japanese Kabuki mask doll on Japanese silk,
collected in Tokyo, Japan, 1958
p.177

Japanese kimono, purchased at the Smithsonian
Institution, Washington, DC, 1996
p.178

Burmese road, 1976
p.189

Storyteller/food peddler on Rangoon street, 1958/59
p.190

Chinthe at an entrance to the Sule Pagoda,
Rangoon, 1958/59
p.203

Large sitting Buddha at the Shwedagon Pagoda, 1958/59
p.205

Shwedagon Pagoda, 1958/59
p.206

Laquered betel box, collected in Rangoon, 1958
p.225

Burmese postage stamp
p.227

Birthday party, Rangoon, 1958
p.228

Mother of pearl and ivory pins, charms and earrings,
in teak box, collected in Rangoon, 1958/59
p.237

Burmese dancer from unattributed postcard, Burma,
1958/59
p.239

Dressed up to Burmese dance in the living room
of 58 B Golden Valley Road, Rangoon, 1958
p.240

After the Water Festival, Burmese New Year Celebration,
Rangoon, April 1958
p.247

Street scene, Rangoon, 1976
p.249

Costume contest, Rangoon, 1958
p.250

Invitation to Burmese wedding,
Rangoon, 1959
p.257

Burmese birthday party, Rangoon, 1976
p.259

Passport from 1958/59
p.260

Burmese children, Rangoon street, 1958/59
p.271

Night pwe at Burmese New Year, Rangoon, April 1958
p.273

American teens in Rangoon, 1958/59
p.274

Advertisment from Rangoon International Cook
Book, the Woman's Society of Christian Service of the
Methodist English Christian Church, Rangoon, Burma,
(1956 uncopyrighted edition)
p.287

Sami, Bachi, Than Swe and Ma's children, Rangoon,
1958/59
p.288

Burmese Ivory Lion, traded for Ham Radio, 1959,
p.301

With Mary, Josephine and 1958 yellow Chevrolet under
the portico of 58 B Golden Valley Road, Rangoon, 1959
p.302

Burmese Fabric, collected in Rangoon in 1958/59
p.309

Burmese postage stamp
p.311

Telegram, the only way to communicate fairly "quickly"
with the U.S. from Burma in 1958/59
p.312

Jungle growth, Rangoon, 1958
p. 319

Peace Memorial, Rangoon, 1958/59
p.321

General Ne Win, from unknown newspaper photo
p.322

Chinthe outside an entrance of the Shwedagon Pagoda,
Rangoon, 1958/59
p.331

Rice paddies in the heart of Rangoon, 1985/59
p.333

American ladies in Burmese attire, Rangoon, 1959
p.334

Papier mâché and lacquer gold owls in front of bamboo
Burmese stools, collected in Rangoon, 1958/59
p.345

Pencil sketch of pongyis on scrap paper, 1963
p.347

Family moving, Rangoon roadside, 1958/59
p.348

Unknown Pagoda, 1976
p. 360, 361

GLOSSARY

A
Almirah: wooden wardrobe used in lieu of a closet
Alaungsithu: King of Pagan, 1113-1167 AD
Anglo-Burmese: the child of a British and Burmese union
Angyi: sheer silk, traditional Burmese blouse, with asymetrical front, toggle closures and a high-cut neck
Animisim: the belief in the existence of individual spirits that inhabit natural objects in the world. Ancient Burmese were animists and many animistic beliefs were blended into Burmese Theravada Buddhism
Aung San: famous general, instrumental in the Burmese movement for independence, assasinated in 1947, six months before the British gave independence to Burma
Aung San Suu Kyi: daughter of Aung San, she is a Nobel Peace Prize winner and a noted Burmese Nationalist, who has long been held under house arrest in Burma due to her anti-totalitarian stances

B
Bael Fruit: round to pear shaped fruit used as food and to treat dysentery
Banana Palm: commonly called a "banana tree", is actually an herbaceous Asian pseudo-tree
Balachaung: ground, fried shrimp combined with onions, 10-20 cloves of garlic, tamarind paste, shrimp paste, turmeric, oil and chili powder; popular dish accompanying rice.
Basha Hut: hut with split cane walls and thatched roof; basic home to many of the poor
Bearer Sweeper: house boy
Beloo: an ogre, sometimes a man eater
Betel Box: a cylindrical, slightly round-topped, decorated lacquer box with trays inside that fit one on top of the other in order to store Betel Nut and other indgredients sometimes added to the nut when chewed
Betel Nut: the nut of the Betel palm, sometimes chewed with the leaves, stains the teeth red and is a euphoric, addictive drug.
Bodhi: a Buddhist term for wisdom found in an ideal state of intellectual and ethical perfection
Buddha: Buddha refers to anyone who has reached enlightment, but frequently refers to Sidhartha Guatama, a prince who got caught up in the world's suffering and became an ascetic, seeking higher truth. He became a teacher from the age of 35 until his death at age 80, around 486 BC
Buddhism: although frequently thought of as a religion, many Buddhists consider Buddhism to be a philosophy based on a set of teachings and practices, without a system of worship or faith. It was founded by Sidhartha Gautama, who lived in the 5th century BC

GOLD LEAFED BURMESE BUDDHA

Burmese Sandals: traditional footwear of the Burmese, looking much like flip-flops, but made of leather or suede with rubber or leather soles, and fitting tightly to the foot.

BURMESE SANDALS/ SLIPPERS, FROM 1958

C

Cheroot: a Burmese cigar smoked by women and men alike

Chinese Cabbage: from the mustard family, has an elongated head, crinkled leaves and can be eaten as a vegetable

Chinlon: a 1500 year old game, played with a woven cane ball, that must be kept in the air without use of hands or arms. It is played in a circle of 6 people, with the focus being on how beautifully it can be played. There are over 200 ways to kick the ball, with position of body, legs, feet and head of great importance to the form.

BURMESE LADY, SMOKING
A CHEROOT. OIL PAINTING

Chinthe: leogryph that guards the gates to the Burmese pagodas

Choli: the short Indian blouse worn under a sari

Cousin Brother: a term used to indicate a close friend, or even the close friend of a friend of another family member who is treated as extended family.

Custard Apples: heart-shaped, edible fruit of white to yellowish flesh

D

Dhamma: [Dharma] means truth, that which really is; also the law that exists in each man's heart and mind and in the universe. If one lives by Dhamma, one can go to Nirvana.

Drumstick: elongated green-striped and slightly ridged pods of a tree, used as a vegetable.

Durwan: watchman or guard

Durian: fruit that has a hard prickly rind and soft pulp, bad odor but a pleasant taste

Dysentery: an intestinal disorder caused by bacteria, parasite or protozoa, resulting in severe diarrhea, fever and pain

BACHI, 2ND DURWAN

F

Flame of the Forest: tropical, deciduous evergreen with five-petalled, orchid-like red flowers. Leaves are fern-like in shape

G

Gecko: small lizard whose padded toes are equipped with suction cups that allow it to climb vertically. It inhabits the inside of houses, feeding on small insects, and derives its name from the chirping it makes that sounds like *gecko*

Guava: edible reddish, sweet fruit from the Guava tree

H

Hnè: oboe-like Burmese instrument

I

Imperial Hotel: built between 1916-1922, this Tokyo hotel was designed by Frank Lloyd Wright to withstand earthquakes by using a series of shifting plates in its foundation

Irawaddy River: Runs 2000km beginning in the Kachin state and flows the entire length of Burma, ending in the Andaman Sea

Ike: a reference to President Dwight D. Eisenhower, who played golf at the Burning Tree Country Club in Maryland, outside of Washington, DC

J

Jack Fruit: large edible fruit from a tree with unisexual flowers and fine-grained wood
Jasmine: any of a number of shrubs or vines native to Burma with a very sweet scented blossom frequently used in making perfume

K

Kachin: tribe living in Northern Burma since the 15th c. who farm hilly tracts cut out of the forests
Karen: hill tribe, members of a Thai people living in southern and eastern Burma
Kawanda: passion fruit
Khamma: [Kharma] means "action" and in the greater sense means the cycle of cause and effect of all good and bad actions. Khamma is not fate. Man can modify his actions and affect his future
Knol Kohl: Kohl Rabi a member of the mustard family where the stem is eaten as a vegetable. Also known as turnip cabbage.
Kyat: Burma's national currency

L

Lemon Grass: tropical grass with aromatic oil used as a flavoring
Lepers: victims of Leprosy
Longyi: three yards of fabric sewn by a single seam into a tube and worn as the traditional garb of both Burmese men and women. Men knot it at the waist and women fold it over and tuck it in at the waist. When people want to shower in public, they loosen the longyi, pull it up under the arms and open it so water can flow through, thus making a tempoary "shower curtain"

LONGYI FABRIC

M

Machete: a long knife with a broad blade used to cut the grass and vegetation in Burma
Mahabodi Tree: a fig tree like the one Buddha sat under to receive enlightenment
Mali: gardener
Mandalay: city north of Rangoon, capitol of the Kingdom of Burma from 1860-1885
Mange: a skin disease caused by parasitic mites, exhibited by skin lesions and loss of hair. Seen in many dogs along the roads of Burma, and communicable to other mammals, including humans. Hence the phrase, "mangy dog"
Mangosteen: large edible berry with a hard rind and sweet juice from a Malaysian evergreen tree
Marrow: very large, elongated green edible squash
Moulmein: 3rd largest city in Burma, the British administrative center from 1827-1852
Monsoon Season: rainy season
Mudras: the different positions of hands and fingers which give different spiritual meanings to statues of the Buddha. These positions are also used in meditation.

N

Nat: spirits that were worshipped in the early animistic religions of Burma, and which have been incorporated into Burmese Buddhism. A Nat was a spirit with dominion over certain people or objects. Altogether, there are 37 national and personal Nats
Ne Win: Burmese military commander who staged a military coup d'etat in 1962 and became a brutal dictator until he resigned in 1988. He died 2002

Nirvana: the state to which all Buddhists aspire, it is the end of suffering when all personal desire is quenched. It is the dying of the Khammic forces, an ascent to peace, the ultimate goal of all Buddhists

P

Padaung: a tribe of Mongolian descent who has been assimilated into the Karen group. They are known for their "long-necked" or "giraffe women", who beginning at age five, wear brass rings around their necks, adding to them throughout their lives until their necks are stretched to extreme lengths

Padouk: 2nd densest wood in the world

Pagan: capitol of the first Burmese empire, established in 1057 and fell to the Mongols in 1257. In the 12th century it was called "the city of three million pagodas"

Pagoda: a stupa, which in Burma is a conical shape, topped by a spire

Pali: the litrugical language of Theravada Buddhism

Palwé: flute-like Burmese instrument

Pomelo: a large citrus fruit that looks something like a huge grapefruit

Pongyi: Burmese monk, always dresses in saffron colored robes as decreed by Buddha

PADAUNG LADY

Pukka(h) House: a western-style house built during British Rule

Putma Drum: Large cylindrical drum, which hangs horizontally over the shoulders

Pwè: a festival celebration that might include drama, dance, puppet shows and music

Pya: coins used as change for Kyats. 100 pyas equaled one Kyat in 1958

R

Ramayana Tales: ancient Sanskrit epic, it is an important part of the Hindu Canon Consists of 24,000 verses telling the story of Prince Rama and his quest for his wife Sita who is abducted by a demon

Rangoon: the capitol of Burma from 1885 until 2005 when it was moved by the ruling, military junta to Pyinmana

Reserpine: a sedative and anti-hypertension medicine

Rambosteen: fruit of the Litchi tree, filled with sweet white pulp in its fresh state

S

Sanskrit: An ancient Indic language, the language of Hinduism

Sari: the traditional garb of Indian women, made of 6 yards of fabric that is wrapped around and tucked into the waistband of an underslip and the tail of which is thrown over the shoulder, or can be draped over the head for protection from the sun

Shan Bag a woven bag with a long strap made by the Shan tribe, one of the largest tribes in Burma, traditionally rice cultivators, shop keepers and artisans. They call themselves "tai" which means "free men"

Shwedagon Pagoda: Most sacred and largest Pagoda in Burma, built between the 6th and 10th centuries according to archeologists, but Buddhist monks claim it was built before the death of Buddha in 486 BC. Genuine gold plates cover its brick structure

Snake Gourd: strikingly long green fruit, used as a vegetable and medicine

Stupa: a dome shaped monument used to house Buddhist relics or commemorate impor-tant Buddhist events

SHAN BAG

Sule Pagoda: 2200 year old pagoda, smaller than the Shwedagon, the focus of social and religious activity in Rangoon

T

Tactoo: large lizard that is attractive to snakes as a food source

Tasaungmon: on a night of the full moon, a festival commemorating Gautama's return from visiting his mother's reincarnated spirit. Fire balloons are sent into the air on this festival

Tamarind: long pods with small seeds embedded in an edible pulp from an Asian evergreen.

Tapioca Root: beady starch from the root of a cassava, used as a thickener in cooking

Tazung: a shelter built as a shrine over an image of Buddha. Can be extremely intricately carved and even gold leafed

Therevada Buddhism: conservative branch of Buddhism, adhering to Pali scriptures, practicing a non-theistic ideal of self-purification and nirvana

Thabeiq: a Burmese pongyi's begging bowl, usually a large round black laquer bowl in which pongyis collect food for the poor

BEGGING BOWL or THABEIQ

Tiffin Carrier: stacked trays held together by a locking handle used to carry prepared foods in south Asia

Top-knot: Burmese traditional hair style, mainly for children, where the hair is cut bowl style except for the top, which is left long, parted in a circle, then knotted on the top of the head.   CHILD WITH TOP- KNOT

Trishaw: a cart or small carriage, powered by a man on a bicycle. Used for both transportation of both people and goods. A rigshaw is a similar conveyance, except it is pulled by a man.

U

U: means mister and is pronounced as the "oo" in boot

U Nu: the first Prime Minister under the 1947 constitution of the newly formed Union of Burma.He was also a Buddhist scholar and author of several books

W

Water Festival: celebrates the Burmese New Year in April with a wild dousing of water from buckets, fire hoses and any other means that is handy, followed at night by pwès

White ant: any one of a number of pale members of the order Isoptera (termites), usually living in warm climates

Z

Zats: story dances

Zedi: stupa

Zeya [Zeyya]: means 'success' in Burmese

TWO ZEDIS AT PAGAN

*Note: Burmese is a tonal language with its own script, therefore all transcriptions into English spellings are subject to variation. Pronunciation in Burmese is key, as even a slight change of tone can give a word a different meaning.

FURTHER READINGS ON BURMA:

Back to Mandalay, Burmese Life, Past and Present, Abbeville Press Publishers, ©1996

Burma, Around the World Program, Nelson Doubleday, Inc ©1976

Burma at the Turn of the 21st Century, edited by Monique Skidmore, University of Hawai'i Press, ©2005

Burma Under the Japanese, by Thakin Nu (U Nu), St Martins Press ©1954

Burmah and the Burmese by Kenneth R.H.Mackenzie, George Routeledge & Co. ©1853

Burmese and Thai Fairy Tales Retold by Elenaor Brockett, Frederick Muller Ltd. ©1965

Burmese Art by John Lowry, Crown ©1974

Burmese Days by George Orwell, Harcourt Brace ©1935

Burmese Design and Architecture by Facloner, Moor, Kahrs, Birnbaum, Di Crocco, Cummings; photography by Tettoni, Periplus Editions ©2000

Burmese Family by Daw Mi Mi Khaing, Orient Longmans, Ltd. ©1947

Burmese Looking Glass by Edith T. Mirante, Atlantic Monthly Press ©1998

Burmese Sunshine by Maung Maung Pye, Khittaya Publishing House, Rangoon 1956

Colourful Burma by Khin Myo Chit, Rangoon:Theidkdi Sarzin ©1976

Finding George Orwell in Burma by Emma Larkin, Penguin ©2005

From the Land of Green Ghosts by Pascal Khoo Thwe, Harper Perrennial ©2003

India and Burma by Prof. W.S. Desai, Orient Longmans, Ltd 1954

Inside a Soviet Embassy, Experiences of a Russian Diplomat in Burma, by Aleksander Kaznachcev, J.P. Lippincott Co. ©1962

Perspective of Burma, An *Atlantic* Supplement, The Atlantic Monthly Co. ©1958

Rangoon (Sites and Institutions), Ministry of Union Culture, Government of the Union of Burma, circa 1955

Selections from Burmese Folk Tales by Maung Htin Aung, Oxford University Press, 1951

Splendour in Wood, The Buddhist Monasteries of Burma, by Sylvia Fraser-Lu, Weatherhill ©2001

Textiles from Burma, edited by Elizabeth Dell and Sandra Dudley, Art Media Resources ©2003

The Land and People of Burma by C. Maxwell-Lefroy, The MacMillian Co. ©1963

The Shwedagon by U Aung Than, 1946

The River of Lost Footsteps by Thant Myint-U, FS&G ©2006

The Trouser People by Andrew Marshall, Counterpoint ©2002

The Vanishing Tribes of Burma by Richard K. Diran, Amphoto Art ©1997

Thirty Burmese Tales by Maung Htin Aung, Oxford University Press, 1952

They Reigned in Mandalay by E.C.V. Foucar, Denis Dobson, Ltd. 1946

AFTERWORD

In 1947, Burma won its hard fought independence from British rule. Thakin Nu was elected its first Prime Minister and except for one year, remained as such until October of 1958, when a bloodless coup was staged by General Ne Win. For those brief years between 1947 and 1958, Burma, then called *the rice bowl of the world*, rich in natural resources, driven by freshly won independence and optimism, was a fledgling socialistic democracy. In order to assure Burma's place in the world, the U Nu government decided to hire consultants from the West to come into the country and help the Burmese to develop their resources and hone their skills for the world market.

In late 1957, my dad came home one evening to ask my mother if she wanted to move to the other side of the world to Rangoon, Burma. He had been offered a job with the consulting firm of Robert R. Nathan & Company to advise the Burmese government on how to market their rice. My mother thought he was teasing her—or else crazy, but sure enough in early 1958, when I was eight years old, my family traveled through Asia to Rangoon where we lived until I was almost ten.

When Ne Win took power in 1958, he canceled all or most of the foreign contracts including the one my father had been hired under and we left the country in March of 1959 to travel the rest of the way around the world through India, Turkey, and Europe before returning home. Before we saw the U.S. again, we had been to Tivoli Gardens in Denmark, and Tiger Balm Gardens in Hong Kong; seen Hagia Sophi, the Taj Mahal by moonlight, the Parthenon, the cathedrals at Cologne and Notre Dame; and visited museums that held the greatest works of art in seventeen countries.

In those days, few people in my suburban Maryland community had been to that number of countries, and coming home as a ten-year-old only confirmed the sense of otherness that going to Burma had defined for me, and that I have carried with me ever since. The world there was as alien as any world I have ever imagined or written about. Differences in cultural language changed my perspective, changed my own cultural language, and permeated my life. I am forever grateful for that experience which led me to write this book, which is a strange amalgam of what was and what might be in the future.

Marking the 50th anniversary of when we moved to another world, I present this book to you, a combination of fact, history, memoir, fiction and science fiction. I hope it fills the reader with a sense of the beauty and fascination that I treasure in otherness.

Most of the letters in this book were written by my mother and father, Mindel and Frank Lowenstein, and sent back to relatives and friends who saved them for us. My mother has passed away, but my father (who is ninety-three at this writing) has kindly permitted me to use both the letters and his slides and photos in this book. I did edit the letters for rhythm and sometimes combined several parts of different letters. A very few I devised out of my memory for the purposes of the book. The names of family and friends were changed, but not of our employees. In addition to my father's photographs and slides, there are several images that came from unattributed postcards I got in Burma, as well as scans and digital photos I took of objects we collected there. Both the drawing of the Pongyis and the oil painting of the Burmese woman in the glossary were done by me from memory in my early teens.

Writing this book gave me back the voices of my family, our friends, and our servants, and like Zeyya in the book, I will hold them dearly close to me for the rest of my life, but sadly, in the fall of 2007, as I was preparing this book to go to press, the brutal story of the continued repression of the Burmese people burst into the headlines again, as yet another cry for freedom was squashed by the ruling junta. As the world watched and protested to no avail, I felt eerily as if I had lived, all those years ago in that "one, brief shining moment that was known as Camelot."

Sallie Lowenstein, December 2007

More information on books by
Sallie Lowenstein is available at:
www.lionstonebooks.com

To contact the author send emails to:
Sallielowenstein@gmail.com